Infatuation

RIVER SAVAGE

Infatuation

First edition: October 2015

Edited by Becky Johnson of Hot Tree Editing
Cover design ©: Louisa Maggio at LM Creations
Cover Image: Furious Fotog
Cover Model: Dustin Sherer
Formatted by Max Effect
Information address: riversavageauthor@gmail.com

Author's Note

This novel contains adult/mature young adult situations.
It is only suitable for ages 18+ due to language, violence, and
sexual situations.

Infatuation explores the damaging effects of a spouse's emotional
and physical abuse and may cause possible triggers related to
domestic violence.

Past

Mackenzie

"**YOU'RE NOTHING BUT A STUPID FUCKING BITCH. DO**
you know that? You think I don't know what you're doing?"
The insult rolls off him with ease, twisting my insides into knots
with each word.

"I'm sorry." I try to placate him, still unsure what's happening here. It's not the first time he's lost his temper or called me
a name; in fact, it's become a weekly occurrence the last few
months, but tonight something's changed. It's like he's come
unhinged.

"You're sorry? You're always fucking sorry." Spit hits my
face, just above my eye, but I don't reach up to wipe it. Fear
freezes me, anchoring me in my place.

"I didn't mean it, Chad." The admission falls from my lips,

but I still don't understand why he's so angry.

"You didn't mean it?" His bark echoes around the confined space of the bathroom he's cornered me in.

"No." I shake my head. My mind races, cataloguing everything that transpired tonight.

We were at a benefit for his dad. Mayor Morre's annual fundraiser. I was polite, stuck by Chad's side all night, smiled and only spoke when spoken to. Exactly how he expects me to act. Judging by the state he's in right now, I know I messed up somewhere during the night. I just don't know where.

"Do you know how pathetic you looked? Like a fucking whore." He continues to unleash his verbal abuse. I know they're only words; I shouldn't let them affect me, but each one tears away at my confidence. Tears away at the love we've shared.

"Do you want to fuck him?" His voice drips in venom, disgust chasing every word as he takes a step closer.

"Who, Chad?"

"WHO?" he shouts my reply back at me, as his hand comes out hard and fast across my face.

The bitter taste of copper fills my mouth, but I don't have a second to register the blood pooling before his hand roughly takes my chin and forces me to look up at him.

"You want to fuck him, don't you?" The question hangs in the air between us. I should try to put his mind at ease, deny everything and try to calm him down, but the ringing in my ears makes it hard for me to concentrate. He hasn't hit me before. He's come close a few times, but I've always managed to diffuse the situation.

"ANSWER ME, MACKENZIE!" My face is pushed with

brute force, and I stumble back in fright. Tears roll down my cheeks, over my lips, and underneath my chin.

"N—No," I cry out, my hand moving to my face, hoping to soothe the burning flesh.

"DON'T FUCKING LIE TO ME!"

"I'm not," I deny it again, but it's not what he wants to hear. Before I figure out where I'm failing in easing his mind, his fist connects with my face. This time, the knock takes me back another step. The backs of my legs hit the coolness of the bathtub. He follows me back, his rage spilling out of him at a rapid pace and suffocating me. My unease turns to full-fledged fear. The hard reality this isn't going to end well moves through my body at lightning speed.

"Please, Chad," I cry, but the continuous flow of tears leaking from my eyes does nothing to convince him this isn't who we are.

Before I can protect myself, Chad's fist connects again.

Stars explode behind my eyes. The sensation of falling envelops me so swiftly I can't find my bearings, and then everything goes black.

1

Mackenzie

"EXCUSE ME, HOW MUCH LONGER?" I SWALLOW THE quiver in my voice and pray it's not much further.

"Five more minutes," comes the reply. My hands shake at my side and my leg bounces to its own erratic beat while I sit in the back of a cab on my way to the only place I have left.

Rushford.

I have no idea what I'm doing, or if they will want to help me, but I have no other options and nowhere else to go.

I check my surroundings again before my eyes move back to the dashboard and the time displayed on the digital clock.

6:01 p.m.

"You sure I don't know you from somewhere?" The older man driving the cab breaks the short silence and pulls me out of my head. His eyes find mine in the rear-view mirror and his graying brows bunch up, like he's trying to figure out how exactly he knows me.

Jesus, please don't let him figure it out.

Not wanting him to recognize me, I avert my gaze out the window.

"No, just making a pit stop in town." The lie falls from my lips with ease and precision. It's one of my best talents. The cool, calm and collected manner I've learned to hone and perfect over the years has always stayed with me.

"And your first stop is the Knights Rebels' clubhouse?" I look back up at the disbelieving tone of my nosey cabbie, but don't reply.

I know it's probably the worst idea coming here, considering I'm so close to home, but if I have any hope of surviving this, I need them.

"Are you sure you're okay, miss? You don't look so good."

"Yeah, I'm all right. Just have a bad headache." I push all my conviction into my answer. The cab driver's growing questions are putting me on edge, but I can't lose it. *Not yet.* The old man takes the hint and quits with the interrogation. I'm almost relieved, until the scene back in Ohio starts playing out in my mind.

"I don't think so, Mackenzie." Chad races behind me, his hand snaking out, fisting my hair and pulling me back. "You and I have things we need to discuss," he seethes, tightening his grip. I fight back, reaching over my shoulders and slapping him. He recoils, letting me go, but before I can pull away, he slaps me hard. A stinging sensation covers my cheek. I drop to the floor at his force, my towel falling away from my body, exposing me.

5

"Miss, did you hear me?" The cab driver's question rips me from the nightmare and brings me back into the here and now.

"Sorry?"

"We're here." I look up at the large building and gather my nerves. Briefly, I second-guess my reasons for coming here but then shake those thoughts out of my head.

You need his help, Mackenzie.

"That will be fifty-seven." The cab driver turns in his seat, looking back at me. I reach for my bag and pull out three twenties and two one-dollar bills.

"It's all I have." I cringe at the tip, but his soft grin tells me he doesn't mind.

"You okay with your bags?" His head moves toward the clubhouse and my gaze follows.

"Yeah." I nod and reach for my backpack. "Thank you." I force something I hope resembles a smile, but only end up wincing in pain.

"Stay safe, sweetheart." I don't reply, just close the door and turn to face the large brick clubhouse. The old building stares back at me, calling to me like a long lost friend, so I give myself a moment to take it in. The place is huge, bigger than what I had pictured in my mind. Turning to gaze to the right, I notice a shed nearly the same size as the clubhouse. The roller doors are pulled down, and a low light shines from a small gap where the door and the concrete meet. Multiple motorcycles are lined up in front of it.

Coming from a life like mine, and marrying a man like Chad, the last place you would ever expect to find me is here: standing out the front of Rushford's very own MC clubhouse needing help. But life has a funny way of putting everything into perspective.

"Can I help you?" A man's voice startles me and I lose my composure for a second. Doubt coils in my stomach and catches me off guard.

No, this is a bad idea.

My flight reaction sets in, and I twist back toward the cab, but the distant glow of the red tail lights stare back at me.

Too late now, Mackenzie. You're stuck.

Turning back around I take a deep breath and will myself not to lose it.

"My name's Mackenzie Morre and I'm here to see Beau." I force confidence into my voice, hoping he doesn't see how afraid I truly am. The guy is a lot younger than Beau, maybe by twenty years. His dark gray eyes roam over my face, before traveling down my body then back up. I want to say he looks like a nice young guy, but from his annoyed stare, I could be wrong.

"Come with me." He turns and guides me to the front door. Not wanting to be left behind, I pick up my pace. "You hurt bad?" He pushes the door open and shifts to the side, letting me step past him into a dimly lit hall.

"No, I'm okay," I tell him as he guides me down to a large open area. The smell of leather and smoke fill the air, the scent reminding me of Beau.

"He's out back. Wait here." He holds his hand up for me to stop as he steps forward. Not wanting to disobey any orders, I hold back and take a look around.

The place is enormous with the open living area taking up most of the floor. A fully stocked bar runs along the right side of the clubhouse with a pool table to the left. The wall above the pool table holds pictures of members in their cuts, some mug shots, but more family shots. The Club's insignia, carved in a large wooden display, sits in the center of the wall, Knights Rebels inscribed above the skull head. A few young men standing around the table look up as the young guy calls out across the room.

"Umm, boss, we have a big fucking issue."

"What the fuck now?" The annoyed grumble of the man I'm assuming is the boss has my stomach shifting with unease.

Beau might not be dangerous, but maybe coming here was.

"Spit it out." The deep timbre of Beau's voice calms me instantly and my feet move forward and step in view.

"Mackenzie?" He stands instantly, and the loud thud of his chair falling back has my eyes dropping to the ground in front of me. I'm not sure if he's angry, or shocked, and I can't bear to look and find out.

"Beau, I'm so sorry I came, but I really need your help," I rush out, hoping it's just shock. Seconds feel like minutes before the same two hands that carried my broken body out of my hometown of Redwick and away from an abusive husband eighteen months ago, come to either side of my face forcing me to look up.

"What the fuck happened?" His deep blue eyes roam my face, inspecting the damage. I don't answer right away, my own eyes reacquainting themselves with his. His dark brown hair is still long, and pulled back away from his face. Instead of a low ponytail like I remember he wore it, it's up in a messy sort of man bun. His beard has grown longer and possibly more gray. Not that he looks old, far from it. He looks good.

Too good.

Dark wash jeans, black Henley pulled tight across his chest, and a Knights Rebels leather cut—just how I remembered. It's as if eighteen months haven't passed. I'm looking at the man who saved me, the man who gave me a second chance, and hopefully can save me again.

"He found me, Beau."

2

Bean

"YOU HAVE ANY JOBS THIS WEEK?" BROOKS ASKS, HAND-
ing me a beer.

"Haven't heard anything yet, but we'll see." I take a pull of
my beer and stretch my legs out in front of me. It's a Friday
evening and because I'm on call for Tiny, it's my first, and only,
beer for the night, so I'm going to savor it.

"I'm free to help out if you need a hand," he offers and I
know I'll probably take him up on it. Between the club and Tiny
putting more work on me, I need all the help I can get.

"Thanks." I nod then zone back in on the conversation
happening among the women at the table.

"So when do you leave?" Holly asks, taking a seat next to
me.

"We fly out tomorrow with Ava." Bell looks up, the tears she just managed to control start up again and her old man, Jesse, reaches for her hand.

Bell is the newest woman to walk her ass into the clubhouse and tame one of the Knights Rebels. I say newest, 'cause she isn't the first. Besides Brooks, who's been tied down with Kelly for longer than I can remember, our club Prez and my best friend, Nix, was taken down first when his kid's teacher knocked him on his ass and he willingly handed his balls over. It was fucking agony to watch. The last thing we needed was a pussy whipped Prez around the clubhouse. I gave him shit for a while, but in the end, I knew Kadence was good for him. *For all of us.*

Next there was Sy. The moody motherfucker was the last person I expected to take on an old lady. But the little blonde, Holly, who has a smart mouth on her, was able to fuck with his head enough to have him giftwrap his balls and send them to her.

Then there is Jesse, the latest bastard to be tied down. He might have fought his way against it happening, but he got there in the end. I can't say he's as whipped as the other fuckers, but wouldn't be surprised if the prick has his balls sitting in Bell's handbag.

"I'm so happy for you, Bell." Kelly reaches out and takes her hand. The news is good. They found Paige, Bell's sister who has been missing for the last six years.

"Thank you. I still can't believe it. If it weren't for all of you, this wouldn't be happening." Her eyes move around the table looking at all my brothers before landing on Nix.

"You all helped make this happen and I'll never be able to

11

thank you enough."

"Nothing we wouldn't do for family, darlin'." Nix shrugs it off, but I know he's tense. The people we've had to walk over to find Bell's sister and the markers we've called in are going to come calling one day, and we will have to pay up one way or another.

"I know, but you'll never know how much this means to me."

Jesse throws his arm around her shoulders and kisses the side of her head. She relaxes against him and I quietly watch them.

They've come a long way the last few months. Jesse even more. The shit he pulled would have sent a weaker woman away, but not Bell. For that, I'm happy to accept her into our fold.

"Just bring her home safely," I say when she catches me watching them. She looks taken aback for a moment before she nods. I'm not surprised by her reaction. It's not like I'm a complete asshole, but I'm guarded. I don't let people in easily. And I don't talk for the sake of talking.

Her wobbly smile tells me she's hanging on by a thread, but I know the strength inside of her won't allow her to shatter; instead, it fuels her to keep it together.

"Umm, boss, we have a big fucking issue." Hunter the club's newest member's voice carries across the club, halting all conversations.

"What the fuck now?" Nix looks up, fingers moving to his temples. I know he's over all the shit we keep finding ourselves in. The last year and a half has been fucking drama after drama. Mostly to do with the business I'm in. Every time we catch a break and shit cools down, it all hits the fan again in the blink of an eye.

Hunter looks to me first before answering and I know right away I'll be responsible for this shit.

"Spit it out." My impatience isn't lost on him, but before he can tell me about my next fuck-up, movement behind him takes my attention. A brunette walks around the corner. Her hair disheveled, face messed up, lip busted, and the start of a bruise dances over her cheekbone. My heart stops instantly as I take her in and realize who it is.

"Mackenzie?" I stand from my chair so fast it falls back with a loud thud; causing her eyes to snap down in submission.

"Oh, fuck," someone curses, but I can't place the owner's voice because I'm too caught up in the fact that Mackenzie Morre just walked into our clubhouse, walked back into my life.

Fuck me.

"Beau, I'm so sorry I came, but I really need your help." Her eyes don't find mine again, staying glued to the floor in front of her. Her hair is shorter than the last time I saw her and she looks to have lost a few pounds. *Has she been eating?* An overwhelming urge to take her in my arms and carry her to my room pulls at me, but I don't. I barely know this woman. I've spent no more than forty-eight hours with her, yet she has a hold over me, a hold I can't explain, and not sure I want to.

Keep it together, asshole.

"Fuck," I think I say before getting my shit together and rushing toward her. She trembles when I step in closer, but doesn't back away as I reach her. "What the fuck happened?" I question as I place my hands on either side of her face. She finally looks up at me and I have a better view. Her dark brown

13

eyes are drowning in fear, but I can see she is trying to fight the current. Her lip has been split and her cheek is bruised. It takes everything in me to keep calm.

"He found me, Beau." Her voice is small, scared and it fucks with my head.

"Where?" I try to keep the disbelief out of my tone because I didn't know where she was the last year and a half. How the fuck did he find her?

"In Ohio."

Ohio? How did she end up there? Why did she end up there?

Shaking my head from all the questions running through my mind, I step back from her and turn, only to find the whole club watching us. I don't have time to acknowledge the concern on their faces before I zero back in on Bell.

"Bell, can you grab the medical kit." Bell nods then moves to the kitchen.

"Tell me what happened." I look back to Mackenzie, needing to know everything before we can figure out how much shit we're in. Her eyes fly to mine before flicking back to the others.

"You can talk in front of them, darlin'. You're safe here." I try to encourage her, but I can already see her walls going up.

"Beau." My name is delivered in a plea and just like that, it's as if the last eighteen months haven't passed and I'm back in our safe house breaking all my rules.

The truth is I barely know Mackenzie. I met her one night on a pickup in the next town over in Redwick. She was messed up so bad we had to deviate from the usual routine and get her into a hospital. Little did we know her fucking asshole husband was none other than Chad Morre, son to Mayor Morre. Chad and his father have done everything in their power to find Mackenzie, even going to the extremes of hurting our own.

"Okay, darlin', come on." I place my hand on the small of her back and motion her to the living room. She relaxes noticeably before moving over to the sofa. Nix hangs back near the bar as the rest of the group move out, heading either into the kitchen or out to the patio.

"Nix is gonna stay. This is his club," I tell her how it is and watch her flick her gaze back to him. I can see she wants to argue, but there isn't anything she can say that will change my mind. Nix won't leave and I don't want him to. We just became an open target now she's back. We need all the information we can get.

"Just start from the beginning. What's happened since I saw you last?" I ask when she settles on the edge of the sofa and fidgets, her hands in her lap.

"Well, after staying with Larry and Mary for the week, I was moved on to Phoenix."

Larry and Mary were the couple I dropped her off to. It was her first safe drop out of Redwick and the last time I saw her.

"I stayed in a women's shelter for six weeks in Phoenix until I healed properly." She runs her finger along a faint scar on the inside of her arm. Anger boils inside of me hating she has a constant reminder of what her husband did to her.

"Once I was able to do everyday things I left there, ended up in Ohio. Found a nice small town and settled down." Bell comes back into the room and opens the kit, setting it up on the coffee table. I offer her a slight nod and then wait till she leaves us alone.

"You found your safe place." I reach forward into the first-aid kit and pull out some sterile wipes.

"It wasn't home, but I tried to make it so." I show her the wipe and motion to her lip, a silent question for permission to use it on her. She nods before twisting her head slightly and offering me better access. It looks like she's attempted to clean it up, but didn't do a very good job.

"I had a job, a nice apartment, and everything had been quiet." She flinches when I gently wipe at her lip, but quickly recovers. "I don't know how he found me. I've been so careful." She shakes her head, berating herself.

"So what happened?" I drop the wipe and reach for a sterile strip. She waits for me to place the small strip over the cut on her lip before answering.

"I came home two nights ago and he was there in my bed." Her hands start to shake in her lap. Without thinking, I reach forward and place my hand over them. It soothes her a little, but not much. "He had a gun, said he had been looking all over for me." My grip tightens in reflex as the vision plays out in my mind.

Motherfucker is gonna burn for this.

"How'd you get away?" Nix steps forward, not as patient as me, and takes a seat across from us. Mackenzie holds his stare briefly before answering.

"Ahhh, I've been taking some classes." Her eyes flick up to mine, unsure and maybe a little shy about her admission.

"Classes?" I push, wondering how far she really has come the last year and a half. Right now she's scared and coming out of her skin, but she's clearly been trying to better her life.

"Self-defense. I wanted to be prepared." A sense of pride— I'm not sure where it comes from—fills me knowing she's been looking after herself and staying ready.

"Good girl." Her eyes soften a little at my encouragement, and the start of a smile pulls at the corner of my mouth, but I stop myself before giving her anything more. "You lay him out?" I already know the answer, but I want to hear her say it.

"Ah, yeah," is all she says before diverting her eyes. I look to Nix and watch his brow dip in question, before giving me his something-isn't-adding-up look.

"What happened then?" I push a little harder trying to connect the dots.

"We wrestled a little. He got a few hits in." She points to her face "And then I just kind of grabbed my bag I had stashed for an emergency and got out of there." Her voice drops low and her eyes fall to her lap.

"And Chad? Were you followed?" We really don't need this fucker back on our doorstep. The last time we dealt with the cockhead didn't end well.

"No, I made sure." I don't really know how she can be sure, but I don't question her.

"Coming back probably wasn't the smartest idea." Nix's tone isn't impressed, and I can see why. After everything we did to move her out of town, the shit we endured, having her just walk back in the door is only going to fuck everything up.

"I know, and I'm sorry if this is not a good time for you, but I didn't know what else to do, Beau."

"No, you made the right decision." I put her at ease. What else was she supposed to do? The last time I saw her I told her we would keep her safe.

Yeah, so fucking safe.

"We will help you any way you need. You can stay here,

under our protection until this shit is sorted." I lay it out for her without even discussing it with the club. Hell, even I'm not thinking it through. I don't give a fuck. There are times in life when you just act and, right now, I'm calling the shots and acting. I know my brothers will have my back, even if they are worried.

"I can't ask to stay here." She shakes her head, but I don't let her decline my offer.

"Mackenzie, you need protection." She starts to argue but stops right away, as the realization I'm right dawns on her. The only way to really keep her safe is if she's under our roof.

She turns her gaze toward Nix, seeking his agreement. His eyes find mine, one brow raised. I know he's trying to figure out what's happening right now, but he still wants to give me the lead on this situation.

"You'll be safer here," he agrees and I watch her shoulders drop in relief.

"I can pay. I'll find a job." She looks back to me.

"Let's just get you sorted first, see what we're looking at. Until we figure all this out, we'll take it as it comes." She nods, agreeing to the plan.

"You won't even know I'm here. I promise."

"Yeah, I doubt it." She lifts her lips to attempt a smile at my joke, but it doesn't reach her eyes. She must be fucking wrecked. A bus trip from Ohio to Nevada not knowing if you're being followed would be more than draining.

I'm going to kill the motherfucker for touching her again.

"I'll ask Kadence and the girls to set the guest room up." Nix stands. "Beau, we need to talk and we need to have Tiny in on this." It's not an invitation for chitchat; it's an order.

Nodding once, I come to my feet and hold out my hand for Mackenzie. She looks down at it, and for a second, I want to drop it. But I don't. I don't know what's wrong with me. It's not how I usually act, but this thing with Mackenzie is affecting me more than I care to admit. Even when I first met her, I knew she was someone who could possibly change me into something else. What, I don't know, but it's messing with my head and I'm unsure how to process it.

"You can go with the girls. They'll get you settled in, Mackenzie," I encourage. Her gaze moves from my hand to my face.

"Are you sure this is okay?" Her reservations aren't lost on me. Maybe later I'll ask myself the same question: Is having her here going to be okay? But right now we have a mess to clean up and if I'm completely honest, I've never felt surer of anything before.

"Yes, Kenzie. Trust me." Her body tightens at my words, but somehow she works through it. Taking a deep breath, she places her hand on mine and comes to her feet.

"Thank you, Beau. I don't know how I'll ever repay you."

"You don't have to, darlin'. We've got your back." This time I allow a smile, something I don't give freely, to form and spread across my face. She returns it with one of her own and I don't think I've ever seen anything so fucking beautiful before in my life.

Jesus Christ, in less than twenty minutes my life has just taken a drastic turn.

I know I'm fucked. More fucked than any of these assholes have ever been. So why doesn't it scare me? *Because you want what they have and she has the power to be the one to give it to you.*

Fuck me.

I can already feel my balls going numb.

God help me.

3

Mackenzie

"SO HERE'S THE BATHROOM. I'LL MAKE SURE YOU HAVE some clean towels in a moment." The woman who introduced herself as Kadence motions to the small bathroom to the left of the room. I follow her line of sight and peek inside. A little basin sits to the left with the toilet in the back corner. A bath and shower sit along the right-hand side of the room. A pale pink shower curtain hangs open, inviting me to get in. I let out a small sigh, eager to soak in a hot bath.

"Thank you so much again." I look back at the four ladies Beau left me with, watching me carefully. "It's perfect."

"It's our pleasure," the other blonde replies as she steps forward. "If you need anything, please don't hesitate to ask." Her eyes are warm, inviting and for a minute, I want to let her comfort me. It's been a long time since I've felt relaxed. Safe.

"Do you all live here?" I look to each one of them, trying to remember their names. Holly is the younger looking blonde; she's tall, lean and her body language radiates confidence. Standing across from her gives me a small case of anxiety. *What I wouldn't do to be confident like her.*

Kadence has dark hair that flows down her back. She comes across as the most relaxed out of the four. With dark-wash jeans, and a tight Harley top, she is gorgeous in an understated way.

Bell is the one who gave Beau the first-aid kit. She looks the youngest and also has dark brown hair. She's quieter than the others, sweet but more reserved. And Kelly is the other blonde. Closer to my age than the others, she's definitely more reserved, almost experienced. I don't know how to explain it, but her eyes hold an understanding I haven't seen in a long time. Like I could open up to her about anything,

You can't get close with these ladies, Mackenzie.

"All the guys have their own rooms here, but we generally stay at our houses," Holly answers, pulling me out of my head.

"I haven't taken anyone's bed?" I ask Kadence, hoping I haven't messed with anyone's space.

"No, this room is for guests."

"Oh, good." I relax and drop my backpack into the chair that sits against the wall.

"Do you want to see the rest of the place, Mackenzie?" Kelly asks. I nod, not trusting my voice. I'd rather draw a bath and soak, but knowing where everything is around here is important too.

"Great." She claps her hands and steps toward the door.

Bell and Holly move next. I follow behind them and Kadence takes up the rear.

"These doors are club members' rooms. Jesse's, Brooks' and Beau's are here." Kelly points to each door, naming off the owners. I pay extra attention to Beau's door, but push it out of my head when I realize what I'm doing. I'm not here to get myself caught up with Beau. I'm here to make sure what happened in Ohio doesn't come back to me.

"Laundry is in here." Holly taps on another door. *Laundry.* I look down at my clothes and realize they could use a wash. Sooner rather than later I will need to go shopping for more clothes. I add it to my mental to-do list. I barely have any clothes; in fact, the only thing I have is my small escape bag.

"You can help yourself to anything, whenever you need." Kadence lightly touches my shoulder, reassuring me. I nod, grateful these people are so welcoming.

We take the corner and walk back through the front room. I notice all the men have moved on.

"So this is our living area, pool table, and bar." Kelly keeps up her tour, pointing as we pass through the room and around the bar.

"And in here we have the kitchen." She stops at the door and lets me pass by her inside. It's bigger than I expected. Kind of like one of those industrial kitchens. Stainless steel counters and appliances. A dark-oak eight-seater table sits to the left. An older man who I can only assume is Nix's father sits at the table. He looks up as we walk in, and the similarity of facial features between the two is striking.

"Red, this is Mackenzie. Mackenzie, this is Red, my father-in-law," Kadence introduces us. Red gives me a nod and then

23

moves his attention back to the small baby girl sitting in his lap. A young boy who looks around thirteen sits to the side of him. There's a baby in a highchair and a little girl is sitting in her own chair.

I don't know what I expected when coming here, but seeing the family vibe happening tonight is the last thing I thought of.

"You looking after my boy, Z?" Holly steps forward and places a kiss on top of the baby's head.

"Of course." The young boy, Z, puffs his chest out like he has the most important job. It's too cute really to see him so protective of the younger kids. "When are we having dinner, Mom?" Z shifts and turns to look to Kadence.

"I suppose I should get that started, huh" Kadence leans forward and scruffs his hair.

"Would you like something to drink? Coffee?" Bell asks as she moves to the coffee pot.

"Ahh, no thanks, I'm good." The last thing I need is coffee right now. Not when I plan on crashing as soon as this little tour Kelly is giving is over. Bell smiles and nods. I watch as she reaches for her own coffee.

"This kitchen is huge." I continue to look around, checking out my surroundings.

"It has to be with all the people around here." Kelly shrugs, like the idea of anything smaller would be ridiculous. "Shall we keep going?" she steps toward the door.

"You guys go on ahead. We'll start on dinner." Kadence waves us off, leaving Kelly and I alone.

"Sure," I reply and follow Kelly out towards a glass door that opens out to an outdoor area.

"The boys spend a lot of their time out here," Kelly offers.

I nod and look out. A large outdoor setting sits in the middle of the patio. Chairs, crates, and a few other makeshift seats fill the area. Past the patio, acres span around the clubhouse, closed in by full fencing.

"It's amazing." I shake my head at my choice of words. I guess when you've been living in a small one-bedroom matchbox unit, something as big as this *is* amazing. I turn back and follow Kelly inside. We step back to the kitchen bypassing a massive oak door that sits closed. I don't ask what's behind it because somehow I know it's where Beau and the others are. *Talking about me being here.*

"Did you want something to eat?" Holly asks, pulling down some plates while holding her son.

"No, thank you. If it's okay with you guys, I think I just want to crash. I'm so tired. I haven't slept in over two days." Holly's eyes darken and I know she's probably mad for me, some kind of woman-to-woman sympathy thing that happens when women hear about your past, but I can't deal with anyone right now. I just need to sleep.

"You go on ahead. I'll let Beau know you can find your way around the clubhouse, and now just need some shut eye." Kadence lets me off the hook.

"Thanks so much, I wish I could stay and get to know you all more," I offer the weak line. I know they probably want some sort of explanation about why I'm here, but if I hang around any longer, I'm not sure I'll be able to keep my calm composure.

"Don't sweat it, girl. We'll be here tomorrow. We can chat then." Kelly steps forward and brings her arms around me. I can't help but tense. Forcing myself to relax into her hug, I focus on my breathing. Over the last eighteen months, I've been working on my reaction to any sudden movement. The self-defense classes have helped, but sometimes it gets the better of me and I react.

"Okay, well thanks for everything. Umm, can you tell Beau thank you." I start to fidget in my spot, anxious to leave. I feel terrible ditching them after they have just welcomed me in, but I need space to process the last forty-eight hours.

"We will, sleep well, and know you're safe here." Kadence steps forward this time. She doesn't put her arms around me; instead, she reaches for my hand and squeezes it firmly in a comforting gesture.

"Thanks." I pull back, and look over at Bell and Holly, giving them a wave before turning on my heel. The idea I am safe settles over me as I make my way to my room.

Safe.

When was the last time I truly felt safe?

The night Beau sat with me in hospital.

Forgoing a bath like I had planned, I pull back the covers on the double bed and crawl in. My eyes are so heavy I don't know how I've functioned for this long.

Letting out a defeated breath, I pull the blanket up to my neck and close my eyes. It doesn't take long for sleep to take me, and for the first time in a long time, I know I'm going to sleep well.

I'm not sure if it's because I'm here, or because of why I'm here.

Only time will tell.

Past

Mackenzie

"OKAY, I'M HEADING OUT." I STOP AT THE DOOR ON MY way out to say goodbye to Chad.

"Where do you think you're going?" He looks up from the television and eyes my outfit. Dark-wash jeans and a pale pink camisole set off with a black jacket and matching heels cover my body. I was going for casual with a hint of sexy and judging by his stare, I might have just pulled it off.

"With Heidi."

"What about my dinner?"

"I told you last week, Chad. I'm going out for dinner for Heidi's birthday." A look I can't read washes over his face before he stands and walks toward me.

"So you're just going to leave me here with no dinner and

go out?" At first I think he's joking. The last few months have been great between us.

"Quit playing, Chad. I'm going to be late." I shake my head just as he steps in front of me. He's the same height as me when I'm wearing heels so I don't have to look up to make eye contact with him. "You can cook your own dinner or there are leftovers in the fridge if you don't want to."

"But I want *you* to cook for me." His voice is controlled, his pout only just gracing his lips. I roll my eyes, thinking we're playing a game here, not realizing how wrong I am. My slip in my reserve costs me. Before I can react, I'm pushed up against the wall. Hand to my chest, pinning me with his weight.

"Chad?" I ask. Fear ignites, working its way through my body and washing away the last four months he hasn't laid a hand on me.

The last time Chad hit me I passed out in the bathroom. I woke up in our bed with him hovering over me with the most distraught face I had ever seen on him. At first, my instinct was to leave. No man was ever going to hit me and expect me to put up with it. But stupid me believed him when he broke down in tears and promised me he would never do it again. Who was I to throw a good marriage away for one mistake? So I stayed. And everything went back to normal. We had our fights, sure. But not once has Chad raised his hand to me again.

Until tonight.

"You ever roll your eyes at me again, you'll regret it, Mackenzie." His alcohol-tainted breath hits my face.

"I didn't mean it." My need to placate him takes over. I've gone back to the woman he needs when he's like this.

"I thought you were learning, Mackenzie." His free hand

moves to my face, holding my jaw in his tight grip. I know it's not a question, but I answer anyway.

"From now on, Chad. I'll remember. I'll learn. It was a slip. I'm sorry." I sound like a pathetic, weak person to my own ears, but I don't care. I just need to stop this before it gets out of hand.

"Do you like it when I punish you? You like being taught a lesson?" His fingers tighten, making it harder to talk.

"No." I barely gasp through the hold he has on me.

"Then why do you insist on pushing me?" I don't have an answer right away. Do I like pushing him? Maybe some part of me wanted to push. Do I deserve this as a result? No. Do I want this type of love?

"I... I don't know why. But I promise it won't ever happen again." I scramble for the words he needs to hear, attempting to calm the beast I know is almost free of his cage, but I'm too late. It's too late.

The slap comes next. The sting burns my face, bringing stars to my eyes.

"You do know why. Don't lie to me. You like it when I'm angry. If I put my hand down these jeans, I'd know how much you like it. The thought alone makes my cock rock hard." I swallow, forcing the impending vomit from coming up as he eases his zipper down. *He wouldn't.*

"Please, Chad. Not like this," I beg. The last time he touched me, I believed he loved me. I thought we were moving past the ugliness he had tainted our marriage with. Now, in this moment, it only brings back the hate, fear, and disgust I felt that night in our bathroom. And as much as I despise him for making me experience all those emotions, I hate myself just as much for believing he changed. For what I have let happen to me at the hands of the man I pledged my love to.

He holds my stare for a moment, neither one of us speaking until he finally comes back to himself, re-zipping his pants.

"You're right. Not here. I have a better idea. Go clean up. You and I will be eating out tonight. Call Heidi. Tell her you're sick and won't make it." I nod, watching him step back and run his fingers through his hair.

On shaky legs, I begin to walk back to our bedroom. The last thing I want to do is cancel on Heidi, especially on her birthday, but there is no other option. He won't let me leave tonight, not after what just happened. He's on the cliff and I don't want to push him. *For your safety, Mackenzie, don't push him.*

"Oh, and Mackenzie, you know how much I despise disrespect. Don't make it hard on yourself. Next time, I won't be so forgiving." A shiver runs through me at his words. It isn't a threat, but a promise. One I know he will keep. I don't know how but I have to get out of here. If the last four months have taught me anything, it's that people don't change.

I've been stupid to think he could.

4

Beau

"YOU WANNA TELL ME WHAT THE FUCK'S GOING ON,
Beau." Nix's first words spoken since we took a seat at the club
table don't hold back his concern or frustration at what having
Mackenzie here could possibly mean for us.

"I'm just as fucking surprised as you are, Nix." I give it to
him straight. The last thing I was expecting when I sat down for
a quiet night was to have Mackenzie Morre walk into the
clubhouse.

"Fuck. You know what this means? More fucking shit we
don't need." He rubs his hands down his face roughly and I
almost laugh at the predictable action from him. It's his tell,
something the asshole does every time he's stressed and trying
to regain his composure.

Nix has been Prez of this club for over ten years with me as his VP, and my best friend for even longer. Growing up together we never had plans to follow in our fathers' footsteps, but when shit happened with a rival club, involving the death of Nix's mother, our future was decided right then and there for us. I don't regret it or hold on to any what ifs. There's no reason to. We've always been family. Our choice was simple. I've seen the way our pops' lived their lives, and while it wasn't what I wanted, once Nix and I took the lead, life has been a hell of a lot better. We've grown both individually and with the club. We moved away from the illegal shit, and now we own three businesses that keep us busy. *Only one said business just landed us in more shit. Shit we could do without.*

"What do you want me to do? Tell her we can't help her?" I pull my head out of the past to respond to him. The rest of the table is quiet as they let us talk this shit out. We don't normally butt heads, both of us usually agree along the same lines, but if I have to go head-to-head with him over Mackenzie, I will.

"Just clue me in on where you're at, Beau. What are we getting ourselves into here and for who?" His tone drops from pissed-off Prez to the friend who has always had my back, so I take a second to gather my thoughts and process this entire situation.

What is really going on here?

In the brief time my path crossed Mackenzie's, we connected. It may have been fleeting, maybe even one-sided, but the night I took her out of her hell, something changed. Yes, my mission is to assist Tiny in helping women escape abusive homes, to aid anyone who truly needs the help of this club, but now having her back, what are my real motives? Part of me wants to say it's my need to make sure we follow this through, ensure Chad Morre doesn't win. But it's more than that. Maybe it's only a small ripple in a roaring sea, but it's deeper than a simple act of service. This hold she has on me is something I'm not ready to acknowledge yet. I felt it the moment I picked her broken body up and placed her in the back of the van. When I held her in my arms and took her to the hospital for emergency surgery to fix the damage her fucking asshole husband caused her. But then I lost it all when we finally managed to move her to the next drop off point.

Knowing I wouldn't see her again, it fucked with me in a way I haven't experienced in a long time. Since...her. *My sister.*

"He's messed up by her." Sy, the quiet fucker of the bunch, speaks out, pushing all thoughts of Missy away. If anyone knows how messed up I am over Mackenzie, he would. He was there the night we saved her. Sy saw firsthand how affected I was by her.

"Don't think you know what you're talking about, brother." I flick my gaze briefly to him, but don't give him the pleasure of seeing what his words do to me.

Messed up is a fucking understatement.

"Ever since we picked her up, you haven't been thinking right. Taking chances when you shouldn't be. Bringing danger to the club because you aren't executing well thought-out plans." I keep my stare on Nix while Sy lays it out. I know he's right. I fucking have. The shit I pulled a few months back with one of the Warriors' women was dangerous, but he can hardly blame Mackenzie for it. That's just me. I saw the woman in danger and I reacted.

"You done?" I ask when he stops throwing me under the

bus.

"You gonna deny it?"

"I don't have to fucking do anything. You think you understand, but you don't. Any one of those women I've helped over the last two years walked into this clubhouse asking, seeking, fucking looking for help from us and I'm gonna do the same thing I'm doing right now for her." I fold my arms in front of me waiting for his comeback. The room keeps quiet and I know he's done.

"I want you to keep your head clear on this one, Beau." Nix finally speaks again. I know he doesn't want to undermine me on this. This club is just as much mine as it is his. We've both been through our own shit, but we've always had each other's back no matter what.

"Not gonna lie. She's under my skin, but I'm not going to go there. She's not what I need and I'm sure as fuck not what she needs." I give it to him straight. No point fucking around. Yeah, her being here is messing with me, but fuck if I can have a taste of it. We're both way too screwed up for each other.

Nix holds my gaze a moment longer, still not speaking. I let him have his play and wait to see where he goes with it.

"What's the plan then?" He finally sighs, and I hold my breath a little longer before relaxing back into my chair.

"We give Tiny a heads up, see what he has to say. Either way, it's out of his hands but we'll need his help. Jesse, I know you have shit with Bell going on this week, but we get Jackson in on this, see what we can throw at Chad, legally, and we go from there." Jesse's slight nod tells me he'll set it up.

"Other than put feelers out, what else can we do?" I look back to Nix. This issue with Mackenzie isn't going to be an easy one. Chad is dangerous because he has powerful connections. We need to go about this carefully, so we don't become caught up in all of his political shit.

"She stays here on lockdown until we know what they know. She needs something, we bring it to her. Until we know for sure what they're planning, we play it safe," Nix gives his orders and I agree with everything.

"I give him to the end of the week before he knows we have her, so we have to keep our eyes and ears open. We should bring a lawyer in on this, see where we stand. Maybe we can look at a protection order for her. I'll make the call and give him the run down," I add, looking around the table. They all nod, agreeing with the plan I just laid out. "And she's off limits." I look directly at Hunter considering he's the only fucker left without any regular pussy.

He laughs to start off with then stops immediately when he sees I'm not fucking around.

"You think I'm fucking stupid, Beau?" His body shakes with laughter, but I don't know what's so funny. I'm fucking serious.

"Just nod and agree." Brooks knocks his shoulder giving him some sound advice. Hunter does as he's told, but it only placates me a little. I know I'm probably overreacting. If anyone needs to stay away from Mackenzie, it's me, but it doesn't mean the others don't need to be warned. Hunter specifically.

"Right, well let's get this shit done." Nix taps the table, ending the meeting just as fast as he had called it. The rest of the guys stand without another word and walk out one by one. I don't shift from my chair, knowing Nix well enough to appreciate he'll want a word with me privately. My prediction is

35

right when Sy walks out, leaving us alone.

"You sure you know what you're doing here, Beau?" He closes the door and rests his shoulders against it.

"You know me, asshole. I say I have it under control, I have it under control." I look up and watch him regard me carefully.

"I know, but they don't. You sure this doesn't have anythin' to do with Missy?" My sister's name grabs hold of me and I'm thrown back into the past. The past I wish I could change.

"You know this is why I do this gig, not gonna hide it."

"No, I know why you do it. We're all aware. But it's no secret the last few months have been messing with your head and clouding your judgment. It can't happen with this, with her, Beau. If it does, we're gonna have problems. Problems we might not be able to come back from."

"I do it for Missy. I fucking miss her every day. But this shit right here, by no means is messing with me. I've got this," I assure him one last time. It will be the last time I do it too because I don't have anything to prove. Yeah, I'm twisted, but not for the reasons he might think.

"She's hiding something."

I laugh, not because I don't believe him but because he picked up on it too. "I thought so too, but I don't know why. Could be just jumpy from the run in?"

"We'll give her a few days, see how she settles," is all he says, and I know he won't question me any further.

"Your wife staying to cook me some dinner?" I change the subject, eager to end this conversation for good, so I can go out and speak to Mackenzie.

"Fuck off, find your own wife." He flips me off, then turns and walks out leaving me on my own. I laugh at the asshole and his protectiveness over Kadence's cooking. The truth is if I had a wife who cooks like Kadence, I'd be the same way. *Lucky bastard.*

Taking one last breath to keep myself in check, I stand and follow him out.

Whatever happens from here on out, I gotta keep my cool. The last thing I need is to lose my head, especially over Mackenzie. And the last thing she needs is more fucked-up shit in her life.

This is going to be interesting.

Taking a sip of my third coffee the following morning, I force myself not to look at the clock again. It's been less than a minute since I last checked, and it's not moving any faster.

After we had come out of our meet last night, I was disappointed to learn Mackenzie had gone to bed. I was tempted to knock on her door, make sure she had settled in, but Kelly was pretty adamant about not bothering her, promising me she was fine. So I stewed the rest of the night. Spoke to Tiny about the predicament we found ourselves in, then called it a night. It was a waste of time anyway. I tossed and turned all night wondering if Mackenzie slept well, if she was second-guessing coming here, if we would be able to keep her safe. Every fucking scenario played out, and every one of them ended with me fucking up with her.

Yep, I'm screwed up beyond all fucking belief.

"Morning." Mackenzie's voice breaks me out of my thoughts a few minutes later. Not expecting her company, I jump a little in my chair, my coffee spilling over the side of the mug and burning my hand.

"Morning," I reply as I wipe my hand on the back of my shirt. She doesn't step forward right away so I encourage her. "Come in." She doesn't make eye contact; instead, her hands fold over the front of her and clasps her upper arms. "You sleep well?" I ask, wanting her to look at me.

"Like a baby. Haven't slept like that for God knows how long." As she speaks, the tension leaves her body slowly and she finally looks up, giving me her eyes. She doesn't make any further attempt to talk, so I take a minute to look her over. Besides the cut on her lip and the small bruise on her cheek, she shows no other sign of injury. Her dark hair is pulled back in a short ponytail. I want to ask her why she cut it all off, but I don't. It's not like she owes me an explanation. She's wearing the same jeans and shirt she had on last night and I make a mental note to ask one of the girls to sort out new clothes for her today.

"You want some breakfast?" I stand and point to a chair, hoping she takes the direction so I can feed her. Like I thought yesterday, the woman hasn't been eating. I'm only going by what I remember the night I met her, versus what I see now. She looks skinny, too skinny, where before she was definitely more than just skin and bones.

Nothing a few weeks of her eating enough food can't fix, though.

"Ahh, I'm pretty hungry, but please, I can fix it."

"You sit. I'll cook," I order and watch her recoil at my tone and command. Shaking my head at my stupidity, I step forward and try to reassure her. "I have it sorted today. Maybe you can cook tomorrow." It almost feels strange compromising on something like this with a woman. I mean I'm not a complete dictating asshole, but there are certain tastes I have.

A willing and submissive woman is one of them.

Something Mackenzie is not, which only makes the line already drawn even more vivid.

"Sure, we can take turns," she agrees quickly and takes a seat next to where I was sitting.

"Coffee?" I hide my pleasure at her agreeing and reach for a cup.

"Yes, please," she answers, and I fill the cup with the black liquid I brewed half an hour ago. I walk back to the table and hand her the cup. She doesn't bother with cream or sugar. Instead, she takes a sip and rests back in her chair. Before I get caught watching her, I set about making eggs for the both of us. I'm sure some of my brothers will wake up to the smell of breakfast and probably give me a hard time for not cooking enough, but I don't give a fuck right now.

"Kelly said she gave you a tour of the place last night?" I start an easy conversation hoping to relax her a little more.

"Yeah, the place is huge. I might get lost, but I think I have it." I nod, cracking two eggs at a time into the pan. "And sorry I didn't speak to you again, but I was just so exhausted."

"No problem, but we will need to have a chat with Nix today."

"Oh, did you decide something in your meeting?" I hear the panic in her voice before I turn back and watch it slide over her face.

"No, we wanted to talk to you about pressing charges against Chad." I set her at ease, but it only serves to push her further.

"No, Beau. It's not worth the hassle, with his connections." Her head moves from side to side. I'm not sure if she's trying to convince me or herself.

"It will help. Having him caught up in the courts can give us more time."

"No cops, Beau." Her hands fist in front of her, turning her knuckles almost white.

"Kenzie, you have to trust who we bring in on this."

"No cops," she repeats, this time with more force. I hold her stare for a beat trying to get a read on her.

"Okay, darlin'. No cops." She holds her breath for another few seconds before letting it out in a loud exhale.

"Thank you, Beau." I nod, then turn back to the eggs. I shouldn't be surprised by her distrust of cops considering Mayor Morre's connections. I suspect he has a lot of men in the force on his books.

"So do you live here full time?" she asks, her tone lighter than only moments earlier. All signs of her apprehension are gone.

"I have my own place, but I stay here from time to time," I answer, knowing from here on out I'll be staying at the compound.

"You stayed last night?"

"I did, and will continue until you're settled." I reach up to the cupboard where the plates are kept and pull down two. She doesn't say anything at my admission, so I don't push it. Instead, I plate up the eggs and place some bread in the toaster. Mackenzie stays quiet while I finish making our breakfast. The silence isn't awkward, more calming and I find myself not wanting to break it.

After a few minutes pass, I quietly place her breakfast in front of her and wait for her to come out of her head.

"Oh, this looks great." She comes back to the moment and looks over at me.

"Just eggs and toast, darlin'," I play it down, not wanting her to make a big deal about it.

"I've barely eaten in three days. It's not just eggs and toast," she states with a shrug, unfazed by her revelation and how it might affect anyone knowing exactly what she's been through. She owns it and it practically has me coming apart.

"Well, don't delay. Dig in." I force myself not to react. Her fingers reach for the fork I placed beside her plate and I watch as she picks it up. I don't want to seem like a fucking creeper, but I just want to make sure she's eating. Before she can put my mind at ease, she returns the fork and reaches for me instead. Her hand lands on my arm, her touch soft and unsure.

"Thank you, Beau. Not just for the breakfast, but for everything you've done for me. I'll never truly be able to repay you." I nod once, not looking for gratitude. Any decent person would do the same. It's what I tell myself, but I know it's more than that. The emotion she awakens in me causes my words to fail. But it doesn't matter, not right now. Words are not needed in this moment. I look at her, from her eyes to her hand still resting on my skin and then back up again. Neither one of us speaks or attempts to break the connection. It's like time only exists outside of us.

You can't have moments like this with her, I remind myself, pulling myself out of it.

Clearing my throat, I turn my head. "Eat." The demand comes out harsh, rough, even a little angry. She doesn't act as shell-shocked as she did at my last command, but she retreats nonetheless, and for reasons I can't figure out, I fight the urge to promise her I'll never use the tone with her again. Instead, I take a seat and pick up my own fork, and satisfied the woman across from me is at least eating, I take my first mouthful.

Who knew making sure she finished her breakfast could have me so twisted.

5

Mackenzie

"YOU HAVE TO TRUST US, MACKENZIE," BEAU TRIES TO reassure me later that day. We're sitting on one of the sofas in the living area of the clubhouse. Most of the members are outside setting up for a club BBQ, while Nix and Beau sit with me to discuss what's happened over the last twenty-four hours.

"I understand what you're saying, but you don't know them like I do. The whole sheriff's department in Redwick is in his pocket," I try to reason with them. The last thing I need is to have the cops brought in on this.

Jesus, the thought alone makes me want to run.

"Not all the men in the department are dirty, Mackenzie," Nix adds, shaking his head, not agreeing with me.

Knowing I'm not going to get anywhere with Nix, I turn to

face Beau. "Please, Beau. Don't make me go to the police." I know they're only trying to help me, but they really have no idea what their helping might result in.

Beau regards me for a minute before turning his gaze to Nix.

Nix is the Prez of the Knights Rebels, and from what Beau has told me over breakfast this morning, his best friend.

"Your call, brother." Nix shrugs, leaving it up to Beau.

"How about we see how you're doing over the next few days? Let you settle in, find your feet. We hear anything with Chad or the Mayor, we act. If not, we leave it." I let out a low breath and nod.

Yes, I can do that.

"Nix, I'm so sorry to interrupt, but I need some help." Kadence steps out from kitchen. One arm trying to carry a plate of steaks, the other holding her wriggling daughter who is almost out of her hold.

Nix stands, and moves to his wife, relieving her of their daughter. She squeals in delight, her small chubby hands slapping his face.

"You got everything you need here?" Nix turns his gaze back on Beau.

"Yeah, I'll fill her in on everything else." Leaving us alone, Nix takes the plate of steaks too, and follows his wife outside to grill.

"Fill me in? Do you have a secret code I need to live by?" I turn back to Beau and attempt to joke.

Seriously, Mackenzie?

"No secret code, but I do need to fill you in on some club rules. Make sure you know how we run things."

"Are you sure me being here is okay?" I ask, before he breaks down the rules. Rules I can handle. If there are certain things I need to know while staying here, I'd rather learn them now.

"Already told you, you're under my protection now. You're staying." I swallow hard at my unease and accept what he's offering. I know the last thing I should be doing is bringing Beau and his club in on my mess, but it's not like I have much choice. I need time to think this through and at this point, it's my safest place to do it.

As long as the cops stay out of it.

"So what do you have to fill me in on?" I move the conversation along. I know the club has a family BBQ planned so I want to wrap this up so I can get back to my room.

"Not too much. You're free to come and go around the club, but until we know more on Chad, it's best you stay here."

"I can't leave?"

"Not until you give your statement." He tries one last shot at getting me to make a statement.

"That's not fair, Beau. I have nothing but the clothes on my back and what I was able to grab and throw into my bag, which is basically nothing. I need more clothes and bathroom toiletries."

"I have it under control. Holly's on the clothes and Kelly's on your girly bath shit."

"Beau—" I start to complain then realize how selfish that would make me so I stop.

"I got you this." He ignores my reaction and places a plastic bag in my lap.

"What is it?" I reach in and pull out smallish box with a

picture of an android phone on the side.

"Thought since you're back, you might like to get in touch with your old friends now."

"What friends?" I'm not sure if he's confused me with someone or he doesn't understand how by myself I really am. "When I left Redwick, I only had one friend left," I admit, hating how low I was at that time in my life. My parents died when I was twelve, and I lost my nan five years earlier. Chad and Heidi were the extent of my family.

"The woman who arranged for you to leave?"

"Yeah, Heidi. Being married to a man like Chad made it difficult to keep friends," I confess, knowing how hard Chad tried to push her out of my life. But Heidi wouldn't take no for an answer.

"You talk to her since you left?"

"About a month after I left, I called her house from a pay phone. I just needed to check in, you know? See how she was. She said Chad had been giving her a hard time. We talked for a bit, filled her in on everything, and I told her I would call back on my next stop. She told me not to, said it wasn't safe. When I called back a few weeks later, the number was disconnected."

"You think Chad got to her?"

"I want to say no, but I don't know. He was giving her a hard time."

"I'll put some feelers out, see what we can find out."

"God, I don't know, Beau." The thought of knowing Chad has something to do with Heidi moving or worse, possibly hurting her, is too much to handle right now on top of what is already going on.

"She was your best friend, right?"

"She was."

"My experience tells me no one puts themselves in that much danger to save their best friend only to cut them off, darlin'." I know he's right, which is why it scares me more. What if Chad hurt her because of me?

"Okay, thank you," I concede, knowing he's right. Heidi wouldn't cut me off unless she had to.

"Now, as for clubhouse rules, what you see or hear stays inside the clubhouse. There are a few guys who come and go, regulars you'll see around, some on the weekends. Not everything you see will be your cup of tea, but no one will bother you and if they do, you let me know. You understand?" I nod, still trying to keep up. I had no idea when I stepped foot in here how busy their lives are inside the club. Beau's cell starts ringing in his pocket, interrupting him from telling me how things run around here.

"Yep?" he answers on the second ring, lifting his hand and signaling one minute with his finger. "Ahh, yeah I'll have to check." He stands and pulls the phone away from his ear. "I need to take this. You all right to hang out with the girls for the rest of the day?"

"I might just head back to my room and have a nap. I'm still beat." I know Beau wants me to feel comfortable around everyone, but it's only been a day. I'm sure he can understand that I'm still a little uneasy.

"Okay, darlin'. Whatever you want." He offers me a quick smile, then turns and walks out, leaving me sitting alone. I don't waste any time in standing and walking back to my room. The last thing I want is to hang out with everyone at a club BBQ. Especially with Beau not around.

I may not have seen him in eighteen months, but something about us clicked. Maybe it was because he saved me that night or maybe it was more. Whatever it is, I don't want to question it.

He's the only one I can trust. Until I know the threat is gone, I can't get close to these people.

It's for their own safety.

"Oh, hi. Didn't realize anyone was still up." I step into the kitchen later that night for a midnight snack.

"Yeah, couldn't sleep." Kelly looks up from the table at my voice.

"Coffee probably doesn't help." I point down at her mug, offering some sound advice.

"I know, but you know how it is." She shrugs. "You hungry? You missed the BBQ."

"Yeah, I'm starving. I went for a nap. Didn't realize I'd sleep through," I admit, still awkwardly standing on the threshold. I wasn't expecting anyone to be up. To be honest, I prayed no one would be.

After Beau left to deal with some business, I went back to my room. I didn't want to come out while the clubhouse was so busy, so I decided to try to get some sleep. Only problem is I slept right through dinner.

"That's understandable, love. Help yourself. There's plenty of food." She points to the fridge and it only takes my stomach grumbling to take up her offer.

"Thanks." I step up to the fridge and pull out a couple of

containers. I haven't eaten since Beau's eggs, so anything would taste amazing right now.

Kelly is silent while I put together a small plate of salad, chicken and fresh bread rolls.

"Did you have a good time tonight?" I ask after I put the containers back in the fridge and take my plate over to the table. I'd much rather take my food to my room, but I can't be rude and leave her here.

"Always fun at club BBQs. You should have stuck around."

"Maybe next one," I offer, not sure when the next one is happening or if I will still be around. Kelly nods, but doesn't say anything.

The silence hanging between us lasts for a few minutes before Kelly speaks again.

"You know, Mackenzie, if you ever want to talk, I'm here. We all are."

"Thanks, Kelly," I say right before I place a mouthful of salad in my mouth. I know she means well, but I don't really want to talk to anyone here about my past.

"About fifteen years ago I was in a situation not too different from yours." I look up, intrigued she's sharing this with me. "I was young, in love, and he had me like a fish—hook, line and sinker. A real charmer. We'd been dating through college and one night we went out with some of his friends. He'd been drinking all day, and then his ex-girlfriend arrived. I was upset because she sat on his knee and kissed him, and he didn't do anything to stop her. I went to sit in the car and he came bellowing over, annoyed I left him there, so I locked the door. That was the first time I realized how strong he was. He put his fist through the passenger window then dragged me out. After punching me around for a bit, one of his friends drove me home. The next day when he arrived at the dorm, he was full of remorse. He promised me things would be different, he wouldn't drink anymore, and he would never hurt me again. The whole sob story. I believed him. I loved him." She lets out a sad laugh and instantly my insides twist in reaction. I know that laugh, understand where it comes from.

Kelly, missing my moment of recognition, continues her story. "Things improved for a few months, but then I got pregnant." My eyes grow wide at her admission trying to do the math. I know Kelly is married to Brooks, and I know they have a daughter who's only five years old, so she's not talking about Mia.

"He was happy to begin with. Things were looking up. But one night a few weeks later, he came around drunk. He was a mean drunk and I was pissed off at him for going against what he promised me. We argued. He said some terrible things. Then he punched me in my stomach." Her eyes shine with unshed tears and I fight my need to comfort her. "I lost the baby two days later."

"I'm so sorry, Kelly." I place my fork on my plate, my appetite now lost.

"I'm not telling you this so you feel sorry for me, or so we can bond on some sisterhood level. I'm telling you because I want you to know I understand your reservations about seeking help. I was lucky I had a close family who had my back, but sometimes, even with all the support, I still felt alone. Sometimes I wanted to just pretend it never happened. But the problem with that is it doesn't always go away."

"Kelly—" I know what she's saying without really saying it,

and I want to put a stop to it. "Did Beau ask you to talk to me?"

"No, I just overheard them talking about you not giving a statement. I want you to know that I get why you don't want to, and I respect that. But unlike me, you don't have the support I did. So I'm here if you want to talk. Whenever, you know?" She reaches across the table and places her hand over my forearm.

"Did you press charges?" I don't know why it matters but I ask anyway.

"No, like you I didn't want to draw it out. I was scared. He came from a wealthy family and it was his word against mine." I'm almost relieved at her answer. That someone around here understands me.

"I know how that feels."

"You're brave, Mackenzie. Doing this on your own shows just how strong you truly are. Just promise me if you need to talk, you'll reach out. Okay?" I nod and take onboard her advice. The last eighteen months I've kept to myself, holding everything in. Maybe a friend wouldn't hurt. Maybe opening up wouldn't be so hard, knowing she went through the same thing.

"Thanks, Kelly. I think you're brave and strong, too." I place my free hand over hers. I watch a smile spread across her lips briefly and I can't help but return it.

"Well, that's enough deep stuff for the night. I better get to bed." She drops her hand from mine and stands.

"See you in the morning." She places her cup in the sink and leaves me sitting alone thinking about her words.

I know why I don't want to involve the police, and I know why I should.

Neither decision is going to help me. All I know is, right now I'm safe. No one is coming for me. No one is asking questions, and after having my world come down around me, I'm not going to go looking for trouble.

If trouble comes knocking, then I will be ready.

"You have to be shitting me," I curse while trying to flip the damn omelet for the fifth time.

"You okay there?" A voice startles me, causing me to jump back in a scream. "Shit, I'm sorry, sweetheart. I didn't mean to sneak up on you." I turn around at the voice and come face-to-face with someone I've met before. Almost black hair, green eyes, legs molded into dark jeans.

"Detective Carter, what are you doing here?" I back up, knocking the handle of the pan, watching it and the omelet I've been trying to perfect, fall to the floor.

Oh, God, is he here for me?

"Didn't Beau tell you I was coming?" He steps forward, tears a napkin from the roll and starts to pick up the mess on the floor.

"Umm, no?" I calm my breathing and force myself to relax.

"Well, that explains the jumpy reception." He chuckles as he comes to stand in front of me. "Sorry about the omelet."

"No problem, it was already ruined." I watch him place the pan back on the stovetop and step back. My hands flex in front of me. My initial instinct is to run for it, but I push the feeling away. In the past, I learned the hard way the police can't be trusted. Not when they were under the influence of Chad's father, Mayor Morre.

"I can see your head running a mile a minute there, sweetheart. I'm not here to bring you any harm. I'm just here to take your statement." A slight grin pulls at the side of his face, only relaxing me a little.

"Statement for what?" I blurt, forcing another breath into my lungs. Beau and Nix both discussed with me the possibility of going to the police last week. But I said no.

Apparently, he didn't agree.

"To press charges against your ex."

"I-I…" My voice of caution whispers softly not to react, but it doesn't break through my body's need to retreat. I shake my head from side to side. "I'm not interested. I told Beau I didn't want to press charges." I go to step around him, but he stops my escape.

"I understand your apprehension with talking to me, Mackenzie, but I'm on your side." I nearly scoff at him. My side? The man works in the same sheriff's department as men who have ties to the Mayor, why would I want to talk to him?

"There are no sides for me, Detective Carter. I'm sorry you wasted your time coming here, but I have nothing to say." I try to keep my breathing steady as I attempt to stay calm.

Cops are a no go. I found out the hard way last time.

"He put his hands on you. You should make a statement." I stop the eye roll from forming, but can't help the scoff this time.

"Like that's helped in the *past*." I casually take another step back. If he's not going to let me out of the kitchen, I at least want to put some distance between us.

"I know you had a hard run, Mackenzie. I'm not excusing

anyone in our department, but not all cops are crooked." I hold his stare for a beat, and try not to read too much into his conviction. I know he personally didn't mess me around, but the department he works in did.

"Yeah," is all I manage to say, wishing I could be anywhere but here. The last thing I want to do today is reminisce about the time I reached out to the police for help and it was brushed under the rug.

"So, Chad hasn't tried to contact you since you've been back?" Detective Carter presses on.

"No. And I'd like to keep it that way." I take another step back, this time less casually. His eyes follow my retreat, picking up on my unease.

"No one knows I'm here."

"And it will stay that way. As far as we're concerned, you being here is a on a need to know basis."

"Yeah, and what about the Mayor?" Anyone in the Mayor's pockets can easily tell him I'm here.

"The Mayor is more concerned with trying to find his son. Seems he's gone underground. No doubt in hiding after what he did to you."

My heart twists as a white light almost blinds me.

"Do you know how long I've been looking for you?" His jaw ticks and his eyes flash with something I've never seen before. It's almost crazed. Feral.

"You okay, Mackenzie? You look pale." Jackson's voice chases the memory away.

"Of course." I hold his stare. In any other circumstance, I would have pulled off my lie with a smile and a quick change of the subject, but not today. Today, I tug at my shirt, and wonder

54

if he can see right through me. With each tug, my unease grows, and I can practically see his mind racing with unasked questions.

"Is Beau around?" He doesn't push my reaction. Instead, he pulls a chair back and takes a seat at the table, his large frame looking just as uncomfortable as I am.

"He had a callout last night. He just got back in. I think he's in the shower."

I force my mind to not picture Beau in the shower. Naked. Wet. His hair dripping.

Shit, it's not working.

"I'll just wait around for him if you don't mind." His eyes don't leave mine and I force myself not to show any reaction.

"Of course, can I offer you a drink, coffee?"

He nods, giving me my answer. I move to the coffee pot and pour him a fresh cup, refilling my own too.

"Looks like you've settled in." He attempts to make conversation when I hand him his coffee.

"The club has been very accommodating," I reply, not wanting to be rude. "Cream, sugar?"

"I'm good." He winks, bringing the mug up to his mouth.

"What the fuck you doing here, asshole?" I jump back at Jesse's booming voice as he enters the kitchen.

"Hello to you too, brother." Detective Carter doesn't take his eyes off me as he greets Jesse.

"You're brothers?" I look between the two men, taking in both of them. Where the detective has dark hair and green eyes, Jesse has blond hair and blue eyes. If I stare long enough, I might be able to see the resemblance.

A little.

"Unfortunately," Detective Carter answers first.

"I'm the better looking one," Jesse replies, flipping his brother off while taking himself to the coffee pot.

"You think you are." Detective Carter takes another sip of his coffee.

"Nope, I know I am." They keep going back and forth until Jesse stops the banter with his own question.

"What the fuck happened here?" I turn and watch him pick up the pan holding my failed omelet.

"Umm, that would be mine." I try not to react when his horror-filled eyes come to mine.

"Jesus, Mackenzie. Beau wasn't lying when he said you can't make eggs." He empties the messed-up omelet into the trash and wipes out the pan. "I think I need to step in."

"What? It's not too bad."

He turns, and cocks his brow. "Woman, I wouldn't feed my dog this." I'm not offended by his comments. In the last week, I've come to learn Jesse just says it how it is. *All the time.*

In this case, it's no different.

"You don't have a dog, Jesse." Detective Carter laughs from the table.

"Well, if I did, I wouldn't feed her it," Jesse counters.

Before they can get back into it, I interrupt. "Okay, well show me how you do it then. Beau won't teach me and I know omelet is his favorite. I just want to get it right." I take a moment to process what I just said, then try not to read too much into it. I just want to be able to repay him in some way.

"All right. Be prepared to learn, Mackenzie." Jesse starts cracking some eggs into a bowl. "I'll show you how it's done." I look over at Detective Carter. He lifts his shoulder, almost daring me to let him. Knowing I'm better off keeping Jesse around to ward off any of Detective Carter's questions, I step over to the stove and stand next to Jesse.

"It's all in the wrist," he says, and then sets out to teach me how to create some kind of edible breakfast, completely oblivious to my slight freak out.

Who knew last week I would be here, in the kitchen of the Knights Rebels MC, sharing coffee with two brothers. One, who has close work ties to the family I'm running from, and the other teaching me how to make eggs for the man who I owe more than my life to.

The same man who frightens me more than anyone because of the things he makes me feel, the things he makes me want. Things I have no business wanting from a man like him.

Yeah, I need more than a minute to process this.

"Kenzie, did you hear me?" Beau's voice calls me out of my trance. I look up, coming back to reality and find him standing at the door of my room. His hair is pulled back in some sexy male bun, making his beard look longer. He's not wearing his cut today, which disappoints me, but the black Henley, pulled tight over his arms, is just as good to look at.

"Sorry? What did you say?" I place the book I was reading down beside me and sit up.

"Have you eaten?" He rests his shoulder against the door-frame, his booted feet crossing at the ankle.

"Ahh, not yet." I look at the time and realize I've just day-dreamed my whole morning away.

It's been a week since Detective Carter came around to see me. Much to my chagrin, Beau came out from his shower, and ripped Jackson a new one for talking to me without him. It's not that I needed him there when Jackson questioned me; in fact, I was glad I didn't have him there. Beau would have only tried to convince me to press charges. It's not that I don't understand where they're coming from, but it's just easier this way. The last thing I need is a paper trail.

"You gotta start eating, Kenzie," Beau pushes off the doorframe and steps into my room. The name my mom and dad called me sends me back to the good memories of my childhood when my life wasn't tainted with fear and pain.

"I'm not trying to starve myself, Beau." My feet find the floor next to my bed and I stand, stretching out my kinks. Eating has been the last thing on my mind lately, not when my stomach is constantly in knots with fear.

"Doesn't look like it to me," Beau pushes, throwing me off more with his comments. I don't know when he's teasing or being serious. Even after spending two weeks with him, I'm still trying to figure him out. He's changed a lot since I saw him last. Not that I really knew him. It was only a brief time we spent together, but it didn't matter. As cliché as it might sound, we had a connection. One that brought us together.

"Trust me, Beau, between you, Hunter, and Jesse, you would think I have some kind of eating disorder." I shake my head at their over protectiveness.

Over the last two weeks, I've come to know all the guys here, but Jesse and Hunter have been around the most. When Beau isn't around, I find myself either in the kitchen with Jesse, or playing pool with Hunter.

"What've Jesse and Hunter been saying?" His brows pinch inward as he steps into my room.

"Nothing, just that I should be eating more," I tell him, unsure why he's so concerned. He says the same damn thing every day. Ever since my first day here, Beau has been on my back about eating. I know over the eighteen months I haven't been eating as well as I should have been. I can see it in the way my clothes hang off my body. So even if I do find his pestering about me eating annoying, I know why he's doing it.

"Tell them to mind their own fucking business." He grunts, folding his arms over his chest.

"Ahh, no. I can't tell them to mind their own business." I pick up my cardigan and slide my arms though the holes.

Is he crazy? These guys have taken me in to protect me, no questions asked. Made me feel comfortable. Offered me clean clothes, food. I'm not going to tell them to get off my back when I know they mean well.

"I'll tell them." He shakes his head, pulling on his beard, his expression guarded. I don't know much about Beau, but from what I've learned, he keeps to himself a lot and rarely shows emotions, but this here is new. This is deeper.

"It's fine, Beau. I'm a big girl. I can handle myself." He holds my stare for a minute and I wait for him to respond, but he doesn't.

"All right, *now* I'm hungry." I take a step toward him, my stomach grumbling on cue.

"Before we eat, I need to talk to you about Heidi." All thoughts of food flee faster than a gambler from a bookie.

"You found her?" My voice is hopeful, but dread offers my mind only one thought. *He got to her.*

"She's missing, darlin'." I had anticipated the worst, knowing she wouldn't just up and leave like she did, but I wasn't expecting the ferocity of guilt and how it almost blinds me.

"She's dead."

"You don't know that. For all we know, she's gone into hiding."

I know it's more than that. Deep down I know. Regret washes over me. How I wish I could go back and take a different path, a path that includes taking Heidi with me all those months ago.

"She wouldn't just leave like this, Beau. You and I both know this. Stop giving me false hope. Be realistic here."

"I'm not giving you false hope, darlin'. I refuse to give up. We're gonna keep looking." He pushes off the doorframe, takes two steps toward me, and reaches for my hand. Instead of flinching like I normally would, I let him take it, let him soothe the raging storm brewing inside me.

I believe him when he says he won't give up, but I also know Chad. Know what he was capable of. If Heidi is missing, I know with everything inside of me, Chad is responsible.

We stand deep in silence, my mind fighting with my body on how to processes it, until Beau whispers, "Come back to me, darlin'." His words are the resuscitation I need to finally let my body gasp for much-needed air.

"I'm here."

"You're not," he argues, but he's wrong. Two weeks ago, the news of Heidi being missing would have sent me into a full-blown breakdown. This reaction is me processing. I'm not saying every part of me doesn't want to break, or retreat into myself, I just don't want to show Beau that kind of weakness.

"I'm here as much as you." I drop his hand and let out a breath. "Now, how about that lunch?"

"Don't put a mask on with me, Kenz. I'm not saying you can't feel, just don't give up hope." I don't reply right away. The fact he just called me out shocks me. That's one thing I respect about Beau. He doesn't let me play my bullshit.

"You're right. Every part of me wants to lie down right now in defeat. But that's not fair to Heidi." I give him the truth. Until we know for sure, I'm going to stay positive.

"It's not fair to you," he corrects me.

"Yeah, well, I don't care about me."

"Well, I do." His wide eyes reflect his conviction, and his hand tightening in mine proves he won't be convinced otherwise. For a millisecond, I let it pull me to him. It's been so long since I've willingly let someone care. I don't know what it is between Beau and I. This tension has been growing rapidly from day one, and every time he's close, my body reacts.

Which is crazy considering I haven't been with anyone since Chad.
"Well, someone should." I laugh to hide my unease. "Come on, I really am hungry." Beau doesn't say anything, he just steps back to let me pass. My arm brushes against his hard chest as I pass him. "What would you like to eat?" I ignore the flutter in my stomach as I look up at him. He's so tall and broad. The top of my head barely hits his shoulder and standing in front of him, my insides grow unpleasantly warm realizing he could probably do some serious damage with his arms.

No, he's not Chad.

"I'll make something." His short monotone voice makes me cringe only for a second before I relax. I'm starting to learn it's

Beau's way. In the beginning, it rubbed me wrong, taking me back to when Chad was angry with me, and no matter what I would try to do to fix the situation, he would still lash out in a cruel way. Beau is different though. He might be short with his answers, and sometimes he might come across as harsh, but there is nothing cruel about him.

"I can cook, Beau. I don't know what the problem is." I roll my eyes. I'm actually a good cook. I bake and love to try new recipes. I'm just not good with eggs, apparently.

"You roll your eyes at me again, we're going to have other problems, darlin'." His hot breath hits me first, then the slight tickle of his beard before the words wash over me.

I freeze instantly. The pressure of his hard chest pushing me against the wall suspends me from the present to the past.

I know Beau wouldn't hurt me, know it with every fiber of my being, but it doesn't stop my body from reacting.

"Step back," I manage past my dry cottonmouth. My stomach turns as the memory grows stronger. My heart heaves in my chest.

He doesn't argue, his weight is off me in one second. But it's too late. I'm spiraling head first back into the past.

Past

Mackenzie

"I'M SORRY, BABY, SEE WHAT YOU DO TO ME? YOU MAKE
me crazy. I love you so much it drives me insane." The stars
dancing in front of my eyes still linger, but I manage to find my
bearings.

It's happening all over again.

"You mean everything to me, Mackenzie. Seeing you taunt
me like that is too much for me. You can't speak to me like that
and not expect me to react." He continues to excuse his
behavior and push the blame onto me, but I don't have it in me
to listen this time. It's going to be the same old story. Only I
already know the ending.

Ignoring his apology, I start to shift from my position on
the tiled floor and attempt to stand on my feet. I was cleaning

the kitchen after our guests had left, right before Chad came at me with his fist.

"Here let me help you." He reaches for me, but a panicked plea leaves my mouth before I can stop myself.

"NO!"

He recoils at the level of my voice and I take the brief moment to find my feet on my own.

"You can't be angry at me, Mackenzie. You deliberately provoked me." I slowly and painfully turn back to face him and finally see what I have been missing since the night he changed. The man is crazy. He's not going to change. Tonight proves it.

"Provoked you, Chad?" I shake my head of thoughts of our beginning and contemplate how we're going to end.

"Don't fucking act dumb. It doesn't suit you, sweetheart." Forcing a breath into my lungs, I take a minute and try to figure out how to play this.

"I'm dumb all right, Chad. Dumb to think you would change." With false bravado, I move to our bedroom. Each small step burns my innards like boiling water.

"Where the fuck do you think you're going?" Fingers wrap around my forearm, stopping me before I can run away.

"Take your hands off me." The shriek in my voice echoes off the high walls of our house, but he doesn't react, his hold staying firm.

"You're not fucking going anywhere. You're my wife." The vein in his temple bulges as his grip grows stronger. His alcohol-laced breath hits my face and I force myself not to breathe in the offensive smell.

"You don't beat your wife, Chad." I tug harder, desperate to be out of his hold.

"Maybe if you weren't acting like a whore all night, I wouldn't fucking have to."

I know arguing with him right now isn't going to help me. He's drunk, angry, and he's already hit me, but I can't help it. The fact he's calling me a whore hurts more than the fist to the face.

"Whore? Tell me how I was a whore?"

"You don't think I saw the looks you kept throwing the asshole. The smiles, the way you fucking let him kiss you goodbye." He pulls me to his chest.

"You're fucking crazy." I fight his hold. The man has lost his damn mind. I was only playing the part he has drilled into me since becoming his wife.

"Yeah, crazy for you, baby." His nose comes to my hairline and he breathes me in. I keep fighting, even though I know it's pointless. He's too strong.

"I'm leaving, Chad. We're done. You promised, and I believed you. I trusted you wouldn't put your hands on me again."

"You're not going anywhere, Mackenzie." He spins us in one fast movement and pushes me against the wall. Air leaves my lungs in a rapid surge at the force of the impact. He steps in closer, one hand leaving my arm and moving lower, slipping past the hemline of my shift dress. Chad starts to glide it up the outside of my thigh. I fight the tears threatening to fall. It shouldn't be like this. I know that. But the most terrifying thing is, I don't think Chad knows it. To him, there are no boundaries or lines that shouldn't be crossed.

"Don't. Please don't." Repulsion aches through me at his touch and I fight it when his fingers slip into the side of my panties. I've never felt so hopeless in my life, standing against the wall inside of my home with my husband's unwelcome touch.

"Don't what? Touch my whore wife." I kick out at his shin, fighting once more for a brief moment to break free, but I'm met with a backhand to the face. My cheek stings and I cry out, not in pain but in fear, not sure how far he is going to take this or how I am going to get out of this. I don't know if I can. The thought alone has my knees buckling under me.

"The more you fight me, Mackenzie, the worse this is going to be for you." He holds me up against the wall.

"Why are you doing this, Chad?" A sob escapes my lips as he forcibly drives two fingers inside of me. How could the man I love try to take this from me? The man who promised to love and cherish me.

"Because I love you, Mackenzie. No one will ever have what belongs to me. Do you understand me?"

I don't answer because I have no idea how he could think this is love.

This isn't love. This is the devil's kingdom and I don't belong here. The flames from the pits of hell are burning my flesh from the outside, working their way underneath my skin, waiting to turn the flicker of hope I have left in me to ash.

I have to find my way out of it.

Somehow I have to.

6

Bean

"THAT'S IT, DARLIN', DEEP BREATHS," I ENCOURAGE. Her eyes remain closed as she slowly starts to come back to herself. She's been like this for over five minutes now, and it's as if my breathing labors like hers, gasping each time she does.

If only I could just get her to come back.

"Is she okay?" Hunter asks, coming to stand next to me as I wait for Mackenzie to recover from her panic attack.

"Yeah, go grab some water," I order, still waiting patiently. I'm careful not to touch her. Knowing my closeness pushed her into a memory and caused her panic attack, fucks with me. The last thing she needs is for my hands to be on her, which could possibly push her right back into another one. It's the last thing either of us need.

"Beau," she tries to stand, but I don't let her. All thoughts of not touching her flee and my hand comes down on her shoulder forcing her back into her seat.

"Keep breathing, darlin'." Her eyes squeeze shut and she takes in another large, deep breath.

"Oh, God, how embarrassing," she says when she finally catches her breath and calms herself.

"Forget about it," I dismiss her concern. It's the last thing I'm thinking.

As soon as I stepped into her space, forcing her back to the wall, I knew I fucked up. The fear washing over her face, the blank look glazing over her eyes... it was nearly too painful to watch. I managed to move her to the sofa and maneuver her head between her legs to control her breathing. What I just did to her in the hall has played out for her before, and judging by her reaction, last time it ended a whole lot fucking worse.

Which is the reason why I should have known. Any sort of fast movement can set her off. I know this. I fucking see it every day. The women we pick up, at all stages, can react the same. I don't even know why I felt comfortable enough to tease her. Maybe it was the way she was smiling at me, acting like her ex isn't out there waiting for a chance to get his hands on her. In the last seven days, I've watched her relax into a comfortable routine. The scared, broken Mackenzie who showed up on our doorstep is still there, but as each day passes, her confidence has started to grow.

After a few more minutes of running the whole scene over and over in my head, and how I messed up, Hunter finally returns with a glass of water. Taking it from him, I step forward slowly and press the edge of the glass to her lips. She takes a few sips before pushing the glass away. I hand it back to Hunter and nod toward the door, silently telling him to fuck off. He begins to retreat as Mackenzie's hand reaches out and grabs me.

"I'm sorry, Beau. I can't believe I reacted like this." She moves to stand, breaking our connection.

"Don't ever apologize, Kenzie. I shouldn't have trapped you in." I follow her up, not ready to leave her alone just yet. She looks back, eyes wild with distress and shame. "Hey, I'm serious, darlin'. You don't ever have to hide from me. There is nothing you have to be embarrassed about. I get it."

"You do?" Her voice is small, almost overly controlled. A façade. Only I can see right through it.

"It was my fault. I should be the one apologizing. Not you," I offer, hoping to relieve some of her embarrassment. She doesn't say anything, but something silent passes between us. Like we both know it's less about whose fault it is, and more about what just happened between us, but we're not discussing it.

"I'm still hungry," she finally says before turning and moving toward the kitchen.

I want to stay where we are, ask her about the exact moment she was taken back to in her panic, but I'm not sure I can handle what she'd say. So I don't. I keep my questions to myself and follow her into the kitchen.

"So, how was your day?" She sets about pulling out food from the fridge as if nothing happened. I move toward her with the intent to take over, wanting her to fully recover from the anxiety I know is still running through her.

"Stop, Beau. You sit, I have this," she orders the same way I would and I nearly laugh.

"I'm helping. Don't think you can boss me, woman." She narrows her eyes on me but doesn't say anything else. The tension between us still stirs from earlier.

"Can't you just let someone do something for you once, Beau?"

"I don't like to be told what to do," I tell her, trying to explain the way I am.

"I've noticed. Why?" She stops and waits for my answer.

"Because I like control, darlin'." I wait for her reaction. There's a possibility she might pull away from me, put her walls back up at my confession, but I'm not going to hide who I am around her.

"You know I spent too many years with someone who wanted control, Beau." She pulls out a fresh loaf of bread and lays out four slices.

"There are many types of control, darlin'." Her hand is still on the mustard jar but she doesn't reply. "The difference is I wouldn't hurt a woman like your ex hurt you."

"You know there was a time when I believed Chad when he said he wouldn't hurt me."

I practically come out of my skin at her comparison, but manage to control it. "Do you think I would ever hurt you, Kenzie? You think I'm like him?" She doesn't answer at first and it guts me. A small sliver of pain aches its way through my body until it reaches my heart. We both know I'm nothing like him, but I need to hear it from her. Need to know she doesn't think of me the same way. *Like him.*

"No, Beau. Of course not. I didn't mean... I know you wouldn't hurt me. It's just Chad took so much from me, and I've fought so hard to come back from there. I just don't ever see myself in that sort of situation again." Her reasoning makes sense, but it doesn't stop my displeasure at hearing it.

Get over it, fucker.

"I understand why you think that. I do, darlin', but the difference between the control Chad took and the control I crave is, if it's done right, it can be more than you ever thought you would like."

"I doubt it." She scoffs before moving about the kitchen. I don't want to get into it with her anymore. Clearly, we're both so different, on two separate sides of the universe with our wants and needs. I'm not even sure she knows what I'm getting at, but at least she has some understanding of what I'm about.

Not that it matters.

It will never matter.

"You find any info on Chad yet?" Nix asks later that night when the clubhouse is in the full swing of a weekend party.

"Nope, fucking dead end after dead end. Tiny is working a lead, but to tell you the truth, Jackson might be right. Maybe the fucker got messed up in something bigger than this." When Jackson was here last week talking to Mackenzie, he commented that the Mayor was riding him to follow some leads on Chad going off-grid.

"You'd think the Mayor would be on it, plastering his face over the TV if he were really missing," He kicks his legs up on a chair across from him.

"Yeah, something doesn't add up. Jackson said he has a re-election coming up. Still, you'd think he'd put something out there. Maybe he knew Chad fucked-up with Kenz again." We fall silent for a bit, both of us trying to piece it all together. Over lunch today, I tried to get Mackenzie to open up some more about Chad, but she shut right down again. Part of me thinks she's still shaken up by Chad finding her, but a small part of me thinks it's something more. I don't want to keep pushing her, so I've decided to let it go. If she wants to talk, she can come to me.

"So, how you doing otherwise?" I let the Chad subject go, wondering the last time we checked in with each other outside of club business.

"Besides the shit with Mackenzie and the shit with Paige, never better." His laugh is dry and I can sense his concern.

"You getting shit from the markers we called in for Paige?"

"Not yet, but I know it's fucking coming. Knowing T, who the fuck can tell what he'll want."

T is the President of the Warriors, another club just outside of town. While we keep our business legit, the Warriors walk on the opposite side. Owing them a marker is bad for business. Those assholes don't give a fuck what side of the law you walk on. They call a marker, you deliver.

"No point getting yourself twisted over it. We'll deal with it. Simple." Nix nods, but doesn't say anything. I know he's stewing on it, but the way I see it is we can't undo it. And I sure as fuck wouldn't want to. It brought Paige to safety and out of the monster's hands she was thrown into. Hell, after only hearing the basics of what Bell's sister endured for more than five years, I'd be happy to owe T five fucking markers if it meant we saved her.

"How's Mackenzie settling in?" He changes the subject

when he sees her walk out with Kelly and Kadence. I can still see her unease when everyone is around, but she's growing more comfortable with them.

"She's doing okay. Had a meltdown today. Besides that, she's adjusting as good as she can under the circumstances." I'm surprised it took this long for her to show her vulnerable side. She was getting so good at pretending she was fine, I almost forgot she had a past.

"You still doing okay with her here?"

"Don't know why I wouldn't. Things haven't changed." Nix's eyes come to mine at my quick fire response.

"She's fucking with your head living here. Don't deny it." I don't reply right away. Trying to get a handle on how I'm coping with her being here.

"I have a handle on it." I clear my throat, watching her laugh at something Kelly says. She's only just started laughing and interacting with the rest of the club. At first, it was just small moments with me, our quiet mornings in the kitchen encouraging her to open up. But as the last two weeks have passed, she's finally opening up to everyone.

"Fuck, dude. You're so fucking messed up. Everyone's too scared to fucking talk to her." He knocks my shoulder at my growl. "You've been walkin' around like someone pissed in your breakfast ever since she came here. You haven't slept at your own place, and you've been cookin' for her. Should I alert the boys, tell them your balls have been compromised?"

"Fuck you. I'm not talking about this with you, Nix. Go talk your girly shit with Sy and Brooks."

"Quit sulkin'. You don't have to talk to me about it. Just know everyone else is noticin'.

73

"Noticing what?" I bark, pissed these fuckers are even talking about this shit. The last thing Mackenzie needs is to have the clubhouse discussing us.

"That you're pussy whipped." His grin grows at my horror-filled face.

"I am not fucking whipped." I grit my teeth, not at all agreeing with his assessment. *Fuck no.*

"When was the last time you had a woman warming your bed?"

"And on that note, I'm out." I stand, not at all interested in the conversation anymore. Nix might be my best friend, but I don't talk pussy with him. *Ever.* That shit is between me and the woman welcoming me between her thighs.

"I'll keep you posted on what we find out." I take my beer and walk back inside. Nix doesn't call after me. He knows when I'm done. And after hearing the club is just waiting for something to happen with Kenzie and me, I am done.

7

Mackenzie

"CAN YOU DO A LOAD OF MY SHEETS PLEASE, MAC-kenzie?" A voice startles me from behind as I bend down and fill the washer with my sheets.

"Sure, just leave them here and I'll put them in the next load, Hunter." I don't bother turning around. I know all the guys well enough now to recognize their voices.

It's been a month since I came to Rushford and moved in with the Rebels. It's taken that time for me to settle in, and get to know everyone. In the beginning, I only opened up to Beau. His constant presence wouldn't allow me to retreat into myself. Kelly was the second person I let in. Her sharing her past gave me something I could relate to and a closeness I haven't had since Heidi. Kelly has been patient and understanding and before I knew it, the closeness we shared moved on to the rest of the ladies in the club. All of them have taken me into their circle.

"Don't you dare, Mackenzie." Kadence's voice echoes through the laundry room, and this time, I turn.

"It's no problem, Kadence. It's the least I can do. Besides, I like keeping busy." I watch as her brow drops into a scowl at the news I'm going to be washing Hunter's sheets.

"Please tell me you don't always do this?"

"Err." I turn to Hunter not sure how I'm going to get him out of this one.

"Jesus, Hunter. You're a grown-ass man." Kadence shakes her head putting two and two together.

"It's not a big deal." I try to save Hunter from the lecture he's about to receive. "It makes the days go by." I stop and take note of how depressing I sound.

Jesus, I've come to enjoy washing sheets. Call me your modern-day Cinderella.

"Go find something to do, Hunter." Kadence turns to face the youngest member of the Knights Rebels. He doesn't need to be told twice before hightailing it out of there. I know what's about to come next, so I turn back and finish my load.

"You need a job." Kadence's next words are not what I was expecting. I was expecting my own kind of lecture, not for her to say what I've been thinking the last few weeks. I'm going crazy holed up in here.

"I know, but Beau doesn't think it's a good idea," I tell her exactly what Beau said when I suggested it. One night after I had changed all the sheets, cleaned the kitchen, tidied behind the bar and still found myself walking around bored, I

76

mentioned looking for a job to Beau and he quickly shut me down.

"Well, I'm sure we can think of something other than cleaning Hunter's sheets. I mean, who knows what's on them."

"I honestly don't mind." I cringe, knowing she's probably right. I don't pay too much attention to who Hunter takes to his bed, but I have noticed since his main girl left him a couple weeks ago, he has a new woman on his arm practically every night.

"I know you don't, which is what makes this even worse. You *want* to clean Hunter's sheets. Girl, this is bad." I laugh at her disgusted tone, but don't argue anymore. She's right. This *is* bad.

Seriously, who likes doing laundry anyway?

"Well, what do you have in mind?" I ask, moving from the laundry and back out to the kitchen. Besides cleaning everyone's sheets, I've kept myself busy with baking. Something all the members are grateful for, even Beau when I make his favorite brownies.

"What did you do for work before you came here?"

"Before Chad I was a receptionist, and after I was a waitress." My mind flicks to Fred and Carly. My boss and his wife from the diner I worked at in Ohio. It wasn't the most glorified job in the world, but I miss it. My boss was a good man, and even though he didn't know the extent of my past, he still helped me out more than anyone else has done in my life.

I need to call him, and let him know I'm safe.

"So yeah, I'm an all-round go-getter." I force Fred and Carly out of my head and laugh at my own joke.

"What are you two talking about?" Holly looks up from the

77

table, joining in on our conversation.

"Mackenzie needs a job." Kadence takes the seat next to her and I move to fill my coffee cup.

"Oh, I was going to suggest something this week. I don't think I've ever seen the clubhouse so clean." She points around the kitchen. She's right. I've spent virtually every day cleaning over and over.

"Not that we don't appreciate it, but I think it's time to step outside the clubhouse," she adds and I nod in agreement. I've been here hiding out for over a month and no one has come for me. I think it's safe to say I'm not in any immediate danger.

"Okay, so do you know anyone who's hiring?" I move to the oven to check on the cake I'm baking. Chocolate mud cake, with orange glaze today.

"I know Jesse is," Holly offers and I take a minute to think about it. Working with Jesse? It might work.

"It could work."

"No," both Kadence and Nix say at the same time. I look back watching Nix enter the kitchen and move to his wife.

"Not at the club, I mean help with his books." Holly ignores Nix and Kadence making-out like teenagers, and explains her suggestion.

I hold in my smile as she rolls her eyes waiting for them to come up for air. After what feels like a minute, she gives up.

"Hello, important discussion happening here. Get a room." A giggle escapes my lips when Nix pulls back from Kadence and a slight blush coats her neck.

"Sorry." She smirks but there is nothing to be embarrassed about. I wish I'd had a marriage where my husband walked in and literally took my breath away with a passionate kiss.

"So Jesse needs help with the books?" She straightens herself, her eyes following Nix's ass as he walks to the fridge and pulls out a beer.

"If Jesse can't use you, you could help me out. We have three businesses to keep on top of and I'm always behind." Nix cracks the top of his beer and bends down to check what's in the oven.

"You own three shops?" I ask, unaware of this news. The club has been welcoming with me being here, but it doesn't mean they talk much about their business.

"Yep." He stands, his eyes coming to mine. "You making a cake?"

"Yeah, it's nearly done." His grin grows full, making him a hell of a lot less scary. Out of the guys here, Nix and Sy are the two I know least about. Sy still scares me. Ever since the night Beau saved me, Sy's made it clear I'm too much trouble for the club, and Nix is the Prez of this club. He intimidates me.

"Come find me when it's ready," he orders, and I can't help the smile as it lifts the corner of my mouth.

"Sure. And if you need help, I can start right away," I add, eager to start.

"You can start tomorrow." He moves toward the door, done with the conversation. I nod, trying not to show too much excitement. I mean, it's not like I'll be leaving the clubhouse, but at least it will get my mind off things and give me my own income, hopefully enough to help me find my own place. As much as staying here has been great, I'm slowly starting to feel comfortable enough to leave and be on my own. The need to always watch my back is fading and with each day, my confidence grows.

Maybe it's really over?

"So it's sorted then. No more washing nasty-ass sheets." Kadence stands, her eyes shining with achievement.

"I can still do washing," I add, not really caring either way. Over a month of free rent, feeding me and keeping me safe? These people are my saviors. Cleaning and washing are the least I can do.

"No, no more washing, Mackenzie." She levels her stare at me. I don't want to piss her off, so I don't say anything. I don't bother arguing. A few loads won't hurt anyone. She doesn't need to know.

Past

Mackenzie

HIS ARM RESTS HEAVILY ON MY CHEST, PINNING ME down to the bed. Paralyzed with fear, I continue counting in my head. Starting at one and finishing at one hundred. Over and over I repeat it. I've made it through counting to one hundred over fifty times now. Each one bringing me closer to my freedom.

Not knowing if he's feigning sleep, I force myself to wait it out another twenty rounds of counting. Chad is a heavy sleeper most days, but I can't trust he isn't waiting for me to make a move.

Once I count through the final hundred, I slowly shift my weight praying to God he doesn't wake. Each small movement cracks at the carefully constructed armor I've erected to stay strong. Once I know he's asleep, I untangle myself, and tiptoe my way to the bathroom and make quick work of changing out of my nightgown.

I know leaving Chad may bring more pain, but it doesn't stop me from trying. I know out of anyone, Heidi will help me. Most people don't want to know about the ugliness that hides behind people's doors. They prefer to look away, pretend to not notice the bruises, the busted lips. But Heidi has never been one to shy away. She's been begging me to leave him.

In the beginning, Chad would leave marks that wouldn't raise suspicion, until he didn't. On one occasion after he had blackened my eye he told me that he liked to see his mark on me. The sick bastard enjoyed it. I didn't know then how bad it would get.

Until tonight.

After the big blow-up earlier, that ended with me lying on our hallway floor used, abused and broken, I knew it was the end. Knew I had to leave. I wasn't sure if next time I would survive.

Trying to forget the nightmare of earlier, I give one final look at a sleeping Chad, and then slowly creep out of the room, down the stairs and out the front door to my escape. I know this is risky walking out the front door, but there is no other way. Our house is closed in on both sides.

Josi, Chad's dog, would have a fit if I walked out the back door and didn't take her out and there's no way I can take the car. Sparing one last thought of Josi, I swallow my tears at leaving her and continue my escape. I can't think of her or anyone but myself tonight. *For once think of yourself, Kenz.*

Careful to keep looking back to make sure I'm not being

followed, I keep my pace until the end of the street. Only then do I start to jog, freedom calling me forward the further I move away from our home. My jog turns into a run when I get three streets away. The flip-flops I managed to put on in my rush were kicked off five minutes ago. Gravel, stones, and sharp objects pierce my feet, but I don't let it slow me down. After ten minutes of running, I turn down my best friend Heidi's street. It's not the smartest move coming to Heidi, but if there is any chance of me getting out of town tonight, she is it.

Managing to make it to her front door, I hope my panicked knock is enough to bring her to the door before I'm seen. My prayer is answered when after just thirty seconds, she answers.

"What in God's name?" She takes one look at my face and pulls me inside. "I'm going to kill him." She moves me straight to the kitchen as I try to bring my breathing back under control.

"I need you to get me out of here right now, Heidi. We don't have much time." I finally find my voice as she wets down a cloth, preparing to clean me up.

"I need to take you to the damn police and the hospital, is what I need to do," she counters and I know this is going to take some work to get her to listen.

"Heidi, we don't have time for this. I need to leave town now before Chad has every cop out there looking for me." I start pulling her back to the front door.

"Just wait a second, Kenzie. Tell me what happened." She breaks free from my hold. My panic is only growing each second she fights me on this.

"PLEASE!" I scream, starting to see my chance slipping away. The idea of freedom is teasing me. I'm so close. Yet so far.

The distress in my voice is enough to make her realize just how serious I am.

"Fuck," she curses, finally listening. "Let me pack a bag." We really don't have time for her to pack a bag, but I don't want to push it. I've just shown up in the middle of the night and demanded we leave.

After pacing for a few minutes, Heidi comes back with an overnight bag. Dressed in yoga pants and sweatshirt, she hands me a pair of shoes. I take them with a thank you and we move back to the front door. I don't know where we're heading; all I know is I need as much of a head start as I can get.

"You sure about this, Kenz?" she asks one last time.

"I've never been more sure about anything. I only have you here. And as much as I love you, I need to get as far away as I can." I admit the ugly truth. I don't have anything holding me here. No family. No loved ones. If I stay any longer, I'm not sure I will survive.

She doesn't say anything or try to change my mind. I can see the understanding in her eyes, see the pity she feels for me. The concern. As much as I love Heidi, I can't let our friendship deter me from leaving.

"Come on," she finally agrees. I know this will be hard for her, but she knows deep down it's my only option. We walk quickly back through her house but before we can get to the front door, the bell rings.

Our eyes find each other quickly, both of us coming to a standstill.

"OPEN UP, HEIDI! I know she's in there." Chad's enraged voice comes through the front door and washes over me, blanketing me with his own particular kind of terror. He rings the bell again and bangs on the door.

I wasn't quick enough. It's only going to be worse now.

"Oh, God, no." My legs become jelly, no longer able to keep me up, and I fall to the floor in a heap.

"Don't you dare give up," Heidi whisper-yells at me. She comes forward and leans down. Placing her hands under my arms, she helps me find my feet.

"It's too late, Heidi. He's found me." The words find their way out over my distress. *If I thought tonight was bad, when he has me alone after this, who knows what he will do.*

"Call the police. Now!" she orders as the front door is kicked open. Chad stands in the doorway, his face distorted with rage. I want to run, take my chances and hope I can get away, but I can't. I failed to be out of his clutches for less than twenty minutes, and the pain of that realization hurts more than my busted-up face.

"Mackenzie, there you are, sweetheart." His sugar-coated voice fills the hall, sinking me further into the depths of despair. "What are you doing here?" He looks at me, a frown spreading across his face.

"You better fucking get out of my house. I'm calling the cops, Chad." Heidi steps in front of me, but we both know she's not going to stop Chad from getting what he wants.

"I'm just here to take my wife home."

"To her prison?" She scoffs, making the situation worse. She has no idea what he's capable of.

"Come here now, Mackenzie. You should have known I would find you. Wherever you go, I will always find you." Just as the words leave his lips, a lone tear rips its way through me and slides down the apple of my cheek. I'll never be rid of him

85

and he'll never let me go.

8

Beau

"WHAT DO YOU MEAN IT'S A MISSING PERSON'S CASE?" MY hand comes down on Jackson's desk. My patience is wearing thin and I'm about to fucking lose it.

"I mean he's off the grid, Beau. The Mayor has the whole department trying to find him. We're treating it like a missing person's case." Jackson delivers the news I don't want to hear.

"Bullshit, the asshole probably has him in hiding so he can protect him."

"You don't know that."

"No, I don't. But I know his family's ties, know what they are all capable of. We can't just sit around and wait for Chad to pull some shit. He's messed up. You've fucking seen how far he was out of line at Jesse's party last year and how he got off." I think back to when he held a broken beer bottle to Holly's throat trying to find Mackenzie. We thought the crazy fucker would be put away, but he pleaded out and was slapped with a misdemeanor and community service.

"I don't know what you want from me, Beau. I'm doing what we can here. For all we know, he fucked with the wrong person and he's in some shallow grave. We need to look at all possibilities here."

"Fuck, I wish." I scoff, knowing it's where he belongs.

"I didn't hear that." Jackson counters.

I smirk, then hold his stare for a minute before running my hand over my beard.

"So that's it. Just some bullshit play from the Mayor and it's filed away for never."

"Trust me, it's far from over. But you're blowing up for no reason. Keep your head straight. No one knows she's back in town and *if* Chad is missing, he's not going to bother you."

He has a point, but it doesn't placate me.

"I don't believe for a second he's missing. He's waiting."

"Well, we have an APB out on him. We're waiting too."

"Fuck the APB. You think some bullshit police protocol is going to protect her from this sick fuck?" I stand and begin pacing. Jesus Christ. How hard is it to find the fucker? "You sure you can trust these assholes here?" I point out the door to the officers on the case. "They're not working for the Mayor?"

"Trust me, I understand your frustration, Beau. But I told you this wasn't going to be easy. You need to let us do what we can."

"No, fuck this shit. If you can't even find the fucker, how am I supposed to trust you have her back?" I stand and move toward the door.

"Beau, don't do anything stupid," he calls out, and I stop and turn.

"I won't, but if I have to, you won't know." I walk out of his office without a backward glance. The last thing I need to do is bring us into more shit, but Chad needs to be found, not only for Mackenzie's sake, but also for my own. If the asshole gets to her again, I'm not sure I'd be able to forgive myself. I'd rather take the fucker's life than have him hurt her.

"Think this through, Beau," Jackson's warning across the station doesn't stop me. I know I should just leave it, let Jackson and his men sort it out, but knowing the fucker is out there, probably trying to come up with some sick way of getting her back, is consuming me. I don't want to think about why this is messing with me. If I were honest, it's more than a need to protect her. It's something more. Something I'm not sure I'm ready to admit. Just being under the same roof appears to tame the growing need though.

"I won't be able to protect you if this goes too far."

"Catch ya, Jackson." I ignore his warning, step outside and head to my bike. I've been relying too much on the law to put an end to this. If Jackson can't sort this out, I'm going old school. I'll call in my own markers and make sure whatever we find out will be handled in house.

Once and for all.

I pull up at the clubhouse two hours later and take a moment to contemplate going in. I know I probably should just head home to my place. I mean, it's been over a month since I've slept in my own bed, but the thought of leaving her alone doesn't sit well with me. Every night since Kenzie showed up, I haven't spent a night away from the clubhouse. From her. Even though she sleeps in the furthest room from me, I'm relaxed knowing I'm close. Doesn't mean I don't wish I could climb into her bed, hold her and tell her I'll never let the asshole touch her again though.

"Hey, fucker. What you doing out here?" Jesse's voice cuts through my thoughts.

"Nothing. Just got in." I climb off my bike. *Yeah, no way I'm leaving her tonight.* "Where you off to?" I take the focus off me and notice his tidy appearance.

"Dinner with Bell's parents," he answers as he climbs onto his own bike.

"How's everything going? Paige settled in?"

"It's been tense. But she's adjusting. They all are."

"Bell doing okay?"

"Yeah, just relieved to have her sister home. The whole thing has been a fucking mess, but it can only get better, right? I have to head out, can't be late. We can catch up later. You gonna be in tomorrow night?" He stops, letting a grin take over his face. "Of course you will."

"What the fuck does that mean?" I bark. I'm ready to go at him for his smart remark. Of course all my brothers know how messed up I am over Mackenzie. They've been very vocal about it.

Fuckers.

"Nothing man, fucking chill. It's just you've been spending every night here and taking less call outs."

Deciding not to have it out with him, I flip him off and walk to the door. He laughs at me, but I ignore it and the fact he's right.

Yeah, I've spent every night here. *So fucking what?*

Doesn't mean shit.

And the call outs are only less because I've taken on more of an administration roll to begin taking over the operation. Not that he gives a fuck.

His bike starts up, the rumble of the pipes filling the air just as I step inside.

"Mackenzie?" I call out when I walk into the main living area.

"In the kitchen. Go clean up. Dinner will be ready in ten," she shouts back and I can't seem to hold in my smirk at the routine we've found ourselves in.

Jesus, who would have thought?

Not wanting to delay in seeing her, I make my way to her. The clubhouse is quiet for a Wednesday and I'm grateful for it. Between work and dealing with trying to find Chad, I haven't had much alone time with her this last week, so dinner has become our thing.

"Hey, darlin'." I rest up against the door and watch her move about the kitchen like she owns it. She may as well, she spends most of her day in here, cooking and baking. The whole clubhouse is in love with her and her baked treats.

"Oh, you're ready?" She spins around and graces me with one of her smiles, and just like the first time I ever saw it, it fucking hits me. "How's your day?" She goes back to the pots on the stove, stirring one with a wooden spoon. It smells good, and as I enter the kitchen all the way, I try to spy what she's making tonight.

Fettuccini Carbonara.

"Busy, had a meet with Jackson." I decide to fill her in and take a seat at the table. I've learned over the last month she likes to fight me when it comes to food. It's starting to become our thing. Tonight I'd rather just sit and let her feed me.

"Detective Carter?" She stops and looks up. "Is everything okay?" She stills as a flash of panic distorts her smile before she covers it up.

"No, still no word. The Mayor has the department looking into it like a missing person. It's all bullshit if you ask me. They're just protecting the fucker." I deliver the bad news wishing I could wipe the disappointment away.

"Well, maybe it's not such a bad thing he's missing. Maybe something happened. Maybe he's not coming to find me anymore." Her voice lowers to a whisper.

Yeah, maybe not, darlin'.

"Do you honestly believe Chad is going to give up?" I call her out on it. We both know who we're dealing with; this asshole won't rest till he wins.

"I'm just trying to stay positive." She moves back, grabbing some plates from the cabinet and setting them on the counter. I watch her face. With the worry marring her forehead, I can almost sense her despair from across the room.

"You should be positive, Kenz." I rise from my seat and take the few steps to stand in front of her. "Your asshole ex is not going to get to you here. I won't let him, I promise."

"You can't promise that, Beau. I'm not always going to be here. You're not always going to be able to protect me."

"That's where you're wrong, darlin'. I'm always going to

protect you." She looks up, eyes blazing, and it breaks me. The uncertainty calls to me. Like I've been where she is and I'd do anything to stop her from feeling like this. I know I'm close to overstepping some kind of line here, but it's like I don't give a fuck anymore.

"And when I leave?" She hands me a plate of fresh steaming fettuccini and I have to force my fingers to grip it tighter to stop myself from dropping it.

"Leave? What the fuck are you talking about, darlin'?" I stand there confused, watching her set herself up at the dinner table.

"Well—" She stops, realizing I haven't followed her over. "Come sit." She pats the spot next her. Clearing my throat, I follow her over and take a seat.

"So, I've been thinking. They're no closer to finding Chad—"

"You don't know that," I cut her off, not wanting her to lose hope.

"I know, but I need to begin moving on with my life."

"What the hell are you talking about, Kenz?" I bark, taken aback by where this conversation is going.

"I was talking to Kelly and Hunter today. I didn't even know they were related, did you?" She starts to ramble, but gets back on track. "Anyway, Hunter said there's an empty apartment in the complex he lives in. I've been saving my pay from Nix. I have enough for a deposit."

"Hunter?" Rage boils in my body the second his name leaves her lips.

Fucking Hunter.

"Yeah." She eyes me slowly, catching on to my change in

demeanor.

"Kenzie, you can't move out, not when Chad is still out there." My hand moves to my beard and I rub hard trying to calm my anger.

"I can't just sit around here anymore, Beau. I'm going crazy. I need normal. I need to be away from the parties, the women. You've all been so welcoming here, taking me in and giving me protection, but Chad hasn't come for me yet."

"It's too dangerous, Kenzie." I'm not okay with this plan and I'm not backing down.

"So I should stay here until you find him? Living in fear like I was doing in Ohio."

"I don't understand you, Mackenzie." I stand and move to the fridge for a beer. I think I'm gonna need a few for this conversation.

"You don't understand I want to be happy?" I pop the top of my beer and take a seat back down.

"I don't see why you would want to risk your safety." I pick up my fork and dig in, twisting it to roll up some pasta.

"Are you happy, Beau?"

I swallow a mouthful of food before I answer. "What does that have to do with you leaving our protection, Mackenzie?"

"Just answer me, Beau."

"Yeah, I'm happy." I shrug, not really sure what she's trying to achieve here. "I mean there have been times I haven't been," I add, deciding she needs the truth. "There've been plenty of times throughout the last ten years I've questioned myself, what I've been doing, where I'm going. But I finally found a head space I'm happy in." I fill my mouth with another serving of pasta.

"You think it's a head space?" She looks back up, my answer surprising her.

"I don't know. Sometimes I think it has to do with in here." I tap the side of my temple. "You just need to be in the right headspace and make it happen."

"I've been trying for a long time you know, even when I was in Ohio. I made some friends, had a good job. I thought I was happy. But in the quiet times like this, I wasn't. It didn't matter how hard I wanted to be happy or tried to make it happen, I couldn't." I know life hasn't been good for Mackenzie in a long time. First living with Chad, then escaping him, but I didn't realize how low she has been feeling.

"Maybe because there wasn't where you needed to be, Kenz." I reach my hand across the table and place it over hers. She doesn't pull back like I expect her to and I celebrate briefly at the win.

"You think this is where I need to be? Here. Hiding from the world." She shakes her head, not accepting this as her fate.

"You're not hiding, darlin'. You're surviving."

"Hiding under the protection of the club isn't surviving." She pulls her hand back, breaking our connection.

"I don't know what you need for me to say here, Kenz. I thought this is what you wanted? Why you came back. You just want to leave now?" I want to give her a decent shake. Make her see she's not thinking right.

"I do. I want to be out on my own. I'm just so frustrated. I thought I could come back and have it all. I realize now it doesn't work like that."

"You *can* have it all."

"Not here I can't, Beau. I need more independence. I'm

thirty-five years old. What am I doing with my life?"

The room falls quiet between us, our dinner growing cold in the unease of the conversation.

"You want out, then move into my place." The words leave my mouth before my brain can think it through.

"What?" Her brows furrow in confusion.

"You want out of here, I want to keep you safe. Move in with me." Again with my mouth blurting before I can think. *Fuck.*

"Beau—"

"Mackenzie, I promised you the night I saved you I would protect you."

"And you did."

"And I will continue to, darlin'. I can't stop you from leaving, but I can offer you a place where I can protect you." I can't let her move out on her own, not when I know Chad is just waiting for the perfect time.

"Beau, you're not always going to be able to protect me."

"I will if you let me." She draws in a deep breath, her hands going to her temples.

"We'll drive each other mad. Have you ever lived with a woman before?" I can tell she's clutching at straws; this back and forth is almost funny. But I'm going to keep coming back at her.

"I have a big place, and we've practically lived together here since you've been back."

"I don't think it's a good idea." She's fighting it, but the more I let the idea grow, I think it's the best idea I've had.

"You stay with me, or you stay here. I'm not budging on this." I need to be able to keep her safe, and I can't keep her safe when she isn't close.

"Do you really think this is the best idea?" She folds her arms in front of her, and from what I've come to learn about Mackenzie, this move means she's ready to argue with me.

"No parties, no women. You have your own space and I'll still be looking out for you." I hit her with all the pros. She doesn't reply straightaway and I can see her resolve start to slip.

"What's happening here? Between us, Beau?" I don't know what to take from her question, so I answer it like I would if Nix had asked.

"You know what's happening here, darlin'. I'm just doing what I promised," I lie, not sure what I really need or want from her. She is nothing like I've ever wanted before. Part of me knows offering her this is too fucking dangerous, but the other part of me—the part that connects my dick to my heart—thinks it's the best idea ever.

"So we're just friends?"

"You want to be friends with me?" I tease, not impressed with labeling us as friends. Do friends want to fuck each other's brains out? I don't think so.

"Quit playing. I'm serious, Beau. Living together, it's not something I thought about, so you can't just come in here and demand I live with you. I need to know how this works."

"Nothing changes. You stay at my place until Chad is found."

"Until it's safe."

"It's only going to be safe when he's found, darlin'." She diverts her gaze like she wants to argue, but she doesn't.

At this moment I'm torn. As much as I want the fucker found, I'm not sure I'm ready for Mackenzie to stop needing me.

"And I'll be free to come and go as I please?" she presses for more leeway, darkening my mood.

"You let me know where you're going so I don't worry." I'm not okay with these stipulations, but if it means I have her in my home, why the fuck argue? She won't know I'll have a tail on her at all times.

She thinks about it for a few moments before she holds her hand out for me to shake. "Deal." I raise a brow at her, but she doesn't drop it. "Shake on it, Beau." I give in and place my hand against hers. Her touch is soft, but firm and my mind moves straight to how it would feel wrapped around my cock.

Shit, down, boy.

"Thank fuck we're done with arguing. Now, can we eat?" I release her hand and pick up my fork.

"Yep, dig in." She picks up her own fork and places a small mouthful of pasta in her mouth then follows it with a soft moan and all I can do is watch.

Jesus, I'm a fucking idiot.

This woman will be in my home. How the fuck will I control myself then?

"Okay, I'm heading to bed." Mackenzie breaks the silence an hour later. After eating dinner and our normal light conversation, I managed to convince her to leave me to wash up. As with everything else, she put up a fight, but eventually gave in and ended up sitting on the counter telling me about her day working for Nix, and about a girls' night Kelly and Holly invited her to next week.

Like I'd be okay with her going out for a girls' night right now when she's meant to be laying low.

I kept her talking and we moved it out to the back deck to have a few beers.

"Yeah, I should too." I stand from the chair and start picking up the empty beer bottles. She walks inside while I check everything over one more time. Security fencing surrounds the club, but having Mackenzie here has opened us up for an attack. By who, we don't know, but I wouldn't put it past Chad to put a hit out on us.

"Thanks for dinner, Kenz," I say when we move to our rooms.

"You're welcome." She slows then comes to a stop just outside my room. "It's the least I could do after everything you've done for me." She goes up on her toes and presses her lips to my cheek. Before I can stop myself, my hand moves to her lower back, holding her close to me. I wait a minute, expecting her to freeze under my touch.

"Beau." Her breath is warm, and I anticipate more of an argument, but she doesn't say anything. Instead, she presses in closer.

Using my free hand, I place my finger under her chin and tilt her head back. Her tongue runs along her bottom lip and it all but invites me to join it.

"Darlin'," I warn. I'm not sure if it's a warning to her, or to me. I can see how much she wants this. Can see the fire in her eyes matches my own need. I know one taste of her won't be enough, but it's like my body isn't listening to my brain.

"Please, just kiss me, Beau," she pleads, shutting down my

reservations. It's all the encouragement I need. She parts her lips as I lean in closer, and when my tongue seeks its entry, I own her mouth.

I don't move slowly. My tongue fights with hers, desperate for a connection. Her taste is fucking addictive—vanilla, strawberry and I don't fucking know what—but I can't get enough. Moving her tongue with mine, my hand on her back pulls her closer. I'm hanging on by a thread here, but does it stop me? Fuck no.

The kiss grows wild, her soft moans stirring my dick to life. The poor bastard has only been seeing my palm since the night she moved in. If I'm not careful, he might blow just from hearing her needy groans.

Taking two steps forward, I reach down and twist the handle. Using my boot, I kick the door open and drag us over to my bed.

She comes willingly, her mouth and hands just as desperate as mine, but as soon as I push her back to my bed, she freezes.

"Oh, God," she blurts, coming up from my bed and finding her feet.

Shit.

"I'm so sorry." She starts to walk past me to leave, but my hand reaches out, stopping her escape.

"Mackenzie." My voice is a lot calmer than the frustration building in me, but she still flinches under it.

"That was a mistake. I didn't mean for it to happen." She pulls out of my hold, and as soon as she was there, she's gone, blowing all chances of taking this any further out the window.

Fucking awesome.

9

Mackenzie

"That was a mistake." I turn to rush out of his room as fast as I can, hoping he doesn't come after me.

"Mackenzie, stop." His tone has me halting before I reach the door, but I don't turn to face him right away.

How could I be so stupid?

Shit.

Deciding it's better to hash this out now, I spin and face him. "I'm sorry, Beau, I shouldn't have. I don't know what I was thinking." He looks taken aback for a second before his dark mask sets in place.

"You didn't do anything, darlin'. I shouldn't have touched you." His voice loses the spark that stirs something in me whenever he talks. "This isn't what you need right now."

He's trying to make me feel better, but it's not working. I'm an idiot for coming on to him then pulling away.

What the hell was I thinking?

"I should go to bed." I ignore my body telling me how much I'd like to go to bed with him and step out of his room.

"Good night, Mackenzie." He uses my full name and for once, I hate it. Only Beau calls me Kenzie and hearing him call me anything else just feels wrong.

Seriously so messed up.

"'Night, Beau. See you in the morning." I lamely wave then spin, walking as fast as I can to my room.

Forgoing a shower, I change into my pajamas, climb into bed then play over every single detail that happened tonight.

Seriously, it's too much to process.

Between Beau offering me a room at his place, and me practically begging him to kiss me, the night has been a hot mess.

I didn't expect when I sat down to talk with Beau about moving he would freak out like he did. I knew he would be apprehensive, maybe put up a little fight, but to flat out deliver an ultimatum? No. That was unexpected.

I didn't know what to say. Short of telling him the truth, I had to agree. What else could I do? The last thing I want to do is upset this awkward situation, especially with things growing between us.

Ever since I came to Rushford things between Beau and I have been tense. Small sparks between us have been building, pulling us closer every chance we're alone. Initially, I thought it was one-sided. My need to forget about Chad and everything in my past pushed me forward, but after a couple of weeks, I started noticing it wasn't just me feeling this draw. Every small touch, every slight look, it's like an unspoken conversation between us.

And now I just ruined everything.

Deciding I can't even go over the kiss, or the way being in Beau's arms felt, I reach over and flick the lamp off.

I don't need to have the scene playing over and over in my head. Maybe tomorrow everything will be clearer.

Maybe tomorrow I'll wake up and realize it was all a dream.

The tingling in my lips tells me otherwise.

Stupid girl, Mackenzie.

I wake the next morning still feeling like a complete fool, a fool for probably making this situation ten times worse. Determined not to deal with any of it right this second, I kick off my blanket and roll out of bed. My alarm clock tells me it's barely after six. Knowing I won't be able to go back to sleep, I change into my favorite dress and fix my hair. It's not like I have plans to go out today, but since I'm up, I should get a start on breakfast before Beau wakes up. Even if eggs aren't my strong suit, I still try to make them when Beau isn't in the kitchen looking over my shoulder. Somehow over the last few weeks, we've fallen into some kind of routine. I cook dinner and he fights me on breakfast.

Stealing a quick look out my door, I spy Beau's door still closed. It doesn't mean he's not up, but hopefully I beat him to it. With no other option but to risk it, I exit my room and walk down the hall and out to the main area. The clubhouse is silent this morning, and I take a second to look around. I've come to like living here. Yeah, the parties and the women can get a little out of hand, but the club family has accepted me as one of their own.

This is one of the reasons you need to leave, Mackenzie.

Pushing all the reasons of why I should leave aside, I head for the kitchen but come to a stop when I turn the corner and see Beau standing there, his back to me, cooking over the stove.

Damn it. He beat me.

Not sure if I should make my presence known or race back to my room, I take the time to have my fill of him.

His bare feet grab my attention first. There's something seriously sexy about a man barefoot in a kitchen. Taking one last look at them, I slowly move my gaze up his body. His shorts hang low, showing the dip on his tanned, inked back.

Of all things holy, my stomach dips at the sight.

His hair is free from his band in a wild and sexy mess and I kick myself knowing not eight hours ago this man was making love to my face and I freaked out.

Kill me now.

Shaking my head free from our kiss, my eyes move over the rippling muscles of his smooth back and zero in on his ink. Most of his back is covered, the largest, a Knights Rebels insignia sits in the middle of his back. I can't make out the rest from this distance, but nonetheless, I still crave to explore them.

Keep your cool, Kenz.

Forcing the kiss from my mind, I decide to get this over with.

"Morning." I step into the kitchen like I just turned the corner and didn't spend two minutes checking him out.

Beau turns at my voice and gives me one of his rare smiles.

"Sit, breakfast is ready." I follow his order and take a seat without even thinking. I don't know why when he speaks to me like this I don't react. His bossy tone no longer rubs me the wrong way. I've become used to it.

"I thought it was my turn to fix breakfast." I eye my plate then try to contain my excitement when he places my favorite in front of me. *French toast.* Even better. *Beau's* French toast.

"Are you keeping tabs, Kenzie?" I hold back my smile hearing he's gone back to using the shorter version of my name and nod.

Okay, maybe we can just act like nothing happened last night.

"I had all these plans to show you up with my mad omelet skills."

He throws his head back at my admission. A deep rumble spills from somewhere low and I'm thrown by the easiness of it so I just sit and stare.

Holy shit, I could just listen to him laugh all day.

"I'll wait patiently for that day, darlin'." Beau pulls me out of my trance and takes a seat next to me.

"Whatever. One day, I will perfect it." I huff before taking a bite of my breakfast. Seriously, so freaking good.

"So I thought we could head over to my place today." I stop eating and look up at Beau's suggestion.

Okay, this is not what I was expecting.

"Are you sure it's wise, Beau?" I place my fork down on my plate and reach for my coffee.

"Told you last night, you're either here or my place."

"Yeah, but after what happened last night?" The last thing I want to do is relive what happened, but it's better to get it over with now than later.

"Last night was my fuck up. It didn't mean anything. I don't think of you that way, Kenzie." He places his fork beside him and gives me his full attention. I ignore the pang of rejection hearing him say he doesn't think of me in that way and nod instead.

"Yeah, of course. I'm not interested in anything more, either. It was just one of those moments. When two people spend a lot of time together, it's bound to happen. Now it's done, we can move on," I agree as heat spreads over my face and neck.

How embarrassing.

"So we're good then." I force what I hope is a smile and dig back into my breakfast.

"Yep," is all he says, before picking up his own fork and pushing a mouthful of food into his mouth. We don't talk again after that, both of us avoiding each other's gaze. I know we just said what happened last night was a mistake, but it doesn't change the fact we're both going to be different now. There's nothing we could do to control it.

"I'll clean up," Beau says when I stand and take my plate to the sink.

Not wanting to argue with him today, I nod and hang back, enjoying a second coffee and letting him take control of the situation.

Ugggh, he is a pain in my ass.

After ten minutes of me watching him tidy up, we finally make our way out to the front.

"Only have my bike. You okay with that?" he asks, locking up the clubhouse.

"Sure." I nod and push down my unease of having to be close to him so soon after our slip. He motions to a bike to our left, and we walk over. I don't tell him I haven't been on a bike before. I just lift my leg and mount his ride like I've done it hundreds of times.

He watches me carefully, eyebrow cocked, hands on hips, but doesn't comment. Instead, the corner of his mouth lifts up in a knowing smile.

Yeah, yeah, whatever.

"Will you be joining me?" I ask when he continues to just stare.

He doesn't reply with words but climbs on in front of me. Not wanting to be too close, I squeeze my thighs tight against his side. Careful not to put my hands on him.

"Don't be stubborn, darlin'. You're not going to last this fifteen-minute ride without holding on to me." He leans back and picks up my hand. I roll my eyes 'cause he's right. I am stubborn. Getting over myself, I slide forward and place my hands around him.

"See, wasn't so hard, was it?" His question is light, playful and I want to reply with some smart remark like I normally would, but today I can't come up with anything. So, rather than dwell on it, I hold on tighter, ready and willing to go wherever he takes me.

Past

Mackenzie

"THEY'RE A FEW MINUTES OUT." HEIDI PLACES THE phone back in her pocket and moves back to where I'm lying down on the sofa. Every inch of my body is on fire and in pain, aching more than I've ever ached in my life.

"Are you sure this is going to work? What if he finds me again?" I can't help the scared plea that leaves my lips as I wonder just how far Chad will go. I only just tried to escape last night to Heidi's place and I'm already attempting it again.

"Sweetheart, these men are good at what they do." Henry, who Heidi found to help me escape, tries to reassure me. I have no idea who he is, all I know is he works with a group of people who help remove women out of bad situations. I don't know if this is going to work, but I have to believe it will.

"Okay, we need to move her now. They're coming up the drive," Henry's wife, Dorothy, calls from the back barn door.

I don't even know how this all came about so fast. After Chad found me at Heidi's last night, I agreed to go home with him. It was my only option. I needed to keep her safe. Heidi fought her hardest to get me to stay, but when she realized Chad wouldn't give up, she hugged me tight, and promised she would come up with something and to be prepared. I never imagined she would pull this off in less than twenty-four hours.

"It's gonna hurt, babe. But we don't have much time." Heidi gives it to me straight as Henry and Dorothy move into position.

"I think I can walk," I offer, knowing it's going to hurt but wanting to make it easier for them.

"I'm so sorry I didn't come sooner," Heidi whispers, wincing in sympathy with me as they help me find my feet and we slowly move to the back door.

"It's not your fault, Heidi. This is what I get for trying to leave. One way trip down the stairs." I try not to let my emotions take over. I knew trying to escape last night with no plan was a bad idea. Knew the minute he showed up at Heidi's I would get my punishment. I'm just lucky he had a work function he had to attend and Heidi could get me out before it was too late.

"Okay, they just pulled up." Henry opens the back door.

"I can't thank you all enough. I'm not sure this is going to work, but either way, I'll always remember what you've done," I tell both Henry and Dorothy.

They both nod, but Henry talks, "We're just doing what any good person would do. These men, they might seem a little rough, but I give you my word, they won't harm one hair on you." I want to cry at how nice these people sound, but I stop myself when a man appears at the door.

"We don't have much time. You have everything you need?" The deep grumble of the stranger's voice rolls through me. I look up at the man and in the low light, I can only make out his frame and part of his face. This stranger is taking me out in the middle of the night. I don't know what he looks like, but for reasons I can't explain, I trust him and what he believes in. I trust Henry when he tells me he will keep me safe from Chad. But most of all, I trust Heidi, who promised me she would help me escape.

"She's good to go," Heidi answers for me then steps forward and carefully wraps her arms around me. It takes everything in me not to cry out in pain, but knowing this will be the last time I see her, I let her hug me tightly anyway.

"Are you sure you want to do this alone?"

"I have to." The last thing I need is for Heidi to become caught up in all of this. "I love you, Heidi."

"I love you, too, girl." She gives me another squeeze before stepping back with glassy eyes.

"Don't you dare cry. You'll make me cry," I tell her with a shaky smile, my eyes filling with tears. We give each other one last look, reassuring one another this is the only way.

"Thank you." I turn to Henry and Dorothy, wishing I could offer something more.

"Time to go," the gruff voice growls, rushing us along. I give one last look to my friend before telling the man I'm ready.

He doesn't reply, just steps forward and picks me up in his massive arms.

"Shit!" I cry out in pain from the fast movement.

"I'm sorry, but it's quicker if I carry you," he states. Part of me should be scared of him, but for the first time ever, I trust this stranger is going to save me, so I hold on tighter, willing to go wherever he takes me.

10

Beau

WE PULL UP TO THE FRONT OF MY HOUSE TWENTY minutes later. The ride took longer than it should have because I'm not gonna lie, I fucking loved having Kenzie on the back of my bike and didn't want it to end.

Yep, fucking goner.

"Wow, it's beautiful, Beau." Her head tilts back as she takes in the front of my home. I bought the house a few years ago, just after my mother died. I sold our family home, then used the money to find my own place. I wasn't interested in living where I grew up, and being constantly surrounded by the memories. I don't know if I plan to stay here forever, but it's kind of perfect for me right now.

"Yeah, it's okay." I brush off the compliment. I haven't

brought a woman here before, and knowing Kenzie is the first does something to me.

Jesus, keep it together, fucker. You told her we are just friends. Stick to it.

"It's perfect. Come on, show me around." She looks back at me, eager to see more. I don't waste any time. I push the kickstand down on my bike and climb off. She's too busy looking at the house to notice my semi-hard cock from her tits pressed into my back, so I quickly adjust myself.

"Okay, let's go." I place my hand in the small of her back and guide her to the front porch. She doesn't flinch at my touch today and I can't help wanting to celebrate the small win. After the kiss last night, I wasn't sure this was going to be a good idea, until I realized the alternative. As much as having her in my house, in my space is going to fuck with me, I'd still prefer it to her living on her own. When she raced back to her room last night, I thought for sure she'd pull right back, and I was prepared for it. But then I felt her come into the kitchen this morning, and I knew there was no way I was going to let her. So I told her I didn't think of her that way. I lied to save face. And yeah she said it back, but I know she was lying too.

We both played it our own way because whatever is happening between us can't progress.

Not yet anyway.

"How long have you lived here?" she asks as we take the stairs to the front porch.

"Three years now." She nods before her eyes find the swing hanging at the end of the porch.

"Oh my, I've always wanted one of these." She walks over to it and plants her ass smack down in the middle.

"It was my mom's," I tell her, watching her smile fade away.

"Oh, I'm sorry." She stands from the swing instantly and I regret dropping it on her like that.

"Don't be, darlin'," is all I say, not because I don't want her to know about my mom or my family for that matter. It's a fucked-up situation and today is not the day to visit it.

"My mom and dad died when I was twelve. Car accident," she shares, and I take a moment to catalog the information. The last month, Kenzie has barely shared anything personal with me. Sure I know her favorite food, what she likes to drink, what makes her laugh, even what she's been doing the last eighteen months, but deep shit like this she keeps to herself. We both do.

"Sorry." I give her the same words back.

"Don't be." She grins then shakes her head. "You gonna keep me out on this porch all day, Beau, or you gonna show me your house?" She breaks through the dismal moment, pulling us both out of the past.

Needing the reprieve, I nod and step up to the door. "I'll have a second key made for you," I tell her as I unlock the door and step into the foyer. She stays close as I move to the alarm and disarm it.

"How am I going to remember all those numbers?" she asks over my shoulder when I punch in my code.

"We can reprogram it," I offer, hoping it will make it easier. I push the door open and let her pass. "So this is my home." I direct her through the front entryway into the living area. The house is an open concept. The kitchen and dining are to the left, and living area to the right. All rooms open up to each other with a hall that takes you to the back of the house where the bedrooms and bathroom are.

"Living area." I point to the room, but continue on to the kitchen. "Kitchen and dining, and through the glass door there is a patio." She follows each direction, taking it all in.

"Down the hall are the bedrooms and bathroom." I continue to guide her through the rest of my house.

"I love the wooden floors." Mackenzie follows closely, taking in everything and offers her commentary. Even though the house only had one owner before me, I still gave it a coat of paint and polished the floors up before I moved in.

"First room is a junk room. Don't even bother trying to clean it up," I warn, knowing what she's like. She'll have it organized and tidied before the week is out.

"Second door is the bathroom." I tap on the door. "It's all yours. I have one in my room. This room is empty." I tap on the third door. "And this room is yours." I stop at the door closest to mine and turn back. She's still checking out the bathroom so I wait.

"This one?" She finally catches up, pushing the door open and stepping in.

"Yep." I stay back and watch her take in her new room. It's nothing special. Queen bed, nightstand on each side, and a dresser against the far wall.

"It's perfect, Beau." She turns back and smiles up at me. "Are you sure this is okay? Me moving in?"

"Wouldn't have offered if it wasn't, darlin'." I'm sure it's going to be hard having her in my space and keeping my hands to myself, but I'll get there.

"I know. I just want to make sure." I watch her eye the door of my bedroom before looking up at me.

115

"My room," I offer and then watch her blush. Seriously, I rarely call a woman cute, but everything she does makes me wanna kiss her and tell her to quit being cute before she makes me lose my head.

"Great." She starts to walk back up the hall, out into the living area. I watch her ass as I follow her. The motion of her movements causes my cock to twitch. "So when can I move in?" She turns around slowly and I divert my eyes immediately before she can catch me.

"We can go and grab your stuff now."

"On your bike?" She looks a little concerned.

"I have a truck. We'll take it back."

"You have a truck?" Her question is sharp and piercing, like she's surprised.

"Yeah. Why?"

"I just always see you on your bike. I guess there's a lot I don't know about you." She shrugs, still looking around. She's right. We might have just spent a lot of time together at the clubhouse, but we still know so little of each other

"Same could be said for you, Kenz," I reply, watching her eyes shoot up to mine.

"Well, what do you want to know?" she asks, opening herself up to me.

"Don't know. Let me think." I grin and watch her place her ass down on the arm of my brown leather sofa. "When's your birthday?"

"Ugggh, the worst day of the year," she groans, rolling her eyes.

"Christmas Day?" I ask, thinking of the first day that comes to mind.

"No, February twenty-ninth."

"Get the fuck out?" I blurt, thinking she's messing with me.

"February twenty-ninth, nineteen-eighty. I'm not kidding. Why?"

"February twenty-ninth, nineteen seventy-six," I reply with my own birthday.

"Are you serious?" Her brows rise in surprise, but her ass stays planted. "That's crazy. What day do you celebrate your birthday?"

"I only celebrate on the date. Which makes me a hell of a lot younger than most assholes my age. How can you think it's the worst day of the year?"

"I hate it. I celebrate on the first of March." She shrugs and I can't move the smile off my face knowing we share a birthday. *What are the fucking chances?*

"Well, I still think it's better than Christmas. Christmas you have to share all the presents. My sister was born Christmas Day and she hated it."

"You have a sister?" she asks. "Jesus, we barely know each other." Her words pull me out of my happy mood and into somewhere darker.

"Missy. She would have been thirty-two this Christmas." I step back, done with this conversation. Kenzie's hand reaches out and seeks mine. I stop at her touch but don't look back. I scarcely talk about Missy. I'm shocked I even shared.

"I bet she was amazing," she whispers, not apologizing for my loss, but giving me something else. *Understanding.*

"She was better than me in every way, darlin'. I miss her every day." I return her squeeze and release her hand. She doesn't ask any more questions, and I'm grateful for it. We've

117

dived deep enough for the day. Hell for the month. At least I have.

"You ready to head out? If we leave now, we could have you moved in by lunch," I tell her, walking back to the door.

"Yeah, but I just have one condition before I agree to move in." I spin back, waiting to hear her terms.

"Yeah, what's that?" I almost tell her I don't make bargains, but like a lot of things with Mackenzie, I let her have her play.

"I get to cook breakfast." Her arms fold over her chest, pushing up her breasts and it takes everything in me to stop my eyes from lingering.

"No," I simply say and turn around ending all discussion.

"Come on, Beau." She begins to argue her reasons, but I just shut her out. The woman cooks a mean meal. I'll give her that, but breakfast is and will always be my gig.

11

Mackenzie

"I THINK I'M DONE." I WIPE MY HANDS ON THE BACK OF my jeans and step back to look at the end result.

It might not be much, but it's a start.

"You sure have accumulated a lot since you've been here." Holly sits on my new bed while holding her son, X, in her arms.

"Thanks to you and the girls. I would still only have the clothes I arrived in if it weren't for you all helping me out." I move to the closet and slide the door closed.

I've just finished moving into Beau's place. It only took one trip, but Holly and Kelly both decided they needed to be here and followed us back when they heard I was moving out.

"It's no big deal. I had heaps of clothes from before X." She shrugs, but I know she's lying. Half the clothes given to me had new tags on them.

"Well, either way it means so much to me."

Before Holly can answer, Mia, Kelly's daughter comes running and falls down, tripping over the rug in the middle of my room.

I scoop her up instantly just as her tears come.

"It's okay, sweet thing." I console her, holding her close in my arms.

"You're a natural." Holly smirks, eyeing me carefully.

"Oh, I love kids. Some days I wish I would've had one, but then I realize I'm so glad I didn't. Having a child in a marriage like mine would have been tragic." Mia finally settles, her little five-year-old fingers playing with the gold necklace my nan gave me.

"Well, it's not too late, Kenzie."

"Please, I'm thirty-five. I missed the baby making boat."

"*Please,* you're like the average childbearing age these days, right? You still have time."

"Well, I don't see myself dating, getting married and having a kid all within the year."

"I think you're off to a good start, moving in with Beau."

"What?" I nearly choke on the shock that she just called me out.

"Oh, come on, Mackenzie. You're telling me this is just a housemate situation?" She lifts her right hand and bounces her pointer and middle finger on the word housemate.

"I have no idea what you're talking about." I avoid her eyes. The last thing I need is her putting any ideas in my head.

Beau and I are friends and we don't think of each other as anything more.

I almost believe it.

"If you say so." She smirks, letting me off the hook.

"Kez." Mia pulls back and points to something over my shoulder. I spin around and follow her direction. She can't manage my full name, so she settles with Kez.

"What is it?" I ask, watching her point to a packet of Starburst. "Ahhh, candy. You have to ask your mom." I place her on her feet and she runs out as fast as she came in to ask Kelly for permission.

"You hungry?" I turn back to Holly, ready for lunch.

"I have to get going. My mom and dad are coming over for dinner tonight and my house is a mess." She stands, adjusting X as she goes.

"Well, thank you for helping me settle in." I follow her out and down the hall back to the living area.

"I barely did much." She winks, then bends to pick up X's diaper bag off the sofa. "Kell, Beau, I'm out," she calls to them in the kitchen.

Beau appears first, Kelly following close behind with Mia chomping into a cookie. *Guess she forgot about the candy.*

"Yeah I should head out too." Kelly turns and walks back to the kitchen to fetch her belongings.

"I'll help you put him in the car." Beau steps forward and reaches for X.

"No, it's fine, you stay." She pulls back, only to offer him her cheek for a kiss.

"You still pissed I'm taking your girl?" Beau lifts his brow, not missing her attitude.

"Who's gonna bake me all those goodies every week?" She winks at me but levels her stare back at Beau.

"She was gonna go and live in some crappy apartment complex Hunter lives in. It probably didn't even have a functioning oven. I have one that works. She's better off here." He leans down and pecks her cheek as she rolls her eyes, realizing he has a point.

"Behave," she warns, pulling back. She then turns and leaves.

"Okay, I'm off, too." Kelly returns all packed up and ready to go. "If you need anything, Mackenzie, you have my numbers." She kisses my cheek then lets me kiss Mia goodbye.

"I'll be sure to let you know," I tell her, watching her say goodbye to Beau.

"And don't forget, Beau. We have the meeting with the lawyer on Wednesday, to go over everything." Beau turns to me. A strange look falls over his face before answering.

"Yeah, I haven't forgotten. I'll be there."

Feeling like he doesn't want me to know what their meeting is about, I leave them to talk in private and set about making some lunch. Not sure what Beau's plans are for the rest of the day, I make us both a sandwich. His cabinets and fridge look miserable and I make a mental note to start a list. Now I'm living here at minimal rent, the least I can do is keep on top of these things. When I've managed to put together a decent lunch, Beau walks in.

"You hungry?" I ask, handing him his plate.

"Starved." I follow him over to the table and take a seat opposite him. "Looks good, darlin'." He digs in then looks up and gives me a wink, mouth full of food.

Friends.

I remind myself as I start eating.

It's what we've been doing at the clubhouse anyway. There's no reason for this to be awkward. I continue to have my conversation in my head.

It isn't until I've finished eating, cleaned up lunch and found my way back to my room, I realize we didn't say another word to each other.

Oh, God, it's already awkward.

"Mackenzie! Have you seen my coffee mug?" Beau shouts down the hall a few days later. I just stepped out of the shower and was about to dry my hair when I hear him banging around.

"In the cabinet," I shout back as I run my comb through my hair.

"It's not!"

I roll my eyes, ignoring his annoyance and walk out to the kitchen. He's searching in the wrong cabinet with his bare back to me when I walk in.

"It is. I put it in there last night," I tell him, reaching up and opening the door to show him the mugs.

"That's not where the mugs belong." His head spins toward me, brows dipped low.

"Ahh, yeah, they do. It's where I found them." I pull down his mug and hand it to him. "It's also the cabinet above the coffee maker. So makes sense." I drop my hand when our fingers graze sending an electric current all the way up my arm.

"I don't know why you think it belongs there, but it doesn't. It belongs here." He opens the cabinet under the microwave to reveal the plastic containers. "The fuck?" He looks up. "Did you tidy up in here?" I shrug, not prepared to answer.

I might have tidied a little.

I didn't however move his mug. His mug has been in the sink every day I have been here, and when I did sort out the kitchen yesterday, the rest of the mugs were in the cabinet above the coffee maker.

"You don't need to clean and organize shit here, Kenz. It's not required and I sure as shit don't like not being able to find my mug."

"I'm sorry. It's a bad habit. I'm used to having everything perfect," I admit, not wanting to get into it with him over the mug. The truth is, it's the least I can do after everything Beau has done for me.

"Well, break those habits, darlin'. You don't have to clean up after me. I can look after my own shit."

"It's really no problem, Beau. I have free time."

"Not arguing with you on this." He steps around me to fill his mug, ultimately ending the conversation.

"Are you always like this in the morning?" I ask, not really sure what the big deal is. His kitchen is clean. What's the issue? Chad always expected a spotless kitchen and if it wasn't, he sure would let me know about it.

"Only when I haven't had coffee in my favorite mug." He takes a sip from his basic black coffee mug and moans briefly.

Jesus.

"Are you feeling better now?" I ask after few minutes of letting him get acquainted with his coffee.

"Getting there," he mumbles taking another sip.

"Good, you can thank me later for tidying up your kitchen." I nod then make my way back to the bathroom, hearing his grumbling about how I'm gonna be the death of him.

"Oh, and if you think the kitchen is too organized, I'm just going to go ahead and apologize in advance for the junk room," I shout my reply and then quickly flick my dryer on, blasting out whatever he has to say.

He can't be angry. I'm only helping him out in the long run. Right? Right.

12

Beau

"YOU HAVE HER AT YOUR PLACE? WHAT THE FUCK ARE you thinking, Beau?" Tiny asks the following week at Fireside Bar. He called a meet after finding out we had moved Mackenzie in with me.

Tiny acquired his name 'cause of his size. The guy stands at six-foot-nine. A real big fucker. He's been a friend of the club dating back to when my dad was VP. He's had his hands in a lot of things. Ex- military, former cop, he's also the guy who started this whole gig with helping abused women. I came on board two years ago knowing it was something I wanted to do to honor Missy. At first it was pick-ups, drop-offs and a few recoveries, like Mackenzie's situation, but then it turned into something bigger. Something I wanted to fully commit myself to.

"Yeah, well it was either with me or have her living in some shitty apartment in a fucked-up neighborhood where he could easily manipulate his way in."

"What's to say he's not gonna come knocking on your door, boy? This is fuckin' wrong and you know it." He shakes his head, and I have to give it to him, he's not as pissed as I thought he would be.

Ever since Mackenzie has been back, Tiny's wanted to move her into one of his safe houses to ensure she was protected. But I would have no part in his plan. She came to me for help. I wasn't going to palm her off.

"He comes to my house, I'll have my Beretta '92 waiting for him." Tiny doesn't reply but I can see his mind ticking over what I just said. "If you're so worried, you put a man on her. Keep her in your sights." I finish my beer and keep an eye on the clock above the bar.

"You don't have men on her? What the fuck, Beau? You're meant to be fucking helping."

"You think I'm stupid? Of course I have eyes on her, asshole. But if you want your own set of eyes on her, then fine, I'll give you that, but she's not leaving my place to be holed up in some fucking cheap unit where he can find her again." I give him a long look, telling him I'm still pissed she was found in the first place.

"Don't look at me like that. I have no fucking idea how he found her. For all we know, it was the missing friend. She could have tipped him off."

"It wasn't her. She didn't even know she was in Ohio. The last time she spoke to her she was in Phoenix."

"Well, he obviously had someone working on it. I don't know." I'm pissed at his blasé reply.

"Well, maybe your fail safe fucking system isn't working well," I call him out.

"You have your head messed up on this one, brother." He ignores my look and gives me his opinion.

"Only thing messed up here is that this fucker hasn't been found yet. Until he is, she's staying with me. Simple." I drop a twenty on the table to cover my two beers and stand.

"And when you have another call out? You're just gonna leave her as an open target?" He drops his own twenty on the table and stands with me. "You know I'm about done with this shit. I'm ready to hand it all over. I need to know you're serious about coming on board." I know he's worried about this, but he also knows my reasons why I do this. He loved Missy like his own daughter. But he has nothing to worry about. Yeah, I might want in Mackenzie's pants. But she's the only one. I'm not some fucking sick fuck who wants to fix every broken woman I help.

"I told you, I have eyes on her. My commitment is still the same, Tiny. Don't fucking make it a problem. Now, I gotta head out. You have anything for me to work with?" We're coming up to two months since Mackenzie has been back and not one fucker in this town nor a marker out of town has seen Chad fucking Morre.

"It's like he's dropped off the face of the earth. Same with the friend. Friends and family say she moved away, left no forwarding address."

"How the fuck is that possible?" I'm fucking pissed. I thought for sure bringing in some markers would have pulled something up. He's either killed her, or she went deep into hiding.

"Your guess is as good as mine. We'll keep looking but in the meantime, we need to sit down and talk about how we're gonna integrate the shelter with the runs." I nod because I know he's right. We have a lot of work to do for this project to work.

"Let me know the place and time and I'll be there." He pulls me in for one of those slap-on-the-back man hugs. I return the sentiment.

"You sort this out, Beau, whatever is going on. She's in your home. You make sure you keep her safe."

"On it, old man."

We don't say anything else, both of us leaving at the same time. I make my way over to my bike and send a text to Hunter to check in.

Me: Everything all good?

I mount my ride and wait for a reply while thinking about Tiny's warning. Having her in my space is opening us up for more drama, but if I didn't offer her my house, I'd be a fucking mess.

After a few minutes, my phone beeps.

Hunter: All good. Quiet.

I pocket my phone, kick my stand up and reach for my helmet. Before I can put it on, the cool metal of a gun meets my temple.

"You better hope you're brave enough to pull the trigger, motherfucker." I keep my eyes straight ahead trying to assess my options.

"Brave bastard, aren't ya? Don't think I won't use it." The voice isn't familiar to me, so I rule out Chad and try to go through the list of who I've pissed off the last few months. *It's a long list.*

"What the fuck do you want?" I ask, kicking the stand of my bike down. If this asshole hurts my bike, I won't be responsible for what I do.

"Where the fuck is she?" He presses the gun harder against my temple.

"Who?" My back straightens. Maybe this is about Kenzie.

"Sandra and my kid. I know you fucking took them, with this underground shit gig you have going on with Tiny."

Fuck.

Sandra was the woman I took from one of the Warriors a few months back, her *and* her baby daughter. I didn't plan on taking her and she definitely didn't come to me looking for a way out. I found her crying at the front of the local store one morning. Took one look at her and knew I couldn't walk away. At the time, I didn't know she belonged to a Warrior, not that it would have changed anything. I offered her an out and she took it.

"I don't know where your information is coming from, asshole. But I don't know anyone named Sandra. Now either pull the fucking trigger or remove it from my head before I remove your arm from your body for you." I don't have a death wish, far from it. But this asshole is desperate to find his family. He's not going to risk shooting me Unluckily for him though

130

'cause I'm gonna make him fucking pay for even trying.

His laughter rings loud in the parking lot and I take my chance to overpower him. He doesn't see it coming. My elbow connects to his jaw, knocking him back. Twisting my body, I reach for his gun. He steadies himself and hits back. The butt of his gun hits just above my eye. Warmth pours from my brow and I know he just split it open. *Fucker.*

His arm pulls back, ready to bring his fist back down on my face, but I'm faster this time. My fingers twist his wrist back, forcing him to drop the gun. He shouts in pain as I manage to slide off my bike. He comes at me again, his fist rearing back, but before he can connect I force my head forward, connecting with his nose. He falls down fast, blood flowing from his nose. The gun is out of sight, and I don't worry about it now. I kick at his chest, forcing him back to the asphalt before my boot finds his throat and I push down. Hard.

"I just want to find my family." His words are strangled by the pressure of my boot and normally I'd take it easy on a desperate man, doing desperate things, but the fucker just had his gun to my head and split my eyebrow open. I'm not feeling so forgiving today.

"The family you beat on?" I sneer down at him.

"So you do know where she is?"

"I fucking took her away from you, asshole. And I'm not fucking telling you where she is." I dig a little deeper with my boot. His back arches in pain, but it doesn't stop me. This piece of shit thought he was a man by putting his hands on his woman. He's not a man. He's pathetic.

"Please." He gasps, his fingers scratching at my legs.

I step back, giving him a chance to fill his lungs. He spurts

131

and coughs, rolling to his side.

"You wanna know where she is?" I ask, eyeing the gun. It's fallen close to my bike out of view. I pick it up and point it at him.

"You know I do. You have no fucking clue who you're messing with. The truce will be done with when my Prez finds out what you did."

I laugh. "You think I give a fuck about the truce? I don't. Means nothing to me, or our club," I lie, knowing how far we've come with the Warriors. Blood has been shed, and the last thing we need is to have them coming into our territory.

"Tell me where she is and I won't go to my Prez," he tries to threaten me.

"You don't know who you're playing with. You think your Prez is gonna start a war for you." I release the safety on his gun and watch panic flash across his face.

"Put the gun down, Beau." I hear movement to my left, but I keep the gun trained on the fucker on the ground.

"Ain't gonna put it down." I don't bother looking around. I know I have one guy to my left, and another to my right.

"Just fucking shoot him." The weasel on the ground shouts to his friends, but no one reacts.

"What the fuck you doing, Baz? Told you to cool off with this Sandra shit," another voice asks, this time from my right.

"I don't want any fucking trouble. Your boy, Baz, here had his gun to my head. Misunderstanding. He has the wrong man."

The air is quiet as everyone waits for someone to make the next move.

"I will find her." Baz comes to his feet, but doesn't step closer.

No fucking chance in hell he's finding her.

"I wish you luck, but I don't know who you're looking for." I lower the gun and place it in the waistband of my jeans.

"That's my gun, asshole."

"And now it's mine. Next time you put a gun to a man's head, make sure you pull the trigger." I mount my ride, confident neither Baz nor the two guys will push the matter. There's no proof. I made sure of it. And they'd be stupid to push it either way, especially on our turf.

They all stay back as I put my helmet on. My eye is already swelling and my head is pounding. Baz begins to say something, but I start my bike and let the rumble wash away his voice.

I'm sure something will come out of tonight. I just fucked up a Warrior and took his gun. But I don't give a shit. He's on our territory. He's lucky I didn't use his gun on him.

I give one more look back at Baz and take off. I take the long route home, taking extra back streets to weed out any tail I might have. I don't think I do, but I won't take any chances with Mackenzie now living with me.

After making sure I'm clear, I pull into my driveway and shut down my bike.

The house is lit up like a Christmas tree, and I shake my head.

Damn woman, I don't know why she has to have every light on in the house.

Before I go in to see her, I walk across the street to the truck Hunter sits in. He lowers the window when I'm close enough.

"What the fuck happened to you?" He notices my eye right away.

"You should see the other guy. Everything okay here?" I

ignore his question and ask the important shit.

"Yeah, nothing happening."

"Good. You can head out now. I'm in for the rest of the night." I tap the top of his truck and turn to walk away.

"Oh, ya might wanna tell your woman, maybe not come out on the porch wearing what she's wearing tonight." I turn and watch him put his hands up in surrender, just like Baz did earlier. "Just saying, bro. Had both neighbors out earlier practically eye fucking her." He starts his truck and peels down the street before I can tell him to fuck off.

Great. More shit to deal with tonight.

13

Mackenzie

I HEAR THE RUMBLE OF HIS BIKE AS HE PULLS INTO THE drive and I race to the sofa, quickly opening my book and finding the page I was on, not wanting to look like I've been waiting for him.

Even if I have been.

It's been just over a week since I moved in. A week of living in each other's space. Of pure hell. Pure sex-god, hot-body, sexy-as-sin, beard-wearing, and fantastic hair hell.

The man is under my skin and living in close proximity is not helping at all.

Apparently, I didn't think this through when I agreed to live here. Yeah, I admit there was something between Beau and I. Something pulling me to him. I don't deny it. The kiss alone back at the clubhouse proved it, but I didn't realize how intense those feelings would grow since living in *his* space.

After the first day of awkwardness, things just seemed to fit into place, both of us settling back into our relaxed way. We've always been able to talk comfortably with each other, even with the slight tension to begin with, and it is no different here than at the clubhouse.

Until it became complicated with what I've been calling the first incident.

It happened on day four. I had left my body wash on my bed before my morning shower. I didn't realize until I had stepped under the water. I knew going by the first few mornings Beau didn't wake until I had finished in the shower, so I decided to risk a mad dash back to my room in a towel. I made it safely, undetected. His door still firmly closed.

That wasn't the problem. It was what I heard when I stepped into my room.

Moaning. A lot of freaking moaning. And my name. Beau moaning my name.

I nearly came apart right then and there. He was pleasuring himself, and calling out my name. At first I didn't know how to respond. I knew we both were hiding our real feelings, but I never imagined it would come to this. It was almost like we were both punishing ourselves for no reason at all. Not sure how I felt about it, I grabbed my wash and raced back to the shower as fast as I could. I tried to push the image out of my head. It didn't help. It's all I could picture for the next two days.

Until the second incident played out on day six.

I was watching a movie on the sofa late one afternoon. Beau had been moving around the house for most of the day doing his thing and leaving me alone, until he came and joined me. I was lying on my side, taking up all the space. I moved to sit up and make some room for him, but he beat me to it and lifted my legs, planted his ass at the end then rested my feet in his lap.

"Stay," is all he said when I tried to lift my legs. How was I going to argue with him? I couldn't, so I gave up and forced myself to focus my attention back on the movie while he held my ankle in his hand and used his thumb to circle a soft pattern into my skin. At first I didn't think anything of it. It felt nice and maybe I just needed nice for once. But then a hot steamy scene came on and the room reached sky-high tension. I felt it. He felt it. My vagina felt it. I'm sure Barry the old man next door I met two days ago felt it. I tried not to react. My eyes stayed firmly planted on the TV and I willed myself not to read into it.

But I couldn't help it. It was like my foot didn't want to listen to my brain and instead of keeping still it started searching. Searching for what, I don't freaking know. He was getting hard. My foot apparently wanted more.

His thumb stopped stroking me and we both kind of paused. Then next thing I knew he was out of the chair, and heading to bed before dinner. I didn't see him again until the next morning for breakfast.

I don't know what's worse. The jerking off or the erection. But both have messed with me.

Plus on top of those two major mishaps, I have taken to dreaming about him. Every night I find his beard between my legs. His tongue, which I have no idea how talented it really is, brings me to orgasm just as I wake.

It's torture.

Pure torture.

I don't know how to stop it or if I want it to.

"Mackenzie!" Beau's voice fills the room cutting through my daydreaming.

"What are you yelling for?" I drop my book and stand when I notice his face. All thoughts of playing it cool fade away and I gasp. "Oh, God what happened to you?" I step forward, needing a better look. Blood has dried from his brow down his face and all through his beard.

"Nothing. What are you wearing?" He runs his eyes over my nightgown before coming back up to my face.

"Errr, my nightgown?" His lip curls at my reply and I take a step back.

Ummm, what the hell?

"Mackenzie, you can't be wearing this shit here. Not out on the porch. Half the fucking street probably jerked off to the sight of you tonight." I ignore the fact he just said men are masturbating over me and zero in on him using my full name.

"What's going on, Beau?"

"You've got no fucking clothes on, darlin'." I look down at the black nightgown I'm wearing. The man's crazy. It's not like it's revealing. The length hits just below my knee. The neckline is a little low, but it's not like I have a large rack to put on display. In the grand scheme of things, it's barely risqué.

"This?" I look back up, waiting for him to tell me he's joking around.

"Yes, that. You can't wear it." He drops his helmet to the table and stalks into the kitchen. Ignoring his ridiculous comment and pissed-off mood, I follow him into the kitchen.

"What happened to your face?" I walk to the cabinet where

the first-aid kit lives.

"Had a disagreement," he answers, searching the fridge for food.

"I cooked dinner." I wait for him to turn and face me. "I'll fix it for you if you let me look at your eye."

"What did you cook?"

Damn, he's stubborn.

"Chicken pot pie." He huffs then moves to the table with a beer in his hand. My pie's clearly good enough to have him caving. I follow him over and open up the kit.

"Some disagreement then?" I lean down to have a closer look. He moans almost like he's in pain and I step back.

"What? I didn't even touch you." He doesn't say anything; instead, he takes off his cut and pulls his black shirt over his head.

"Put it on." He offers it to me.

"You can't be serious?" I scoff, caught between the thunderous glare he's giving me and checking out his naked chest.

Seriously, this man.

"Darlin', I'm fucking wired right now. Your tits are in my face. And this fucking sexy getup leaves nothing to the imagination. I'm not sure I'll be able to hold it together."

"Beau?" I take another step back at his tone. I'm not sure if I'm turned on or scared. He's never been this intense before and I take a minute to calm my breathing.

He won't hurt me. I know this.

"Don't even go there right now, Mackenzie. You have nothing to be scared of." He notices my reaction and drops some of his tension. "Just put the shirt on, darlin'." I know he's right. I have nothing to be scared of with Beau, and I feel a little foolish for reacting. With quick fingers, I manage to pull it over my head.

"Fuck, it's almost worse," he mumbles, and if I weren't freaking out, I would laugh at his displeasure.

"Should I leave?"

"Fuck no. Just let me stew for a while." He draws a deep breath in and then slowly lets it out.

"Feeling better?" I ask when a few minutes of awkward silence pass.

"Getting there."

I roll my eyes. "Are you going to let me clean you up?" I fold my arms in front of me. He follows my movements and shakes his head before lifting his mouth in a sexy smirk.

"Have at it." He rests further back in his chair and allows me to proceed.

I step forward, open an antiseptic swab and begin removing all the dried blood first. I don't know what the hell happened to stir this kind of reaction in him tonight. Beau's never spoken like this to me before. Yeah, he has his moments of shortness and bossy ways, but this, this was something else. And I'm not sure if it really has anything to do with the nightgown.

"This part might sting." I grab a clean swab and lean back over him. His eyes stay closed as I make short work of cleaning up the cut.

"It's not too deep. I'll just put a bandage on it to keep it closed." I reach back to the first-aid box and search for some sterile strips. "So what happened tonight?" I ask when I find them.

"Nothing you need to worry about." His eyes are still

140

closed, his jaw tense. Being this close with free run to stare at him is dangerous.

What would he do if I pressed my lips to his?

"Well, I will if it means you're gonna come home and be an ass, I might worry." His right eye opens at my sass and I shrug.

What does he expect? He pulls it out of me.

"Club business, darlin'. Not gonna talk about it with you." He shuts down my questions.

Club business. Don't ask.

"Fair enough." I let it go, and place the first strip over the cut. He doesn't flinch or show any sign of hurting. I use a second strip to make sure it's secure, this time pushing a little harder. Again he doesn't react and it doesn't surprise me. The man is a pro at keeping his emotions in check.

"Done," I announce then step back and start clearing the wrappers from the strips and swabs.

"Thanks, darlin'." He opens his eyes, the fire slowly fading behind them.

God, he's handsome. The dark eyes, tanned skin. Beard. Ugh, the beard.

"No problem." I clear my throat and step over to the trash can. He doesn't say anything else and I wonder if I should push this. "Now that you're cleaned up, let's discuss the nightgown." I take a seat next to him. My mind and body are at war with each other. Some messed-up part of me wants to please him and not wear it just to make him happy. But at the same time, he doesn't get to tell me what to do.

"You can't wear shit like this if you want to live here."

"You're serious? What's wrong with it?"

"Everything." He keeps his eyes on his beer and I don't

know if I want to slap him or kiss his face. Even just sitting there, in his pissy mood, he affects me. I regard him for a minute, willing his eyes up, but he doesn't react.

"Okay, I'll start looking for a new place tomorrow." I stand and begin to walk away. I have no idea where this is all coming from. Yeah, sometimes it can be tense between us but this is a whole new level for us. One I'm not okay with.

"Why? Because I don't want you to wear the stupid dress around me?" he calls out. I turn back to face him.

"No, because clearly this living arrangement isn't working for us. And because you don't get to control me, Beau."

"I'm not trying to control you, Kenz."

"No? 'You can't wear your nightgown if you wanna live here, darlin'.'" I deepen my voice and quote his words back to him. "Is that not controlling?"

"I'm just trying to protect you." He growls, still not making any sense.

"What from, the cold? Last time I checked it's eighty out."

"Don't be a smartass. You know what I'm saying. You can't walk around here wearing shit like this and not have me react. It's the last thing you want." His honesty shocks me for a minute before I draw his meaning from it.

Okay, we're doing this now.

"Did you bother to ask me what I want, Beau?" I'm starting to lose my composure. Me standing here, exposed, yet he can barely look at me.

"You don't know what you want, Mackenzie."

"Oh, I know what I want. Maybe you're the one confused here." There, I said it. No point hiding it. Surely by now he knows this tension isn't going anywhere. Ever since I came back, it's been there. Both of us lying to each other isn't working anymore.

"Jesus, you're so fucking clueless."

"And you're so annoying."

He stands, pushing the chair back and takes two significant steps toward me. I fight my need to cower. Instead, I straighten my back and hold his stare.

"You really wanna know why this will never work, Mackenzie?"

"Yes!" I practically shout in his face.

"Because you're right. I want to control you, darlin'. Not in the way your fucking ex did, in a way that makes you come apart."

A hot pulse of need shoots through me, igniting me with his words.

He leans in closer and I have to tilt my head back to keep eye contact.

"I want to fucking claim you. Tie you to my goddamn bed and force you to submit to me." He presses his mouth to the shell of my ear and I don't fight it, I wait.

Wait for everything and more.

"I want to do dirty things to you, Kenz. Things only dirty girls enjoy. I want to push every one of your limits so no man will ever be able to make you come like I do." His hot breath moves over my ear and I can't help the shiver that rolls through me.

"I. Want. To. Own. You." He pulls back when he's finished. Both of our breathing thick with need.

Holy shit.

How do you respond to that?

"Beau." I step back, unsure what to say. His eyes narrow at my retreat, but he doesn't say anything.

My body is alight, buzzing with need but also uncertainty.

If it were anyone other than Beau saying these words, I'd probably be thrown back into the past with Chad. A past I want no future in. But this is Beau. He doesn't frighten me or want to hurt me. He cares for me and I care for him.

"I don't—" I begin to reply but stop because I have no idea what I want to say.

"Save it. I'm not doing this with you. Wear your fucking revealing nightgown. I don't give a fuck." Beau takes my pause the wrong way, turns and walks out, leaving me alone to process the last ten minutes on my own.

Holy shit, what just happened?

"Kenz?" A knock at my door and Beau's voice stirs me out of my sleep. My room is dark, the low glow of the hallway light peeks through under the bottom of the door.

"Yeah?" I call back before checking the clock.

Just after ten. I've barely been asleep an hour. After Beau left me standing in the kitchen highly aroused, I closed the house up, turned everything off and made my way to bed.

"Can I come in?" he asks and I roll to sit up. I quickly fix my hair and look down.

Shit, I'm still wearing his shirt.

"Ahh, yeah, come in." I pull the cover up, hoping to hide behind it. He pushes the door open and steps inside. "Is everything okay?" I lean across to the bedside table and flick the bedside light on.

"I fucked up, darlin'. That shit out there, it wasn't right." He sighs, resting his shoulder against the wall.

"It's okay, Beau. Things were heated," I agree, wanting him to know I'm not angry or scared like he thinks I am.

"It's not okay. It's not me, or more than that, it's not how I want to be when it comes to you." He runs his fingers through his beard and I want to tell him to piss off with his sexiness. But I can't.

I can't because I care for him, and I can see he's struggling with all of this.

"I'm not sure what you want me to say, Beau," I offer, just as lost as him. He kind of just left me hanging out there for me to process everything alone.

"I don't want you to say anything. I don't want you to think about any of this. It's the last thing you need right now."

"Well, it's kind of hard not to when it exists between us. Has ever since I've been back," I counter, still not sure exactly how to process all this.

Did his words stir something in me? A need I didn't know I would or could want? Yes. But if I'm honest, it also frightened me a little. I mean I'm not some blushing virgin who doesn't know her way around her body. Yeah, I haven't been with anyone since Chad, but before I met Chad, I had a couple of partners, each one opening me up to a new experience. But what it sounds like Beau is into, is something entirely different.

"Yeah, I know and I didn't mean to put it on you at all. I know you have your past, and I'm a fucking idiot for thinking it would be okay to lay it on you like that. This can't happen." I try not to be affected by his words, but I can't help it. In the beginning, I was this person who wouldn't even consider what he is offering, but I've been working so hard not to be that broken woman anymore.

"I don't need to be handled with kid gloves, Beau. I'm not saying what you shared didn't affect me, but I'm not cowering away from it."

He doesn't say anything for a while, and I worry it's too late.

"I'm not trying to handle you in any way, Kenzie. Clearly, we're both feeling this, whatever this is between us. Since you showed up at the clubhouse, it's been there. But you came to me for help, darlin'. Not for me to introduce you to my kind of kink."

I begin to argue, but he holds his hand up, stopping me before I even begin.

"No, let me just get this out. Now, I'm not gonna lie, you've come to mean something to me, darlin', and as much as I want this, I'm not prepared to go there with you. You have your own shit to deal with. Chad *and* getting your life back on track. This thing between us now isn't the right time. We need to focus on the other issues and keep our heads clear."

I let out a breath I didn't know I was holding.

I know he's right. Now isn't the time to be caught up in a relationship with Beau, regardless of how we both feel. It's stupid to think I could handle anything right now, not with an unknown future that could come back to bite me at any time.

"You're right, Beau. I agree," I finally say, hating this for what it is.

"You do?" I don't miss the change in his tone. I'm just not sure how to read it.

"Yeah. I think things are still fresh. It's clouding our judgment. We should take a step back, focus on what's important."

We're both old enough and wise enough to know this thing between us could end badly, with my past and his tastes. We shouldn't mess anything up by forcing it.

"Well, shit. I wasn't expecting you to agree."

I laugh a little at his confession. Maybe an hour ago I would have argued for more, but sitting here now, I can see it. "Well, I don't always like to push you," I joke, hoping to break some of the bad tension still hanging around us.

"Could have fooled me." He chuckles, the tension lifting a little.

"So we're good. Tonight didn't happen. We'll just move forward and forget it." *Again.*

"I think it's for the best, darlin'."

"Okay." I force a smile and hope he doesn't see through it. I honestly don't think it's possible to forget what happened tonight.

"Okay. Night." He returns my smile then reaches for the door, preparing to leave. "Oh, and Mackenzie?"

"Yeah?"

"I'll be needing my shirt back," he adds before pulling the door closed and leaving me red-faced.

"Well, it's this or the scandalous nightgown. You choose," I yell back, not sure if he heard me. His laugh travels through the door, but it does nothing to bring us back to where we were before.

Shit, can I do this? Stay in this house with this man when I have these feelings and urges for him?

I want to say yes. I can move on, staying just friends and hope I stop thinking of him this way, but I'm not sure it's possible.

It has to be, though. Beau is my friend. He came into my life for a reason, and that reason changed everything. I wouldn't want to lose what friendship we had built. Not now. Not ever.

It's going to be hard to push these feelings away, and maybe I'm not strong enough, but I have to try.

Only time will tell.

Past

Mackenzie

"YOU'RE DOING GOOD, DARLIN', JUST A LITTLE LONGER."
The man who held me close to his chest for fifteen minutes in the back of a van keeps repeating his reassuring words.

"Hurts so bad." I wince when he picks me up and then lowers me down to a sofa in a house, sending a sharp pain through my chest.

"I know, darlin'. We're gonna have you looked at," he tells me. His voice is deep and husky.

"What's your name?" I ask, needing to know what to call him.

"Beau," he answers instantly and it sets me at ease. He's good-looking in a rough, biker kind of way. His dark hair is pulled back away from his face in a low ponytail. Blue eyes and tanned skin hidden by a beard covering most of his face.

I've never understood the fascination with men and long hair, I always just thought it was strange, but staring up at this stranger, I can see how it might be appealing to some.

"Beau, where are we?" I'm not sure if I can take much more of this pain. I need something. Anything.

"We're at a safe house. There's been a change in plans."

"What? No. I was told we were heading out of town. I can't stay here." I start to fight as much as I can, but it doesn't get me far. My muscles tire and my eyes drop as I begin to slip away.

"You can and you will. Trust me. You need a doctor. We can't drop you off at the next stop until you've been checked out. Sy and I are going to take good care of you," he promises, but I don't know him or Sy. How can I trust he won't send me back to the pits of my own personal hell?

"Hurts so bad, Beau," I whisper again just as the darkness takes me.

"Darlin', you with me?" Beau's voice breaks through the heaviness around me and pulls me back.

"Yeah?" I manage past my lips. I open my eyes, fighting past the blurriness.

"How're you holding up?" He's sitting in a chair next to me, not touching me, but still somehow comforting me.

"Okay, how long have I been out?" I wheeze. My chest is still heavy, and my discomfort is increasing in waves. The small lulls giving me false hope of an end, do nothing to calm me.

"About thirty minutes." He leans down and brushes some

hair off my face.

Thirty minutes?

"We need to leave, Beau. He's going to find me." Panic threatens to overwhelm me knowing I'm still in town.

"No one is going to find you. This wasn't in the plan, but we're gonna work with what we have." Beau tries to assure me, but it doesn't help.

"You don't know Chad as I do. He *will* find me. He did this because I tried to leave him." I whisper.

"Listen, Mackenzie. We'll do everything we need to do to get you out of here safely, but we have to have this arm set. It's too badly damaged to move you to the next drop off. We have the connections here. I promise you he won't get to you."

A car pulling up into the gravel drive takes his attention.

"Did the doc call?" Beau stands and moves through the cabin.

"No, he said he'd call five minutes out." The other guy picks up two guns, handing Beau one.

"Whatever you do, don't make a sound," Beau places his finger to his mouth. I nod, my eyes locking on his gun.

"Move her to the back room, Sy," Beau tells the other guy as he walks to the front window.

"It's him. I know it is," I cry, not listening to Beau's command. I knew I wouldn't get far.

"Woman, be quiet," Sy orders, coming to stand over me. I nod, silent tears clouding my vision. "I need to move you. It's gonna fucking hurt, but you can't make a sound, you hear me?" Sy leans down into my space.

"Okay." I nod, my breath coming out choppy.

"Bite down on this." He hands me a clean towel. "Okay. One, two, three," he counts then picks me up over his shoulder.

Shooting pain burns in my ribs but I bite down to muffle my screams. "Good girl," he whispers, placing me down on the bed in the back room. "Hang on." He steps up to a freestanding closet and pushes it aside.

"What's going on?" I remove the towel from my mouth.

"Whoever is out there is not meant to be here. We have to hide you 'cause if it's the police, they're here for you." He flicks the lock on the secret door hidden in the wall.

"I can't go in there." I shake my head, looking at the small, dark space. Fear pricks my skin at the thought of being trapped.

"It's either in there or back to your husband. What do you want?"

A dark, scary hole sounds like heaven compared to Chad. Even with the apprehension and the fear of someone being outside to take me back to him swirling around in my belly, I know what I have to do.

"Okay." Slowly and painfully, I stand from the bed and walk toward him. "But, please don't leave me in here long," I plead as he helps me down to my knees to crawl in.

The room is no more than six feet wide. It's dark, dirty and musty.

"As soon as we get rid of whoever is out there, we'll be back," he promises, closing the door. The darkness closes in on me, blanketing me in a new kind of hell. I hear the sound of him dragging the closet back into place and I sit and wait.

Wait for an unknown future.

I HEAR THE SHOWER TURN ON THE FOLLOWING MORN-
ing and I can't help a groan from leaving my mouth.

Fuck, not again.

My cock stirs to life, images of her standing under the spray of my shower play out in my mind. My hand travels down my stomach and wraps around my now hard cock.

Jesus, I'm going to hell.

Deciding not to fight it like I've been trying to, I fist myself. Rough to begin with before loosening my grip and stroking my hand up and down my shaft. Ignoring my dry callused palm, I imagine what her grip would be like wrapped around me. Would it be soft and unsure? Or would it be firm and confident? I can almost sense it, the touch of her delicate fingers wrapped around me.

Resting back onto my pillow, I pick up my speed and imagine Kenzie in the shower. It doesn't take long for my mind to put me in the bathroom with her.

She looks up as I walk into the bathroom, her body slick and wet.

"Join me," she whispers as she squeezes a healthy dollop of soap into her hand, spreading it all over her tits.

Fuck me.

I strip out of my boxers and waste no time joining her under the spray of the water. My cock stands hard between us, throbbing in anticipation. She hands me the bottle and I squeeze the liquid in my palms.

"I'm really dirty, Beau. I need to be washed again." She pushes her tits forward, an invitation for me to get to work.

I don't need to be told twice. I reach forward and coat her tits in the soap. Her nipples pebble, the rose pink buds begging for my attention.

"Harder, Beau." She moans my name and I comply, twisting and pulling her nipples between my thumb and finger.

Her hand glides down my body, her soft grip wrapping around my aching cock.

"I think you need to be cleaned." Her grip tightens, and I jerk at the touch. "Do you need me to clean you, Beau?" She drops to her knees. I nod, words lost on me.

Her pink tongue flicks out and swipes at the tip, lapping up a small bead of pre-cum.

"Fuck, baby." I moan. Her hot breath and wet tongue almost have me blowing my load right there.

"Put it in your mouth, darlin'." I push my hips forward,

needing more.

She doesn't disappoint. Her mouth encases my length, her suction soft and gentle.

"Yes, suck it good, Kenz," I encourage, pushing my cock to the back of her throat. She takes it all, her head bobbing up and down with wild abandon.

"Jesus, fuck." My head falls back as she takes my balls in her hands, rolling them between her fingers. She knows exactly what I want. What I fucking need. My balls grow heavy and I know I'm about to fucking blow. She senses my impending explosion and picks up her pace. A low growl vibrates over my cock and it's the catalyst to push me over the edge.

"Mackenzie!" I shout my release. My warm cum covers my hand, breaking my visual of Mackenzie on her knees and bringing me back to my room. Back to reality.

"Fuck." I sigh, coming down. I slow my strokes, milking the last of my orgasm.

A bang from Mackenzie's room has me stilling.

Fuck. Please don't tell me she heard me. I listen carefully for more movement but don't hear anything else. Pushing the thought out of my head, I reach for my shirt and clean myself up.

This is what it's come to. Me jerking off every morning while she showers.

Yep, I'm fucking sad.

"Thank fuck you're here, another minute of this daddy day-care bullshit and I was about to lose it." Jesse stands when I walk into the clubhouse the following morning.

"Says the man who stole my daughter from my arms the minute I walked in," Kadence quips, not letting Jesse play his bullshit.

"Whatever," he dismisses and hands Low back to her.

"Where the fuck you been? And what the fuck happened to your face?" Nix walks out, coffee in hand.

"Slept in, and got in a disagreement," I tell him the same thing I told Hunter and Kenzie as I follow him into church with the rest of the guys. This morning is our weekly club meet. I'm only five minutes late, but judging by everyone's mood, I may as well have been an hour.

"You have an alarm clock, asshole?" Sy takes a seat in his chair next to me putting his own two cents in. Jesus Christ, what the fuck is up everyone's ass today? If anyone has a pass to be pissed off, it's me,

I screwed up last night. Lost my shit at Mackenzie, then told her everything I've been dreaming about doing to her since she came back to me. My tight grip on keeping everything platonic is slipping. I don't know how much more I can keep denying this.

"You have a problem, Sy?" I force all thoughts of Mackenzie out of my head and give Sy the same attitude back.

"How about you both shut the hell up so we can get this shit over with," Nix cuts off Sy's reply and addresses the table.

"What's gonna piss me off this week?" He starts the meeting like he always does, going around the table and checking in on the business side of things. Brooks runs the bar Fireside, Jesse runs the club, Liquid, and Sy mans and runs the tattoo shop, Ink Me.

A couple of months back, Kelly and I put it forward to Nix and the boys our plans for opening a women's shelter in town. With me taking over from Tiny, I wanted to change some areas. Not all cases run the same. Not all women want or need to leave town. A local women's shelter in town will help cut down on unnecessary runs, and still keep the women safe. We were going to go ahead with or without the club's input, but we wanted them in on it since it's gonna take up a lot of time for both me and Kelly.

Our goal for the shelter is to provide safe accommodation with twenty-four-hour emergency support, but also community support. Along with shelter staff and volunteers, we will be able to assist women with job training and hunting, housing, medical, and legal services. The length of time a woman or family can live there will be based on their individual needs and goals. Some may come through for emergency housing, others may stay on for over six months.

The vote came through as a yes from the club and, after some back and forth, we finally secured the perfect place big enough for what we need here in town.

"How did you go on getting licenses for the shelter?" Nix asks when everyone has gone through all the usual day-to-day dramas. On top of sourcing qualified staff and volunteers, we've been jumping through hoops to make sure all paperwork is up to date so we can legally receive donations and government grants.

"Have everything we need, bar a name. Any suggestions?" I ask the table, hoping someone has something. This part of the business holds the least interest to me, which is why Kelly is a perfect business partner.

"Well," Brooks speaks up. "The boys and I were thinking maybe you wanted to name it, Missy's Place." I hold my breath, trying not to react.

My sister.

The reason I started all of this.

"You don't have to." Nix takes my silence for a no, letting me off the hook. But it's not what I want.

"I think she'd like it." I bite the inside of my cheek until the metallic taste of blood fills my mouth.

"Then it's settled Missy's Place it is." Nix reaches over, slaps me on the arm, before moving on to the next topic. I miss it entirely, my mind's too lost in the memories of Missy and what this means for me. For her.

I never thought I'd ever come to a point in my life where I'd be able to honor her name.

Until now.

It might have taken ten years, but fuck it feels good.

"You still with us?" Nix asks a while later, pulling me back. I look up and notice the boys have all left, leaving Nix and me.

"Yep." I stand, ready to go.

"So you wanna tell me what happened to your face." He stops my exit like I should have known he would.

Taking a seat back down, I prepare to lay it all out for him. "One of T's boys jumped me after leaving Fireside last night."

"How's he look?"

"Lucky to be alive."

He draws a breath in and slowly releases it. "This gonna come back on us?"

"Depends if he has the proof he says he has."

"Is there a chance he has proof?"

"I don't think so, but he seems adamant."

"You don't think so? Jesus, Beau. You either know or you don't."

"I don't fucking know. I can't be sure. It wasn't a planned rescue. It happened so fast. You know this already. I saw her and took her."

He taps the table three times, thinking through our options. "Well, where is she?"

"She's still in town. Tiny has her in one of his safe houses. She doesn't want to leave in case he files kidnapping charges. Tiny's dealing with it." It's probably not the best place to have her considering Baz is losing it, but after this, I'll make sure I talk with Tiny.

"Well, keep an eye on it. If this fucker gets out of line again, don't be so easy on him next time."

"Oh, I look forward to it," I tell him, knowing I don't need my Prez's permission to take this shit further. If Baz fucks up again, I won't have a problem taking the asshole down.

"You really okay with using Missy's name? Didn't mean to throw that shit out there when you're unprepared." Nix changes the tone of the conversation, but I'm prepared.

"It's fine. I'm good." His brows dip a little, watching me for a reaction.

"You just seem a little wired. Everything okay at home with Mackenzie?"

Fucking wired is an understatement. I'm on fucking edge and don't need to be sitting around fucking talking about it.

"I'm good. Look, I gotta head out to the new building with Kelly. She wants to discuss furniture shit. We done?" I stand and look down at him.

"Yeah, we're done." He finds his feet and follows me back out to the bar.

"You ready?" Kelly stands when she notices me.

"Yep. You bringing her?" I ask, looking down at Mia playing at her feet. I don't have a problem if she does, but I have a feeling we're gonna have to go shopping and, fuck, shopping with Mia where she runs around touching everything is gonna drives me nuts.

"Don't be an ass, Beau." She shakes her head, before digging through her bag.

"What did I say?"

"She has a name. It wouldn't hurt for you to use it." She pulls her keys from her bag and starts to walk out to her car.

"You're a dick," Jesse shouts across the clubhouse, happy for once I'm copping it and not him.

"Yeah, says the biggest dick of all." I flip him off.

"I know I have a big dick, thanks." His laughter can be heard all the way outside as I follow Kelly.

Jesus, I'm losing my touch. I fucking walked right into that one.

15

Mackenzie

"PLEASE, TELL ME THIS DID NOT ACTUALLY HAPPEN?" I laugh at Kadence's reaction as Holly relays a story involving Nix, Valentine's Day and Viagra.

"Oh, it happened," Kadence answers, laughing just as hard as the rest of us.

It's a Friday evening, five nights after my tense encounter with Beau where he told me he wanted me as much as I wanted him but wouldn't act on it.

I had planned on having a quiet night in until Beau was called into work, and he didn't want to leave me alone, so I told him I would call Kelly over to keep me company. She showed up with alcohol, Kadence, Holly, and Bell, turning my quiet night into a girls' night.

"So what did you do?" I take another sip of my drink, my third for the night, and I sit back in the chair I now call my own. I know it's not really mine, but I've claimed it as my own whenever I sit down to watch TV or read a book, it's the comfiest spot.

"We had to go to the ER. It was so embarrassing. Everyone knew." Kadence giggles, hiding her face in her hands.

"I can't even imagine." I laugh along with them, picturing it all play out.

"Enough about us. We want some gossip on you." Kelly leans forward and tops up her cocktail.

"What? I don't have any gossip." A warm blush creeps up my neck and four sets of eyes fall on me.

"Girl, you're hot gossip at the moment. Don't leave us hanging," Kadence encourages, and I almost feel disappointed I have nothing to gossip about with them.

"I swear, I have nothing." I shrug, those four sets of eyes, fading from excitement to suspicion.

There is no way I can tell them what has or rather hasn't happened between Beau and me.

"You mean to tell me, you've been living under this roof, living in your own bubble with no interruptions, no nosey club members to cramp your style and you have nothing to share?"

"Believe me, if I had something to share, I would." I let out a huff at my own displeasure.

Ever since that night when Beau told me what he wanted to do to me, then told me we can't, he has been reserved, keeping to himself and staying clear of me. It's been tense and somewhat awkward, but I'm trying to put it behind me with hopes maybe things might change.

"So you *do* like him. I knew it!" Holly stands to raise her glass.

"Sit down, fool. We all knew she liked him." Kadence rolls her eyes and turns back to me.

"So what's the issue? He's too moody?"

I laugh at her question only to find them all staring back at me blankly. "Beau is not moody. He's just composed," I defend him, watching as each of them share a look.

"Girl, the man is so moody, some days I wonder if he's PMSing on the same cycle as me," Kadence fires, and I can't help but laugh along with them.

"He's not that bad." I shrug, not seeing Beau the way they do. He's direct and quiet, but moody? No.

"We have bets to see how many words he can say sometimes. I think the most I've ever heard in one night was fifteen. Fifteen, Kenz. Fifteen." Kelly shakes her head, disturbed by the number.

"He talks to me," I offer, hoping to show them he's not the moody asshole they seem to think he is.

"Yeah, 'cause he likes you, probably wants to tie you up and spank you." Bell's hand slaps over her mouth just as fast as the words leave her lips.

Oh, God, did everyone know about Beau and his wants but me?

"What. Do. You. Know?" Kadence turns to face the younger woman, whose eyes are practically falling out of her head.

"Oh, God. No, nothing. I know nothing." She shakes her head, denying it as much as a kid caught with his hand in the candy jar would.

"Bullshit. Don't you dare hold out on us," Kelly pushes this

163

time.

"I can't say. I wasn't meant to say. Oh, I'm gonna be in so much trouble." Bell starts rocking.

The thought of her knowing something she isn't supposed to doesn't sit well with me. A spark of jealousy settles in me. *What does she know?*

"Well, the cat's out of the bag now. Just spill," Kelly adds, just as eager to know.

"Shit, guys." Bell stands and starts pacing.

"If it's bad, you shouldn't say." I try to pull the conversation back, not wanting to know.

"It's not bad, bad. Just, I was sworn to secrecy. And now I've gone and blabbed."

"What if we guess?" Kadence asks, offering her a way out of her guilt.

"Yeah, okay. If you guess correctly, I'll just nod, that way I'm not actually telling anything." I nearly laugh at how serious Bell's taking this.

"Let me guess. Beau is the kinky fuck who tied Lissy up, spanked the fuck out of her ass while we were in Vegas." I spit my drink at Holly's guess and watch all color drain from Bell's face.

Lissy? Oh, my God. This is worse. He's had sex with Lissy. Is he still having sex with her? Is that why he doesn't want more from me?

"How did you know?" Bell sits, her hands moving back to her mouth. "Shit."

"'Cause Lissy told me." Holly shrugs, a slow smile pulling at the corners of her lips. "She didn't swear me to secrecy, so we're cool," she assures Bell before turning back to me.

"Are they still?" I stop to think how to phrase it. I've met

Lissy a couple of times in the last two months. She's a little crazy and loud, but a nice girl. I never once suspected her and Beau had or even have a fling.

"Oh no. It was a one-time deal. You know Lissy, she's just having fun. You have nothing to worry about. It's all in the past." I look at Bell, silently pleading with her to stop.

"Why, do you have a taste for kink, Mackenzie?" I fight the blush that runs over my face and offer Holly my innocent look.

If only they knew.

"I don't have a taste for anything." I clear my throat and push all images of a naked Beau spanking Lissy out of my head.

"I bet ya that's why he hasn't made his move. Innocent Mackenzie is messing him up." Holly, oblivious to my panic, starts running through all the scenarios. *Jesus, is this woman psychic?*

"Beau just isn't interested in me, guys." I try to put out the fire they started with their questions and let them down easy. It's not like I can tell them he wants me, but because of my past is too afraid to go there, and I was too clueless to understand any of this until I practically begged him.

Yeah, I'm a hot mess.

"Are you deaf, blind and stupid?" Kadence asks this time. "The man is so into you, I'm concerned for his own health."

"I kissed him then kind of freaked out. Now he says we can't go there, and I've tried to forget about it ever since." This time I slap my hand over my mouth, realizing I just revealed too much.

"HA! I knew it." Kelly stands, dances in her spot then holds her hand out. "Pay up, bitches." She waits patiently as Kadence, Holly and Bell place ten-dollar bills in her hand.

"You made a bet?" I ask, not sure if I should be offended or laugh along with them.

"You'll get used to them, don't worry," Bell offers and for reasons I can't explain, I believe her.

Yeah, they're crazy, brash, loud and over the top, but it's not all there is to them. They're kind, funny and caring. They opened their lives to accommodate me, look after me, and now in such a short time, accepted me as a friend. I'm more than lucky to have them in my life, especially when I still have no idea if Heidi is in hiding or if Chad has done something to her.

"So what was the bet, then?" I ask, wanting to know the odds.

"Well, I bet you had already fucked each other's brains out." Holly shrugs, before taking a sip of her drink. "You could have taken one for the team, babe." She winks and I laugh.

"I bet you hadn't done anything," Kadence adds, not at all worried she lost out.

"And I bet you made it to second base." Bell blushes a little and I want to say sorry I couldn't take it further for her.

"And I, of course, won the bet," Kelly says, counting her money.

"Huh." I look at each of them, still not sure what to say.

"You're not mad, are you?" Kadence asks, looking a little guilty.

"No, I'm just trying to figure out how I can get in on these bets." I smile, setting her at ease. I'm not mad; I knew there were whispers about us. Who wouldn't talk?

"Well, we have a pool for when Bell announces she's getting married." Holly offers.

"What? You do?" Bell shouts, not clued in on the bet.

"Yeah, I lost out already." Holly clearly has high hopes for everyone getting it on and getting married.

"Okay, well, can I be in on that one?" I ask, trying to figure out when she and Jesse would want to settle down. I know they just started living together, but I might have an advantage here.

"Yeah, the pool is at two hundred." Kelly smiles, ignoring Bell's shock.

"Okay, I bet $50 they're engaged by Thanksgiving." My mind goes back to the morning Jesse taught me or should I say tried to teach me how to make an omelet and I remember Jackson telling Jesse he needed to put a ring on Bell's finger. He said soon and dropped the subject just as quick.

"Done. Locked in."

I turn to look at Bell and watch a knowing smile spread across her face.

"What?" I question, wonder what she's hiding.

"Nothing." She shrugs but I caught it. She's keeping something. I just hope it doesn't happen until Thanksgiving.

I could do with $200.

"Ugggh." I wake up the next morning to the smell of coffee and bacon. Normally, this combination would have me rolling out of bed eager to start my day. But after the six cocktails I consumed last night, my head and my stomach are telling me otherwise.

"You awake?" The deep voice of Beau echoes around my head, causing me to flinch in pain.

"Don't yell so loud." I pull my pillow over my face and try

to block out the daylight.

"Come on. Up you get, you've slept the whole day away." I peek out the side of the pillow and check the time.

Just after twelve.

Holy crap, he's right. I've slept half the day away.

"I want to die." I groan, my stomach rolling in protest.

"I made you something to eat. You'll feel better with something in your stomach."

"Can't move. Dying. Send for help." I ignore his chuckle and force my eyes closed. Maybe if I sleep some more, I'll wake up not feeling like death.

"I am the help." The blanket is ripped off me and I'm thankful I'm still wearing the clothes I wore last night and not my scandalous nightgown.

"Beau," I complain, but before I can say anymore, Beau has me up and out of bed in his arms.

At first I freeze, but then I realize nothing is going to change, so I push hope out of my head and relax.

We're just friends.

"If I puke on you, it's your own fault." I bury my head into his chest, still not ready to face the day. His shirt smells like pine and a hint of lacquer.

"If you puke on me, darlin', you're getting in the shower to clean me up," he replies and my stomach does that dip thingy that happens just as you free fall on a roller coaster. "Shit, sorry," he quickly adds, realizing his slip.

Ugggh, this is why it's hard to move on when he oversteps the friend line.

"Why do you smell like pine?" I change the subject, not because I don't want to shower with Beau, because I do. But

168

talking about it anymore than I have to will only make things worse.

"Why do you smell like vanilla one day and strawberry the next?" he counters my question with his own.

"'Cause I use two different body washes," I answer as he places me on the kitchen counter.

"Why do you have two different body washes?" He hands me a mug of black coffee, just how I like it, and refills his own.

"I like to keep it fresh. Spice things up." He lets out a low chuckle at my answer but doesn't comment any further.

"So why do you smell like pine?" I ask again, wanting to know why he really smells like he took a bath in lacquer.

"I re-varnished the porch swing." He steps up to the stove and begins to fill up a plate with eggs and bacon.

"You did?" I slide off the counter and walk out to the front porch. I throw open the door and walk out to the swing. The faded peeled wood has been sanded back and now shines with new varnish.

"Came out good." I turn back to see Beau standing at the door watching me.

"Yeah, it looks great. When will it be ready?"

"Tomorrow it should be good to go. I know how much you like sitting out here and reading."

"You did this for me?" I spin back, trying to gauge his reaction.

"No, been meaning to do it for a while. Had the time today." He turns and walks back inside like it's no big deal.

He so fixed it up for me.

I follow him inside and take my seat back on the counter. I don't push the swing, not wanting to make a big deal, but I can't help smile about it. It's a small gesture, but to me, it's huge.

"What time did you come in?" I watch him carefully as he hands me my plate. I don't bother moving to the table. My appetite's coming back, so I dig in right away.

"You don't remember?" He takes my plate out of my hands and brings it to the table. I only pout for a second before following the food.

He's bossy even without words.

"No. I remember the girls leaving, Holly was last to go then I started to clean up. The rest is blank."

"I got in around midnight. You were passed out on the sofa."

"I was?" I look up, trying to remember. Shit, yes. I sat down when the room started to spin. I must have fallen asleep.

"You snore when you're drunk," he teases between mouthfuls of food.

"I do not." I hide my face behind my coffee cup.

"You do. You even drooled a little." He wipes his mouth, showing me how much I dribbled. My eyes must convey my horror because he starts laughing.

"You're lying." I don't believe him. No way.

"I'm not lying, darlin'. You were snoring, drooling, and even mumbling in your sleep." My head hits the table, as his laughter grows louder.

"Stop, just stop." I look up and watch him enjoying himself way too much.

"Okay, so you don't want to know what you proposed when I managed to put you to bed?"

I don't answer, his laughter telling me it's just as bad, if not worse. Instead of stressing about what I might and might not have said, I finish my breakfast, top up my coffee then take my ass to my favorite chair and decide to wallow for the rest of the day.

I'm never drinking again.

16

Beau

"So, how's Mackenzie settling in?" Holly asks a couple of weeks later at a Friday night club BBQ. Nix had called a club meet earlier to discuss some shit with the Warriors and follow up on how Chad is still completely off the grid. Not one sighting. How the fuck it's even possible I have no idea and I don't want to get my hopes up, but it's starting to look like he's not going to make a move.

"She's okay," I answer and take another sip of my beer. I should probably be heading out, but tonight I'm finding it hard to go home. The last few weeks of having Kenzie in my home haven't been easy. Especially after the night I told her just what I wanted to do with her.

The first few days after that evening were quiet, both of us treading carefully, but just like everything else, time has healed things and now it's like we're back to normal.

An ordinary Hell that leaves me not wanting to go home most nights.

It's not that I don't want her there. Fuck, far from it. She cooks dinner every night, keeps the place tidy, and last week even started on bringing back the garden I've managed to kill off.

The problem is more than all those issues. It's knowing she sleeps next door to me every night, a thin wall the only thing separating us. It's the showers every morning that force me to jack off to stop me from kicking the door down to join her. It's the fucking nightie she continues to walk around in every night. The same one I told her not to fucking wear. It's every single day knowing this woman, who wants me just as much as I want her, is so damn perfect, I know I can't ruin her.

She's driving me crazy, but it doesn't stop me from going out of my way to find ways to talk to her, sit with her and even watch the stupid shows she likes to watch. I even went as far as fixing up the damn porch swing for her.

I'm twisted up over pussy and I'm not even fucking her.

"I'm surprised she's not here," Kelly continues to question me, only making my pissed-off mood darker.

"She worked earlier and decided to go home," I answer, still not sure why I'm annoyed she didn't want to hang back with us. I thought she would eventually get used to the club, the parties, and women, but it doesn't seem she wants to. Not yet anyway.

"How about you? Are you doing okay?" Holly asks.

"I'm fine, Holly." I let out a frustrated breath. It's not like I want to be an asshole to her. I just don't want to fucking talk about Mackenzie when I'm wound so tight.

Maybe I need my dick wet? Fuck her out of my head.

"Hey, Beau." Lissy, Bell's friend, interrupts my thoughts and takes a seat next to me.

"Hey." I keep my eyes on my beer, the irony she just sat down not lost on me.

"Wanna get out of here?" She leans in closer so no one can hear. That's Lissy, straight to the point.

Like me.

I think it over for a bit. Maybe it would help? I haven't fucked anyone since Mackenzie came back into my life, maybe it will help break this connection we can't seem to shake. It would be easy. Lissy and I spent a night together in Vegas a few months back. She knows what I like and clearly knows my tastes.

I look up and catch Holly watching. She looks away before I can tell her to fuck off.

"Nope, not tonight," I reply to Lissy, my eyes on Holly. Lissy doesn't say anything, not bothered by my rejection and again, I kick myself for knocking her back.

Fucking hell, what the fuck is wrong with me?

"I'm out for the night. See ya'll tomorrow." I stand and give a few head nods around the table before making my way around the clubhouse to my bike. I need out of here before I lose my cool.

"Beau, wait up," Lissy calls out as I make it around the front and mount my ride.

"Lissy, don't. You knew the fucking score back in Vegas. It was one time, not gonna happen again." My tone isn't nice, but she doesn't seem fazed.

"I know, of course. I just wanted to say sorry. I wasn't thinking. It's why I followed you around here." I look at her for a minute. She was a good fuck, into everything I put her through, but staring at her now, my head and my dick know she's not what I want. Not what I fucking crave.

"No problem," I finally say and start my bike up. The rumble of the pipes cut off anything else she could possibly want to say.

With one final head nod, I back out and take off, hoping a ride clears some of my head and I decide right then to take the long route home.

Maybe it's not such a good idea to have Mackenzie in my space anymore if it's messing with me so much.

But it's not like I could ask her to leave.

I could send her back to the clubhouse?

No, there's no way she would go for it, especially after demanding she move in with me. No fucking way.

After riding for over an hour, and no closer to coming to a decision, I pull up out front of my house, kick the stand down and climb off. The front porch light is switched off, but the kitchen light still glows, so I know she's still awake.

"You're home?" Mackenzie looks up from the porch swing when I climb the stairs.

"Jesus, darlin', didn't see you there." I take stock of where she's sitting and try to curb my displeasure that she's out here in the dark.

"Sorry, was just enjoying the cooler air." She pushes a blanket off her legs and stands.

"What the hell you doing out here in the dark?" I scold when I see her in her fucking nightgown.

175

Fuck me, she's trying to kill me again.

The fabric molds to her body and exposes her erect nipples for the world to see.

Fuck, think of puppies, and babies. Puppies and babies.

"I'm fine, Beau. Relax." She bends and picks up a mug, and then walks to the front door. I don't fight her anymore on the subject because truthfully, I don't have the energy. The woman fights me on everything and tonight I just don't have it in me.

"You had dinner?" I ask, watching her walk into the kitchen. Her hips sway as she walks, drawing me in like some sort of siren.

I stay back kicking my boots off at the front and dropping my helmet on the table next to the door.

"Yeah, there's leftovers in the fridge." She looks up from washing out her mug when I make it to the kitchen.

"Thanks." I head for the fridge, suddenly pretty fucking hungry.

"How was your night?" She pulls herself up on the counter, watching me dig into some chicken pie dish.

"All right. You should have stayed. The girls wanted to talk some girly shit with you," I tell her with a mouth full of food.

"Umm, the parties get pretty full on." She picks at a thread on her nightgown and looks up.

"Does it still make you uncomfortable?" I place my plate on the counter and pull a bottle of beer out of the fridge.

"No, it doesn't bother me at all. Just didn't want to see some things."

"What things?" I push, not sure what she's getting at.

"Well, you know, what you do is your thing and I respect that. I just didn't want to risk seeing something I'm not sure I'd be able to handle."

"You think I'm gonna be all over some club whore in front of you?"

"Why not? You don't owe me anything. Like you said, we're friends, and I know you and Lissy were—" She stops for a beat and arranges her face. "Anyway, it's not my business." She slides off the counter.

What the fuck? How the fuck does she know about Lissy?

"I'm gonna head to bed. I'm tired." She brushes past me and before I realize what I'm doing my hand reaches out and grabs her. Her body locks, tensing under my touch. I wait a beat, pausing for her to realize I'm not a threat. It's only a few short seconds before she relaxes.

"You don't have to worry about that, darlin'."

"Oh, I'm not. I know you have needs. We both do." She steps back out of my reach and I can't help but want to pull her back.

"What's that supposed to mean?" The question comes out as a growl because she's pissing me off. Fucking needs. What fucking needs is she talking about?

"You really want me to answer, Beau?"

"Yeah, I really do."

"Okay, well, I haven't seen you with anyone since I've been here. You don't have to hide it from me, Beau. I mean we have to be okay when one of us brings someone else home."

I think my chest tightens and my arm grows numb. The thought of a man in my house, in her bed, could warrant a heart attack, right?

"Darlin', you won't be bringing a man into my home." I shut that shit down right now. I wouldn't be able to control myself if some fucker was in my house touching what's mine.

"Well, I'm not talking about tomorrow, Beau," she argues, making it worse.

"You won't be ever."

"Beau—" She starts to explain, but my mind blanks, white noise blocks her out. Need, fear, and anger simmer through me and before I think it through, I step into her space, dip my head and smash my mouth to hers. She fights it to begin with, her hands pushing at my chest. Until I reach around and pull her closer. A soft sigh dances from her lips and my tongue sweeps, seeking an opportunity.

I know we've been here before and I told her I wouldn't go there with her again, but in this moment, none of that matters. What started as simmering desire transforms into intense infatuation. To have her, taste her, make her mine, it's too much to resist.

I'm fucking done fighting it.

17

Mackenzie

THE KISS TAKES ME BY SURPRISE. MY FIRST RESPONSE IS to fight it, push back and end it. Until his hand moves to the small of my back and pulls me in closer while his tongue whispers along my lips coaxing my mouth open. Desperation replaces my shock, and I meet his hunger with my own.

I know this is what we both agreed shouldn't happen, but I can't stop. I can't step away from him. Ever since the night I kissed him, I've been dreaming of this. I've been dreaming of a hell of a lot more than this.

Deepening the kiss, I rise to my toes and reach up to run my fingers through his hair. He has it pulled back in one of those knots on top of his head today, so I rip it out and help it fall free.

He pulls back slightly and for a second, I think he's putting a stop to this until he places his hand on my waist, picks me up, turns and plants me on the kitchen counter. His mouth finds mine again while my hands make quick work of disposing of his cut. Moving away from my mouth, his lips slide down my neck to my collarbone. His breath is warm, his beard a mixture of rough yet soft.

"Beau." His name creeps past my lips. The hunger burning in my body brings the fire out in me.

His kisses stop, while he pushes the straps of my nightgown down my arms, exposing both my breasts to the cold air.

"Jesus, you're more amazing than I could have imagined." He lowers his mouth and takes a nipple between his lips and rolls it.

"Holy shit." My hands find his hair again, pulling hard as his teeth graze my tight bud.

"Fuck, your tits are perfect, darlin'." His gravelly voice shoots a jolt between my legs and a thrill down my spine. I don't think I've ever had a man make me need this much.

"Don't stop, please don't ever stop," I beg, dragging his head back to my breast. His mouth descends again, showing my nipple the same attention as before.

Rolling, nipping and tugging, the dampness between my thighs grows, arousal pulsing through me.

Pulling him off my nipple, I drag him back up to my mouth. He doesn't waste a minute. His tongue darting past my lips and curling against mine.

My hands work his belt, breaking it free before flipping the button of his jeans and moving my hand down his front. My fingers find the base of his thickness instantly.

Jesus, he's so fucking hard for me.

Hard and thick.

Before I manage a full grip around him, he freezes.

"Wait." He steps back, breaking our connection. "Darlin', we need to cool it down." A pained look falls over his face and it's like having a bucket of ice water thrown over me, dousing all need and want. I push my arms back through my straps to cover myself up.

"Are you kidding me?" I slide off the counter and rush past him. Rejection flows through me, the burning flame of need he just lit now doused by my insecurities.

Am I not enough?

I need the earth to open up and swallow me whole. *How could I be so stupid?* A seed of embarrassment starts to grow inside of me, and I know if I don't get away from him, I will be flowering a new shade of red on my face.

"Kenz, wait!" he calls out, but I can't bear for him to see me like this.

"No don't, Beau. Just leave it," I manage to say before escaping the kitchen.

"I'm no good for you, Mackenzie. This—"

"Is a mistake. I got it." I stop, turning back to finish his sentence and holding the disappointment from my voice. The last thing I need to become is some desperate woman in an off and on sort of relationship.

"No, darlin', I'm just looking out for you. You don't need this kind of fucked up."

I shake my head, done with his excuses. I've lived fucked up. I was married to it. Beau is not fucked up. I know it with everything in me. The totality of his commitment to me proves he is nothing like Chad.

He's the one who gave me hope when Chad took it away. He's the one responsible for giving me a life I never thought I could be worthy of. Because of him, it's as if everything has been wiped clean.

"Do you *want* to be with me, Beau?" His eyes close at my question as if it pains him to answer.

"So much it hurts, darlin'."

"Then be with me, Beau. Be with me how you want to be with me." I offer what I think he needs from me. Not because I want it, because the truth is I don't know if I will, but because he does and I want him any way I can have him.

"Kenz, it doesn't work like that."

"Why not, Beau? I need this as much as you do."

"Because I don't want you to give it to me, darlin'. I want to take it. And as much as you think you're ready, you're not."

"How do you know I'm not ready? I'm willing to try." I am. I'm willing to do anything for him. And maybe it's stupid, maybe it's dangerous, but I trust him. Trust him more than I trust anyone in my life.

Beau would never hurt me.

"I know, darlin', believe me I know, but I'm not prepared to push it." The room falls quiet as we both process what is happening here. *We both want the same thing, but in different ways.*

"Then I can't live here with you like this. I thought I could move past this, but I can't. It's too much. It hurts too much." He looks up at my confession.

"You're right. It's not fair. I'll stay at the clubhouse," he offers, and it almost pains me as much as his rejection.

"No. I don't want to be here. I'll move out, find my own

place. You've done enough for me since I came to you."

"Don't make any decisions tonight. We'll talk in the morning." He shakes his head, not setting anything in stone.

"Yep." I sigh, turning to continue walking to my room.

Tomorrow we *will* talk. I will make it clear I'm not staying here. I need to be away from Beau. Away from everything that reminds me of him.

If it means leaving Rushford, then so be it.

18

Beau

"WE'LL TALK IN THE MORNING," I TELL HER, KNOWING she won't see any reason tonight. How can she after what I just did.

"Yep." She turns and walks out. I want to call out to her, tell her to come back, but I don't. I let her go.

Like you should have before you fucking touched her, asshole.

Grabbing another beer from the fridge and my cut off the floor, I decide to skip the rest of my dinner and call it a night. I know I just fucked up everything we've been trying to hold together, and to be honest, I wasn't sure how we were going to come back from it. I had her, willing and ready, yet I froze.

Switching off the kitchen light, I make my way down to my room. Mackenzie's door is to the left of mine and I force myself to pass it without a glance.

I open my bedroom door, walk inside and throw my cut across my bed.

Why did I pull away?

It's not like I don't want her. Fuck, I don't think I've ever wanted someone so much. It's more about what I want to do to her. What I want to make her do to me.

I've tried to push her out of my head, tried to keep my mind off the small detail of wanting to bury myself balls deep inside of her, but everywhere I turn in this house, she's there.

Her smile. Her laugh. Even the way she fucking smells.

"Fuck me dead." I let out a puff of air and fall to the bed.

I know thinking of her this way is only going to make it harder for me. She's everything I don't need. I need control, something we both know she struggles with. Maybe with time she might be able to, but what if she never gets there. Would it be enough for me? Would my natural desire to control just fade away?

No. I doubt it.

Sitting back up, I finish off my beer deciding I need to get out of here. I change my shirt, put my cut back on, and make my way back out to the hall. I don't want to, but I decide I should let Kenzie know I'm leaving. Walking to her door, I stop right outside of it.

"Kenzie, I'm heading out. Will you be all right on your own?" I call out to her but receive no reply. Her door is ajar a few inches, so I knock, letting the force push it open further.

She is standing there. Her pert tits take my attention first and instantly my cock stirs back to life. She doesn't stop to cover herself and I don't look away.

"I'm heading out." I manage some cough mumble thing, my throat becoming dry. She doesn't say anything and her eyes don't leave me. I should turn away, let her change in private, but I'm lost in the sight of her.

The soft glow of her bedside lamp highlights her against the dark room but even from this distance, I can see every one of those goose bumps glazing her skin.

We continue to stand silent for what feels like hours, until the soft whisper of her nightgown falling to the floor shocks me back, like the first momentary sonic boom that fills the skies on a Fourth of July weekend. My eyes follow its descent, pausing at the lace covering her pussy.

Jesus, fuck, turn around, man.

I swallow past my hunger and try to will myself to leave, but fail when her fingers hook into the side of her lace panties.

"Mackenzie, don't." My warning comes out strangled, my resolve slipping, but it doesn't stop her. She continues to undress, sliding her panties down her legs then stepping out of them, leaving her completely exposed to me.

She's beautiful. Fucking perfect. Every fucking inch of her. But there's an innocence to her. One touch, one taste is going to destroy me.

What the fuck is wrong with you, man? Go to her. Fucking take her.

"Darlin'," I say with a heavy breath, forcing my eyes away from her naked body and back up to her face. Her pink, plump lips, swollen from our kisses, slightly part as she draws in a long breath.

"You're making this really fucking hard to stay away." My voice cracks as my gaze catches her hand sliding between her legs.

"If you're not going to help me, then leave." Her voice is barely a whisper as her finger slips between her pussy lips disappearing from view. And fuck it turns me on.

Before I realize what I'm doing, my legs carry me to her. Not giving it a second thought, I slap her hand away from her pussy and pull her naked body to me. She comes willingly, a small cry filling the room at my touch.

"Fuck," I groan, knowing I'm close to losing control. "I need you to think this through, darlin'. Be real fucking sure, 'cause once we start, I don't think I'll be able to stop," I tell her when her chest hits mine.

"I've never wanted anything more, Beau." My name coming from her lips in a plea cancels out all my reservations, and before I can comprehend what's happening, I have her on her back on the bed.

Pulling off my cut and shirt in record time, I flip the button of my jeans. Mackenzie comes up on her elbows and watches as I lose my jeans.

"Holy shit, you have it pierced." She looks down at my cock, intrigue turning to wonder.

"I have two." I point to the Apadravya piercing. The small barbell runs through the head of my penis. I then pull to show her the Frenum piercing on the underside of my cock.

"Did they hurt?" She bites her lip, her eyes not leaving the piercing.

"I survived. Had it done years ago." She nods but doesn't say anything.

"You keep looking at me like that and I don't think I'll last long," I admit. Her inquisitive eyes move from my piercing up to my face and I realize it wouldn't matter what way she looked at me. I'm wound up so fucking tight from not having my cock in a woman for God knows how long, I'm not going to last long regardless.

"Like what?" She looks back down at my cock and it bounces its own hello.

"Like you want to wrap your mouth around my dick and milk it dry," I offer the visual, the picture playing out in my mind.

Yep, there is no way I'm going back on this, now.

"No one has ever spoken to me like this before." Her teeth graze her bottom lip, and I don't know if she's afraid of me, or fucking turned on.

"You want me to stop talking to you this way?" I ask, placing a knee down on the bed and moving over her.

"I don't think so." She lays back, her dark hair spilling around her.

"You don't think so? It's a yes or no question, darlin'." I keep my eyes on her, like I need to memorize every inch of her body.

"No," she answers instantly.

"Then I won't." I lean down and circle her nipple with my tongue. Her hands glide back into my hair, pulling as I bite down.

She's a responsive little thing. Just how I like it.

I switch to the second nipple, showing it the same amount of attention. Her tits aren't huge, but they fit comfortably in my hand. Her rose-tipped nipples are on the larger size, and I have to control the urge to want to place nipple clamps on them.

Too soon, man.

Pushing the image out of my head, I focus on the soft little moans I pull from her as I continue to tease her swollen nipples with my teeth and tongue over and over.

"Yes," she hisses between her teeth as her fingers tighten around my hair.

"You like that?"

She moans her reply and I pull back to admire my work. The creamy flesh is now covered in my marks. Nothing too crazy, but they're there, and her nipples are more swollen than before. I press my lips against each nipple before kissing my way back up her neck.

"This is how we're gonna play this, Mackenzie." I kiss the corner of her mouth. "Tonight, I'll do whatever it is you want. You're running the show here." I give her the one thing I don't usually give. Control.

"But you said—" She looks up confused at what I'm offering and I quickly interrupt her.

"I know. And I will. Fuck me, I will have you tied and submitting to me, darlin'. But not yet. We do it this way, or no way." I know what I told her and know what I like. But now that I have her under me naked and willing, I can't stand the thought of pushing her away because she can't handle it.

"Okay." She nods before releasing a long breath. There's no way she's ready for what I want to give her.

"What do you like, baby?" I whisper my question against the shell of her ear and watch as goose bumps come back to surface over her skin.

"I like to be touched." Her voice is husky, her tone desperate.

"Where do you want me to touch you? Show me." I pull back and watch her hand slide down between her legs. "You want me to touch that pretty cunt of yours, darlin'?" Her fingers slip through her folds and her eyes roll back at my words.

"Yes." Her back arches with each flick of her clit and I take a moment to enjoy the show. Mackenzie has always been beautiful to me, but this right here, her touching herself is fucking breathtaking.

"You want my fingers or my mouth." I lick my lips. The very thought of tasting her, having her juices on my tongue drives me wild.

"Mouth." Her hips start to roll in time with her finger and I quickly guide myself back to the edge of the bed. Her legs open wide, and I can't help the smirk that spreads across my lips at just how eager she is.

"Fuck, baby. All this for me?" I dip my head low and breathe in her sweet scent. She's wet, weeping with need, and my cock aches knowing I made her like this.

She doesn't answer, her finger still working fast. So I take her small wrist in my hand and pin it to the bed.

"No." A cry of displeasure tears from her lips, but I don't let it deter me. She's done touching. It's my turn.

"I don't want you coming too soon, darlin'." I smirk at her pout. "Don't worry, I'm gonna make you scream with my tongue." I lower my face to her pink lips and slowly and painstakingly, glide my tongue from her opening to her swollen clit.

She lights up at the contact, her hips rising from the bed. Wanting to drive her wild, my hand finds her belly and I gently push her back down.

"Still," I order, repeating the same action over. Her taste is sweet, with a hint of spice and fuck, if I could be drunk off it, I never ever want to be sober. Moving my tongue faster, I focus on her clit.

"Yes, there. Don't move from there!" she calls out, pressing her hips into my face trying to lift for more friction.

"Darlin', I know how to eat pussy. How about you just relax and let me." I smile against her when she looks down her body at me.

"Seems to me you just like teasing," she sasses, my dick bouncing in fucking delight.

"That's the point, babe. Gonna light you up like a Christmas tree till you're crying for release." I ignore her panting and plunge a finger inside her. Her walls grip me tight, and I fight the urge to forget about her needs and sink my cock into her snug heat.

Soon. I remind myself.

Replacing one finger for two, I slowly hook them, searching for the right spot.

"Holy fuck, yes!" Her voice cracks in arousal, pushing me further along. I ignore the way my cock jumps at the husky sound and pick up my pace.

"Beau, Jesus. Don't ever stop." My name comes out as a growl, pulling my own groan from deep in my gut. She's close. I know it. My cock feels it. Knowing I need it, I hook my fingers one more time, push down harder, and work her clit over and over. She thrusts her hips one more time, then cries out just as a small rush of her orgasm sprays against my tongue.

Holy fucking shit, she's a squirter.

I don't think my cock has ever wept with joy before this moment.

Her screams fill the room, and deep-seeded accomplishment

flows through me. I can't wait to fucking explore this.

Pushing the little nugget of knowledge away for another day, I keep my fingers hooked and fuck her clit with my tongue, lapping up her juices. She writhes under me, her screams making her voice raw.

"No more," she pants, begging me to stop. With one last hook of my fingers, I give in to her request. Slowing my tongue, I carefully remove my fingers. Her juices glisten on them. I pull back and look down at her. She watches me closely, her cheeks flushed pink, a slight sheen of sweat covering her skin.

"Jesus Christ, Mackenzie, this is fucking something I wasn't expecting." I keep my eyes on hers as I lick my fingers clean.

"Beau, don't." She covers her face with one hand and I chuckle.

"I'm sorry, did you want a taste?" I tease, knowing by her reaction she's probably never tasted herself before.

"NO!" She drops her hand. She looks almost embarrassed, but I don't care. She'll soon learn there is nothing to be embarrassed about with me in bed.

"Okay, next time you can lick them clean." Her eyes bug out of her head, and I can't help but laugh at her reaction.

Fuck me, so fucking sexy yet innocent.

"I've never, um, done it," she admits, looking everywhere but me.

"You haven't tasted yourself after a man's gone down on you?" She shakes her head as I hover over her body then lower my mouth to hers.

She opens instantly, her tongue darting out to taste herself.

A soft moan gets trapped between us. I'm not sure who's more turned on, me or her.

"You like?" I ask, moving my lips over her jaw and down her neck.

"On you, yeah." She gasps as I sink my teeth into the soft flesh above her collarbone. She smells like strawberry today.

"You want more?" I ask, still wanting her to direct what happens next. Her head nods, but it's not enough.

"Need words, Kenz. Always words."

"I want you. Give me more."

"What do you want, darlin'?" I lick around her nipple, before moving to the next one.

"You. I want you in me."

"You want my cock?" I push, wanting her to say it. Needing her to say it.

"Yes, Beau. I want your cock." She starts panting, the harder I roll my teeth over her tight nipple. "I want you to fuck me." I pull back and line my throbbing cock at her entrance.

"Condom." She exhales and I still. Fuck, how the hell could I forget?

"You on the pill, darlin'?" I ask, not wanting to put a hold on anything. My cock is practically weeping in delight. He's not ready to give this up for a glove.

"Yes, and I'm clean," she says, pulling me out of my pity party.

"I've never had sex without one," I admit, not sure why I'd be willing to let her be the first.

"We don't have to." The need in her voice matches mine, so instead of thinking about it anymore, I thrust deep into her.

"Fuck!" We both cry out. Not in a painful kind of way but with relief.

"So fucking good." I take a minute to let her adjust to my

size as I get used to not wearing a condom. Her walls hug me tight and the sensation of flesh on flesh almost pushes me to lose my load.

"I need you to move, Beau," she begs, ready before I am. I don't comply with her needs; instead, I let myself sink deeper.

After a few moments of controlling the urge, I start to rock my hips. Slow to start with, building my rhythm, each deliberate stroke pulling her closer to the edge with me.

"Faster," she moans, tipping her hips up to meet each thrust.

"Put your hands above your head, darlin'. Wanna see those perfect tits," I order. My balls tense getting ready to explode. She follows my orders, and if my cock could be any harder, it would.

"Good girl, keep your hands there, you hear me?" She nods, her eyes rolling back.

"Words, Kenz. I need words."

"Yes, Beau. I won't touch. Even though I want more than anything to touch you, I'm going to keep my hands on the boring bed." My grin grows wider at her unconventional way of submission.

Fuck, what I could do to her and her sassy mouth.

I pick up my speed, my resolve all but gone and start to unleash faster, rougher strokes into her. Her fingers fist the blanket.

"I'm there, oh, yes, yes, yes!" she cries out, her hands move to her head, pulling her hair as her walls spasm around my cock, gripping me as she rides out her release. It's enough to set me off. My balls squeeze tight before exploding into her. Waves of pulsating pleasure roll through me as I empty the longest release of my life inside of her.

"Fuck, darlin'." My pulse quickens as I thrust my hips over and over. The sounds of my balls slapping against her fade out as our ragged breaths fill the room.

"It's never..." She sucks in a sharp breath. "The piercing..." Her head falls to the side as she gives up. I keep sliding slowly in and out of her. My cum mixed with her arousal spills out between us with each motion, but neither one of us moves to stop it.

Jesus when was the last time I came that hard?

Never.

"Darlin', I don't even know where to start." Pulling a deep breath through my nose, I will my racing heart to calm as I finally pull out of her.

"Is it always like that?" She starts to laugh, her body shaking underneath me.

"I'll let you know after the second round." I look down at her. A deep, red blush covers her chest and a small sated smile paints her lips.

I really fucking hope so.

19

Mackenzie

I WAKE WITH A STARTLE THE FOLLOWING MORNING. Naked and exhausted, my mind's full of images from the night before.

"Oh, God. Yep it happened," I tell the empty room. I roll to sit up, and my body protests in a good way.

Turning my head, I check the time on my alarm clock. Ten-o-five. Though I'm not surprised, I still curse myself. I hate sleeping in this late.

The price you pay when you stay up till sunrise, letting a man fuck you silly, Mackenzie.

My mind flicks back to the moment Beau walked into my room last night and saw me getting undressed.

I was angry, hurt, but most of all I was done. Maybe it was

the way he was looking at me that gave me the confidence to stand there and expose myself to him, or maybe it was my need driving me.

Need to be wanted. To be devoured. By him.

I'm not sure what made me do it, but I knew standing there would be our last chance. He reacted, thank God, but what shocked me the most was how he handed all control over to me. He said it wasn't something he wanted to throw me into, but I still picked up the subtle commands, the way he reacted when I sassed him back, and how he decided when I came. They were only indirect, but I still caught them and obeyed immediately.

It was unlike anything I've ever experienced before. If anyone had asked me prior to last night if I've had hot and heavy sex before, I'd have said yes, plenty of times. But now? Now I can honestly say after last night, I've only experienced that level of arousal with one man. Beau.

He was different. He took the time to take me there. To make me come apart before even thinking about trying to get himself there. Yeah, the men I've been with always made sure I came, but not like Beau. Not where I was begging to stop.

After the first round, we took a shower, both of us exploring each other. By the time we were dry, we were ready for round two. Beau took control the second time, and surprisingly, I wanted more. I never thought I would see myself handing over so much. I know Beau hasn't even begun to show me what he likes, and while it scares me a little, it's not enough to push me away. I want to try to please him. I want to show him I would and could do anything he asked.

Even if my comfort level is tested.

The smell of coffee brings me back to the present. Pushing all of last night's activities away for now, I roll out of bed and throw on his shirt. I forgo panties and go in search of him.

I find him in the kitchen, resting against the counter. Feet crossed in front of him, coffee mug in hand. His only clothing is boxer shorts, and I can't help but stare.

His body is a contradiction of hard and smooth: broad, high shoulders, firm chest with pecs that bulge beneath the skin.

Smooth line after line separate ripples of ab muscle. His waist is narrow, hips lean and his ass. Ugggh, his ass is tight.

Seriously, the man is dangerously sexy.

"Morning." I stop my ogling and step over the threshold, a little unsure how to act. Do I go to him? Pretend like nothing happened?

There's no doubt last night was incredible. We both gave into temptation, and spoke about taking things slow, but would he regret it today? Would he pull away from me like he did last night in the kitchen?

He looks up at my voice. "Morning, darlin'." I hang back, still feeling self-conscious and maybe even clueless. "You gonna stand there making this awkward, or you gonna come give me a kiss?" he asks, driving my nerves away.

"I thought I would just watch you there in your underwear all morning," I sass back, before moving toward him.

He places his mug on the counter next to him and opens his arms for me to step in close.

"Is this a new dress code I'm not aware of?" he asks just as I press my mouth to his. His beard brushes against my lips, sending a zing straight to my clit, reminding me how it felt to have him between my legs.

"Hmm," I murmur as his tongue traces the seam of my lips, coaxing them open and reclaiming my mouth. He tastes like coffee and Beau. The perfect mix I need this morning. The kiss takes on new life, as our tongues tangle, reuniting like long lost loves. Beau's hands come to either side of my face, cupping me closer to him.

"Geez, woman, I've been missing out on this every morning?" He pulls his lips away and leans his forehead to mine.

"What can I say, it's the beard." He throws his head back in a deep laugh before planting a kiss on my forehead.

"I need coffee," I tell him, almost desperate. He releases his hold on me and lets me step back. I don't waste any time and take myself to the glorious coffee pot.

"Gotta say, I'm liking our new dress code, darlin'."

I look over my shoulder at the playful tone in his voice and catch him checking out my legs. I turn back, roll my eyes and reach up into the cabinet for a mug. His shirt rises with me and I feel a little naughty knowing I just teased him.

Seriously, who knew yesterday morning we would be here, less than twenty-four hours later, acting like we hadn't spent the last two months pretending we weren't into each other.

"Please tell me you're wearing panties." Beau's pained growl rolls through me as a new wave of need takes over. Everything becomes an unimportant blur as my body awakens.

"Ummm." I laugh awkwardly, filling my mug with the black liquid. I don't have a chance to taste my coffee before Beau's front is pushed up against my back. His hard cock nudging me between my ass cheeks.

Holy hell.

"Woman, are you trying to kill me?" His hot breath skirts

over my ear while his hand glides up under the shirt.

I sag against him as his finger finds my pulsing clit.

"You sore?" The soft rumble of his voice warms me as his finger glides down then drags my wetness up to my clit.

"No." I whimper when he flicks my bud once. Okay, maybe a little sore, but I don't tell him. I want him any way I can.

"Good. Spread your legs, darlin'," he orders, and like a good girl, I do as he asks.

He sighs his approval, leaning closer to my ear. "This for me?" I become lost in my arousal as the words vibrate over my ear. "Answer me," he urges, dipping his finger lower again, moving more wetness to my clit.

Oh, God, bossy Beau is here and I'm going to combust.

"Yeah." I nod, my hands finding the counter to hold on.

"New rule, no panties at breakfast," he commands, before sinking his teeth into the side of my neck.

"Good rule," I pant, thrusting my hips upward seeking more friction. He lets me have my play, stepping closer to give me support.

"Now, seeing as you came to breakfast with easy access, do you want me to make you come with my mouth or my cock?"

"Mouth," I answer too quickly, a little too desperately.

Way to play it cool.

"I'll give you my mouth, darlin' as soon as you give me yours." He steps back from me, taking his finger with him.

I turn to face him ready to bargain, but my eyes fall to his cock, standing tall and proud in his boxers.

"You want me to suck you off?" I ask as a new wave of hunger takes over. We didn't do this last night. In fact, he barely let me touch him.

"I want your mouth on my cock. Yes. Not sure if I'm gonna let you suck it, or if I'm gonna fuck your mouth." I inhale a startled breath, the thought of him fucking my mouth leaving me wheezing.

"You want me to fuck your face, Kenz?" he asks, seeing my reaction.

I nod, but remember his rule of words. "I think so," I answer before he can remind me. "Yes, I mean yes." He smiles a crooked smile before giving me a wink.

Holy shit, can this man ever not be sexy?

"You remembered. Good girl. Now on your knees, darlin'." I want to argue. I don't know why. I want to be on my knees, but the defiance in me decides to question him.

"Here?" I ask, looking down at the kitchen floor.

"Here," is all he says, pushing away any discussion otherwise. I nod and then step forward. My arousal between my legs grows, and for the first time this morning, I regret not putting on panties. The slick wetness slides between my thighs as I step forward and go down on my knees.

Without taking any more instructions, my hands reach for his boxers. Slowly and carefully I pull them down. His cock bounces free and before I can touch him, feel him, his hand fists it.

I look up at him, his gaze burns through me as he strokes himself, each one a sharp, rough caress.

"Is this for me?" I smirk up at him, using the same words he used on me.

"And then some," he answers, releasing his cock. "Put it in your mouth," he orders, pushing down on it to line the bulging tip with my lips. The small bar piercing through his head glistens with pre-cum. I want to reach out and lick it, play with it, but I know he's testing me. Challenging me to push him. Not wanting to disappoint, I lean forward and open my mouth.

My eyes stay on his as he slowly guides himself inside.

"Fucking hell!" He hisses as I mold my lips around his width. A shudder runs through me as I accommodate his size. My arousal grows, sliding between my thighs.

Squeezing my legs together, I focus all my attention on what's happening in my mouth. The cool bars from both of his piercings glide on my tongue and I take a moment to let my mouth memorize it.

"You control this, Mackenzie." Beau coaches me, moving his hands to either side of my face. He continues to glide back and forth between my lips. I can't take him all without needing to gag so he stops short, knowing just how far to push.

"You want to stop this, you stop. Simple," he reminds me, giving me an out.

"Hmmm," I acknowledge his words with a slight nod.

"Good girl. Now, I want you to relax your throat. I'm not going to hurt you, but by the time I'm done, you're gonna take me whole." He smiles down at me before picking up his pace. I keep my breathing steady through my nose, careful not to lose it. I haven't given head like this before. Not with someone else in control, that fact alone makes it more erotic.

"Fuck, baby, your mouth is heaven." His encouragement relaxes me more, a new need taking over. A need to please him. Beau continues to control his strokes, in and out. Deep and precise. His moans grow wilder the faster he pistons his hips. The bar starts to hit the back of my throat, but it's not uncomfortable. If anything, it ignites me.

Can I come without even being touched?

Not sure it's possible, I slip my hand between my legs and find my clit. My own touch is electric, consuming as I work myself toward my own release.

"Stop touching," Beau barks above me, and instantly my fingers freeze.

"Hmm," I growl back. Frustrated doesn't begin to describe my feelings. I need this release.

"Not yet, beautiful. Want you to come over my mouth." His admission soothes me a little, but not much. I purse my lips tighter and relax my throat, with hopes to move this along so I can have the attention I too am craving.

"Fuck, Kenz, gonna come too soon you keep it up." I suck deeper, wanting it as much as he does. His hands tighten in my hair, pulling my hair in a sharp tug, and for a split second, I tense. The sensation of being trapped between his hands threatens to freak me out, but I force myself to let my fear go. *This is Beau, not Chad.*

Beau, not missing anything, reads my reaction. He releases my hair instantly and slows, but I don't want him to end this. I want him to come.

Moving my hands to the thick muscles in his thighs, I pull him back to me, showing him I'm not ending this. He gets the hint and picks up his pace. Careful not to grip my hair again, he fucks my mouth over and over. His groans grow wild, his strokes desperate, until an uninhibited cry of satisfaction fills the kitchen, and warm cum explodes at the back of my throat. My stomach dips, the sounds of his orgasm sends spasms through my pussy. Trying not to focus on the taste, I swallow everything he gives me until his moans of pleasure quieten and he slows his movements. Allowing me to make sure I take everything he offers, he stills briefly before letting his still hard cock fall from my lips. I lean forward and run my tongue over his piercing. I look up under my lashes and watch him draw a sharp breath through his teeth.

"You have no idea how breathtaking you look down there, darlin'."

I feel powerful. Sexy. Unstoppable.

"Come on, dirty girl. Your turn." He bends at the waist and helps me up to my feet. Before I can wipe my mouth, he smashes his lips to mine, finding my tongue in desperate need, and strokes me to a new kind of ecstasy. *Lust.*

I'm consumed by everything he gives me. Everything he takes from me.

Jesus, the man can kiss.

He continues to kiss me for what feels like hours, until I'm pushed back against the counter.

"Up." He drops to his knees, while I climb up and spread my legs open for him.

"Jesus, I'll have to fuck your mouth every day, darlin'. You're dripping for me." He pushes his tongue between his teeth and with a devilish grin lifts it in two quick flicks.

Oh, God, yes please.

"Hands beside you, flat on the counter," he orders, but this time I don't want to comply.

"No. I want to touch you." His eyes narrow at first, waiting for me to submit, but I don't.

"Please, Beau," I push, needing this more than he knows. I know he said it would be like this, but I need to connect with him on this.

"I'll give you this one today, but next time you learn what happens when you disobey me." He shakes his head before lightly nipping at my thigh.

My fingers move to his hair, spreading wide to pull the length between them. I want to ponder on what kind of punishment I would find myself taking, but time ceases to exist when the rough tingle of his beard lets me know his mouth is there. A moment later, his tongue spears my clit and two fingers fill me.

I block out everything else, too lost in what his fingers and his tongue are doing to me.

All thoughts of punishment gone.

"Do you have any other family alive?" I ask later that afternoon as we lay in bed naked. After Beau made me come with his mouth on the counter, twice, we sat and ate breakfast before racing back to bed where Beau made me come apart with his cock.

We've spent the rest of the day switching between the kitchen and Beau's bed. I shouldn't be able to walk, let alone talk with how many orgasms I've received in the last twenty-four hours. But I can and now we've started, I don't want to stop.

"Only the club left," he answers, his finger trailing soft circles along my neck.

"Did you grow up in Rushford?" I keep the questions coming. It's the first time I've ever felt Beau is completely relaxed to open up.

"Yeah, grew up with Nix and the club. What about you? You always lived here?"

"I grew up in Los Angeles. My mom and dad were actors."

"Yeah? Movies?"

"No." I laugh. "I should say aspiring actors. They were in a few TV commercials, but my mom and dad were free spirits. They never really had a serious job, always floating from place to place."

"How did they die?"

"When I was twelve they were in a car accident. I was at a friend's house for the night. They were driving out to a party when a drunk driver ran a stop sign. My mom died instantly. My dad died three days later."

"Sucks, darlin', losing your parents so young." He presses his lips to the side of my head, offering me comfort.

"Yeah, it was hard, I had to move to Redwick to live with my nan. I hated it at first, but every day was better than the last. My nan was great. She let me adjust, and have my moments until I finally came around. I took it hard when she died five years ago. She was the last of my family." He squeezes me closer, breathing in my scent.

"I felt the same way when my ma died." He offers his own story. "My sister, Missy, died first. It was tough on all of us, but Ma, she was a mess. Thinking back now, part of her died that day too. Then two years later when we all just got back to a good place, Dad died suddenly one morning. Aneurism. Fucking brutal. By the time she was diagnosed with cancer the following year, she was ready to go. It was bittersweet. I knew she didn't want to fight, so in the beginning, I was fighting harder for the both of us."

My heart breaks a little for him. To suffer the loss of his whole family over a period of a few years can't be anything short of agony.

"It took a while for me to forgive her, leaving me for them. But I understand it now. She lost too much."

I don't know what to say. I mean what could I say?

Nothing.

I don't offer words. I simply let him continue to stroke my hair, the silence comforting enough for both of us.

We must have drifted off shortly after, because the next thing I know, Beau's shifting me off his chest to answer his cell phone.

"Yeah?" he answers in greeting.

I roll to my side and check the clock.

Just after six.

We'd fallen asleep for four hours.

"Yep. Can do." He opens the drawer of the nightstand, grabs a pen and a pad of paper, writing on it quickly.

"Yeah, probably four hours." He continues to write. "Okay, thanks." He ends the call and then starts typing out a text.

"Everything okay?"

"Sorry, darlin'. I gotta head out." He drops his phone to the nightstand, presses his knee to the bed, and leans over to kiss me. I want to ask him why, but I know it's for someone in need.

"Okay," is all I say, before returning his kiss. He doesn't take it deep, just peppers three more along the corner of my mouth then pulls back.

"You wanna stay at the clubhouse tonight, or I can see if one of the guys can keep an eye on the house?" He moves toward his dresser and takes out a pair of boxers, stepping into them.

"Don't be ridiculous. I'll be fine here. And don't bother anyone." I know Beau has been having some of the guys come and sit out the front whenever he's away. Something I feel guilty about.

"Not gonna leave you all night. Gotta go out to Henderson, and back. Won't be home till early morning. It's either clubhouse or one of the guys will come around." The last thing I want to do is head into the clubhouse. I just want sleep.

"I'm sure I can handle one night on my own." I shake my head at his concern. Beau has the whole place set up with a security system. I'm as safe here as I am there; besides, there's no threat to me here. Surely by now he realizes it.

"I'll call Hunter." He ignores me and tugs on a pair of jeans, this pair almost black.

"No, don't. I'll be okay. I'll have a bath, find something to eat and then head back to my own room," I add, not sure what the etiquette is. We live together in the roommate capacity. Does that mean we still sleep in our own beds?

"You're not sleeping in here?" He looks over at me, still half-dressed.

"I mean it's your bed. I have my own bed next door." I shrug, not really sure what to say. Does he want me to stay in his bed when he isn't here? Do I only come in here when we have sex?

Why does sex make you stupid?

"Want you in my bed, darlin', but if you're more comfortable in your room, I'll climb in there." He sits on the end of the bed and pulls his boots on.

"You don't think it's weird me being here while you're

gone?" I press on, voicing my unease.

"Fuck no. The only thing wrong with the idea is I'll be thinking about it all night. Probably have a semi half the night. Jesse will probably give me shit."

I laugh at the image. Yeah, Jesse will so give him shit. "I'll see how it goes," I finally say, watching him stand and put on his cut.

"Okay, but so you know, coming home to you in my bed would be a fucking dream." He leans down and kisses me one last time. "Be thinking of ya, darlin'." He stands to full height, and without a backward glance, he leaves me naked in his bed.

It's not until later when I see Hunter's truck parked across the road I realize he didn't listen.

It makes me fall a little more for him.

Past

Mackenzie

"I DON'T KNOW WHAT YOU'RE FUCKING THINKING HERE."
A voice pulls me out of my groggy sleep and back to reality.

The past twenty-four hours come flooding back and then I realize I'm in a hospital.

"Don't start your shit right now, Sy," Beau's voice answers and I keep still, wondering what they're talking about.

"She's fucking dangerous. Look who she's connected to. This is bad shit, Beau."

Me. They're talking about me.

"What the fuck is your problem, Sy? You think I'm gonna walk away from her? I'm following this through. If you want to leave, fine. Fuck off. But we're all this woman has right now. I'm gonna take her out of town away from that abusive-ass husband, with or without your help." I hold my breath, then slowly let it out as I realize this man is truly going to save me.

"I'm not saying to leave her here. I'm saying call Tiny in. Have someone else do this. I'm worried about you. I haven't seen you like this before."

The room falls silent, the insistent beeping of the machine grows louder the longer no one talks.

Like what?

After what feels like ten minutes I decide to give up my façade and release a soft whisper, like I'm just stirring from sleep.

"Mackenzie?" My name is called and I slowly open my eyes. Beau is sitting in the chair next to the hospital bed, Sy standing by the door.

"How did it go?" I take stock of my body, but can barely lift my head. The drugs are doing their job. Even my face is numb.

"Everything ran smoothly. They were able to reset your arm."

I don't answer, but nod as I try to move myself up to a sitting position. "When can we go?" I look toward Sy and see him quietly assessing me.

Oh, God. He scares me.

"Tomorrow. They want you to stay the night here, and then once you receive the all clear, we'll be on the road." Beau stands and passes me the remote to control the bed.

"I'm gonna go check in with Nix. Be back." Sy turns and leaves us alone.

"I don't think he's too happy," I murmur, more to myself than Beau.

"He has his head up his ass over his woman. Just ignore

him. I do." He rests back in his chair and stretches his feet out in front of him. Faded jeans, scuffed boots. I don't say anything for a few minutes, until I can't help but want to engage with him.

"Beau, why do you do this? Help women." He regards me for a long while, and I wonder if I've overstepped some line I didn't know was drawn.

"Ten years ago, someone close to me lost their life because she didn't leave." His face darkens, his brow dipping low, and then he shakes his head clear. Like he can't believe he just shared a little of himself.

"I'm sorry to hear that, Beau."

"Nothing to be sorry about. Now get some sleep. We have a long day tomorrow." He shuts down any more chances for me to talk. Deciding sleep sounds appealing, I rest my head back and let my eyes fall shut. He's not leaving. I'm safe.

"Beau," I call one last time, hoping he answers.

"Yeah?"

"I bet your special someone would be proud you do this." I hope to offer him some kind of peace.

"Thanks, darlin'. I hope so." His reply is soft, gentle and if you could breathe hope from my words alone, you'd swear he was trying.

"I know so," I whisper just before sleep takes me.

20

Bean

Hunter: Just got here. All good.

Me: Thanks

I reply back to Hunter's text, feeling a little lighter knowing I can stay focused now there are eyes on her.

"Was that Mackenzie?" Jesse leans over the cab of the van trying to check my phone like a fucking nosey old woman.

"Will you just watch the damn road?" I pocket my phone, close my eyes and rest back into the chair.

"Well, aren't you in a chirpy mood tonight." He scoffs when I don't play along.

"Don't know what you're talking about." I keep my eyes

closed and don't fall for his bullshit. He's right. I'm far from fucking chirpy. I had plans tonight. Plans that included my cock in Mackenzie's pussy, maybe try to work her up a little more, have her coming on my face again. After her first orgasm last night that revealed a little something extra, I wasn't able to get her back there. Instead, I'm stuck on a fucking run with Jesse.

"So how is everything with Mackenzie?" I tense, wondering if he knows, but relax when I realize there would be no way.

"Off limits." He laughs at my reply, still not getting a clue. There's no fucking way I would ever talk to this asshole about Mackenzie.

"So fucking whipped."

"You really wanna go there, Jesse?" I counter, ready to pull every fucking thing he has done the last seven months since Bell's been on the scene.

"I have no problem going there, Beau. Unlike you, I own it. Yes, I'm pussy whipped. I don't give a fuck who knows it." I ignore the smartass and start counting down the hours I have left with the fucker.

"The girls are having a night out next weekend," he says after a few minutes.

"Why would I care?"

"Oh, didn't Mackenzie tell you? She'll be there too."

"Shut the fuck up, Jesse, you're starting to piss me off." I don't bite like he wants me to, but I store the info in the back of my mind to bring up later. I don't give a fuck if Mackenzie goes out, but the club will have eyes on her. I still don't trust her asshole ex. Even if it's been over two months and there has not been one sighting of him. I'm just waiting for something to happen.

"Maybe she'll pick up someone. I know a few of the guys around the club are keen on her." Before he can add in another word, my left hand reaches out, grabbing him by the back of the neck.

"Seriously fucker, I'm about to kick you out and you can take your sorry ass home on your own."

"I'm gonna fucking crash, asshole." He laughs louder, rarely taking anything serious. I squeeze tighter, keeping my grip firm.

"Okay, I'll quit it," he relents. I give his neck one last squeeze before releasing him. I'm not fucking kidding. If he doesn't quit it, he's out.

He manages to keep quiet for another forty minutes before breaking the silence. *Again.*

"So, I'm thinking of asking Bell to marry me." I let a few minutes pass to take in what he just said before commenting.

"You sure you're ready?" It's not like I want to question his reasons, but Bell and Jesse just dealt with some major shit. The last thing they need to be doing is rushing into marriage.

"She's the one. There's no one else for me." He sounds so sure and I don't want to be an asshole, but I ask anyway.

"How do you know?" It hasn't even been a year. They've only lived together for a short time. Hell, Mackenzie and I've almost been living together for the same amount of time.

"Fuck you're such a cynic. Of course you don't believe in love, Beau."

"Didn't say I don't believe in love. I just think giving yourself over to it is dangerous." I shrug, not shy in sharing my thoughts.

"Dangerous? How so?"

"It hooks you with ties stronger than death, Jesse. You of all people can understand that." I give it to him straight. The man just lost his father this year. He should fucking get it.

"Jesus, Beau. Bit fucking deep, even for you."

"It's the fucking truth. I'm not saying you don't love Bell. But are you ready to hand it all over, knowing if anything ever happened, it would hurt more than anything?"

"Hey, maybe it's flawed and complex to you, Beau. But it's not just one layer. It's multiple fucking layers. Not giving yourself over to it because later it might hurt makes no sense. Death can't cancel it out because it's fucking pure. It cancels everything else out." I don't respond right away, my mind still trying to catch up that I'm having *this* conversation with Jesse.

It takes me a while to respond, my head still trying to process it from a different point of view. "The fuck you come up with this shit, Jesse?"

"I'm in love, brother. When you know, you know." His deep laugh resonates from within him and fills the van.

"If you say so." I shake my head and rest back in my chair. The next time he asks me a question, I pretend to be asleep. He's already schooled me enough tonight. I don't need him to know I was already affected by it.

We pull into the clubhouse early the next morning. After picking up the woman in Henderson, we drove her back to Rushford and set her up in one of the safe houses we have here. She will stay there for a week before we move her again with a new identity.

"The gate's open," I say aloud, but more to myself than

anything.

"Maybe Nix is in." Jesse sits up a little straighter. Both of us on alert. I know Nix said he would lock up after we left, so the gate being open puts me on edge.

"At five in the morning?" I pull out my cell and bring Nix's name up. Jesse opens his door and walks toward the gate, pushing it fully open so I can drive through.

"Yeah," Nix grumbles, coming out of sleep.

"You at the clubhouse?"

"No, why?" His voice becomes more alert at the mere question.

"Front gate is open."

"I left after you took the van out. Locked that shit up tight 'cause no one was in."

"Nix?" Kadence's whisper comes through the line.

"Shh, go back to sleep, babe." I hear rustling and I know he's moving through the house. "Check it out and call me back." He hangs up as Jesse gets back in the van.

"Got your gun on you?" I ask, knowing he probably does.

"Yep." He reaches for his gun as I pull up just short of the club parking lot.

"You carrying?" he asks, checking the chamber, the click and release ringing out between us.

"Yep. You take the front. I'll take the back." I put the van in park, both of us pushing our doors open and moving out.

I reach for my gun and watch Jesse head swiftly toward the front door. He clicks his tongue, pointing to the busted lock on the front door. I nod, bringing my gun up and walk around to the back of the clubhouse.

Instantly I'm alert, ready to act. The back door has been

217

smashed in with a chair, shards of glass both inside and out. It cracks under my feet as I gently lift the chair out of my way and step over the debris and into the clubhouse. I walk through quietly. The rooms are dark with the sun not up, but I continue to clear each room as I go.

The place has been ransacked, both sofas are shredded, the top of the pool table sliced. The bar has been smashed up, every bottle cracked over the Oakwood countertop with shards of glass and liquid everywhere. It's a complete fucking mess.

I catch movement to my left, and I clock Jesse clear the front hallway. He looks up, his gun still trained in front of him. I point to my right, signaling for him to go first toward the bedrooms.

He nods once and then steps forward. We search each room one by one. They show signs of being torn up. Beds slashed, mirrors smashed, furniture thrown across each room. The dirty fuckers even pissed on some of the beds. *Fucking hell.*

After we clear every room, we meet back out front in the main area.

"Jesus Christ. Cunts pissed on my bed." Jesse kicks at one of the broken stools.

"What a fucking mess." I look around. I wouldn't even know where to start.

"How the fuck did they pass the alarm?" Jesse asks, moving to Nix's office.

"I don't fucking know. I'm gonna check the shed. Get Nix down here." I head back through the clubhouse the same way I came in. As I clear the back door, I notice a figure to my right crouching down behind the shed. Not wanting to draw attention to myself, I keep my pace smooth. The asshole can't see me, but he can still turn at any time.

Making quick work, I clear half of the space between us, before he looks back and notices me. His hat is slung low, so I don't get a good look at him before he stands, aims his gun and shoots off three rounds.

"Fucker." I fall to the grass, taking cover and watching him bolt for the front gate.

"Jesse, out the front!" I find my feet and shout out, hoping he can cut him off. He's too fast for me.

The guy takes the corner before I do, but I pick up speed, not willing to let him get away. He's halfway to the gate by the time I take the corner. Jesse races out the front door, and takes the lead, before managing to spear him to the ground in a loud thud. I watch them struggle with a gun for a bit before Jesse manages to disarm him and pin him down, but not before a bullet leaves the chamber. The heat from it slices right pass me just as I reach them.

"Motherfucker." Jesse presses his knee into his chest and knocks his hat back as I train my gun down at him.

It's the dumb fuck who jumped me three weeks ago.

"You have to be fucking shitting me." I look down at the piece of shit named Baz.

"Fuck you, fucker." He continues to fight. Jesse's fingers wrap around his throat forcing him down.

"You fucked up, man." I squat down beside him.

"Fuck you, asshole."

"You couldn't have made it any easier for me." I bring the butt of my gun down to the side of his head hard, knocking him out cold.

"I enjoyed that too much." I let out a breath as Jesse comes to a stand.

"He got ya." He points to my arm and the slight grazing about three inches long marks my skin. It's nothing to be concerned with. Just a slight burning sensation, but I'm pissed he marked me.

"Help me pull him up." We both grab him. Half carrying him and half dragging him we get him to the shed.

"Find some rope," I instruct Jesse, pulling the asshole toward one of the metal shelving units. I bend down and bring him up against it. Baz stirs, almost coming to. I deliver a punch to his face again, knocking him back out. Jesse hands me some rope and I make quick work, tying his hands behind him and through the metal shelf.

After I've secured him, I search his body, making sure he's clean.

"He have anything on him?" Jesse passes me a rag to tie around my arm.

"Nothing." I stand and remove my cut, wrapping a knot around the graze.

"You get in touch with Nix?"

"Yeah, he just texted. He's on his way."

"Good, gives me some time to play with the fucker before he gets here."

"What the fuck you going to do, Beau?" Jesse regards me carefully, probably thinking I don't have it in me.

"This is the fucker who had a gun to my head three weeks ago outside of Fireside. Roughed him up a bit and warned him. Apparently, he didn't learn. Coming into my fucking place and disrespecting our club." I shake my head and move toward Baz. I should have fucking shot him when he threatened me the first time.

"Well, this will be interesting then," Jesse declares as he pulls up a chair and gets comfortable.

"Wake up, fucker." I lean down and slap Baz's face a few times.

"Hmm," Baz grumbles, his head rolling from side to side, slowly coming to.

"Good morning, sunshine."

He blinks a few times, taking stock of where he is before he starts to fight his restraints. "What the fuck, man. Let me go."

"And where would the fun be in that?" A slow smile pulls at my lips watching him realize he's fucked.

"You will pay for this. I'll fucking kill you." He kicks his leg out trying to connect with me, but I step back.

"You're not smart, Baz, are ya? 'Cause from where I'm standing, looks like it's you who's about to pay."

"What are you going to do?" His eyes briefly flick in fear before he manages to hide it.

"I don't know yet. Depends on what info you give me."

"I don't have any info for ya." He shakes his head, not giving in.

"What you doing on our turf?" I ask, keeping it cool to start with.

"Looking for my woman, the one you took from me."

"You mean the one you beat?"

"I don't know what you're talking about. Whatever she told you is a lie. I hardly fucking touched her." He fights his restraints, but I made sure to secure him good. He's not going anywhere. At least not until I'm ready to let him go.

"See, the thing is, Baz." I squat back down, getting to his

level. "She didn't have to tell me anything. I fucking saw her face the day I picked her up."

"It was an accident," he blurts, only making it worse for him.

"So, you accidently beat your woman." I bark a laugh. This guy is a piece of work.

I pull my arm back, making a fist with my hand as I go and let it surge forward, pounding it into his nose. A nice crack rings out before blood flows down over his lip. "Did that seem like an accident?" I taunt, reaching out, pinching his ear between my fingers and twisting it back.

"FUCK!" He screeches, his body twisting to find relief. "You're fucking dead." He tries to spit up at me, but misses.

"Now, now. No need for the death threats." I release his ear, pushing his head back into the shelf with a thud. "Not yet at least. We still have a few things to get through." I stand and walk toward the tools hanging up on the far right wall.

"W-what are you going to do to me?" His voice trembles as he starts to scramble.

Not so fucking tough now. Just like I thought. A fucking pussy.

"Beau," Jesse warns as I grab a pair of bolt cutters.

"What? We're just gonna play one game."

Jesse curses under his breath knowing what I'm gonna do.

"I wonder if you didn't have your fingers, would you still be able to accidently beat on a woman's face again." I turn back to Baz. A fine sheen of sweat breaks out on his forehead.

"Are you just going to let him cut my fucking fingers off?" Baz looks to Jesse. His plea drips in desperation and fear, and I fucking love it.

"Don't ask him, asshole. You pissed in his bed." I squat

222

down and force his face my way.

"I'll do anything. Anything you say." I grip his shoulder and pull him forward. "Please, I'm begging you."

"Does your Prez know you're here?" He doesn't answer. His claim to doing anything to get out of this only seconds before was clearly bullshit.

"Which finger do you want the least? I'll let you choose which one I take." I reach for his hands not in the mood for his shit.

"NONE! I choose none." He starts thrashing, but it's no use. He's fucked.

"Wrong choice." With a steady hand, I grab his wrist. His fingers are fisted tight, so I pinch his middle finger and pointer. Digging in, I break them free.

"Does T know you're here?" I ask again, holding both fingers firmly.

"NO! No one knows I'm here." I'm not sure I believe him, so I goad him a little more.

"You sure, Baz? 'Cause it looks like it's gonna be two for one." I lower the bolt cutters to just after two of his knuckles.

"I swear, I was told to leave you alone. They're not interested in finding Sandra. They know I didn't treat her good." He starts spilling his guts in an attempt to save his fingers, but little does he know, it's too fucking late for him. I'm just biding my time.

"How did you get through the alarm?" I ask my second question.

He hesitates, "There was no alarm."

He's lying.

"Last chance, Baz."

"There wasn't." He hesitates again, feeding me bullshit.

"Wrong answer." Slowly but deliberately, I squeeze down. The sickening crunch of flesh, muscle and bones is the only thing I focus on, dulling the harsh shriek of his screams.

"FUCK! No! No! No!" His voice cracks in pain and I push a little harder. I continue to torture him, drawing out more pain, more blood, before crushing them entirely between the metal. The faint thud of his fingers dropping to the concrete ends his torment.

"You fucker!" He starts to rock his body back and forth, over and over again. I reach down, picking up his fingers and wave them in front of his face.

"Oh, shit. That was an accident." His eyelids flutter three times before his eyes roll back in his head, and then he's gone.

Out like a light.

"Pansy-ass passed out." I stand, disappointed my fun is over. Dropping his fingers to his lap, I reach for a rag, wiping the bolt cutters clean.

"You have fucking issues, man. That's some messed-up shit," Jesse says, breaking the silence.

"Fucker pissed on your bed, marks me, and beats on his woman, probably in front of their kid. He'll be lucky if I leave him with a finger to scratch his ass." I place the bolt cutters back on the workbench as the rumble of a bike pulls into the yard.

Leaving the asshole passed out on the ground, I walk out to meet Nix.

"He get ya good?" He notices my arm first.

"Nah, graze." I shrug it off.

"Who is he?" He kicks the stand down on his bike and

removes his helmet.

"A fucking Warrior," I fill him in, watching his eyes darken.

Yeah, a Warrior on our turf is serious shit.

"Bypassed the alarm, smashed his way in and ripped the clubhouse apart. Every room."

"The fuck?" Nix moves away from his bike and toward the shed. "How did he manage to get past the alarm?"

"Didn't get it out of him. Could have someone working for the security company. Who fucking knows." We enter the shed, Nix moving toward Baz.

"Jesus, Beau. Tell me he's alive." He kicks at Baz's feet looking for life. He doesn't stir. Blood pools all around him, his fingers lying on his lap.

"For now."

"He the only one?"

"That we know of. Cameras will let us know."

"How much damage he do?"

I look to Jesse allowing him to answer.

"The place is fucked-up, boss. Every room trashed. The fucker even pissed on some beds."

"Jesus Christ." He draws a large breath through his nose and lets it out slowly. "I just would like one fuckin' month where I don't have to deal with this shit." He spins and kicks at a crate, sending it flying across the shed.

"You think it's an attack?" Jesse asks after Nix calms down a little.

"Nah, I believe him. He's just gone AWOL. He was here on his own. T's not fucking stupid." If the Warriors wanted a war, ransacking our clubhouse would be the least of our worries.

"He's right. This isn't retaliation. It's not T's style anyway,"

Nix agrees.

"Well, what do you wanna do with him?" I ask, happy to fuck with him some more.

"Find out how he made it past the security system then get him out of here. I don't care where you take him, but send his fingers back to his club." He starts to walk toward the door. "And then I want everyone down here. We'll need all hands on deck to help clean," he says before leaving us alone.

"How pissed do you think he's gonna be when he finds out he pissed in his bed too?" Jesse asks, a hint of humor in his question.

"I should probably get Baz out of here before he finds out. You think I'm twisted? You wouldn't want to know what Nix would do." I look back at the asshole still out cold.

"Well, I can't say this has been fun. Remind me never to fuck with you." Jesse stands and heads for the door.

"What? You're not staying for the second act? You wound me."

"No, I have piss to clean out of my bed, motherfucker. Now that I think about it, cut a finger off for me too." He waves me off, leaving me alone with Baz, and my bolt cutters.

21

Mackenzie

"MORNING, BEAUTIFUL." A WARM BREATH SKIRTS OVER my ear, stirring me from my sleep.

"Beau?" I stretch out, letting myself wake up. My body aches more than yesterday. Muscles I never knew I had groan in protest.

"Sore, darlin'?"

I look up at his question and watch him strip beside the bed.

"It's a good sore," I tell him, my eyes traveling down his chest, abs, and landing on his hard cock.

Nope, it doesn't get old.

"We don't have much time." He rips the covers off me and crawls over. My legs are bare, only going to bed in a pair of panties and Beau's shirt.

"We don't?" His fingers reach the thin lace of my panties. Dragging them down my legs, he throws them off to the side. My need is instant. It flows through me, awakening me entirely.

"Nope. Need to go back to the clubhouse. It was trashed last night. Nix wants us all there. I just came home for you." He leans forward and presses his lips to mine.

I open instantly, my tongue rushing to meet his. I sigh at the contact, letting him take control, his tongue guiding mine in an intimate dance.

The coolness of his cock piercing rests on my pubic bone. Lifting my hips, I seek a different angle, hoping to find some friction. It doesn't work. Beau only pulls back, breaking our connection when I get close.

"Patience." His lips move against my skin, peppering small kisses along my jaw and down my neck.

"But I thought we didn't have much time." I roll my head to the side, allowing him better access.

"I changed my mind, forgot how sexy you look in my shirt." He moves lower, bunches the shirt up around my neck and wraps his lips around my nipple. His hand glides to my other breast. Using his thumb and forefinger, he pinches my erect nipple, rolling it and pulling it hard.

Groaning, my back arches, and lifts off the bed, pleasure and pain moving through me.

"You have the sexiest nipples I've ever seen." He swaps sides, moving his mouth to my left breast, and his hand to the right. Repeating the same strokes, he gives them equal attention.

"I do?" It's not that I don't believe him, I just haven't had a man so taken by them before.

"Oh, yeah." He traces his finger around my red nipple.

"Look how swollen it is for me." He cups my breast and pushes it up giving me a better view. "Watch." He lowers his mouth and captures it between his teeth, biting down hard and pulling back.

"Ahh." I bite my lip at the pain, but keep my eyes on his mouth. He releases my nipple from his teeth, and then circles it with a soft touch of his tongue. It's the perfect mix of pleasure and pain. After getting his fill of my nipples, he releases my breast and pulls back.

"Haven't stopped thinking about you since I left." His hand trails down my stomach and finds my bare pussy lips.

"You haven't?" I ask, letting him push my legs open wider. He crawls back down the bed, hands around my ankles, and jerks me to the end of the bed.

"I kept picturing my tongue, sliding through this pretty cunt of yours." He drops to his knees, his mouth at the apex of my thighs. "I wanna make you come on my face, darlin'." He blows his warm breath over me before wrapping his lips around my clit and sucking it hard.

"Beau!" I shriek, my hips rising off the bed. Sharp electric currents shoot up through my clit. I've never felt anything like it before. Pain then pleasure. Throbbing then contracting.

"Keep your ass on the bed or I stop." He releases his suction, waiting for me to obey.

Instantly, I drop it back to the bed.

"Good girl," is all he says before his tongue glides through my folds, curls around my clit twice before sliding back down. The roughness of his beard and the smoothness of his tongue ignite every small nerve to life.

He repeats the pattern again, curling around my clit before

sliding down. On the third lap, he wraps his lips around my clit and sucks. This time two fingers enter me at the same time. White flashes explode in front of my eyes, the name of God flies past my lips as I press my hips down against his fingers. The walls of my sex contract around him.

He releases my clit with a pop, hooks his fingers deep, then presses into me over and over.

"Yes," I moan as waves and waves of energy build within me.

"You're gonna come hard in a minute, darlin'. Don't fight it." Beau's voice breaks through my haze. His fingers keep pressing up into me, harder. Faster. Up and down.

He's right. I can sense it everywhere. I'm on the edge of something explosive. Heat coils through me. My breath is shallow, not giving me the oxygen I need to keep a clear head.

He pushes in deeper, presses up harder, and then the explosion hits me. An orgasm, unlike anything I've ever had before rolls over me. Starting in my toes and ending in my nose, it shatters through me. Wave upon wave crashes over me, drowning me in pure ecstasy. Digging my heels into the bed and my fingers into my hair, I rear my hips up, taking Beau's hand with me and begging for more. He doesn't still or stop, his fingers milking my new favorite spot.

"Fucking beautiful." His voice is raw, like it hurts him to speak. His hunger becoming palpable, dancing over the surface of my skin in a soft low whisper.

"Never—" I start to say, but give up, too high on lust to form a coherent sentence.

After what feels like an eternity, when the pulse starts to dull, my hips return to the bed, and Beau's fingers slide out of me and glide up to my clit.

"No more, Beau." My legs squeeze together in protest, trapping his hand.

"One more, darlin'," he coaxes, using both hands to pull my knees apart, and pushing them back down to the bed.

Pressing the flat part of his thumb against my swollen clit, he starts rolling it in slow, gentle strokes.

"I can't." I fight it, knowing what he's trying for. My clit is on fire, my body is spent and I'm pretty sure my face is numb.

"It's happening, darlin', and you're gonna watch it." The wave builds again the harder he rubs against me, and in less than ten seconds, I'm close once more.

"Eyes on me, Kenzie," he warns, flattening my clit.

"Oh, God, Beau. It's too much." The coil starts to unravel, surging and crashing over me.

"Now." He growls as the first squirt of my orgasm hits his face. "Fuck, yes," erupts from his mouth as he leans in closer.

Holy shit.

Rolling harder on my clit, he flicks his tongue out as the next small burst sprays from me, catching it with his mouth.

"OH, GOD. OH, GOD. OH, GOD!" I half chant, half scream as he continues to press down on my clit. The orgasm is short, but powerful as he lets me ride it out.

Holy shit, that just happened.

I'm done.

Exhausted.

Possibly dead.

Beau releases his finger from my now bruised clit, and then dives in. His tongue laps up everything I just gave him with a hunger I haven't seen before.

Where the hell did that come from?

"Fuck, Kenz. Sexiest fucking thing I've seen." He moves his body back over me, hovering above me.

"I can't even right now, Beau," I tell him then watch a triumphant grin spread over his face. His beard glistens with my arousal and it might just be the sexiest thing I've ever seen.

"You come like that for everyone?" I don't have it in me to be shy about it. It's only happened twice before, both times on my own.

"Only on my own." His eyes darken getting my drift, and I need to end this now before he asks for more information. "Your beard," I whisper as I reach up.

"Never washing it again." He snatches my hand away and leans in, nuzzling against my jaw, and down my neck.

"Jesus, Beau." I squirm against the dampness of his scruff. He slides to the other side, showing the same attention. *Claiming me with my own scent.*

"Now I can smell your cunt all day." He places his nose to my neck and inhales loudly. "Fucking delicious. Now, get on your hands and knees. My balls are about to explode after seeing you come that hard." It doesn't take being told twice to roll onto my stomach and find my knees before pushing up with my arms. His hands spread my ass cheeks apart and he slides the tip of his cock between my lips. The cool metal of his piercing hits the hood of my clit and I whimper at the sensitive touch.

"I'm gonna take you hard, darlin'. I need it, baby." I nod, letting him know I need the same. Instantly, he drives himself into me, filling me in one deep thrust.

We both cry out in unison, his piercing giving me a new

level of pleasure with the different angle. I move my hips in small circles, adjusting and allowing myself to take all of him.

"Damn, Kenz. Stop." The quick pinch of fingers at my side has me stilling.

We stay like this for a few seconds, both of us unmoving. My heart pounds erratically at the thought of him releasing more power over me.

I'm about to tell him I need more when he rocks into me, slow to start with, before building his stroke deliberately. The bar that sits on the underside of his cock glides over the ridges of my walls stroking me like nothing I've ever felt before. It's like my own massager, adding a whole new level of pleasure to work with.

"One day, when you're ready, I'm gonna take your hands and tie them behind your back, and fuck you like this." His words are like an electric current running through me, setting every nerve ending on fire.

Would I let him tie me? Allow him total control?

"You're gonna fucking love it, darlin'," Beau answers my silent question, and the way he says it makes me believe him. So I don't argue. I just let my body relax into it and let him take what he needs. *What we both need.*

"Tell me you want it, darlin'," he pushes, needing my words.

Always words.

"I want it, Beau. I want you to do it," I confess, giving myself over to him. I'm not sure I'm ready right now, but the thought of being tied under him excites me more than I thought it would.

"I will." His strokes build faster, harder, more controlled. Then when I think I can't take it anymore, he reaches around, flicks my clit once and I'm coming apart under him.

"Beau, yes!" I scream, letting the orgasm hit me and take me under, dragging me beneath a wild current and forcing me to swim. His piercing drags out my orgasm, pulling me along a little bit further as he succumbs to his own release.

"God, yes. Fuck, darlin'," he grunts out, before sinking his teeth into my shoulder.

"Holy shit, Beau." I buck at the unexpected pain, then soothe myself as his hips slow. His breathing is harsh, but his strokes are gentle so I take comfort in it. This is Beau. Hard and soft. Rough and smooth. For every action, he controls my reaction and I can't help but be drawn into it, into *him*.

"We're gonna be late," I whisper, my voice scratchy from crying out. My words break the moment, causing him to still.

"I decided we're not going. We're staying in bed, not leaving here till I have my fill." He gently slides out of me and then rolls off to the side.

"But we have to go help." I follow him down, falling to my back.

"Not anymore. You're not feeling well." He reaches for his shirt to help me clean up. I let him wipe himself from between my legs then watch him throw his shirt back on the floor.

"I'm not?" I roll toward him and rest my head in my palm.

"No, you have a fever and you're going to need bed rest for at least a few days." I can't help my grin from growing.

"You wanna play hooky with me?" I don't remember the last time I have. It's been years.

"I want to play a lot with you, darlin'. I'm just getting started." He rolls back over me and covers my body with his.

"Just getting started?" I don't know if he's talking about sex or what's happening between us.

"Not ready for this to end." I hold my breath for a second as I process what I think I need to process.

"Has it started, Beau?" I ask, missing the moment we labeled what was happening. Barely twenty-four hours ago, he was fighting this, yet now he's not ready to give it up.

"Darlin', do you even have to ask?"

It's not a label or even really an answer, but I'll take it anyway.

"How can you not be exhausted right now?" I move us away from this line of questioning and settle in closer to him.

"Fucking beat, but something tells me having your naked body in my bed I'm not getting any sleep."

"You could try."

"Or I could fuck you. Better yet, you can fuck me." His hands move to my waist and in one quick movement, he rolls, taking me with him. I land on top of him, his cock starting to grow as it rests at the apex of my thighs.

My eyes fall on the small skin-colored bandage on his arm and I zone in on it.

"What happened?"

"Just a scratch," he dismisses too coolly as he rests his hands under his head and smirks up at me. "I'll give you free play. Then I'll take the lead."

"You're terrible." I shake my head, letting it go.

"I am, but you fucking love it."

"Maybe. Maybe not."

The truth is I do. I love the way he is. Love the way he speaks, the way he treats me. I love it all and yeah it scares me. Oh, God, does it scare me. What will happen when my past finally catches up with me? Would whatever is going on between us fall apart? I want to think no, but sometimes when you grow tired of running, your fears make you insecure. They pull you down and force you to live in darkness, surrounded by whatever it is you are running away from.

I didn't want to be like this anymore. I wanted something more. Even after everything I had done.

Maybe later I will rethink my actions, but right now this is what I want and I'm not going to overthink it. I have to trust this future is better than my past.

If anyone understands that it's Beau.

Past

Mackenzie

"WE'RE HERE." BEAU PULLS UP OUT FRONT OF A RANCH-style house two days later. After getting the all-clear to leave the hospital, we waited until early morning the next day to leave town, driving the four-hour drive straight through.

"You ready?" He turns the van off and releases his seat belt.

"These people, I can trust them?" I ask him again. We've already gone over it on the drive here. I know he said I can trust them, but in the last two days, I've become comfortable with Beau. The thought of leaving him and trusting new people freaks me out.

"They'll take good care of you," he assures me before exiting the van, moving around the front and opening my door. With my arm in a cast, and my chest wrapped tight, I need help to move down.

"I'm going to help you down again." He steps in closer when I nod, then wraps his arm around my waist. "Careful," he whispers, lifting me into his arms. I wince slightly from the movement as my feet hit the ground.

A man and woman come down the stairs to greet us as we move around the van, both older than us. They smile and wait for us to meet them. They look like a sweet couple, but I hang back a little, still unsure.

"How you doing, Larry?" Beau reaches forward and takes the man's hand in a handshake.

"Doin' good, Beau." Larry looks to be around sixty years old. As tall as Beau, he has graying hair, a small potbelly, but a warm smile.

"Mary." Beau nods to the woman and she gives him a genuine smile. Mary looks a little younger than her husband, maybe in her fifties. Her short dark hair is blow-dried in a bob that kicks out at the ends and her face is free of makeup. She reminds me of my nan. Beautiful in a reserved kind of way.

"Mackenzie, this is Larry and Mary Canter. They're gonna be helping you for the next week."

"Hi." I offer a wave and attempt a smile, but it feels dishonest.

"It's lovely to meet you, Mackenzie." Mary steps forward, but I pull back instantly before she can get too close.

"It's okay, Mackenzie." Beau turns his body toward me and lowers his voice. "You have to trust me. They're good people." I let out a shaky breath and relax a little at his words.

"It's nice to meet you, too." I look back up at Mary and decide to trust Beau. He hasn't let me down yet. Why would he start now?

"If you want to come with me, I can show you around." Mary steps back and motions toward the front door. I look back at Beau, unsure if this will be our goodbye or if he will be hanging around a little while longer.

"Go ahead, I'll wait until you're finished." Beau answers my silent question and I relax, following Mary up the porch steps and into her home. She keeps her pace slow, allowing me to keep up with her easily. After my surgery, I've been given some good painkillers. I hadn't taken any today, wanting to be clearheaded when I arrived here.

"So, this is the kitchen and the living area." Mary walks me through her home, showing me the rooms I need to know. "You're welcome to anything, anytime. The fridge is stocked and Larry likes my baking, so there's always something to eat." I nod, acknowledging her offer, even if I won't take her up on it.

We continue on the tour, my mind not really into it. I let everything pass over me, barely taking in my surroundings with the nerves still swirling around in my belly.

"Bedrooms are down here." Mary moves us further through the house. "Yours is the last one." We walk to the last bedroom on the right as Mary continues to talk.

"Everything you need is in here. Your own bathroom, and I've left clean towels on your bed," she says as she opens the door to what will be my room while I'm here.

"Thank you," I say, not sure how I'm going to be able to shower with my cast and ribs wrapped up, but I'll think about it later.

"Now, can I offer you something to drink?" She steps back out of the room.

"No thank you. I think I might just go say goodbye to Beau and then take a nap. I'm really exhausted from the ride."

"Of course, dear. You let me know if you need anything at all." She offers a warm smile before leaving me alone. I don't wait around; instead, I make my way back out to the front in search of Beau. He's sitting on the front porch when I finally step back outside, talking on his phone. I hang back, not wanting to interrupt.

"Yep, I'm done here. I'm heading out now. See you soon." He ends the call then stands, our eyes locking onto one another's. "You settled in, darlin'?" I nod and watch him step forward slowly.

"Good. Okay, well, I gotta head out. You're in good hands here, darlin'." He tries to reassure me once again and for the most part, he does, but I'm still hesitant.

"Thank you for everything, Beau. For saving me." It's not enough, but I have to give him something.

"You saved yourself, darlin'. I just gave you a helping hand." He brushes it off as nothing and maybe for him it is. Maybe he does this sort of thing every week, but to me it's huge.

"You're gonna be all right, Mackenzie. You'll heal up, get your life sorted, settle down somewhere and this will be your past."

"He's not going to stop looking for me, you know? I'll always be looking over my shoulder." I disagree with him and remind myself of the hard truth. "This won't be my past. He won't let it be."

"This life isn't easy, darlin'. I wish for your sake it was, but look at you now. Look what you've been living. Now look at the new chance you have right here. What's the alternative? You want to go back? You say you can't fight him, his connections are too strong. There is only one option here then, you gotta do what you gotta do."

I know he's right. I stayed too long with Chad, and I wasn't strong enough to fight him, nor was I strong enough to leave him.

Until now.

"Well, thank you for giving me that chance." I reach out to touch his arm, but stop mid-air and drop it back down. "I really appreciate it."

"Listen, if you ever need anything, Mackenzie, anything, you know how to find me, okay?" he offers. I don't reply, but I take it in as my last resort. "Anytime. You just look me up." He takes my hand and gently squeezes it before taking the steps and moving back to his van. He doesn't look back and I don't watch him leave. I just step up to the porch swing, take a seat, and look out at the empty sky ahead of me.

I stay out on the porch for the rest of the day, until the blue sky turns inky black. I don't eat dinner with Larry and Mary, my stomach still tied in knots. I don't engage in any conversations, my mind too lost in thoughts. I just sit on their porch swing and think.

Think about what I am going to do with my life. Where I will end up. All these new possibilities and I have no idea how to process it.

I don't think about Chad and how he would be reacting to the news I was gone. I don't think about Heidi, my only friend left behind. And I especially don't think about Beau, or the fact him leaving me in the middle of nowhere felt worse than leaving behind my whole life. Maybe later I will process it, but tonight I don't want to deal. I don't want to feel. I just want to sit.

I am free.

I have escaped.

I don't know how long it will last, but tonight it doesn't matter.

Nothing matters.

22

Beau

"OPEN UP, BEAU, I KNOW YOU'RE IN THERE." THE
knock on the door pulls me out of sleep and back to my living
room.

Fuck, here we go.

"Kenz, wake up." I shift her naked body off me and take
stock of my surroundings. It can't be later than six. The
afternoon sun is just starting to darken the room.

"What's happening?" Kenzie yawns, stretching her arms up
over her head. Her tits push out in front of her and I have to
physically stop myself from touching her.

Keep it together, man. Just get rid of Nix first.

"Nix is here. Go put some clothes on." I help her up then
watch her naked ass walk down the hall.

Fuck, I could just ignore him like I've done the last three days.

"Beau, I'm not fuckin' kiddin'. Open the fuckin' door." Nix's pissed-off voice reminds me why that's not a good idea.

"Hold the fuck on. I'm coming." I reach for my discarded jeans and step into them before heading to the door. I should have known this was coming. Judging by the constant calls I've been ignoring for three days, this was inevitable. Bracing myself for what's to come, I arrange my face and pull the front door open.

"What?" I greet, not giving one fuck Nix is probably about to lay me out. The last three days of having a naked Mackenzie anytime I want was worth it though.

"You missed the meet." He pushes the door further open and storms past me.

"Sorry. Forgot." I'm surprised his fist didn't greet me. Not giving up on it still happening, I close the door and follow him into the kitchen.

"You forgot?" He practically scoffs. "You forget you cut some fucker's fingers off, then left me with the fallout." He flicks the coffee machine on and moves to the fridge, making himself at home.

Fucker.

"I know, shit." I rub my face in frustration. Probably not my best move leaving the club with all my shit.

"You're fuckin' her." It's not a question, but a statement, one that pisses me off.

"Not your fucking business, Nix." I step up to the coffee machine and take over, getting the pot started for a fresh brew.

"It's my business if you're gettin' your priorities messed up,

Beau."

"I missed one meet. Don't get your panties twisted." I press the brew button then turn back to him.

"You're too busy gettin' your dick wet to know this shit with the club is fuckin' important."

"Don't go there, Nix." I force myself to stand down. I'd love nothing more than to take the three steps toward him and fucking knock him on his ass, but I remember Kenzie is here, probably about to come in here and the last thing she needs to see is me raging.

"I'm fuckin' already there, brother. You've been off the grid for three days. Must be some pussy." His remark pushes me too far, and before I can think of the consequences, I manage to step into his space and connect my fist to his jaw, knocking him back against the counter.

"The fuck, Beau?" He recoils, his hand wiping the small amount of blood from the corner of his mouth. "You're out of fuckin' line, Beau." He steps forward, pushes me back and returns a fist to my nose. Pain spreads across my face. Blood spills instantly, but I don't have a chance to stop it before he locks me in a headlock. I don't give him the upper hand for too long before I twist out of his hold and take another swing at him. This time connecting with the side of his head.

"You really wanna do this?" Nix grins as I twist my fingers into the front of his shirt.

"You went there." I hold him steady in my grasp, weighing up my options. I could hit him again, but he'll only fucking come back at me.

"Beau? Wh-what's going on?" Mackenzie's panicked voice breaks the tension, pulling me back to the room.

"Fuck." I twist my face to my sleeve, wiping the blood from my face, before pushing Nix back and spinning to face her. "Darlin'." I step toward her and watch fear wash over her face.

"Beau? Did you cut someone's finger off?" She steps back, her eyes dodging between me and Nix.

"No, darlin'. Nix is fucking around. Right, Nix?" I turn back to Nix and watch him smirk.

"Sorry, sweetheart. I was just messin' with him." He backs me up, but I'm not sure it's enough.

"Relax, darlin'." I force my voice louder, trying to pull her out of her head. She's scared. No fucking mystery there, but she needs to know she's safe.

"Of course you're joking." She takes another look between us both before visibly relaxing. "Is everything okay?"

"All good, darlin'." She holds my gaze searching for truth, but I don't give it to her.

"I might go have a shower." I look down and see she's thrown on one of my shirts and an old pair of shorts.

"No problem, darlin'." I give her what I hope is a reassuring smile then watch her retreat out of the kitchen. After hearing the bathroom door close, I turn back to Nix.

"You're an asshole." I level my stare at him.

"You done?"

"Yeah, I'm done," I hiss, letting out a breath past my teeth.

"Good." He shakes his head then moves back to the coffee machine. "You got yourself in deep over some pussy, brother."

"I'll hit you again, you call her pussy one more fucking time," I seethe, knowing I'm only working myself up again.

"Didn't think I'd ever see it." We both know he's full of shit. This has been a long time coming.

"Just don't fucking talk about my woman's pussy again, we won't have a problem."

"Your woman?" One brow lifts and he tries to stop himself from grinning. He fails miserably.

"Yep," I admit, knowing this is where I'm heading. I never did see myself settling down.

Until her.

"Well, about fucking time." He claps me on the back then hands me my cup filled with freshly brewed coffee. The shower turns on just as I take it and then move to the table to sit.

"What the fuck's been going on anyway?"

Nix follows me over and pulls out the chair next to me.

"Clubhouse is cleaned up. No, thanks to you." I ignore his dig and wait for him to continue. "Had a meet with the Warriors. You missed that clusterfuck, too."

"I take it T received my package?"

"He wasn't happy. But Baz has been giving him a headache since you took his woman. And after this shit, he owes us." I nod, glad we're not in debt to the assholes anymore. After the marker Jesse pulled for Paige, I was sweating what we might have been pulled into.

"Anything else?" I ask when he relays the rest of the meet and fills me in on everything else that's been happening. The shower's been off for five minutes now and I just know Mackenzie's retreated back to her room probably freaking the fuck out.

"Pretty much. Just checkin' to make sure you're eatin'. Looks of things you have it sorted." He smirks, taking a look around. I take stock of the kitchen and notice the mess.

Jesus, we have gone off the grid.

247

"Okay, well, reunion is over. You can piss off now." I finish my coffee and stand.

"Club's having a BBQ on Friday. Can I let my wife know you'll release Mackenzie for a few hours?"

"It's been fucking three days, calm your tits."

"Hey, you're lucky it's me and not Kadence here." He stands and slaps me on the back before walking back toward the front door. I don't stop his retreat, I want him out.

"Tell Mackenzie I hope she's feelin' better. Must have been some virus." He flicks his wrist goodbye then opens the front door and leaves.

Smartass.

Not giving him a second thought, I head back down the hall to check in with Mackenzie. Her door is closed and the fact she didn't come to my bedroom is not lost on me.

"Kenzie?" I knock once and wait.

"Just need a minute, Beau," she calls back, but I don't want to fucking wait a minute.

"Open up, darlin'."

"Beau, I just need a minute."

"And I'll give you a minute. Just not behind a door, getting lost in your head."

"Beau."

"Mackenzie." The air grows silent, and I contemplate kicking the door down before the door swings open. She doesn't come out, so I step in.

"I'm really fine." She looks up and finds my eyes. She's already dressed in tight dark jeans and a black singlet. Her hair is wet from the shower, loose around her shoulders. I can see she wants me to believe she's okay, but I know she's lying. I can see her unease in the way she holds herself. It's almost like she's standing in front of me the first day she came back.

"You don't look fine. You look scared."

"I'm a little worried." She turns and sits her ass on the bed with her gaze on the ground.

"You have nothing to be worried about."

"I walk out and see you fighting with Nix, bloodied nose and you tell me I shouldn't be worried."

"It was nothing, darlin'."

"So you weren't fighting over me?"

"No. Nix was being an ass." Her brows rise calling bullshit.

"I told you it was a bad idea to not go in. The clubhouse was trashed. They needed us." I know what she told me, but it didn't matter. We both needed the last few days.

"Best three days of my life." I step up to her, and lightly push her shoulder.

"Yeah?" She falls back and smirks up at me, and I let it settle over me. This is what I need. Her playful, carefree, not worrying about club shit.

"Especially when I made you come with my mouth." I lean over her, trailing kisses down her neck before settling my weight above her.

"Haven't you had enough?" Her breath hitches as she tilts her head back allowing me more access.

"I don't think I'll ever have enough of you, darlin'," I admit, letting the truth fall between us. We haven't said where this is going between us, but anyone can see this is moving hard and fast.

"You say that now, Beau." Sadness flicks in her eyes before disappearing just as fast. It's not the first time it's happened. At first I thought it was about Chad. But sometimes it's like it's bigger than that. Over the last few days, I've seen it more than I care to admit. I've asked her about it, but she just shuts right down.

"I'll say it then too," I promise her, knowing more than anything it's the truth. Yeah, it's barely been a week of having her in my bed, but this here, whatever the fuck it is, is more. More than sex. More than helping her with her ex. It is more than both of us. Sy was right that night at the hospital. She is dangerous. She has gotten under my skin and buried herself deep.

And I'm not sure I want her out.

No, I know I don't want her out.

"So what do you think?" I ask Mackenzie a week later as she takes in our new venture. We're in town at Missy's Place, and I just revealed to her everything we have planned here.

"It's amazing, Beau. I can't believe you're doing this." She spins, turning back to me. I don't know why it bothers me to know what she thinks, but it does. As much as I'm doing this for Missy, I'm doing it for her too. For all the women like her.

"It's something I've wanted to do for a long time." I shrug, as she steps into my space.

"You're incredible." She reaches up, places her hands around my neck, and pulls me down to her lips.

"One day you're going to have to tell me Missy's story," she whispers over my mouth and I can't stop the tension tightening my stance.

"Not much to tell, darlin'." I press forward and deepen the kiss, stopping all talk of Missy. She knows my sister died. Knows her name is Missy. She just doesn't know the story.

"You're opening this place because of her, Beau. She's your someone special." She reminds me of our past, and I'd be lying if I said the walls around my heart didn't shatter just a bit at the mention of the conversation back in the hospital all those months ago. I remember the night. She asked me why I did this. Why I risked everything to save women. I wasn't going to answer. I didn't want to. But she was lying in that hospital bed. She had no one and I wanted her to know why, understand why she was important. The words fell out before I could put them back in. And then she gave me something no one has ever given me before.

Grace.

Fucking grace.

This woman who I knew nothing about me, gave it to me, and fuck if I didn't want to lie down in the bed with her and beg for more.

"No secret as to why I do any of this. Her asshole husband killed her." I shake my head from all those thoughts, reach up, unclasp her hands from my neck then take a step back.

"It's okay, Beau. I'm sure there's more to her story, but you don't have to talk about it with me." She's not offended by my retreat. If anything, she's composed, reassuring.

"I'm not trying to hide it from you, darlin'. Just don't like to talk about it."

"Okay, honey," she whispers, and then diverts her gaze back to the main room. I'm a fucking asshole, especially when she's so fucking understanding, but I'm not getting into it with her today or here.

"Come on, I'll show you the rooms." I take her hand and show her through to the rest of the house.

The shelter is big enough to accommodate ten residents with full staff at any one time. With twelve private bedrooms, large enough for mothers with children, two large communal dining rooms, and an industrial-size kitchen, they will have the privacy to come and go as they please, with the option to interact with anyone else in the house in the communal areas.

"You know, I wish I had this as an option." Mackenzie steps into one of the bedrooms and walks around.

"Wish you did too, darlin'." I watch her face as she takes in the room, running her hand along the freshly painted wall.

"I was lucky I had Heidi, and you." She looks up, and I take a moment to see how far she's come. She's no longer this jumpy, scared woman in fear of her life. She doesn't let the past hold her back. She's stronger, braver.

"You did good, Kenz. Even without all this." She shrugs, like the statement is questionable. But it's not. She's come so fucking far.

"Maybe, but I still wish I did some things differently. Wish I never went to her that night." She's talking about Heidi.

"And who knows what would have happened to you then, darlin', if you didn't get away."

"At least Heidi wouldn't be missing, God knows where she is because of me, Beau." It's the first time she has spoken about Heidi in a while. I don't want to upset her, but maybe she's willing to open up about it. She's been so shut down, I don't know where her head is at.

"We'll find her, darlin'."

"I doubt it." She worries at her lip, and I wonder what the hell that's supposed to mean.

"I understand your doubt in the sheriff's department, but I've told you before, Jackson is on our side."

"You're right. I'm just over reacting. Heidi probably ran off and got married." She steps up to me, and wraps her arms around my middle. My arms instantly wrap around her, pulling her closer into me.

Her apprehension rings out loud and clear, and I understand it. After all, the last conversation she had with her friend wasn't very comforting for her. I wish I could take it away. I wish I had more information to tell her, to ease the worry in her heart.

The truth is the chances of finding Heidi are slim. But I'm not telling Mackenzie that. She's been through so much, has lost so much. If we discover she lost her friend, too, I don't know if she will ever recover.

Not wanting to keep us in this moment, I don't push the conversation anymore. "Come on, you've seen around. Let's go." I take her hand in mine as we move back through the shelter to start locking up.

"We're going home?" She reaches for her bag.

"No, we gotta head to the clubhouse. Our presence is needed."

"Great." She sighs but grins when I turn to look at her reaction. She acts like she's uncomfortable around them, but we both know that's not the case. She's starting to become part of the family. The girls have accepted her into their fold, and once the guys find out I've claimed her as mine, it won't be long till they're giving her shit over me.

"Don't worry. It's just a family BBQ," I tell her as I lead her out the same way we came in. I didn't take her to last week's one, after Nix specifically told me to; instead, I opted to keep her in my bed, nowhere near ready to share her.

"Maybe I should just hang back at home then." She tries to get out of it, but if I'm going, she's coming. She's family.

"Come on. The quicker we do this, the quicker I can have you back in my bed." Once out, I follow behind her pulling the door closed with me before grabbing the keys out of my pocket and locking up.

"I'm serious, Beau." I drape my arm around her shoulders and steer us back to my bike.

"And this is me showing you I haven't had enough, darlin'." I won't let her try to weasel her way out of it. Before she tries to fight it more, I take her bag and stash it in my saddlebag, plant her ass on my bike, take my seat in front of her, and start it up. She stops her arguing, wraps her arms around my waist and molds her front to my back.

Just like that, she submits.

Fuck me, could she be any more perfect?

23

Mackenzie

"DON'T ACCEPT A DRINK FROM ANYONE UNLESS IT'S from Jesse or any of his staff. And don't leave the club," Beau reminds me of his rules while I get ready for my night out with the girls a couple of weeks later. I know he's only looking out for me, and I appreciate it, but he needs to take a breather.

"Yes, Beau." I hold back my eye roll and step into one of my new dresses Kelly helped me pick out yesterday. It's not my first rodeo with these ladies, but it is the first time without a tail.

"I'm not fucking messing around, darlin'."

"Beau, I'm not some eighteen-year-old girl who doesn't know her surroundings. Do you think I'm naïve? Zip me up?" I step up to my bed and turn my back for him to complete my request.

"Darlin', your crazy asshole ex is still out there. You're lucky I'm even letting you out of my sight." His fingers find the zipper and he pulls it up in a slow and deliberate pace that ends in a kiss on my exposed shoulder.

"He obviously isn't coming back. It's been over three months, or he would have by now. I'm sure we can relax a little more," I reply to his overprotectiveness. I hate that he's still so wired when I've become complacent. Guilt continues to pester me. I have made him this way, asked him to be this person. And even though it hurts me now, there is no way I can undo it. Not now. Maybe with time, he too will let it go.

Then again, maybe not.

"Don't fuck around with me on this, Mackenzie." He spins me back to face him. "I'm not relaxing until he's found." His eyes hold on to mine and a wave of anxiety washes over me.

I wish it didn't have to be like this.

"And if you never find him, Beau?" I croak, quickly clearing my throat.

"Then you're stuck with me." His gaze leaves mine and travels down my body, and I'm thankful. I don't know if I can hide my uneasiness any longer.

"Fuck, this dress isn't good, darlin'." I look down at my black figure-hugging, one-shoulder dress. I wasn't too sure when Kelly showed me it on the hanger, but as soon as I stepped into it, I knew it was perfect.

"What's wrong with it?"

"I'm fucking hard just with one look." He stands and steps in close to me so his erection sits against my stomach.

"I'm not changing." I blurt the first thing that comes to mind.

"Didn't ask you to." He trails his finger along the low dip of my cleavage. He's right. He didn't say anything about changing.

"But you want me to, right?" I remember all the times Chad asked me to change and dictated what I wore.

"I do, for my own selfish reasons. But I'm not gonna tell you to change." He steps out of my space and sits back on the bed.

"Is this like some reverse psychology?" I question, not sure what he's playing at.

"No darlin'. I might not like the thought of some sleazy fucker checking you out, but I'm not gonna tell you to change outfits to meet my wants or needs." He rests back against my headboard and crosses his feet at the ankles.

"You're not?" I ask, watching him carefully.

"Not him, darlin'. I might like to control you when I'm fucking you, but you're your own woman. You wear what the fuck you want to wear. I'll deal." I don't say anything for a second, unsure how to respond. He's right. He's nothing like Chad. My mouth wants to blurt I love you, but my head forces it to shut up. Instead of talking, I spin and move to my dresser to finish my makeup.

The room stays quiet for a few minutes, the soft sounds of me searching around my makeup bag the only thing between us until Beau speaks again.

"So, who is going to this girls' night?" He changes the subject and I take a breath.

"Just Kadence, Holly, Kelly, Bell, oh and, Lissy." I lean close to the mirror and brush my eyelashes with mascara, trying to play it cool, but know I fail when his eyes catch my awkwardness.

"There a reason you just cringed saying her name?" My eyes find his again and I watch him raise a brow.

"Well, you know, because of your past together." I drop my mascara into my makeup bag and keep my gaze on myself. I'm not sure what I should tell him. Am I threatened by Lissy because she had sex with Beau? Yes and no. The woman is stunning, at least ten years younger than me, and she's seen Beau's cock.

Okay, who am I kidding? Yeah, I'm threatened by her.

"Come here, Mackenzie." His request is firm and leaves no room for me to argue. Placing my makeup brush down, I turn back and walk to him.

"You worried about Lissy?" He sits up and shifts to the side of the bed, pulling me to stand in front of him. I shrug my answer, not really sure if I do have a problem with Lissy personally or if it's solely on what she represents.

"That's not an answer, darlin'."

"Fine, I'll be honest. I'm not comfortable knowing you've been with her. I'd prefer I didn't have those images in my head," I concede, giving him the truth. I know he can't help it. We both have our own pasts, mine colorful to say the least, but he doesn't have to go out and pretend like it doesn't bother him.

"Can't change my past, Kenz. Been with a lot of women. Not gonna lie. But there's only one of you."

"You tell those lines to all the girls, Beau?" I force myself not to roll my eyes at his smooth line or the butterflies taking flight in my stomach.

"Never told a woman that line before, darlin'." I still and drop my smile. Something passes between us before I realize he's serious. "This isn't just some fuck for me. I think I made it clear the first night I had you in my bed, darlin'." He did. I remember. But it still doesn't stop the insecurity. What if it doesn't work out? What if I can't be who he needs me to be?

"And if I can't be who you want me to be? I can't give you everything you crave? Will I be enough then?" I lay it out quickly, needing to know.

"You think it's a deal breaker?" His hands come to my waist and hold me in place.

"You're the one who said it was, not me." *I remember the threat, remember the promise. Yet I really have yet to see it.*

"That was before I tasted you, before I had your body underneath me, my cock inside you. Before I knew what waking up next to you every morning would be like." I look down into his eyes and I know he's telling the truth. I see the conviction in them, but it only hurts me more, because I'm changing him.

"But you want more. You want me tied to your bed while you hurt me?" Images of him and Lissy flash before me and I have to force myself to shake them out.

"Yeah, I'm not gonna lie, darlin'. I want you in more ways than one. But I don't want to hurt you. For me, it's more about the pleasure I can draw out of you, but just like this dress, if what I want and what you need from me don't match up, I'm not gonna push it."

"See, that's the problem for me. I look at Lissy and I can see you doing those things to her. I can see it and I hate it. I hate she could give you that, when I don't know if I can."

"I can't change what you see, darlin', but I can guarantee you I'm not even fucking looking at her. I'm looking at you and I'm more than fucking happy." I can't stop the eye roll on that one. *Please, the man craves something and I have yet to give it to him. In no time, he'll get bored.*

Noticing my eye roll, his arms come around me tighter. "You need me to show you who I think about? Who my cock grows hard for every day?"

"You don't have to." I start to second-guess myself. I shouldn't have brought it up. It's ridiculous. It's my issue. I shouldn't make it his.

"I think I do, darlin'." His fingers find the hem of my dress and bunch it up to expose my lace panties.

"Beau, I'm going to be late," I complain, but don't do anything else to stop him.

"You're also gonna come," he promises, sending a thrill through me.

"Slide your panties down your legs and step out of them," he orders as he rests back further on the bed. I contemplate arguing with him, pushing back and stopping this, but I don't want to. So I do as I'm told. I slide my lace panties down my legs and step out of them.

"See right there, darlin'. You doing what I tell you, when I tell you, how I tell you, that's more than enough. You hear me?"

"I hear you, Beau," I admit, starting to see his side. I might not be able to give him exactly what he likes, but maybe I'm getting there.

"Good girl. Now come here and sit on my face. If I have to spend the next few hours waiting around for you to come home, I want a taste to help me through." I almost laugh at how desperate he sounds, but I don't because I need him just as much. So being the good girl he wants me to be, I listen to his command. Climb on up, lower myself down on his face and let him eat me out.

By the time, he's done, I barely know my own name, let alone Lissy's.

"Oh, my God, just spill the news, it's not like we don't know what's really going on! The man has it bad and we want all the deets." Kadence pushes an hour later as we take a seat up in the VIP section of Liquid. We just walked in and everyone is here. Kadence, Kelly, Bell, Holly, Lissy and two of Bell's friends I haven't met before, Manda and her twin sister, Kate.

"Yeah, spill. I've seen that look before. He wound you up good and now he's holding you tightly in place, isn't he?" Holly laughs, getting in on teasing me. *Jesus, this woman, I have no idea how she always manages to read me like a book.*

"I'm surprised he even let you out of the house," Kelly joins in, letting me know they aren't going to give up tonight. "We haven't seen you around the clubhouse in weeks."

"Can we not do this now?" I flick my eyes to Lissy then back to Kelly. It's not that I want to keep what's happening between Beau and me secret, I just don't wish to talk about us with Lissy here.

"Yeah, let's give her a break." Bell stands up for me. I give her a thankful smile then catch a glimpse of a huge rock on her left ring finger.

"Let's talk about that ring?" I point to her hand, then watch her smile take over her face.

"Holy shit, you're engaged?" Kadence reaches for Bell's

261

hand to have a better look.

"Yes!" She practically screams like she's glad the news is finally out.

"Why didn't you say anything?" Holly reaches for her hand next.

"Well, I was planning to, but you guys haven't let up on Mackenzie since she walked in all sexed up." The girls only look partly guilty before barraging her with every question. *When? How? What did he say?*

"So we took a ride up to Mount Lookout last night." Holly snorts and Kelly laughs. "I know, I know. Make-out Mountain. It's kind of lame, but that's where we had our first time." Bell tries to justify it to them. I haven't been to Make-out Mountain, but I know about it. Growing up in Redwick, we had our own make-out point.

"*The* first time?" Kelly questions and Bell blushes before nodding. I'm totally not getting the significance of what Mount Lookout means to Jesse and Bell, but I continue to listen regardless.

"He had this whole thing planned and then he messed up. He was a nervous wreck, fumbling his words."

"Damn, the man has it bad." Kadence's grin lifts, looking just as excited as Bell.

"It was cute. Then he just said 'Fuck it, will you marry me, sweetheart?' Then of course, I said yes."

"I'm actually shocked," Holly tells the group when Bell finishes telling her story.

"Oh, believe me, I wasn't. Before we moved in together, I didn't think he would be ready for at least a couple of years, but within a week, it was as if a light had been switched. The man traveled from zero to one hundred." She looks down at her ring.

"I heard him talking about it with Jackson when I first moved into the clubhouse," I reveal.

"And you didn't tell us? Girl, we need to have a word." Holly shakes her head in disappointment.

"Well, I didn't want to ruin the surprise for Bell."

"I'm glad you didn't. I already had my suspicions," Bell assures me I did the right thing.

"I knew when I saw your smirk you knew something was up."

"We had only talked about it the night before. I knew it was coming. I just didn't know when."

"Well, who won the bet?" Manda asks, obviously in on the bet.

"Not me, I had them down for next year." Holly shakes her head.

"Me too." Kadence bows out.

"I've been out for weeks. I thought they were gonna announce when they moved in together." Lissy lets out a disappointed sigh.

"Don't worry, I thought for sure it wouldn't be for two years." Manda laughs, way out on her guess.

"I think you were the closest." Kelly turns to me.

"I said Thanksgiving."

"Yep, you were. So you win."

"I did?" I look to Bell and watch her grin.

"Drinks on you, Kenzie!" She cheers, offering me a high five and as quick as they were drilling me about Beau, our girls' night out turns into an engagement celebration for Bell and

Jesse.

I listen to the conversation, but keep my gaze off Lissy, not wanting to draw attention to the discomfort she causes in me. Bell, oblivious to our tension, begins to chat about her and Jesse's plans for the wedding. I tune out for a while, not that I don't care for weddings or planning them, but just to take stock of my life the last few months.

As much as I've finally found the peace I've been searching for since leaving Chad, the guilt is starting to eat me alive. Guilt that my past could come back and hurt these people who have taken me in. On top of the guilt, I miss having Heidi around and having nights like this. I miss the closeness and being able to share everything with her. Sure I have Beau. But there are some things I never want to share with him.

"You okay?" Kadence pulls me out of my head a little while later.

"Yeah, I'm great." I take another sip of my wine.

"You know, if you ever want to talk. I'm here, Kenz." She offers me her hand and I give it a small squeeze.

"Thank you, Kadence, but I'm fine." We don't do deep again, and the night progresses along with more laughing, drinking, and dancing. After finishing off my third glass of wine, I stand to use the bathroom.

"I'll be back, ladies. Just heading to the bathroom." I stand and start to move toward the stairs.

"Wait up, Mackenzie. I'll come with you," Lissy calls out before I can make it away.

Shit.

"Sure." I slow my escape and let her catch up. She smiles as we take the stairs, neither of us speaking.

"Mackenzie, have I done something to upset you?" she asks when we hit the lower floor and start to move to the bathroom.

"No, why?" I push open the door to the bathroom door and let her walk in before me.

"I just wanted to clear the air." She stops short of the toilet stall.

"I don't know why you would need to, Lissy." I decide to play dumb.

"I know you know about me and Beau." I know what she's trying to do, but I don't want to discuss this with her. Not here. Not now. Not ever.

"Lissy, I have no problem with you. Don't make one." I enter my stall and close the door. Maybe that was a bitch move. Maybe I just made it worse, but what does she expect? I would much rather we pretend she hasn't had sex with my man.

After using the toilet, I step up to the vanity and wash my hands. Lissy is already done and stands awkwardly off to the side.

"I'll meet you back upstairs." She turns to leave when I keep my eyes in front of me.

"Wait, Lissy," I call back to her before she goes. "I'm not trying to be a bitch. I just really don't want to discuss you and Beau." I reach for the paper towel and dry my hands.

"I get this is the last thing you want to talk about, I do. I just wanted to clear the air. We have mutual friends. I don't want to make it any more awkward."

"Well, consider it clear," I offer her what she needs. She nods once then leaves. I give it a few extra minutes before following her out. I don't make my way straight upstairs, instead opting for the bar instead.

"You okay, Mackenzie?" Jesse asks when I step up to the bar.

"Yeah, just wanted some water." He gives me a wink and asks one of the bartenders to get it for me.

"Congratulations on your engagement. Good job on the rock." I praise his choice and watch him grin.

"She talking about me?"

"Of course." I watch him look up toward the VIP section with a smile on his face.

"Jesse, I need you." One of his staff members calls out taking his attention. I spin around and check out the club. It's a fancy place, probably the hottest place in Rushford to hang out. When I first heard the club owned it, I didn't believe it.

"Mackenzie Morre." A deep voice startles me, sending chills down my spine at the tone he used to call my name.

Fuck, who is this?

"Who's asking?" I question as I twist my body to face them.

"I have a message for you, from Mr. Morre." He steps in closer, invading my space.

"Step the hell back," I grit out, as unease settles around me.

"You're not going to get away with what you've done." My body locks at his words and I swallow past the bile forming at the base of my throat. On the outside I look like I'm holding it together, but on the inside, anxiety rips through me, clouding my conscience worse than it already is.

Oh, God.

"Have your attention now?" I'm about to respond when Jesse steps up beside me.

"Step the fuck back from the lady now, before I fucking make you." Jesse's warning is enough to have the stranger backtracking without another word. I follow his retreat, watching him fade back into the crowd, disappearing out of my sight.

"You all right, Kenz?"

"Yeah." I keep my gaze out on the crowd as an uneasy feeling washes over me.

Is he watching me?

"Hey, you know that guy?" Jesse taps my shoulder, jolting me back. I turn to face the bar and look up at him.

"Haven't seen him before. He just wouldn't take no for an answer." I grab my glass of water and wash down my lie with a large sip.

"You sure? You look like you just saw a ghost." Jesse's eyes narrow slightly, silently assessing me.

"I'm good," I lie again. This time the water doesn't wash it away so well. I wasn't good, but I wasn't about to tell Jesse.

My past flashes before me and I can't stop it.

I'm not safe here anymore. What I've been running from is never going to leave me. I have to get away.

I can't risk my freedom.

Not for Beau or my newfound family.

Past

Mackenzie

"I'M DONE FOR THE NIGHT IF YOU DON'T NEED ANY- thing, Fred?" I hang up my apron and reach for my handbag. It's my second week on the job and Fred, my new boss, has already taken me under his wing.

"You sit down and let me fix you some dinner," he calls out just like every night this week.

"It's really okay, Fred. I want to head out before it gets dark." It's just after six and I know it's going to be dark within the next twenty minutes.

"Don't argue, sweetheart." His graying eyebrows dip low, waiting for me to agree. Knowing it's not going to get me anywhere, I let out a sigh and pull up a spot at the counter. "Good girl," he says then turns, too happy with himself.

It's been three months since the day Beau dropped me off with Larry and Mary. After staying with them for a week, I was moved to Kansas where I lived in a shelter for nine weeks until my cast could come off and I had some strength back in my arm. From there, I finally was able to head out on my own. I hopped on a bus and traveled east, wanting to be as far away from Chad as possible. This small town in Ohio wasn't meant to be a stopping spot for me, but after a mix-up with getting on the wrong bus, I ended up here and decided to settle down. *At least for a while.*

"We need to talk about you walking home alone at night." Fred pulls me out of my head.

"I told you, I can look after myself." I try to shut it down before it goes anywhere. Fred is a good guy and means well. When I first walked into his diner looking for a job, I felt a connection to him, almost like I knew I had ended up there just so I could know him. That's not to say he didn't scare me, the military vibe I got off him, the way he saw past the bullshit lies I fed him to get the job, it made me hold back a little. But then his wife, Carly, walked in, took one look at me and hired me on the spot, even without reading my resume. Since then, both of them have welcomed me into their life like a long lost friend.

"Carly's brother holds these self-defense classes down at the gym. Now that you're settled in, I think you should find yourself at some of them. I'd feel a whole lot better knowing you're protected." He continues to push the subject. He does it a lot. Push the subject. At first it didn't sit right with me, the bossiness almost reminding me too much of Chad, but then I realized it came from such a different place.

"Fred I—" I begin to argue, but I know it's hopeless.

"No, you listen to me. I don't know your past, or what you're hiding from, but I knew the second you walked in here you had a story. I see the way you jump at loud noises, how you're always keeping your eye on the door. Now, I'm not asking you to share, though I hope one day you do, so I know how to be prepared in case someone comes around, but until then you need to protect yourself, sweetheart."

I don't say anything, not sure there really is anything to say. I thought I was doing a good job at pretending I was okay. Clearly, I'm not.

"Just give it some thought. In the meantime, I want you to keep this on your body." He reaches behind his back, pulls out a small handgun and places it in my hand. The cold metal stings my skin and I have to force myself not to recoil.

"Fred this—" I stop when I see him shake his head.

"Do you know how to shoot?" I nod, remembering the few times Heidi took me out to the shooting range back home. It was the first time she saw the aftermath of Chad's rage. When I refused to leave, she made me learn how to shoot.

"Then take it. Humor an old man and get Carly off my back." I want to hand it back, tell him I don't need it because there is no way Chad is going to find me, but I don't because a small part of me knows I'll never be safe.

"Until I start those self-defense classes," I agree, placing the gun in my bag.

His grin grows before he gives me a wink and then turns back to the kitchen, intent on trying to feed me.

I sink back in my chair, annoyed and maybe a little disappointed in myself. Not because I just agreed to take self-defense classes or even because I took the gun. Those things would keep me safe. No, I was disappointed because the one rule I gave myself when I arrived here was to not let anyone in.

I've failed. Fred and Carly are in, whether I like it not.

I just hope it doesn't come back to bite me later.

24

Bean

"THANKS FOR INVITING ME. I HAD SUCH A GOOD TIME."
Kenzie wraps her arms around Kelly and pulls her in for a quick
hug.

"I'm glad you had a good night." Kelly pulls back and starts
talking about some shopping shit for next week.

It's just after midnight, and I received the text from Jesse
twenty minutes ago saying the girls were wrapping their night
up.

"Any trouble?" I turn to Jesse, interrupting his conversation
with Nix.

"Just some creeper hanging around. She said it was nothing,
but she looked a bit spooked." I turn back and watch Kadence
say her goodbye. She would tell us if it was anything to do with

Chad.

"You get a look at him?"

"Yeah, but didn't ring any bells. It didn't seem like she knew him." I catalog the information to talk to her about it later.

"Okay. We're out," I say to them both, done with hanging around. I've been sitting around the club with the boys shooting the shit waiting for the girls to be done. Now they're done, I'm ready to head the fuck home.

"You ready, darlin'?" I step forward, dip my head low and whisper in her ear. She nods, but doesn't speak.

"Night, ladies." I spin us around and head back through the clubhouse to the front door. Kenzie gives one last wave over her shoulder before turning back. "Did you have a good night?" I ask wrapping my arm around her as I steer her out to my bike.

"Yeah," is all she says, stepping up to my bike and reaching for her helmet.

"You okay?" I place my hand under her chin and force her to look up at me.

"Just tired." She pulls back and diverts her eyes.

The fuck?

Something about her reaction isn't sitting well with me, but I don't push, wanting to get us safely home.

"Then let's take you home, darlin'." I climb on and wait for her to slide forward. It only takes a short second for her to wrap herself around me close. I start my bike, rev the throttle a few times before taking off.

The whole ride has my mind trying to figure out what the hell is up her ass. By the time we pull up to the front of my house, my unease only grows when she slides off and heads straight toward the door.

273

"Kenzie, what the fuck is going on?" I call out as she steps up onto the porch. She doesn't answer this time. Pushing her key into the lock, she steps inside, leaving me standing there.

Climbing off my bike, I take the steps two at a time. I follow her inside, down the hall and into my room.

"The fuck? What the hell is up your ass, darlin'?" I try to rack my brain trying to figure out what could have upset her in the last few hours.

Lissy?

"You have words with Lissy tonight?" I ask, watching her step out of her sexy-as-fuck heels. Her body reacts to Lissy's name and I zone in on it.

"What the fuck happened? If she spewed her shit—"

"She just wanted to clear the air. That's it." She pushes past me and moves to the bathroom.

"This why you're pissy?" I follow behind her, still not getting it. Apparently, I didn't make it clear just how much Lissy is not on my fucking radar.

"I'm not pissy. Can you just leave me alone? I told you I'm tired. Keep pushing me and it's only going to piss me off." She stops at the door, preventing me from entering. I hold her stare, and honestly it's written all over her face. This is so much bigger than Lissy.

"Don't fucking shut down on me now, darlin'." She recoils, her head snapping back at my voice, but she only looks blankly up at me.

"Beau, I told you nothing happened. I'm just tired." She forces some fake bullshit smile then reaches for the door. Attempting to shut it.

Yeah, like that's fucking happening.

"You're not acting like nothing happened." I place my hand on the door, stopping it from separating us. "You're acting like you're lost in your head, darlin'." I rest my shoulder against the doorframe and watch her step back.

"You need to leave me alone."

"Not until you tell me what's happening here. I'm kind of fucking clueless right now." Her arms come around the front of her, wrapping herself tightly.

"You're keeping something from me." Her body stills for a brief second before she quickly hides her reaction.

"You think you know everything." She spins on her heel, moving to the shower and pulling the door open. I watch her sharp, angry movements. She starts the shower, steps back, and tears the zip down on her dress.

Willing myself not to get hard, she practically rips it from her body, unclasping her bra and throwing it on the floor.

"You just have to push and push." Her panties go next. "Can't I just be tired? Can't I just have a moment? Fucking men just have to push. You're just like him." Her whole demeanor has flipped. *This isn't Mackenzie talking.*

"Maybe I don't want to talk about it. Did you think about that?" She twists back to face me, completely naked. "Did you? I don't have to talk to you about everything, you know. You don't get to tell me how I can feel, how to act." She pulls the glass door open and steps under the stream of the water. She dips her head back, letting the water soak through her hair. Her tits push out as she raises her hands to her hair. I don't know if I want to laugh or spank the fuck out of her ass right now.

"Are you done?" I ask when my cock decides he's done with this bullshit play.

Her eyes open as I take three steps toward her. "Are you?" She narrows her gaze when I rip my shirt over my head.

"Not even fucking close to being done, darlin'." I toe off my boots, flick the button on my jeans then pull them down.

"Beau." She steps back when I open the glass door.

"Turn around, put your hands on the tiles, and don't move them." I spin her before she can argue and guide her hands over her head, firmly placing them against the wall. "Don't you ever fucking put me in the same head space as that piece of shit." I step in close to her, my front to her back.

"I didn't mean it." Her whisper is unsure as it echoes around the small shower.

"Don't give a fuck. I'm not him. Never will be." Her head drops forward, chin tucked into her breastbone.

"I know. I'm a bitch. I didn't mean to say it." I press into her closer, my cock now rock hard.

"You're not. But you're gonna tell me what the fuck is happening here." I lean in closer, my mouth to her ear.

"I don't know."

"Don't feed me bullshit. I'm not fucking stupid. This have something to do with Lissy?"

"No. No, it's not her. It's me." She gives me something to work with. "Maybe this is moving too fast for me."

"You freaking out?" I keep her pinned to the shower wall. Her hands still above her head. I'm confused. She's showed no signs of pulling back in the last week. Not for one second have I thought I've pushed her too far.

Until tonight.

"Maybe. I don't know." She shakes her head. Almost like she's as confused as I am. My head is telling me she's full of shit, but my body steps back giving her space. "Wait." She turns back to face me. Her eyes grow wide in panic. "Jesus, I don't know what I'm saying." She shakes her head again.

"Nothing's changed here, darlin'. We go at your speed." She bites her lip and I can practically see the wheels turning in her head.

"I'm sorry. I really am tired. The girls were on my case all night. Then the thing with Lissy. I'm just getting lost in my head." She steps up to me this time.

"Nothing to be sorry for. You want to cool things down. I get it." I wrap my arms around her. I still don't understand what made her flip like this, but I don't push. I've already pushed too far tonight.

"I don't know what I want." She speaks into my chest, and it's probably the most honest thing she's said all night.

"Come on. Let's get you to bed." I decide to end this conversation, at least for now. Whatever she's stewing over isn't going to go away tonight. I've already tried to bring her out of it and was unsuccessful. I'll let it go this evening, but *tomorrow* is a new day.

I reach forward and turn off the water. We step out of the shower, and I wrap her in a towel before grabbing one for myself. She lets me take the lead, drying her off before moving her back to my bed. We don't say another word as we dress for bed. Unsure of what I'm looking at with our situation, I let her run things. She heads back to the bathroom and dries her hair. I climb between the sheets and wait to see if she comes to me. After everything else tonight, I wouldn't be surprised if she made her way back to her room. If it happens, I'll follow. Five minutes later, she steps out of the bathroom and comes to my bed.

I don't show my relief. Instead, I pull the blanket back and let her climb in.

She settles, still keeping the silence, so I turn the light off, bathing the room in darkness. Another five minutes go by and she finally shifts, rolling to face me.

"Beau, I'm falling in love with you. And maybe that's too soon to say, or too soon for you to hear, but I need you to know." She rests her palm over my naked chest.

"Darlin'—" I begin, but she cuts me off.

"I didn't tell you so you can say it back. I just wanted you to know."

Jesus, I'm on a rollercoaster right now. Ups and downs, and fucking looping everywhere.

"Okay," I whisper, pulling her closer to me. The urge to tell her back is strong, but I don't. Not because I don't feel the same way. Fuck, I think I fell in love with her the second she walked into the clubhouse. No, I don't say it back because something's not right. It's almost like she had to tell me before it was too late.

But too late for what?

An unease settles over me, and digs in so deep I know it isn't going away. She's up to something and I don't know what the fuck it is, but I'm sure as hell going to find out.

Sooner or later I *am* going to find out.

Past

Mackenzie

"I'M OUT FRED!" I SHOUT, REACHING FOR MY BAG.

"If you wait ten minutes, I'll take you home," he yells back, but it's the last thing I want. Not tonight. I just want to go home after my long shift.

"No, it's fine. I'm beat. I just want the quickest way into a shower so I can crawl into bed."

Fred pokes his head around the corner and lowers his brows. I can see he intends to argue with me.

"Leave her alone, Fred. She's just down the road," Carly starts on him before he starts on me.

We've been having the same argument since I've been working. Even with the gun and self-defense classes, he's still overprotective.

"I know she's just down the road, Carly." He shakes his head at his wife, then levels his eyes back on me. "You still having problems with your new neighbor?" He changes tactics. "I can stop by and have a word with him." Fred has become my self-appointed father, Carly my mother. They have been so good to me the last fifteen months. I hate keeping them at a distance.

"I spoke to him yesterday. He said he's going to turn the level down a little." I fill him in on my neighbor drama.

"He doesn't, I'll pay him a visit." He nods to himself. I don't argue with him about it. There are some battles you just won't win with Fred. This will be another one.

"Okay, Fred." I try to keep the frustration out of my voice. "Bye, Carly. See you tomorrow."

"Night," she calls back and I make my way to the front door.

"Girly, wait." Fred stops me before I can step outside. "You call me if you need anything. Any time."

"Will do," I promise, before closing the door.

The walk home is quick. Living only two blocks from where I work has come in handy. Especially since I haven't saved enough to buy my own car yet, much to Fred and Carly's displeasure.

The last fifteen months in Ohio have been... I want to say great, but I would be lying. It's been comfortable.

It's not that I don't like it here. I've grown close with Carly and Fred, and I enjoy working at their diner. It's just that I'm not truly happy.

The hiding my past, the not knowing when it will catch up with me, the fear he's going to find me. It's like I'm a caged bird desperate to be freed, and if I were honest, I'm over it.

I continue to dwell on my predicament as I take three steps up to my small one-bedroom apartment. I wish I could just push it all out, relax and maybe breathe easy, but I can't. I can't allow myself to become complacent. Not when he could find me any day.

"Snap out of it." I give myself a talking to as I reach the top of the stairs. *"No more."* I shake my head just as I notice the doormat slightly off center.

What the hell? My senses flare as I check my surroundings.

I live on the bottom level of a low-rise apartment building. With only one level above me, I hardly ever see my neighbor, but it doesn't mean I don't hear him.

Max is a twenty-something-year-old gamer, who only moved in a few months back. Since then, it's been hard to get a decent night's sleep with the amount of noise coming out of his apartment.

Tonight it's quiet, which tells me he's either not in yet or he took my friendly noise complaint serious. Time will tell.

After doing a quick check of my surroundings I decide it's my mind playing tricks on me. Kicking it back in place, I unlock the door and step inside. Everything looks normal and in place. The flowers on the table I picked up yesterday fill the room with a sweet floral scent. Relaxing into my nightly routine, I kick off my shoes, and place my bag down on the sofa, heading straight for the fridge to fill a large glass with my favorite wine.

After nibbling on some cheese, I take my glass to the bathroom and fill the tub. I strip off my clothes and waste no time sinking into the hot water.

Today's been a busy day. The hot water eases the tension in

my muscles and the wine relaxes my mind. This has become my standard routine every night. Wine. Bath. Bed.

After soaking for thirty minutes, the apartment walls start to shake with vibrations of gunfire and explosions, letting me know Max is in fact home.

Great. He didn't take me serious.

Knowing I'm not going to be able to relax with the noise, I decide to call it a night. I stand and wrap a towel around my body. Not bothering with drying off completely, I take my glass and head to my room only to stop dead in my tracks.

"Hello, Mackenzie." The wine glass falls to the carpet as his voice runs through me, and my world comes crashing around me.

"Ch-Chad?" My knees lock as I take in his form lying on my bed. His eyes rake over my body before coming to meet mine. I've been waiting for this moment the last eighteen months. Dreamed about how I would react, *if* I would react. But now that he's here, it's like it's not real.

"Do you know how long I've been looking for you?" His jaw ticks and his eyes flash with something I've never seen before. It's almost crazed. Feral.

"How did you find me?" I still haven't moved. I'm dripping with water, wrapped in a small towel. My heart pounds rapidly in my chest, almost as loud as the noise coming from Max's apartment.

"Fuck, it wasn't easy. You, sweetheart, have cost me a fucking arm and leg trying to find you. I almost had you in Arizona when you called Heidi." My pulse drums in my ears. *Heidi.*

"What did you do to her?" My mind runs a mile a minute.

He wouldn't dare.

"I didn't come all this way to talk about that bitch. Can you tell me why you need a gun, Mackenzie?" Chad throws his legs off the side of the bed and stands, pointing a gun at me.

Shit, he has my gun.

I weigh up my options. I could scream for help, but no one would hear me over Max's game. I could run, but won't get very far, or I can fight him.

Before I can unstick my legs, he's moving toward me. Acting on bad instinct, I react. Spinning in my spot, I hold onto my towel and try to make a run for it.

"I don't think so, Mackenzie." Chad races behind me, his hand snaking out, fisting my hair and pulling me back. "You and I have things we need to discuss," he seethes, tightening his grip. I fight back, reaching over my shoulders and slapping him. He recoils, letting me go, but before I can pull away he slaps me hard, a stinging sensation covers my cheek. I drop to the floor from the force, my towel falling away from my body, exposing me.

Reaching for the towel, I leave myself open. Not missing his chance, he delivers a kick to my side. Air leaves my lungs in a sharp thud before my long lost friend, pain, comes to visit.

Knowing I can't cower, I roll to the side, give up the towel and find my balance as I stand up. I need to keep myself up if I'm going to have any chance.

"You've ruined my life long enough." He reaches for me again, but I shift out of his way. I just need to get the gun out of his hands.

"Please, Chad," I beg as I back out of my room. I don't know why I think it will work, but I need to try something.

"None of this had to happen, Mackenzie." He follows me out, not chasing me, but drawing out my panic.

"You're right. It didn't then and it doesn't now. Please put the gun down and we can talk this through," I try to reason. Maybe if he believes I want to work things out, I might have a shot at this.

"You've made my life hell the last eighteen months. Do you know what people are saying? The rumors that spread because of what you did? I had to file for divorce. Make it out that I divorced you for abandoning me. *You* fucking did this." A wave of relief and sadness washes over me knowing we're no longer married. *Can he even do that?*

"You know what we had was unhealthy, Chad." I attempt to talk to him, not at him.

"How can you say that? I fucking love you." He steps forward, gun raised. His eyes are frenzied, his hands shaking. "You fucking left me." Another step closer.

"Please, Chad." It's almost surreal. After running for so long, this is what it comes down to.

"You promised me till death do us part. Remember, Mackenzie?" My back finds the wall as the gun finds my chest. "I've come to make sure you honor our vows."

25

Mackenzie

"BEAU?" I WHISPER A FEW HOURS AFTER I PRETENDED to fall asleep. Beau doesn't stir so I quickly slip out of his bed and sneak back into my room to grab the small emergency backpack I've kept since living here.

I didn't want to have to do this, but there is no other way. I can't let this come out. My only option is to get out of town.

The house is quiet as I tiptoe down the hall and make my escape. I don't spare a second glance at the home Beau offered me. My only desire is to get out. It's like I'm on autopilot, my mind emotionally bankrupt. There is nothing left to say. With each stride, my resolution grows. It's as if the distance from the safety of Beau's arms gives me more clarity. The truth is, since I've been back, I've invented every excuse for staying, when I should have got the hell out of here. I've been living a lie, a beautiful lie, with fake hope. I know Beau is going to be pissed, but I also know he's not going to understand. I can't have people looking for me here. I need to make a clean break and go back on the run.

Making it to the front door, I don't spare one last look before flicking the lock and slowly opening the door. The glow from the full moon is enough to guide me along the porch and down the stairs.

I'm not sure where I'm going, or how I'm going to get there, all I know is I have to get out of here before anyone finds out.

"Mackenzie?" My name from Beau's mouth startles me as I take my first step on the grass. "What the fuck are you doing?"

"I- I." I take a breath and gather my thoughts. "I have to go."

"The fuck, Kenzie? You're not going anywhere." His brows are bent in and his fists clench at his side. I don't think I've ever seen him look so angry. Before tonight, it would have scared me to see it on him, but knowing what might happen if I stay, I can't let it bother me.

"I need to go, Beau." I shake my head, not sure if I need to clear it, or to stop him from arguing.

"Talk to me, darlin'." He changes tactics, stepping forward, trying to move closer.

"I have to do this, Beau. I have to go," I rush out my words. The early morning air bites at my skin, but my body is hot with fear.

"Why do you need to go, Mackenzie?" He takes another step, and this time I retreat.

"You won't understand. Just let me go."

"I can't do that, Mackenzie. I won't."

"If you care for me, you will." I know I'm reaching, and it's not going to help me, but I can't just give up.

"Not fucking happening. You don't know me very well if you think that's gonna work on me."

"I need to do this."

"You don't know what you need." He keeps coming at me, pushing and drawing me back at every angle.

"Oh, and you do?" I lash out, done with this back and forth.

"Yes, I fucking do. I've been giving you what you need since you've been back."

"Right, because I'm this weak woman, right? I couldn't possibly know how to look after myself."

"Don't put words in my mouth, Mackenzie." His eyes flick up to the road as a car travels down it.

"No, you didn't have to, Beau."

"What the fuck is really going on here?" His arms fold over his chest, forcing the muscles to compress under his shirt. To anyone looking on it might seem concerning, a male exerting his power to intimidate me, but I know that's not the case.

"I have to leave. It's not safe for me anymore."

"So you're running?"

"I'm just protecting you, Beau." He laughs a short, unimpressed laugh, as if the thought is ridiculous. "So you're gonna walk out in the middle of the night, without a goodbye. That's what I fucking deserve?"

"No, you deserve so much more, but I knew you wouldn't let me go."

"You're fucking right I'm not letting you go. I've already let you go once. I ain't doing it again. Not when Chad is still out there."

"You just don't get it." My hands move to my temples, trying to force the pressure down. The lies and the deceit build ten-fold as the man I love stands in front of me, oblivious to what I have done. Visions of that night start to weigh me down, distorting my present with the horrible past. "Kenzie." I hear his voice trying to break through.

"I killed him, okay. He's gone. He's not coming back for me. He never was. I made it up. It was a lie. I even tricked myself into believing he was really still out there when I knew. I fucking knew he wasn't." My breathing halts as the horrible moment I took his life takes over and the ugly truth spills from my lips.

"Kenzie, listen to what you're saying." He takes the last step to me, our eyes connecting as we come chest to chest.

"I did it, Beau. I killed him. It was me or him." My mind starts to slip into the darkness. The truth is just too much for me. I close my eyes and try to breathe through it, but it feels as if a weight has been dropped on my chest, turning my once strong breaths into short, shallow blasts of air.

"Stay with me, Kenz. Just breathe. Deep breaths." I hear the softness of Beau's voice trying to calm me before I'm thrown back to the night my past and present clashed, changing the course of my life forever.

Past

Mackenzie

"YOU PROMISED ME TILL DEATH DO US PART. REMEMBER, Mackenzie? I've come to make sure you honor our vows." A coldness washes over me at the spitefulness in his voice. I shake my head, clearing my mind and body of the fear. *Don't show him you're scared. He feeds off it.* Taking a deep breath, I decide at that moment if I don't fight, I'm going to die.

Using my self-defense techniques, I kick out and connect my knee to his balls, while my hand punches his wrist. He falls forward but doesn't drop the gun. Risking it again, I kick his wrist. This time, the gun slips from his fingers and I dive for it. Just as my fingers wrap around the prize, he rolls me over and pins me with his lower body.

"Why do you keep fighting?" Spit hits my face as the words

escape his clenched teeth. "Why couldn't you let me love you the way I needed to love you?" His disgusting breath hits my face as he leans down closer to my lips. He's so wrapped up spilling his hate and trying to kiss me, he's oblivious to the gun in my hand.

You have to do it, Mackenzie. I look into his eyes and I see the man I fell in love with, the soft man who promised me the world. But then I remember everything he's done. Everything he's put me through. Every bruised cheek caused by a slap to the face, every broken bone and concussion, every black eye, busted lip, and bloody nose and I realize he never loved me, and he would never change. The man who I married was a lie, simply a persona created to fool the world.

"Because I don't love you, Chad." Dread slithers over me, numbing me to what is about to happen. Thick fingers pinch into the soft skin of my neck, and restrict my airways. Black mist swirls around the edge of my mind, drawing me into the sanctity of a peaceful darkness. Maybe this is where I need to be. Maybe I can't fight anymore. Just as my resolve becomes clear, his fingers tighten and the darkness embraces me, promising me an end to all the ugliness.

"If I can't have you, Mackenzie, then no one will." His words are laced with venom and instead of letting them pass, my mind rebuts them.

Why does he get to decide that?

The inky swirls darken, trying to blanket me, but my mind fights it.

This isn't what I've been fighting for, just to give up when he says I have to. All the people who helped me survive deserved more. *I* deserve more.

My stomach lurches and adrenaline swirls. The once comforting darkness instead smothers me, like a musty damp blanket clinging to me. I want to scream out, not in fear or panic, but in a roar of victory.

I can't let him win.

I *won't* let him win.

With fierce resolution, I point the gun at his chest and fire.

Bang.

The recoil shocks me, vibrating through my body as the sound gets lost in the jolting resonance coming from Max's apartment above me.

I fire again.

Bang.

My chest heaves as if bound by rope, straining to inflate my lungs. Everything stills, almost frozen in time and our life together flashes through my eyes.

Each physical and emotional hit to my very being holds me in the past.

"You're a slut, Mackenzie. A whore of a wife. You make me crazy. Why do you make me do this to you? No one will ever love you like me. I will never let you go. I will always find you."

Bang.

Chad's fingers relax, and I drag large gasps of air down. He makes no move for the gun. He just hovers over me, a lost faraway look settling in his eyes.

"I'm sorry," I rasp, wishing it didn't have to come to this, wishing I hadn't just become the same monster as him.

"Ma—Macken—Mackenzie," he gurgles. Deep red blood drips from his mouth and rolls down his chin.

"I'm so sorry. I'm so sorry." My body racks in sobs as his

full weight pushes into me. I shove him off and roll away from him. The tears continue to roll down my cheeks, the wine and cheese I had earlier comes up in violent waves, burning my throat like acid.

I'm so sorry.

I repeat the words over and over, but I'm not sure if I'm saying them because I'm truly sorry for shooting him or if I'm apologizing to myself for becoming a killer.

"I'm so sorry."

I say the words aloud this time, but they're a lie, just like our marriage. Just like our love.

26

Beau

"I DID IT, BEAU. I KILLED HIM." HER BREATHING BE-
comes erratic as she paces in front of me. "I pulled the trigger."

"Calm your breathing, Kenz. Slow it down." She doesn't
listen. Her panic grows as she revisits the night in her head.

"I didn't know what to do. He had a gun, Beau. He had the
gun pointing right at me." Not wanting to lose her to a panic
attack, I reach forward and pick her up. "Come on, darlin'. Let's
get you back inside." She folds into my chest as sobs rip
through her.

Jesus, fuck. What the fuck is happening here?

I knew something was up. I didn't know what, but when I
felt her shift off me, I waited to see what she was going to do.
The last thing I expected her to do was run.

"Beau, I have to go." I ignore her as we step back inside the house. I make sure I lock up before taking her back to my room.

"Please, Beau. You don't understand." She's right. I can barely understand her past the sobbing. I know she thinks this is what she needs, but the woman can barely walk.

"No, you're right. I don't. You're going to make me understand, though." We walk down the hall and into my bedroom, and then move over to my bed.

"I killed him, Beau. I took a man's life." Her tears come faster as she starts to fight my hold on her.

"I have that part, darlin'. Now tell me what happened after you shot him?" I shift her off me so I can see her face.

"I freaked out. There was so much blood. He wasn't breathing. I only had Fred to turn to."

"Fred? Who's Fred?" My mind zeros in on the name Fred as I try to piece everything together. To say I'm fucking shocked would be an understatement. I think back over the past few months and her comments about Chad, about moving on, her reaction whenever he was brought up. And it all starts to make sense. How I didn't see it before now is beyond me, but now the truth is looking right at me.

"My boss at the diner. He's good people. Him and his wife, Carly, took me under their wing like a daughter. He came right away and said he would help me. He told me to pack a bag and he put me on the next bus out of town."

Fucking hell.

"Jesus, Mackenzie. You just left?" I barely manage to rein in my shock, anger and disappointment that she didn't call me, but somehow I do.

"I was scared, Beau." She shakes her head. "I was worried someone would find me. I told Fred about Chad's connections, about his dad and everything he's covered up in the past and he thought it was best to get out of there."

"So what happened then? Why would you come here?"

"I wasn't going to at first, but then Fred didn't think I would be okay on my own, so he said to come back to you for help. He was right. I wouldn't have been able to go it alone. I needed help. I was going to tell you. I swear, but then I thought if Fred did what he said he would, I would be safe. I wanted to wait, see if anyone came for me. So I waited, and I waited some more, and when they didn't, I didn't know how to tell you."

"So you made me believe Chad was going to hurt you?" She looks up, eyes red, nose running and I have to stand from the bed before I take her in my arms and tell her it's okay. Because it's not okay. She fucking lied to me, right to my face. Not only me, but all my brothers as well. "We had people looking out for you, darlin'. Had eyes on you. The fucking club pulled so much shit to keep you out of his sight." I'm angry, fucking furious, but at the same time, I understand it. Fuck, I understand it. *You wanted her to fight and she did.*

"It was wrong. I know. I'll never forgive myself, but I needed someone who would help me. I had nowhere else to go and the last thing you said to me was if I needed anything..." She stands and reaches for my hand. I let her take it, knowing she is right. I did tell her if she needed anything to find me. I meant it then just like I still mean it now.

"I know, darlin'. But fuck, Kenz. You should have told me this. Straight out."

"I know. I screwed up, Beau, which is why I was leaving. I

295

didn't want you in on any of this. Now someone knows."

"Who knows?"

"At the club tonight, I was paid a visit."

"By who?" I press for more.

"A man, I don't know who. He said Mr. Morre had a message. He said, 'You're not going to get away with it.' He knows, he knows Chad's missing. He must know I had something to do with it." *The man Jesse told me about.*

Jesus, fuck.

I drop her hand and take a seat back on the bed.

Could this situation be any more fucked up?

"How well do you know this Fred? You think he talked?" Kenzie takes a seat next to me.

"No, he wouldn't. I only spoke to him a couple of weeks ago."

"You've been keeping in contact?" I remember her talking to someone one night on the phone, but she told me it was her old landlord.

Jesus, fuck, the woman has been lying with everything.

"I've checked in twice since being here. He took me in, made sure I was protected. He covered it up. He wouldn't do that to me." I can see how much she believes it, but I don't know the fucker from a bar of soap. Who knows who he could have told already.

"So if he didn't say anything, then who?" I put it back on her.

"I haven't told a soul. No one knows but Fred, and now you."

"So why run tonight if Fred cleaned it up and the Mayor has nothing on you? He's fucking with you then."

"What else can I do, Beau?" Her hands drop by her side.

"I don't know, darlin'. Fucking fight? Keep fighting." I want to fucking shake her. Kiss her. Fuck her. I don't fucking know, but I need her to see where I am coming from.

"I'm so over fighting, Beau. I don't know if I can do it anymore."

"Kenzie." I place my hands on either side of her face and force her to stop talking and listen. "Don't ever say that. Ever. You hear me." I shake her a little and her hands cover mine.

"He's always going to be inside here." She presses down over my hands, indicating her head.

"Only if you let him, baby, only if you let him. You did what you had to do. You fought. And you won. He can't hurt you anymore if you don't let him."

"But I've done a horrible thing. I'm not even sorry, Beau. He deserved it. He deserved more. And it just makes me sick to my stomach. It eats at me because I'm no better than him."

I close my eyes to gather myself. This woman. *Fuck, this woman.*

"Darlin', you didn't choose that. Your choice was taken from you. He took it from you when he pointed the gun at you. You fought to stay alive. Anyone would say the same. You didn't have to run."

"Beau, but his family—"

"I understand why you did it." I cut her off. She didn't have to run, but I know why she did. All the corruption this family lives in I don't blame her. Fuck, no one would. "You're not an evil person. You survived. I wish you could see yourself the way I do." My thumb wipes away at a lone tear as it rolls down her cheek. I press my lips to hers. They're wet from her tears, but I kiss her anyway, wanting to take it all away from her.

"You're fucking amazing, you know that?" She closes her eyes, almost like it hurts her to hear it. "Look at me."

Her eyes open and I pull back a little.

"I love you, Mackenzie. I fell in love with you the second you walked back into my life."

"You don't have to say it back to me." She tries to pull out of my hold, but I don't let her.

"I fucking love you, darlin'. You amaze me every day. You're the strongest woman I know. I'm not letting this beat you. I'm going to fix this." Her tears fall freely and it fucking guts me. Kissing each of them, I continue to take them away.

"How? This isn't going to go away." She thinks it won't, but I'll make it. Now I know Chad is dead, I don't give a fuck what I have to do to keep this covered up. This shit won't come back to her. Not by the time I'm done.

"Well, first off, I need to go visit this Fred. Make sure he's as trustworthy as you say he is." I release her face then take her hand, pulling her with me as I lay back on the bed.

"He is, Beau. I swear."

"I believe you, darlin', but I'm still going to visit him. He covered this up for you. I need to meet this man, make sure we're on the same page. From there, I'll decide our next step. Until then you're at the clubhouse." She doesn't argue with me on the clubhouse rule, and I'm grateful. I don't think I can deal with it tonight. Not after everything we just went through. "Now sleep. I'm beat. Everything will look better in the morning." I reach over and flick the lamp off, blanketing the room in darkness. She lets out a soft sigh, before snuggling in closer.

"I'm sorry I lied to you. I didn't want this between us. And I'm so sorry I lied to the club." Her voice cracks, and it almost breaks me. "You all gave me a second chance, made me feel safe. I didn't want my ugliness to touch you."

"You gotta know I still would have protected you either way, darlin'." Yeah, I'm pissed she kept it from me, but how could I be pissed at what she did? I couldn't, not when I'm so fucking proud of her. Proud of what she did to save herself.

"I love you, Beau. I don't deserve you. Everything you have done for me is too much."

"Don't speak that shit to me again," I growl, pissed she doesn't see herself the way I see her. "You deserve more. Fuck, you deserve everything, then some. If anyone doesn't deserve this, it's me. Now sleep." I drop my head close to her until my nose finds her skin and I breathe her in.

Fuck, I could have lost her tonight. I nearly did.

Nausea swarms in my gut, and my heart struggles to keep a steady beat. The fact she was willing to walk out like that taunts me, her words replaying like an echo.

You deserve so much more.

I know she thinks she was doing the right thing, but she has to know by now I will never let her leave.

Ever.

Knowing this is far from over, I force myself to keep my head clear. Tomorrow, shit is going down, but tonight, I will hold her and comfort her until her tears dry up and every ounce of guilt she's been carrying drifts away.

Maybe one day she will see just how much she deserves this and then realize I'm not enough, but until that day comes, I am going to give her what she needs. And right now, she needs grace. Grace for taking a monster's life.

And I am going to give it to her.

If anyone deserves it, it's her.

"So you want to go to Ohio, walk into some small town diner looking for a guy named Fred, and ask if he covered up a murder?" Jesse summarizes everything I just told the table, making it sound more fucking crazy than I am right now. It's the morning after Mackenzie told me her secret. After tossing and turning all night, I decided I needed to bring the guys in on this to get their perspective. After all, Mayor Morre could know more than I think he knows and then we'd all be in more shit.

"Need to know this Fred can be trusted. I don't want anything coming back on her."

"You don't want to call Jackson in on this?" he presses.

"Jesse, she fucking killed him then covered it up. Yeah, let's bring the fucking cops in on this, asshole." I shake my head, not in the mood for his shit today.

"I'm sorry. I didn't realize we were back on the other side of the law," he fires back with the same attitude.

"What the fuck is that supposed to mean?" I turn in my seat and give him my full attention. If he even suggests we call this in again, I'll fucking lay him out.

"He means we all like Mackenzie, Beau. But she killed someone. The Mayor's son at that. Then she came back and lied to us all. You really okay with this?" Sy enters the conversation.

"The fucker terrorized her. Beat her to the point she had to run. You think he was looking for her so they could have a fucking candle-lit dinner? He was going to kill her. Regardless of how you or I see it, she did what she felt she had to do in order to survive. So yes, I'm fucking okay with her taking the asshole's life."

"Yeah, and if she stayed, she could have had a better chance of fixing this," Jesse keeps pushing. He just doesn't comprehend it. How could he? His woman hasn't been in Mackenzie's shoes and never will be.

"But she didn't, okay. You can fucking judge her all you want, but we're still going to help her."

"Boss?" Jesse turns to Nix. "You gonna weigh in on this clusterfuck anytime soon?"

"You know what, fuck you, Jesse." I stand, pushing my chair back, done with his shit. I was stupid to think bringing them in on this would be good. Should have just handled it on my own without a single fucking word to them.

"Beau, wait—" Nix calls out, but I'm not hearing it. I didn't come to them for a fucking vote. I came to them for help.

"No, I'm done. This club has done so much shit for everyone sitting at this table. I get it. I really fucking do. We've pulled ourselves out of hell. We don't need this kind of heat. But we are not calling the cops. I'd take the fall before I see her do time for this."

"You're fucking crazy," Jesse scoffs.

"No, he's in love," Hunter counters and my eyes fall on him.

Fuck me, the little fucker gets it.

"She was ready to run to keep us safe. I'm not okay with that. She fucking leaves, I go with her." The table falls silent at my admission and I take the moment to calm my breathing.

301

"You'd do the same for Holly." I turn to Sy, already knowing his answer.

"Fucking A," is his reply.

"Kadence?" I twist back to Nix.

"Don't even have to ask."

I look to Brooks and point him an expectant stare. He nods, giving me his answer. I skip over Hunter, knowing he doesn't have a woman and look back to Jesse.

"I'd do the same for Bell, but she's my woman." He cocks his brow, just pushing me the only way he can.

"Mackenzie is my fucking woman, cockhead!" I all but scream at him.

"So you love her?" Jesse smirks. If I could reach him without moving, I'd punch him.

"Keep up, asshole." I shake my head at his deep laugh. "Nix, I'm not asking for your permission here, not when it comes to her." He gets me. I know he does. But he still takes a minute before speaking.

"Take Hunter with you. We'll keep an eye on her." He gives me his approval, but in all honesty, this would have happened with or without it.

I turn my attention to Hunter, nodding for him to get up.

"I'm leaving in ten. Grab what you need now." He doesn't need to be told twice. He moves out of the room without a word.

"Anything else?" I look back at Nix.

"Don't fuck this up," is all he says before coming to stand. The rest of them follow him up and come toward me. Sy smirks at me and slaps my back as he passes.

"Welcome to the other side." And maybe it's the adrenaline

running through me, but I miss the punch line.

"What side?" I call after him.

"Where you do stupid shit for pussy," Nix answers, passing me next.

"Fuck, been there since she walked into my life," I admit, then listen to them all laugh.

"Not like I haven't been telling you this since the night we picked her up," Sy shouts back.

"Yeah, I'm finally listening," I tell him as Jesse passes. Remembering how much he pissed me off, I land my fist into his arm. "That's for being a fuckhead."

"Love you too, bro." He barely flinches, continuing his exit.

I contemplate going in for a second punch but let it go. I told Hunter ten minutes. The sooner we have this done, the sooner it's over, and we're back in Rushford.

27

Mackenzie
five days later

"YOU DOING OKAY, KELL?" I ASK, WATCHING HER SORT through piles of paperwork. It's almost opening week for Missy's Place and with Beau away dealing with the mess I left back in Ohio, Kelly is here trying to get it all sorted.

"Yeah, just hoping I can pull this off. With Beau away, it's double the stress."

"I'm sorry." I cringe, hating that my drama is only messing this up for both Kelly and Beau.

"Don't be silly. He needed to go. I'm just being dramatic." She tries to soothe me, but it doesn't help. When Beau told me he was heading to meet Fred, I begged him to take me with him. He didn't think it was a good idea, and even though I understand why, it doesn't make it easy knowing he's there and

I'm here.

"Well, if it's any consolation, I'm here for you." It's the least I can do.

"And I'm going to use you. We have to have all this un-packed today." I follow her gaze around the room and prepare myself for some hard work.

"Okay, well, where do you want me to start?" I stand from the chair and move toward the huge living area.

"Let's just work through each room, starting in the living room. We can stop for lunch around twelve and hopefully finish up this afternoon."

"Got it," I tell her, but before I can start, my phone beeps from my back pocket. Pulling it out, I let out a breath when I see it's from Beau.

Beau: Two hours out, darlin'. See you soon.

I quickly type back, my mind running wild with what he found out.

Me: Is everything okay?

Beau: Everything's good. Will talk more when I'm home.

I smile at the text and let out a long breath. I'm assuming 'everything's good' means he met with Fred and we have nothing to worry about.

"Beau?" Kelly notices my reaction.

"Yeah, he's two hours out." I pocket my phone, my day

now perking up.

"Did he say if he found Chad?" I swallow at the mention of his name.

Kelly and the girls don't know about Chad or what I did, and I want to keep it that way.

Having Nix and the rest of the guys know is bad enough. To say they were pissed would be an understatement.

After Beau left with Hunter to see Fred, Nix sat me down and expressed how unimpressed the club was that I had lied to them all. I knew it was coming. Beau was too kind to me to really tell me how angry he was, but Nix didn't offer me the same grace. And rightly so. I lied to them, to everyone, and it wasn't my intention to fall in love with Beau. It happened. But I should have told them sooner. After, he ripped me a new one, made it clear we are family, and that family look after each other. He followed it up with a hug and a warning not to fuck with Beau's heart. I didn't need the warning, but I took it. It was the least I could do.

"I'm not sure." I divert my gaze so she doesn't pick up on my unease.

"I'm sure he has. He wouldn't be heading home without a resolution for you." Kelly pulls me out of my head.

"Yeah." I nod because she's right. It's just the way Beau is, always taking care of me.

After chatting for a few more minutes, we start work pulling open all the boxes and setting up. We don't talk about anything deep, keeping the conversation light and easy. I'm grateful for it. My mind is still messed up with what Beau has to say. The day passes us quickly and before we know it, we've missed lunch.

"Oh, God, it's after one." Kelly looks up when we finish unpacking the third room.

"You want me to go pick something up from the diner?" I ask, taking in all the work we've managed so far. The living area, kitchen and dining room are all set up. Warm tones, dark wood, and brown leather furniture makes the house more homier, welcoming even. I can already see women here, getting the help they need after leaving dangerous situations.

"I should probably go. You stay here." Since Beau has been away, I've been staying at the clubhouse and have had an escort to and from wherever I go. Now Beau is on his way back with what I can only assume is good news, I barely think there's anything to worry about.

"I'll be fine, Kell. It's less than a block away. I have my phone." I scoop up my bag, starving for food. "What do you want?" I pull out my phone and open up the memo app.

"I'll have the California grilled chicken and a diet Pepsi, please." She starts picking up the empty boxes.

"Okay, I'll be back." I flick the lock on the front door and push it open. "Lock the door behind me."

"Got it," she calls back and I wait for her to click the lock.

The cool November air nips at my skin. I wrap my cardigan around my body tighter and pick up my steps to get to Happy Chef quicker.

The lunch crowd is in full swing when I enter. I quickly place my order and take a seat at the counter. Looking around the diner, I'm thrown off kilter when I spy Mayor Morre sitting in the back booth, his graying blond hair is slicked back, almost identical to Chad's. He's wearing a dark blue suit, white shirt, and a gray tie. Playing the perfect part. On the outside, he looks

307

put together, but the strong tick in his jaw tells me otherwise.

He looks in my direction, his cold eyes locking with mine before giving me a quick wave, signaling for me to join him. Knowing if I don't go to him, he will come to me, I contemplate leaving for five seconds before forcing my legs over toward him.

Beau would have told me if he knew something. He's only trying to mess with me, I remind myself when I step up to his table.

"Mackenzie, lovely to see you. Please take a seat." I slide into the booth and decide to beat him at his own game.

"Cut the crap, Morre. What do you want?" I sound braver than I really am, but I run with it.

"I think you know what I want." He tilts his head, quietly examining me, but I don't let him throw me off.

"I don't know where Chad is," I lie, knowing there is no way I'll ever tell him the truth. Not when he has no proof.

"You think I'm stupid?" His voice drips in controlled anger. "Chad knew where you were. He left to go find you. Couldn't get over his fucking obsession." He looks down at me in disgust, and I almost feel it wash over me. "So color me surprised when you end up back here. Alone."

"Well, he didn't find me, clearly." Instinctively I edge my voice with strength, and straighten my shoulders. "Maybe he found something else to finally fixate on. The last I heard, he went off the rails when I left. Who knows where he ended up. Now, unless there is anything else—" I start to move out of the booth, but his hand comes down on mine, stopping my retreat. I react, trying to pull back, but his grip tightens. His short stumpy fingers trap me in their grasp.

"You have no idea who you're dealing with." The vein in his

temple throbs as he leans forward and clasps his hold tighter around my wrist. "I know you know something. I might not want this public, but I will make your life hell until you tell me where my son is."

"Is that a threat, Mayor?" I raise my voice a little, hoping to throw him off.

"No, dear. It's a promise. You might have the protection of the MC, but for how long? I can't imagine them being okay with you bringing trouble to one of their own. Say the lovely blonde you've been holed up with in that godforsaken shelter this week."

My back straightens at his words and a disturbing unease washes over me.

Kelly.

"What have you done?" His hold on me starts to burn, but I can't react. My head is lost in the frenzy of hearing his threat.

"Kelly is it? What a shame you left before my present arrived." Fear drives me forward. Ripping my hand back, I fall out of the booth, and race toward the door. I can hear his soft chuckle from the front of the diner, and it only fuels me faster. Running back the way I came, the trip takes less time, yet feels a hell of a lot longer.

When I make it back to Missy's the front door is open and my heart sinks. *I'm too late.*

"Kelly?" I shout, racing through the front door. She doesn't answer so I keep moving from room to room. My anxiety spikes as each second passes by and there is no sign of her. I make my way to the back room, and every part of me locks instantly when I find Kelly lying face down on the floor.

"Kelly?" I force my body to react and race toward her,

almost tripping over my own feet in the rush. She's out cold, non-responsive, but I can see her back rise up and down with each shallow breath she intakes. "Shit, shit, shit." Afraid to move her, I reach for my phone with shaky hands and dial 911.

Through my tears, I give our location and a brief rundown of how I found Kelly to the emergency operator. They keep me on the line, telling me to stay calm and keep talking to her.

Seconds pass, followed by minutes and I realize this is bigger than we thought it was.

Mayor Morre is worse than his son. And now he had a score to settle.

"Please be okay, Kelly." I reach for her hand and try to fight the tears, but there's no stopping them. I caused this. My past is never going to leave me.

Once again a Morre is set on destroying my life.

I check the clock again for the fiftieth time and bounce my knee in front of me. It's been over thirty minutes since they took Kelly, and now I'm getting concerned.

I called Beau from the ambulance, but he hasn't showed up yet and I'm about to lose my mind.

Scenario after scenario plays over in my head as the hands on the old worn clock start to taunt me. Each second drags me deeper into a sad darkness threatening to destroy me completely. Each minute reminds me of how fast everything can change.

After enduring another fifteen minutes, my nerves settle when Brooks, Beau, and Nix burst into the waiting room.

"Have you heard anything?" Brooks asks first, coming straight to me.

I shake my head just as Beau pulls me up into his arms. I watch Brooks head to reception over Beau's shoulder as he holds me tightly.

"You doing, okay?" He pulls back and cups my face. Panic rages through his eyes and I force myself out of my head just enough to comfort him.

"Better now you're here." I return his embrace, hoping to calm him. Brooks is already losing his shit trying to find out answers on Kelly's condition. We don't need Beau doing the same.

"Tell me everything that happened." Beau forces me to sit back down in the uncomfortable chair. I do as he says, because the need to be closer to the ground is growing.

"I–I don't know. I didn't see. But I know it was Mayor Morre."

"How do you know?" His grip on my arm tightens at his name but releases when he notices my grimace.

"'Cause he was at the diner when I was there to buy lunch. He said I didn't know who I was dealing with and then he mentioned Missy's Place and that Kelly was alone there. He knew everything, her name... Oh, God, this is all my fault, Beau." I fall into his chest as the need to breakdown pulls me closer into its clutches.

"Don't even go there, Mackenzie. It's not your fault. This family has been fucking around with your life for too long."

"But if I didn't come back, if I didn't use you..." I stop my words before I speak them out loud.

"Don't, darlin'. I'm gonna make it better. Gonna fucking fix this. Fix everything."

"So more people can be hurt? No, Beau. Maybe I should just come clean. He already knows something is up." I work my bottom lip between my teeth, weighing up my options. These people don't deserve this, to be dragged into what I have started. Not when they have done so much for me.

"No, this ends. You've come too far for this asshole to fuck with you. He knows nothing, darlin'. He's bluffing." Beau stands and brings me up with him. Just then Holly and Kadence rush in, holding X, and Low, followed by Z, Sy, Jesse, and Hunter.

"What are you going to do, Beau?" I hold on to his cut, keeping him in front of me. I can't focus on filling anyone in on what happened right now. I need Beau to see reason.

"What I should have done before this got out of hand." He presses his lips to mine, and then pulls back.

"Please, Beau. Don't leave," I beg, but we both know there's no point. I can see the determination in his eyes. He's done. "Beau, talk to me."

"What's going on?" Kadence comes into my line of sight.

"Is she okay?" Holly asks from the other side of me.

"Kadence, you need to sit with Kenzie. Nix you with me?" Beau ignores my pleas and shares one of his looks with Nix. One that's code for *I need back up*. Nix nods then pulls Kadence in a quick hug, kisses Low, then tells Z to look after his girls.

"Beau, don't do this."

"Trust me, Kenzie. I've got you," is all he says before releasing my hand and walking back out the doors of the emergency room.

I know he wants me to trust him, but my head is screaming

at me to follow him and stop him from making any rash decisions.

"Kenzie, let him go." Kadence takes my hand, stopping any chance of me running after him. I twist back and hold her eyes, silently pleading with her to let *me* go.

"Girl, I know that look. We've all had that look," she states looking at Holly, who nods in agreement.

"Kadence. Please, don't stop me. I need—" I start to pull out of her grasp, needing to chase after Beau to make him stop.

"No. You need to sit down and tell us everything." She moves me back to the waiting chair. I watch as she hands Z some dollar bills for the vending machine and then points her don't-leave-anything-out stare at me as soon as he is out of hearing distance.

"You have ten minutes before he'll want something else, so start." My eyes land on Jesse, Sy, and Hunter as they follow Beau and Nix out.

"What about Brooks?" I point over to Bell and Brooks. Brooks is still pacing, but Bell is trying to calm him enough to speak to a fellow nurse.

"Bell knows everyone here. If she can get any information, she will," Kadence assures me. "Who did this, Kenzie?" I sit back, no longer sure I can fight it anymore. These people are my friends, even if I don't deserve the title anymore. They have to know why Kelly is here.

Knowing there is nothing left to say, I start from the beginning, not leaving one thing out. I am done lying to my friends. They have to know. If Beau is about to do something we can't come back from, it's the least I can do.

Even if it means losing them all.

313

28

Beau

"WHAT'S THE PLAN?" NIX FALLS INTO STEP WITH ME AS we make our way out of the hospital.

"We're going after Mayor Morre." I reach my bike and place my helmet on. "Call in T. We're gonna need him in on this."

"For fuck's sake, Beau. The Warriors? We can't handle this on our own?" He resists like I expected he would, but I know he'll come around. Jesse, Hunter and Sy come up behind us.

"No, I want everything we can get on him. I don't give a fuck who we call in on it."

"Do you hear yourself right now, Beau? Just take a breath, think this through." Jesse starts his reasoning with me, but it's the last thing I want to do right now.

"This asshole has hurt one of ours. He has nothing on

Kenz, and I'm done spending my time on this fucker. He wants to fuck with us, so we hit him back hard. Find something on him so we can end this shit." Nix holds my stare for a minute before nodding.

"You know for sure it's a hunch? He's got nothing?" he questions, reminding me I still haven't filled them in on what happened when I met with Fred in Ohio. I barely made it back to the clubhouse when the call came through to meet Mackenzie and Kelly at the hospital.

"Yeah, Ohio turned up clean. This Fred fucker was special ops. Crazy, I tell you. He and some buddies sorted everything out. You think I'm messed up? Fuck, this guy is a piece of work. Good guy, but fuck me, I wouldn't get on his bad side."

"Jesus." Nix shakes his head, giving the same reaction I had. At first I was apprehensive. I mean, who the fuck just covers up a murder for one of his employees? But after finding out his past, where he came from, what his own upbringing was like, I soon understood him.

Fucker hates abusive men just as much as I do.

"Yeah, Kenzie was right. He's got her back. Even left there with a new connection. So we're sorted on that front." All the guys relax a little, but I know they'll want all the details when this is over.

"I'll fill you in on the rest later. Now we need to find out what we can on Morre." I kick up the stand on my bike and start the engine.

"Jesse, get back to the shelter, check the cameras. Let's see if we can get this fucker on tape." Jesse moves right away.

"Sy, you're with me. Hunter ride with Beau." Nix takes over ordering the guys and moves toward his own bike, ready to do

315

what needs to be done.

"Later." I give them one last nod before taking off in the opposite direction. Nix and Sy to the Warriors Prez, and me and Hunter to Tiny.

I don't know what we will find out, *if* we can find anything out, but I'm not returning until we have Morre where we want him. Even if we have to make our own shit up.

The fucker is going down today.

We pull up out the back of Pink House three hours later, an illegal whorehouse just outside of town in Redwick.

"You sure you want to do this, Beau?" Nix asks one more time, climbing off his bike and coming to stand next to me.

"Yes," I answer, done with the questions. We are doing this and fucking doing it tonight.

"So how are we playing this? We just gonna walk in there and fuck him up?" Jesse asks, coming to stand with Nix and me. Hunter pulls up in the van, followed by Sy on his bike.

When I left Nix in the hospital parking lot, I paid Tiny a visit. After filling him in on everything, he pulled his connections to see what we could find. It was unreliable to start with, but after a few calls, things become clear. Not only does Mayor Morre have connections inside of the law, the fucker also had more than his toe dipped into far worse shit.

Shit that could be traced back to the men who took Paige.

"We go in, rough the fucker up, then take him with us," I tell them the plan again. We were back at the shelter checking over the CCTV tapes hoping to get a face on who got to Kelly when we received a tip-off from one of Tiny's men. The tip put Mayor Morre here, getting his weekly fill with a whore named Angel.

"Are we going Red on this?" Sy asks, using our code name for taking it to the next level. When Red, Nix's dad, ran the Rebels, jobs like these would be frequent. Something we all hated and were glad when we eventually stopped.

"We're not fucking going Red on this." Nix turns and points his stare at everyone, reminding them we're not crossing any lines here.

Too late.

"If it were Kadence, would you be saying the same thing?" He doesn't answer right away, but I watch his lips tighten. He knows we have to do this. It's our only option. We couldn't get a good look at the fucker on the camera, and if we have any hope of finding out who he is, it's from Morre.

Knowing I won't receive a straight answer from Nix, I start walking to the back door. "Are we gonna stand around playing with our dicks or we getting this shit done?" Before I reach the door and knock, it swings open, and out steps one of Tiny's men.

"You have ten minutes. Cameras are off. But they go back on regardless if you're out or not," he warns looking us over.

I'm not sure who runs this place, but whatever markers they had with Tiny, he just called them in.

"What room?" I ask, not giving a fuck about the cameras. We'll be in and out.

"One level up, three doors down on the right." He steps back and lets us pass.

"You sure he's there?" Hunter questions as we take the

steps two at a time.

"Yeah, apparently it's a regular booking." Mayor Morre likes to stick his dick in barely legal pussy.

"Witnesses?" Jesse asks, wondering if interrupting them will come back to bite us.

"Tiny's set this up. He's not gonna fuck us over on this one." Jesse eyes me, still not looking convinced, which only serves to piss me off. "You want out, leave now." I give him a chance to go.

Jesse wasn't around when Red ran the Rebels. Not to say he hasn't crossed any lines since joining, but this shit could get messy.

"I'm not going anywhere. Just covering our asses. Don't want this coming back on you or anyone." He lays it out and I can respect his hesitation, but even if it does come back on me, I don't give a fuck. If the Mayor is involved with the men who are running a trafficking ring around here, then he deserves everything coming to him.

"By the time this is over, I doubt there will be anything to come back at us with," I tell them, not giving a fuck how out of control it makes me sound.

"Beau," Nix cautions when we stop at the third door on the right. The pink paint is cracked and peeling, exposing the black underneath. But I give it no more than five seconds of my attention before turning to Nix.

"I got this," I tell him, not needing him second-guessing me. With a quick nod, he kicks in the door, and we all move in.

"The hell is this?" Morre shoots up off the bed, pushing the blonde bitch riding him off his cock, and onto the floor with a loud thud.

"Well, well, well. Look what we have here, boys. Mayor Morre? Fancy running into you here." Nix trains his gun on the piece of shit who's been fucking with us, while I step closer to him. Jesse stands at the door, keeping watch. Hunter's at the end of the bed, his own gun trained while Sy moves toward the whore.

"What the fuck do you want?" He makes no attempt to cover himself up, so I point my gun down at his discarded pants on the floor.

"Cover your shit up," I order, and then watch him casually reach for them.

The whore stands from the floor with the help of Sy and reaches for her dress.

"Do you mind telling me what this is about?" Morre asks when he's covered his shriveled dick.

"We're going for a drive. We're gonna have some words," I tell him, pointing to his shirt.

"I can assure you, whatever you need to discuss doesn't interest me." He ignores his shirt and puffs his chest out. Somehow his pants have given him some newfound confidence.

"No? I think the video you just made could be of some interest to you." I nod to Angel, and she moves to the freestanding closet, opens it up, and pulls out a video camera.

Thank fuck Tiny could set this shit up.

"You think your threats interest me?" He reaches for his phone, but I'm faster, snatching it from his hands. I drop it to the floor and stomp my boot into it, smashing it to pieces.

"You think this is a threat?" I step in closer and press my gun into his pasty chest. "You have no fucking idea. Put your shirt on. You're coming with us."

"I'm not going anywhere with you." I point my gun at his thigh and pop a round into his flesh.

"Fuck." He falls to the bed, clutching his leg.

"Last warning. You'll have another hole if you fight this." He looks up, fear, panic, and anger flash all over his face, before resignation.

"Fuck you!" The cocksucker isn't bright. I train my gun on his right leg, and let the pop ring out before his screams take over once again.

"That's two rounds in less than a minute. We need to wrap this up," Nix reminds me over the screams of the Mayor. I don't want to rush this, but he's right. We need to get him out.

"Not gonna tell you again, Morre."

"You're gonna have to kill me," he spits, deciding the next move for me.

"You're not gonna walk. We'll carry you." I bring the butt of my gun down on the side of his head and knock him out cold.

"Get the van ready, Jesse. Hunter, Sy, help me with him." They both move at my command, Sy taking his legs, Hunter on his arms. "Nix, make sure we have a clear path." Nix nods, leaving us alone.

"You okay?" I ask the girl.

"Yep, you go. I'll sort it." She hands me the tape. I slide it into my back pocket as she moves to her bag and pulls out her cell. I don't give her a second thought. I pick up his shirt and then help Hunter with his other hand and start to drag him out of the ratty hotel.

"Fucker better hold up enough for me to have my shot at him," Sy grumbles under his breath.

"Don't worry, I'll take it slow on him. You'll have your

320

shot," I assure him as we carry him down the stairs and into the back of the van.

"Straight to the barn." I turn to Hunter.

"Got it," he says, moving to the driver's side.

"Jesse, you stay here and make sure that everything gets cleaned up," Nix orders, and I'm grateful for it. If this turns Red, I'm not sure he's gonna be able to handle it. The last thing we need is him going green on us.

"Yep, boss." He moves back to the steps, following his orders.

"Let's roll." I pick up my pace as I head back to my bike and watch Hunter speed out of the parking lot.

"You sure you want to do this, Beau? There's no going back from this."

"I've done worse for less to better men," is my only response.

"And you've come back from that. You sure you wanna head back there?"

"The only thing driving me forward now is knowing this will be the end, Nix," I tell him what he wants to hear. He mounts his bike, not saying anything else.

This is happening.

Maybe later my decision will play with me, maybe it won't. But I won't waste another second thinking about it right now though.

I have to do this. For Mackenzie. For Kelly. For this to end.

I already let down one woman in my life. I'm not making the same mistake again.

"I'm not telling you anything." Morre slurs his words, still fighting his restraints as I land another blow to his face.

We've been going at it for an hour, and I'm not sure how much longer I can keep up. I just want the fucker dead, but know I can't take it anywhere close to there. *Not until we have the information we need.*

"You fucking will, even if it's the last words you say." I punch him again, splitting the bridge of his nose. I don't even care how fucked-up he looks, or how clean Nix wanted this. There's someone out there who is responsible for Kelly being in the hospital and I want a fucking name before we finish this fucker off.

"You and that bitch won't get away with this." Before I realize what I'm doing, my fist is connecting with his mouth. He twists his head and spits blood out onto the dirty barn floor.

"Call her a bitch again, and I'll put another bullet in you." I shake my fists out. I'm getting over his bullshit. He has no proof on Chad, but it's in his head, and he's not letting it go.

"Nix, Warriors just pulled up." Hunter's voice travels across the barn.

"What the fuck are they doing here?" Nix pushes off the bench and makes his way outside.

"Listen, fucker, you're dead either way I see it. Give me the name and I'll make sure we go easy." I have no desire to follow my promise through, but he doesn't need to know.

"You have no idea who you're messing with." He dodges my question and continues with his shit.

"No, I know you've been dealing with Axle David." His eyes find mine at the name. "You don't think we know about your connections, Mayor?"

"I can explain." I almost laugh. I doubt there is any possible way for him to explain this clusterfuck.

Axle David is known as the leader of a human trafficking organization in Arizona. One of the largest ones, on this side of the country. Connections to the Mayor tell me Axle's organization runs a lot deeper than anyone knows.

"I don't think you're gonna be able to find a way out of this one, Mayor." I smirk, knowing we have him right where we want him.

"Beau, we have a problem." I turn back and watch Nix walk back in with T and three of his guys.

"He's ours, T. Fuck off," I tell him right out. How the fuck did he know we were here? Someone obviously talked back at Pink House.

"Give him up, Beau. Trust me, you don't want this marker on your head. You kill him, you're only bringing more shit to your doorstep."

"And you expect me to believe you give a fuck?" I fire back. I don't know what T's intentions are here, but I'm not willing to give him up, so the Warriors can settle whatever it is they want with him.

"We have a relationship with them. We also have our own agenda." He offers nothing for me to go off.

"And you want us to trust your agenda is going to sit well with us."

"You owe us."

"Last time I heard, you owe us, T. I'm not giving him up."

"You will if you want your woman to walk away with murder." My mind blanks for a second, before clearing and realizing what he just said.

"The fuck you say?" I take two steps toward him. Nix moves to my right, Sy to my left. I know I'm fucking losing. I'm walking a steep precipice here. But fuck, I can't seem to give a fuck.

"Rumors." He raises both hands in surrender.

"Yeah, rumors, this fucker's been spewing to anyone and everyone." I point back to the piece of shit tied to one of the support beams.

"Let us take care of this, Nix. There are larger things at play here." T ignores my anger and turns to the one person who can put a stop to it.

"Larger things you're not gonna share with us," I surmise, knowing before he even answers.

"This goes way up, Beau. Don't fucking get yourself twisted in it."

I don't say anything for a while. The Mayor's labored breathing is the only sound in the barn.

"He's right, Beau. The less our hands are dirty, the better."

I don't want to agree with Nix so I argue back. "So when he comes back and fucks with us some more?" Men like Morre don't give a shit about threats. He survives this, there will be hell to deal with.

"He's not surviving anything. Trust me, Beau. This shit is bigger than all of us. It's going to be dealt with," T offers and it only appeases me a small amount.

"You clean this shit up like he wasn't even here." Nix makes the decision for me, before I can even question anymore.

"Nix."

"Don't push it, Beau. We have an out and we're taking it. Let it play out in someone else's territory." I know he wants to keep us clean, but my anger is holding me here.

"You want me to trust they have our interests?"

"I want you to trust this is what's best for the club. For our family."

As much as I'd love to put a bullet through the fucker's head, Nix is right. We're better off letting this play out on someone else's territory. For the sake of the club.

"Fuck," I concede, not happy about it.

"You're making the right decision here." T reaches forward and taps my shoulder.

"Get the fuck off me, T." I brush it off, and move back to Morre. "Looks like it's your lucky day. Or maybe your not so lucky day." I bend my knees and crouch down to his level.

"Please, don't let them take me, I'll give you whatever you want." The Mayor's eye grow wide realizing I'm going to hand him over. *Now the fucker starts to plead.*

"You give me the name, I'll see what I can do." I'm not short of lying to the fucker to get what I want.

"Brent Harrison. He's a street thug." It's the first truthful thing he's told us since we've been here.

"Where can I find this fucker?"

"He hangs down by the dock in Redwick."

Knowing this is all I'm going to get from him, I give him one final gift. "I was going to enjoy what I had planned for you next." He licks his lips, his nervous tell showing. "I wondered if you'd piss your pants as much as your son did when I had him tied," I lie through my teeth. If this shit with T and the Warriors falls through, I want Chad's death on me, not Mackenzie.

"You?" His brows shoot up for a second, before lowering into a scowl.

"Yeah," is all I say before delivering my final punch, and knocking him out.

"You clean this shit up, no trace this fucker was here," Nix orders T.

"Nothing will touch you. You walk out that door, we don't talk about it again. He turns up in a few weeks, you don't bat a lid."

I don't know if I believe T or whoever wanted Morre, only time will tell. But I am going to trust my Prez and his decision. Kenzie and the club are safe and we have a name.

Brent Harrison

That's all that matters to me right now.

We will sort out the fucker who laid his hands on Kelly.

For Brooks.

For the club.

For Kelly.

29

Mackenzie

"DARLIN'." BEAU'S VOICE BRINGS ME OUT OF THE FOG IN my mind and back to the emergency room.

"Where the hell have you been?" I look up as he takes a seat next to me. It's late. For over four hours, I've been sitting here in a ball of anxiety and worry.

"It's done," is all he says, and my panic only deepens as Nix walks in next, followed by Sy, Jesse, and Hunter.

"What did you do?" I look at each man and back to Beau. My eyes grow wide when I notice Beau's bloodied knuckles.

"Not here, Kenzie. We'll talk later."

"Oh, God, what happened?" I ignore his warning and find my feet. "Please tell me you didn't kill him." I almost laugh, but I don't. I'm still wired after this mess of a day.

"Calm the fuck down. Not here." He stands and drags me down the hall of the hospital, out of earshot. "I will fill you in back at the clubhouse. Right now, you need to pull your shit together." His grip on me tightens, not enough to hurt me, but enough to anchor me to his words. "Tell me what's happening with Kelly." I calm my breathing, focus in on what he's asking.

"We don't know yet. At first they thought it was just a concussion, but then the CT scan came back and they realized it's worse. She hit the ground from falling or being pushed, fuck, I don't even know, but she hit her head bad. She's bleeding inside, something about a hematoma. They had to take her in for surgery to drain the blood." The tears I've only just managed to bring under control start back up.

"She was hit with a baseball bat." His nostrils flare and his lips curl.

"Oh, God, Beau." My eyes well up. The first tear falls then the second.

"Shit, darlin', wasn't thinking." He pulls me into his chest. *That could have been me.*

"Brooks coping?" He pulls back, and takes my face in his hands.

"He's a mess. Won't talk to anyone. Kadence just left to pick up Mia from the babysitter's and bring Kelly's parents down." He nods, knowing Kelly's parents are too old to drive.

"Bell get him back to see her?"

"He saw her briefly, but they rushed her back for surgery." His eyes darken and his jaw ticks. "I don't know what to do, Beau. Everyone is just so silent, no one's talking."

"Everything is going to be okay. This is Kelly we're talking about. She's going to come out of the surgery and everything is going to be okay." He pulls me back into him, kissing the top of my head. "The woman is just as fucking strong as you, darlin'. I have no doubt she'll pull through. I won't accept anything less."

"Please, tell me this is over for real," I whisper into his chest. Even if I don't want him to have blood on his hands, I need to know this is over. That we can live our lives.

"It's over, darlin'. I promise." He gives me what I need, what I've been searching for. "Come on, let's go be with our family." He reaches down and takes my hand.

"Okay." I steel myself and try to keep it together as I follow him back over to where the rest of the club sit, silently waiting and offering Brooks their support.

"Any news?" He claps Brooks on his back before taking the seat next to him. I take the spare seat next to Beau.

Brooks has barely spoken a word to us girls the last few hours, so I'm surprised he answers Beau right away.

"Nothing. Not a fucking word." He rests his elbows on his knees and drops his face in his hands.

"It's gonna work out, brother," Nix tries to reassure him.

"You find the cunt who did this?" He looks to Nix and Beau.

"We're on it," is all Nix says, before Brooks lets out a long deep breath and nods.

"Fuck, she's gotta pull through. I can't do this on my own." His voice is shaky, and it touches me all the way down to my bones.

"You're not alone, Brooks. She's going to be fine. I know it." I reach across Beau and squeeze his hand. Brooks links his fingers through mine and squeezes back.

"I know, sweetheart." The tension rolls off me as he accepts my comfort and I find myself letting out my own relief.

It was just a small gesture, but to me it's the world.

Things might be still up in the air with Kelly, but everything out here is sorted. Beau made it so and I believe him. I have to believe him.

What other option do I have?

"How you feeling, Kenz?" Holly takes a seat next to me later that night when I stir from the most awkward nap of my life. We haven't been home yet, deciding to sleep it out in the uncomfortable waiting chairs until we heard more on Kelly.

"Oh, God, what time is it?" I stretch, trying to relieve some tension in my back and neck.

"It's after 2 a.m."

"Have we heard anything yet?" I look around the waiting room. Nix is asleep four chairs down, Sy, Hunter and Beau are talking quietly across from me. Kelly's parents are sitting two rows back with a sleeping Mia on their laps. Jesse and Bell are talking quietly between themselves, and Brooks is pacing the hallway. Waiting. Praying. Hoping.

"Not yet, but it can't be much longer."

"Where's Kadence?" She was here before I nodded off, with both Low and Z.

"She took the kids home. It was getting too late. She'll be back up in the morning." I nod then glance back over at Brooks.

Seeing him like this, I can't help but be mad at myself. I shouldn't have left her. We should have left together, or called one of the guys to bring us something to eat.

Turning my head away from Brooks, I lock eyes with Beau. He stands to come to me after noticing I'm now awake.

"You okay?" He hands me a bottle of water and takes the spare seat next to me.

"Yeah, sorry, I didn't mean to fall asleep." I take a sip of the water before handing it back to him. I haven't had anything to eat or drink since this morning.

"Don't be silly. Everyone is tired." Holly rests her hand on my leg and gives it a gentle squeeze. Ever since I told her and Kadence what happened and why it happened, I've been worried they would pull back from me, maybe blame me for everyone being here. But they haven't. If anything, they've rallied around me even more than before, offering comforting smiles, reassuring words and even their shoulders to cry on.

"It can't be too much longer, right?" I look up just as a doctor appears, stopping in front of Brooks.

The room becomes a flurry of movement and questions as we all stand and step forward, all desperate for good news.

"—An induced coma to help with the swelling." I miss the first part, but manage to catch up. "She's stable, but still in critical condition. The next three days are going to be precarious." The doctor is young, almost too young and I wonder how long he's been doing this.

"A coma?" Brooks' panicked voice spears me while I take it all in. "You said the surgery would be enough."

"Yes, the surgery helped relieve some pressure, but we are concerned with the swelling. We need to control it. Our best chance for it to happen is to let her brain rest."

Brooks' hands run through his hair as he takes a step back.

"So that's it? We just wait?"

"I know it's not what you were expecting, but the next few days will tell us more."

"Can I see her? I need to see her."

"Soon. She's being moved to the ICU now. Someone will be down shortly to take you back." He offers a comforting hand on Brooks' shoulder before leaving us alone to process.

We all stay silent, letting Brooks take the lead.

Induced coma.

Swelling.

It doesn't sound good. It sounds downright scary and judging by everyone's faces, they all feel the same way.

"It's gonna be okay, Brooks. Dr. Dawson is thorough. She's in good hands." Bell steps forward and wraps her arms around his neck. He accepts her embrace, holding her while his body shakes in sobs.

"I can't lose her, Bell. I can't."

I almost come undone watching him.

Nix steps in next, wrapping his arm around his back and whispering low in his ear.

Wanting to give him privacy, I turn back and notice Kelly's parents holding each other. Hunter now holds Mia, looking so much younger than I've ever noticed.

It all becomes so real. Our world is spinning out of control.

How are we going to survive if she doesn't pull through? The thought weakens my knees, and before I meet the ground, Beau has me, holding me up.

"We need to take you home," he tells me, moving toward a free chair and sitting me down.

"I can't leave, Beau. We need to stay."

"Beau's right. We should get some rest. Brooks and Kelly are going to need all the help they can get." Holly steps in and stops me from arguing. "We can't be of any help with no sleep."

I don't want to leave, but I understand where they're coming from.

"You guys head out. I'll stay with Brooks until he goes back to the ICU. We can meet back in the mornin'." Nix comes to stand near us, as Jesse and Bell move in to console Brooks.

"Are you sure?" Beau asks him.

"Yeah, you take her home." He nods down to me.

"What about Mia?" I ask, looking back at her sleeping form. "We can take her." I look up at Beau, hoping he agrees.

"We'll take her back to the clubhouse," Holly offers. "She'll be better off waking up there." Nix nods, deciding it's the best decision for tonight.

"We'll stay at the clubhouse, too." Beau agrees. "You call us if you need anything, Nix." Nix nods, and then claps Beau on the back, before turning and doing the same with Sy.

"Come on, darlin'." Beau helps me up and holds me close as we say our goodbyes to everyone. Brooks accepts my hug, and our promise to take good care of Mia before leaning in and kissing her sweet little face.

"You ride with Holly. I don't have a helmet with me," Beau tells me as we follow Sy and Holly out of the hospital. "We'll ride behind."

I nod and take his kiss before planting my ass in the passenger side of Holly's car.

After settling Mia into her seat, we set off, and before I can fight it, my eyes turn heavy, and I'm out again, the warmth of the car lulling me back to sleep.

"Darlin'," Beau's soft voice calls to me as he releases me from my belt. "You fell asleep," he whispers as I come back to myself.

"It wasn't a dream." I start to cry. The day's events finally catching up with me. "It's still real, Beau." I shake my head, fighting to escape the darkness.

"Come on, you need to sleep. You okay with Mia, Sy?" Beau asks, and I think I hear him reply, but I can't be sure. Every second of the day, every action, and reaction washes over me as it all plays out in my mind over and over.

Kelly is in a coma. Beau has done something bad, and it's all because of me.

"Are you ever going to tell me what happened?" I ask Beau three nights later when we climb into bed at home. We just came back from the hospital; it's been seventy-two hours since the doctors put Kelly in a medically induced coma. Every day we've woken up, had breakfast, dressed and headed over to see her. Every day we've prayed for her to heal and be okay, but as of today, she's not ready to come out. As devastating as it is, the doctors assure us it's for the best. Her brain function is good. Her vitals are strong, but the swelling is still a factor, they're not prepared to bring her out of it yet.

"The less you know, the better, darlin'," Beau tells me the same thing he's told me the last three nights before he flicks off the lamp and curls into me with his front to my back.

"Beau, please don't keep this from me. I can't handle it.

With everything else going on, I don't need this between us." I try to roll to face him, but his hold is too firm.

"He's not going to give you more trouble," is all he gives away while pulling me tighter against him.

"He's dead, isn't he?" He doesn't answer me, the room growing eerily quiet. My hands move to his arm that's holding me and I pry it off me. "Don't you dare keep this from me." I sit up and look down at him. "Please." I'm just shy of pleading, but I don't care. I need to know.

He lets out a frustrated sigh, before rolling back over, flicking on the lamp and coming to sit up with me. "If he's not already, then he will be soon," he says casually, like he's just given me the time.

"No, Beau." I shake my head, not okay with this at all. His hands come to my face, stopping my freak out.

"Mackenzie, he fucking put Kelly in the hospital. In a fucking coma. Don't make this out to be anything more. He fucked up."

"But what if it comes back on you?" I push, hating that this is all because of me. Two days ago, Jackson came to the hospital to take my statement regarding what I knew. Unless Beau knows and hasn't told me otherwise, the man responsible for hitting Kelly with the baseball bat is still out there. The cameras at Missy's didn't get his face, so until she wakes up, we won't know who we're dealing with.

"I promise you it won't." He sounds so sure, I don't know if I should be scared, or relieved. I know Beau is capable of being a dangerous man. I know who his club deals with sometimes, but I also know deep down in my soul he would never hurt me.

"I'm scared, Beau. I'm scared for Kelly. For Brooks. For

335

Mia. For you." He drops his hands and pulls me into his lap. I don't fight him. My need to be close to him only grows stronger the more reality seeps in.

"I know you are, darlin', and I wish I could reach in and take your fear from you, but I can't. I can only tell you I have your back. Nothing will touch you. You have to trust me."

"I did this. I made you do this. It's already on me, Beau." Bile creeps up the back of my throat, but I force it back down.

"Bullshit, he did this. Not you. I don't want to hear you say that shit again."

"For all I know you killed a man for me, Beau. How can you expect me not to react?"

"I didn't kill him, darlin'," he whispers, his voice almost disappointed.

"Then what happened?" The air grows thick as we both sit and look at each other, neither one of us speaking until Beau takes my hand. "I love you, Kenz, but I'm not gonna talk about this with you. Do you hear me?" Reluctantly, I nod, in understanding more than anything. If Beau didn't kill him, then someone else did and he won't tell me.

"I need to hear the words."

"Yes, I understand, Beau." I give him the words he needs to relax.

"Do you trust me, darlin'?"

"More than myself," I answer without pause. He has to know how much trust I have in him. How much he could destroy me. We are connected like nothing else. I trust him with everything.

"Then breathe, darlin'. Trust that I have you. That I have this." I nod, giving it over to him and maybe even more. This thing between us is bigger than I've ever felt before; this is on a whole new level.

"Good girl, now come here." He falls back, pulling me down with him so my body covers his.

"Just promise me she's going to be okay." I press my lips to his and close my eyes, almost praying he grants my wish.

"I promise you're going to be okay." I open my eyes when he doesn't give me what I want.

"I don't care about me. I need her to be okay." He rolls us to his left, following me over and covering me with his weight.

"I care about you. I need *you* to be okay." I shake my head, not sure if I'll ever be okay.

Not after this.

When I came here, I couldn't imagine my situation getting any worse. I thought after everything I had been through, surely this time around would finally give me my happy ending.

Look where it got me. I was to blame for bringing this to their lives. I knew it. Beau knew it. Everyone in the club knew it.

But no one is saying it.

No, I won't be okay, not until Kelly is.

Not until this is over.

30

Bear

"MACKENZIE? DID YOU HEAR ME?" SHE LOOKS UP AT MY voice and smiles. But it's not like her usual smile. This one's new. It's the one she started giving after Kelly was hurt. Each day it kills me and each day it gets worse.

After the first three days, Kelly's swelling didn't come down as quickly as the doctors first hoped. She was kept in her induced coma for nine days before they brought her out. Only she didn't respond. Three weeks later and she still hasn't woken up. She's breathing on her own, her brain function is normal, she's shown signs she's there, but she hasn't come out yet. We're all hopeful, telling ourselves she's just taking a little longer to come out of it because her body is healing. Most injuries with the brain vary from case to case, so all we can do now is wait.

"Yeah, just finishing up. You go on ahead." Mackenzie waves me off and goes back to reading.

"Must be some book you have there." I reach down and pull it out of her hands.

"Hey!" She shifts forward to grab it back, but I don't let her.

"Reading time's over. You're coming to bed with me."

"Beau, I was at the best part." She fights it, but I'm done with this shit. I'm not letting her play this card anymore.

"It's still gonna be there tomorrow."

"I'm not tired. I just want to read, Beau." She starts to shut down, just like every time I push a little. Over the last four weeks, I've let her get away with it, thinking it was what she needed. But now it's getting out of hand and she's pulling further away instead of coming back to me.

The last month has been tough for everyone. The club has taken a huge hit with Kelly still in her coma. Brooks is barely holding it together. Mackenzie feels guilty. We're still on the lookout for Brent Harrison and between daily visits to the hospital, and having Mia stay with us off and on, it's been a complete clusterfuck.

"You've been pulling back from me."

"I'm just—"

"You can't lose yourself in a book to get through this, Kenzie." She looks up at me, guilt etched all over her face.

"I'm not, Beau." Her argument is weak, setting in stone what we both already know.

"Darlin', I haven't had you in my arms in four weeks. Tell me when's the last time you came to bed with me?" I try not to sound like a fucking pussy, but Jesus Christ, I'm losing my shit.

"I'm sorry. I just haven't been in the mood. How can you even think about sex with everything going on?"

"I'm not talking about sex, darlin'. I'm talking about holding you. Fucking touching you. Just being with you." In the beginning, I expected it. I knew she would shut down, but this, this is more. This is her letting it eat at her.

"I don't know what you want from me, Beau."

"I want a lot of things, darlin', but I'll settle for you coming to bed with me. You want to read, fine. You read in our bed, with me." I reach out for her hand and wait for her to take it. "Come on, Kenz," I encourage. It's something so small. But right now, for us it's huge. I need her to come back to me. To come back to us.

"Fine," she finally relents. "I'm tired anyway." She takes my hand and stands.

I hand her back her book as I guide her down the hall, turning the lights off as we go. She doesn't talk and I don't push her. After brushing our teeth, we settle into bed. She doesn't roll into me like she used to, and I want to reach over and pull her to me, but I don't. It's enough she's even here.

"The opening of Missy's Place is going ahead next week," I fill her in on what the club decided today.

"What?" her body flings up to a sitting position. "No, Beau. You can't. Not without Kelly."

"We've already postponed it three weeks. We've gotta get it going." I itch to roll over and flick the lamp on, wanting to see her reaction, but I don't want her to shut down again. Not when I just have her talking.

"It's her baby just as much as it's yours."

"You're right, and she would want us to go ahead. Kelly

would want us to help as many people as we can. You know this."

She doesn't come back with anything; instead, she lies back down and settles underneath the covers. She knows I'm right, knows this is what Kelly would want. Pushing back the opening isn't helping anyone.

"I'm sorry, darlin'. I know you wanted to wait. But we have a lot of people expecting to start work, plus all the women we had coming in."

"No, I get it. You're right. She would want it to go ahead." She slightly rolls to the middle of the bed, facing me and I turn to face her. I can barely make out her features in the dark, but I can see her eyes are open and looking into mine.

"I'm sorry, Beau. I didn't mean to pull away," she whispers after a few minutes of silence.

"Nothing to be sorry for. I understand why you have, but darlin', it's gotta stop. I've given you time, and I've let you try to work this out on your own, but I'm done waiting." Her hand finds mine under the blanket and I greedily take it, threading my fingers through hers.

"The guilt, it's just eating me, Beau. Because of me, she's in that hospital bed."

"You can't let this guilt win, Kenz. You need to fight it before it controls you. Fuck, trust me. If anyone knows, it's me." I roll in closer to her. If I could just fall into her to make her see, I would.

"How do you know, Beau? How do you know what this feels like? I can't just stop feeling this. First it was Chad. Then Heidi, because we both know she's not coming back, and now Kelly." The desperation in her voice almost makes me lie and tell her one day it will go away, one day it will stop hurting, but I don't because it doesn't.

"I know because every time I help a woman in a dangerous situation I see Missy's face." I try to give her something to hold on to. Something I haven't given anyone before. "I'm reminded of that look of fear, the look of defeat, and then I'm reminded I couldn't save her. I help these women every fucking day, Kenz, yet all I see is Missy. I see my failures. My regret. My guilt." She stills as I shift my body back, angling to face the ceiling.

"It took me two years to realize something was wrong. For two fucking years I didn't see it. I don't know if it's because I was selfish, lost in my own fucking head, or if I just didn't want to see it, but I missed the signs. The turtlenecks she would wear in the summer. How she all of a sudden became clumsy. Fuck, even the way the light in her eyes just dwindled away. Two years, I was blind. How's that for guilt?"

"You can't blame yourself, Beau." Kenzie finally speaks up, resting her hand on my bare chest. "You didn't bring him into her life."

"No, I did worse. I didn't save her. Instead of protecting her, or insisting she leave him. I drove to his work and roughed him up. Took Nix with me and beat his ass. Told him to pack a bag and fuck off. But he didn't. He was pissed and didn't take too kindly to Missy telling me. She was dead the next day."

"Oh, God, Beau. That's not your fault." She sits up and flicks the lamp on, bathing the room in orange light.

"No? Whose fault is it then?" I put it back on her. She's no more to blame for Kelly than I am for Missy, but it doesn't stop the guilt from being fed.

"His. He took her life. Not you." Her eyes are red from

crying and I'm a complete ass for putting this shit on her, but I can't sit back and watch her travel down the same path as me.

"And you didn't put Kelly in the hospital, darlin'." Her shoulders sag in defeat when she understands what I'm getting at. "I know you want to blame yourself, but you have to fight it. There are always going to be moments in my day where I beat myself up over it. I was her big brother. I was meant to look after her and protect her. I can still see my mom falling to the floor when I had to tell her Missy was gone. I can still feel both of my parents pull away from me, from each other. I didn't just lose Missy, Kenz. I lost my family. But I can't change any of it. I can't go back and save Missy. I can only do what I can now."

"That's why you started helping women? Started Missy's Place?" she whispers, finally getting it.

"Yeah, darlin'. But it took me a long time to get here. Like you, I let it control me, but you don't have to. You have all these people giving you grace and you're pushing it away."

"But how do I accept it when I don't think I deserve it?"

"I learned a long time ago it doesn't matter what you think you deserve. You can't give yourself grace. You have to allow others to give it to you. No one blames you. Yes, this is a fucked-up situation. Yes, Kelly is still in a coma, but she's not dead. You have to stay positive." I reach forward and wipe her face. "You have to have hope. Fight for her. Fight for yourself. Don't give up now, not when it matters the most." Her tears are falling hard and fast now, but I don't care. She needs to feel how real this is.

"You're right, oh, God." She buries her head into my chest. "I've just been so buried under this guilt, I haven't seen anything around me. I've been selfish when I should've been fighting."

"You're the least selfish person I know, darlin'." I hold her tightly against me, wishing she wouldn't be so hard on herself.

"I can't even stand myself right now, how can you?" She sniffles, her hot tears roll down my skin.

"Because the bitterness I've been carrying from Missy's death doesn't taste so sour in my mouth when you're around. You changed me. You made me see everything differently. The way you think I'm seeing you right now, is so far from the truth. If I need to light one thousand candles for you to see yourself the way I do, then I will."

"I don't know what I did to deserve you." She lets out a shaky breath, while wiping her face.

"Been asking myself the same question until I realized I don't think I do deserve you. So I stopped asking myself and started loving you." She looks up giving me one of her smiles. Only this time, I believe it all the way to my bones.

It's the most beautiful smile she's ever given me, because it means I haven't lost her. She is still there. She's fighting it, and that's all I need. I can do the rest.

And I will.

I'll do anything for this woman.

"How you doing, brother?" I ask Brooks a couple of days later on one of my daily visits to the hospital. His face is drawn downward and his beard is unkempt. He's wearing clean clothes only because the girls have been bringing him some in, and he doesn't look like skin and bones because the hospital has been feeding him, but besides that, the man is falling apart and I can't blame him. I don't know how I'd be coping if Kenz was lying in that hospital bed.

"She just needs to fucking wake up. Everything will be okay if she just woke up." He drops his hand from Kelly's and rests his elbows on her bed. I look over Kelly's sleeping form and the overwhelming ache of helplessness grows. We're no closer to knowing when she'll wake. The doctors are saying she can wake any time. There is no reasoning with these types of brain injuries, we just have to be patient and wait it out. It's the worst thing to hear. Sometimes the unknown is more frightening than the horrible truth.

"It's going to work out, Brooks. You have to believe it, brother." He nods but doesn't say anything else. He's probably sick of hearing it. From everyone. The whole clubhouse has stepped in. Always having someone here for when she wakes up. The girls come up every day, making sure someone is always with Kelly. Talking to her. Encouraging her to come around. Brooks hasn't been alone but at the same time, he has. He's alienated himself. And I get it, I do, but it's hard to watch it. Watch him shut down and push everyone out.

We sit in silence for another twenty minutes until Brooks finally sits up and takes Kelly's hand again.

"You find the fucker who did this yet?"

"Not yet. We've still got eyes out." I hate we can't give him the answer he wants. Yeah, Mayor Morre has been dealt with, but the man responsible for this needs to be found.

"I want him, Beau. I want him found and I want to deal with him." I want him, too. After finding out who we're looking for, Jesse and Hunter did some digging. It turns out it's the same guy who threatened Mackenzie in Liquid.

Yeah, I'll make sure we get him.

"We're on it, brother. Rest assured, I *will* find him." I offer the only thing I can: my word. We haven't had any blow back from the Mayor. T's promise on the Mayor turning up dead came through. A week after we left him alone in the barn with the Warriors, he was found dead a few hours out of town. Media called it gang war. Mayor Morre was apparently in the wrong place at the wrong time.

I called it good riddance.

"I want him to pay." I nod, knowing that feeling all too well. Even with the blood on my hands, knowing Chad and the Mayor are gone, I can breathe easier.

"While we're talking about club business, I need to talk to you about Missy's Place. We decided we need to keep things moving on it." I hate being the one to tell him we want to go ahead with it. It's the last thing he needs to think about, but I won't go ahead without him knowing. I'm not keeping it from him.

"Kelly would want you to go ahead. You can't keep putting it off." He gives his okay and I'm relieved. We've already put the staff off for three weeks. I don't want to risk losing them.

"The club is gonna have a fundraiser night for the opening, you want to come?" I know it's pointless asking him, but I told Mackenzie I would, just in case.

"I can't leave her, man. What if she wakes up?"

"You're right. I just wanted to make sure you know you're welcome." A knock at the door stops Brooks from replying. I twist my head to watch Bell walk in.

"Hey, guys, how are we?" She steps into the room and walks

over to Kelly. She's wearing her nurse's uniform today so I know she's on shift.

"Hey, Bell." I nod and watch her lean down and squeeze Kelly's free hand.

"Morning, Kelly. Are you going to wake up for me today?" She smiles down at her before picking up her chart. "How was last night?" She looks up at Brooks.

"Same. Nothing." He lets out a frustrated breath.

"She's showing activity, Brooks. I know it's hard but keep talking to her. Some people say they can hear what's going on around them in this state. Everything helps." She places Kelly's chart back into place then moves around the bed.

"I'll be back in later." She waves us off, leaving just as fast as she came. The room falls silent again, and I wonder if I should just head out too. Mackenzie is at the clubhouse and I'm bringing her up later, so I can always stay longer when we return.

"I think I should head out. Give you some quiet time before the next visitor," I tell him, deciding to leave. Every day he gets more distant and every day, it gets harder to watch it.

"How's Mia?" He looks up, stopping my retreat and I see a flash of pain in his eyes.

"She's doing okay. We're taking her tonight. We can bring her down before dinner if you like." I sit back down, letting this one play out.

"I don't like her seeing Kell like this. The tubes and the machines, it's too much. She was in yesterday."

"I don't think she minds. She just wants to see you and Kelly," I try to reason with him. This subject has been a huge issue within the club the last four weeks. While Mia is being

347

looked after by all of us, there are concerns for Brooks' reluctance to have her around.

"I just can't deal with her questions right now, Beau. She doesn't understand. How can she? She's five." His jaw ticks and his body tenses. Agitation seeps from him, so I don't push it. I know it's his way of dealing, who am I to tell him otherwise? I have no idea how I would react in this situation.

"I get it, bro. It's all good." The last thing he needs is to be getting worked up, not here in front of Kelly.

"I just need more time. I'm not trying to push her away."

"No one thinks you are. We just want to make sure you're both okay." He doesn't reply, so I don't continue pressing it. It's up to him now.

"Well, I need to head out. You want anything before I go?" I look up at the clock knowing Kadence will be in next. The girls have spaced out their visits throughout the day. Kadence, Holly, Bell, then Mackenzie, followed by the boys. I opt to come early in the morning, less chance of dealing with an agitated Brooks, plus fewer people.

"Nah, I'm good."

"Okay, I'll be back later with Kenz." I stand and step up to Kelly.

"Come on, Kell, you need to knock this shit off and come back to him," I whisper in her ear, and then gently kiss her cheek. I hold back, almost anticipating her reaction. Like every other day, it doesn't come and I try not to let it pull me down.

She'll come to when she's ready.

"See you, bro." I walk around the bed and plant my hand on his shoulder. He reaches up and squeezes it tightly for a few seconds, like he is taking in my strength before releasing.

"Look after my girl," he whispers. I squeeze him back, a silent reply I have it sorted.

Without another word, I walk out and head straight for the bathroom.

I make it just before bringing up my breakfast.

It doesn't happen every visit.

Only the tough ones.

The problem is the tough ones were becoming more frequent.

"I don't want to make a big deal with the opening. Let's keep it simple, quiet, and just have it over with," I tell Mackenzie later that day while we're at Missy's Place getting shit sorted for opening next week.

"Not even a celebration at the clubhouse?" She looks up from her notebook. Kelly and I had planned a run to raise some funds, but we'll put it off for a bit. Until she wakes.

"Nope, don't need it. Not with everything going on. Besides we have the fundraiser." Mackenzie nods, making another note.

"Okay, that's fine. We also need to go through the list of volunteers. I know you and Kelly had chosen some, but with the postponing of the opening, we may have lost a few." I stop reading over the list of jobs I have to do before Monday and watch her quietly. She's sitting across the desk from me on the sofa against the wall, with bare feet, denim jeans, and a black Harley Davidson tee. Her hair is down today in a mass of curls and my hand itches to run my fingers through it. She looks fucking amazing.

Too fucking amazing.

"What's wrong?" She catches me staring.

"Nothing." I shake my head and continue to have my fill.

"Then why are you looking at me like that?"

I smile at her as she worries her bottom lip with her top teeth. It's a quirk of hers I've come to love. "Just noticing how beautiful you look today."

She releases her lip and lets her smile take over her face. "Thanks." A small spark in her eyes brightens at my compliment.

"It's good to have you back, darlin'. Here with me. Together." Ever since the night I shared Missy's story, I've had her back.

My woman came back to me.

"It's good to be back." She picks up her pen then drops her head back to her notebook. "We need to set up a meeting with Brie this week, so we know what her expectations are and ours with her." Brie is our full-time social worker. Before Kelly had her accident, we hired her. When she found out about Kelly, she agreed to hold out until we were ready. Luckily, Brie had no problem waiting an extra six weeks to start.

"And we need to sit down and do up a roster. I know Bell, Kadence and Holly are all as keen as I am about getting on it. I've already spoken with Brie about what we can do for training. Do you think that will be okay?" She taps her pen to paper then looks up, waiting for me to process it all.

"Do you want to keep working for Nix at the clubhouse or would you like to come work here?" I ignore her roster plans and ask her right out. Sitting here listening to her ramble about rosters and training, I realize she's just as passionate about this place as I am.

"Here?"

"Yeah, you don't have to if you don't want to. No pressure. But, darlin', I haven't seen you this alive in months."

"Well, what you're doing here is the most amazing thing ever, Beau. You don't have to offer me a job. I'm happy to just help out when you need me."

"You didn't answer me, Kenz. Do you want to work here?"

"What would I do? You have all the spots filled."

"Head of administration." I offer her the one job Kelly and I were going to share.

"I'm barely qualified."

"Not from where I'm sitting. Kelly and I were going to share the job. With Kell not up to it at the moment, it's just me. I'm going to need help."

"I can just help."

"I want you here full time."

"What about Nix? I can't let him down." She keeps fighting it, but I'm gonna wear her down.

"He was doing his books long before you came along. He'll manage." She worries at her lip again, letting it all sink in.

"You really mean it? You want me here?"

"Couldn't think of a better place for you."

"Beau, this is huge for me." She stands, places her notebook down, and walks around the desk to me.

"So that's a yes?"

"Yes!" She falls into my lap and wraps her arms around my neck. "For you, for Missy. It's more than I could ever want."

"I love you, Kenz." I wrap my arms around her, trying to memorize having her back in my arms.

"And I you, Beau." She rests her forehead on mine. I'm about to kiss her when a large bang on the front door interrupts us. Spinning in my chair, I turn and look at the CCTV monitors. We had more installed at the front door after Kell was attacked.

"Is that Detective Carter?" Mackenzie leans forward for a better look.

"Yeah." I shift her off my lap and stand. "Stay here while I talk to him." I kiss her briefly and then head out past the common area and toward the front door.

"Jackson?" I open the door and step outside.

"Beau, how are you?" He offers me his hand and I take it. If he finds it odd I just stepped outside instead of offering him to come in, he doesn't show it.

"Good, busy. You know how it is." I release his hand and wait for him to tell me what he's here for.

"No news on Kelly?" I shake my head, not prepared to talk about it.

"I'm not here on official business. Just wanted to give you a heads up." I still my breathing and lower it to stay composed.

"What's up?"

"Had an envelope delivered to my desk last week. Pretty full on shit implicating Mayor Morre to Axle David, and his clusterfuck of a rap sheet."

"No shit?" His brow rises at my tone, but he doesn't comment. I know the file he has. Tiny was responsible for setting it up.

"Yeah, him and Chad to be precise. Chad's been working some cases for them. Too bad we can't collar him for it. You still have men looking for him?"

"Not gonna do your job for you, Jackson." I know he's

fishing for information right now. Probably knows we know more than we're letting on.

"I'm just concerned, Beau. Mayor turns up dead. Chad's missing—"

"I'm not worried about Chad," I cut him off. I probably shouldn't be so cocky, but I'm done beating around the bush. Chad is gone. The Mayor is gone. I'm not going to play along.

"You're not?" His head tilts slightly.

"Not in the least."

"One would think you had something to do with his disappearance, Beau, with a comment like that. Just weeks ago we were getting hounded to find him and now you aren't worried. What did you do?"

"Nothing. You know we run a clean club, Jackson. Maybe his father's connections caught up with him. Axle David was responsible for Paige's disappearance. I'm sure he's capable of getting rid of scum," I remind him how much he risked last time to help Paige out of her situation. It's a low move, but I don't give a fuck.

"You know we still have eyes in the Warriors." He ignores my dig and delivers his own. I keep my expression blank, trying not to react. Jackson did tell Jesse a few months ago they had a man undercover, but somehow in the stress of things, we seemed to fucking forget.

"Then you'll know we had nothing to do with it," I call his bluff.

Yeah, okay, we fucked him up a bit, but he has nothing on us and the shit with Chad. No body. No crime. Simple.

"You might not have signed his death certificate, but you had a hand in it." I don't bother arguing any more. I'm done

353

with this conversation.

"Well I can't say this hasn't been interesting, but I have a shelter to open next week, sixteen staff and volunteers to train up. You get my proposal for the sheriff's department to come on board?" I change the subject, hoping he drops this. Obviously, he knows what transpired in the barn, but unless he's going to do something about it, then there is no point going back and forth.

"We did. Didn't Mackenzie tell you?" She did fill me in only twenty minutes ago, but I'm not going to tell him that. "We're working to set up a program, have one of our female officers come out and work with your people." I nod, happy he's coming on board.

"Appreciate it, Jackson. We're trying to do a good thing here." My words have double meaning and I'll be surprised if he doesn't get it.

"You are, Beau. Just don't let this good work get messed up with shit I can't pull you out of." It's a warning. One I'm going to listen to.

"You have nothing to worry about."

"I nearly did."

"Your guy was gonna talk or something? Go over your head?" I decide to take the bait.

"No, we're both on the same page thankfully. My point is it could have been someone who plays by the book, word for word and no moral judgment." We both fall silent at the implications of his words.

"Beau, is everything okay?" Mackenzie's voice comes from behind as she opens the door and steps out.

"Everything's fine. Just filling in Beau here on where we're at with the program we're bringing together for the shelter," Jackson answers. I look up, almost shocked he's not pushing it with her.

"Oh, great. Did you want to come in? I just put a fresh pot of coffee on." I level my stare at the bastard hoping he reads my no.

"I'd love to, but I have to head back to Redwick." He starts to move away from the building toward his cruiser.

"I'll be in touch in a couple of days." He flicks his wrist before opening his door. "Good seeing you again, Mackenzie," he calls and then closes his door.

"I thought I told you to stay." I barely control my irritation as we watch Jackson reverse out of the driveway, and peel out down the street.

"When do I ever listen?" she sasses, pushing the door open.

"Never, and I think I need to do something about it." I step in after her and close the door behind me.

"What are you going to do?" She steps into my space, wrapping her arms around my neck. My cock instantly hardens. The last time it's had any attention was before Kelly's accident.

"I'm sure I can think of something." I press my lips to hers, my mind running wild with what we could do.

"You have my attention." Her lips move against mine, but before I even have one taste, a knock at the door has everything coming to a standstill.

"Go away." I groan, not impressed this is the second time in fifteen minutes this has happened.

"Open up, Beau. I have Mia and she needs to use the bathroom," Holly calls back, well and truly ending all hope of this happening now.

"Rain check?" Kenzie asks, before drawing back and arranging herself.

"I'm counting on it." I pull her back, kiss her one more time, and then step away from the door, allowing Kenzie to open it and let them in.

"Uncle Beau, why you take so long?" Mia's five-year-old voice scolds me as she races past us, desperate for the bathroom.

"I think Uncle Beau and Auntie Kenzie were very busy with work." Holly follows her in, handing X to Mackenzie with a knowing smile before chasing after Mia.

"Aww, come on, it's not too bad, honey." Mackenzie catches my scowl before blowing a raspberry on X's cheek.

"I think I enjoyed Jackson's visit over this one."

"Don't let Holly hear you say that." She turns, taking X with her. Her laugh carries all the way back to the office and all I can do is stand here and listen. It's been so long since I heard it, I almost forgot how fucking amazing it was.

Maybe I'd take my statement back, the sound of her laugh lightening my mood a little.

"Uncle Beau. I have my Barbies to play with tonight." Mia comes running back out, reminding me it's our turn to take her. Any chance of my raincheck is well and truly not happening in the next twenty-four hours.

Nope. Mood officially darkened.

31

Mackenzie

"KEZ? KEZ?" THE SOFT SWEET VOICE OF MIA CLOSE TO my ear jolts me out of my sleep.

"Mia? What's the matter?" I come up on my elbows and take stock of my surroundings as I check the alarm clock. It's late, barely after midnight.

"I'm scared. Can I sleep with you?" Her fingers clutch her small little lamb, whose ears look like they've seen better days. Turning my head, I check to see if Beau has stirred. He's out cold and has no idea this little human wants to climb into bed with us.

"Sure, sweetie." I slide over closer to Beau and let her climb up beside me. She settles in next to me and brings her lambie up to her nose.

I want to ask her what made her scared, but like every other time we have had her stay overnight, she doesn't talk about it.

Between Kadence and Nix, Holly and Sy, and me and Beau, we've all been pitching in. Brooks has totally checked out. He knows we have Mia, and we're all looking after her, but that's it. I just wish he would show her she hasn't lost her mom or her dad. The poor girl is frightened, alone, and I don't know how much more she can handle.

"Kez, when is my mommy gonna come home?" Mia's little voice asks, bringing me out of my head.

"I don't know, sweetie. I think Mommy needs to sleep a little longer." I pull her in tighter against me, while I swallow my sobs.

"I miss her. And I miss Daddy too."

"And they miss you, sweet girl. So much." I clear my throat and force myself to be strong. I've spent so many nights crying over Kelly. I can't do it in front of her child. I *need* to be strong.

"I don't like when Mommy sleeps so much."

"Is that why you're scared?" Her little head nods as she squeezes her lamb tighter.

"I had a bad dream."

"It's okay, Mia. Everyone has bad dreams. Everything is going to be okay, sweetie. Close your eyes. I'll be here if you have another one." I lean forward and kiss her forehead. I reach up and stroke her hair, lulling her back to sleep. After a few minutes it works, she's back in a deep sleep.

"She asleep?" Beau shifts closer to me as my silent tears fall.

"Yeah, she had a bad dream."

"Another one?"

"Do you blame her? Poor thing is barely coping," I whisper,

still stroking her hair.

"She's doing the best considering the circumstances, Kenz." He tries to put it all in perspective, but I only see it one way.

"No, she needs stability. Brooks needs to sort his priorities out."

"Darlin', he's trying to get there. He's got a lot of shit on his plate."

"Well, that's not good enough. I'm sorry, but he's also this little girl's only person right now. She's all alone, Beau. She should be with him." I try to keep my voice in a low whisper, hoping not to wake Mia, but I can sense myself getting worked up. I know I'm the last person to judge. The last four weeks I've done the same thing, until Beau pulled me back.

"Darlin', she's sleeping snuggled up close. She might miss her mom and dad, but she's not alone."

"It's not the same, and you know it."

"No, it's not. But we're her family and we're what she's got right now. You can't judge Brooks for reacting. He's hurting, Kenz."

I know he's right. The club is family, and no matter what, we're all here for one another, even when we make bad decisions.

"When did you become so smart?" I tilt my head back and let him whisper a soft kiss over my lips.

"When I met you." He chuckles when I make a snorting sound at the back of my throat.

"Shhh, you'll wake Mia." I pull back and look down at her. Her lambie is still nestled under her arm, and I eye the condition it is in.

"Maybe I should wash Lambie," I whisper over my

shoulder.

"I don't think a wash is gonna save it." He leans over my shoulder and looks down at her.

"It's so cute. Don't you think?"

"It's ugly and probably infested with germs." He pulls back, not at all enamored with the small toy.

"I'll wash it a couple of times," I tell him, freaked out by the thought of it being infested with germs. Gross. And she has it on her face all night. The room falls quiet for a few minutes before Beau speaks again.

"Do you want kids one day, Kenz?" His question shocks me for a second. We haven't had a discussion about our future. Everything kind of happened so fast, before shit started falling apart around us.

"I always thought I would be a mother, have three kids, white picket fence, you know? But I think it's too late for me," I tell him honestly. I'd love nothing more than to be a mother, but I gave up that hope when I left Chad.

"Never too late for anything, darlin'. Still have a few years in you." He pinches my ass and I squirm.

"What about you?" I still, while I wait for his answer.

"Didn't think I did. Then I just woke up and heard you console a scared little girl, pull her into our bed, then stand up for her as any protective mother would. All I can see now is you sitting on our porch swing, cradling our daughter." I shift slightly, trying to process his words. Everything the last month has become *ours*. Our bed. Our swing. I can't help reacting when he does it.

"What are you saying?"

"Fuck, I don't know. I just know the thought of having your

belly swollen with my kid is something I need to happen."

"You're nuts. It's too soon," I try to reason with him. I know what we have going on right now is deep, but we're talking about a lifelong commitment.

"If anything, the last few months have taught me not to wait. It all can be over in a minute, taken from us. I don't want to turn around in a year's time and wish I did things differently."

"Beau, you're talking crazy. Go to sleep." I roll back, willing my erratic heart to calm down. Of course everything he's saying is wheedling its way into my heart, spreading itself through me, giving me hope and possibility, but like I said, it's way too soon.

"You want it. Don't even have to see your face to know it. I can sense it right here. Right now." He leans over, places his hand over my heart and whispers in my ear.

"Yeah, I want it. God, even the possibility of having that kind of goodness in my life is more than I ever imagined. But we're not even married."

"Don't need to be married to have a baby, darlin'."

"Ahh, yeah I do," I whisper back. It's not like a deal breaker for me, but it's definitely something I've always thought would happen. Like a natural progression of things.

"Then marry me, darlin', if that's all you need."

"No, Beau." My breathing practically stops and I have to force it to start again.

"Why not?" He sounds almost offended and I have to take a minute to figure out how to approach this.

"Beau, you're not thinking this through. You're reacting to a situation." I don't dare roll back and look at him. We shouldn't be talking about this.

It's not that I don't want to marry Beau. Jesus, the thought alone makes me want to scream out yes. But I know he's only acting on impulse. And I don't want a proposal based on impulse. I don't want to get married because we're rushing to have a child.

"You're right, I am. I'm reacting to you being fucking amazing and not wanting to waste time and create a life with you."

"I love you, Beau. I've never loved anyone as much as I love you, but please don't ask me like this. Don't make me say no when all I want to do is say yes."

He doesn't say anything for a few minutes, the silence almost deafening before his mouth moves to my ear.

"You're going to be my wife, Mackenzie, and you're going to have my babies. The sooner you're on board, the sooner we can start." A shiver runs through me as his words wash over me. His threat is serious, almost dangerous, and I have nothing to come back at him with.

Because I want this. I want it so bad it scares me.

So instead of responding like I know he wants, I close my eyes and pretend he didn't just threaten me with a beautiful life. A life I didn't think I'd have. A life I want as much as he does.

Only the problem with pretending is it has a habit of hurting you more than the truth.

And I've had enough hurt in my life. I don't need more.

"Hey, Kell," I whisper, taking a seat next to her bed and reaching for her hand. She doesn't reply, the soft touch of her hand missing the warmth I've grown used to the last few months.

"I really need you to wake up, Kell." I squeeze her hand gently, desperate to get through to her. I only have about ten minutes alone with her until Brooks comes back from his shower, so I don't waste any time in filling her in on everything going on around her.

"So much is happening, and everyone needs you. Mia needs you. Brooks needs you. The club needs you." I sit and let her process it. "I need you," I whisper the last part. She doesn't respond like I wish she would, so I keep going.

"Beau asked me to marry him." I spill my secret from last night.

"I mean, it was barely a marriage proposal, more like a threat." I can imagine her laughing at his reaction to me saying no. "I just don't know if I'm ready. After everything with Chad, I didn't think I would ever get married again, but these last few months with Beau has changed me." The room falls silent as I process my own words this time. Babies and marriage with Beau are the last thing we should be thinking about right now, but I can't help it. He's planted this seed in me and it's growing into a possibility with each passing second.

"Anyway, enough about me." I clear my throat and move on. The last thing she wants to hear about is Beau and my issues. "Mia is doing okay. She stayed with us last night. She's still having nightmares. I think it would help if she came and visited more, but Brooks doesn't believe it's good for her. And I understand he's coming from a good place, but she just misses you. Touching you. Both of you." I fall silent again, and try to rack my brain on anything I've missed.

"Missy's opens in five days. Everything's pretty much ready to go. Beau and I met with Brie yesterday. She's amazing." I'm about to tell her more about Missy's when Brooks walks back out. Damp hair and clean clothes on. His eyes are sunken, accompanied by almost black circles, and his beard is so overgrown he looks almost unrecognizable. But at least he's clean.

"Hey." I look up and watch him fall back into the chair he's claimed as his own before reaching for Kell's hand.

"Anything?" he asks without taking his eyes off her.

"Not yet." I try to keep it hopeful, hating how my disappointment grows as each day passes. "But I know with time—"

"Time?" He barks out a bitter laugh and looks up at me.

"'Cause time is all we have, right? Time is just going to stop and wait for her?" I know he's hurting, angry and even scared. His world as he knows it has stopped. I understand his pain.

Knowing there is no point getting into it with him, I stand and give Kelly one last hand squeeze before stepping back.

"I'm going to get going. I'll be bringing Mia up after school today."

"I already told Beau, I don't want her up here too much."

"And I understand why, but she needs to see her mother and father. You can't keep this from her. It's doing more harm than you think." I reach for my bag, step around the bed and come to stand next to his chair.

"Mackenzie—" He twists to look up at me,

"No, Brooks. I know you think this is what's best for her, but it's not. You're right. Time isn't standing still, and while you're here watching it slip by, Mia's left out there living what you're living but times two. Don't make her do it alone. Don't push her out. Let her be here." I bend at the waist and give him a quick kiss on his cheek before standing back to full height. He doesn't react, doesn't tell me to mind my own business. He just sits there looking up at me.

"We'll see you this afternoon." I give him one final look before spinning around and walking out.

I hold myself together until I make it halfway down the hallway. Only then do I let out a shaky breath as the day's first stream of tears come.

Jesus, I'm just a crying mess these days.

I didn't want to have to do this, but I know if it were me in this situation, I'd want someone stepping in. I know Brooks and this isn't him. This is a man too caught up in watching his wife sleep the days away, and he's missing the bigger picture. I'm not going to sit back and allow him to shut down like this. Not like I did, especially when Mia needs him.

If I have learned anything the last month, it is our time is irreplaceable, and it can be taken away in a blink of an eye.

Not only am I going to start living in time, but I will make sure Brooks is there with me.

Mia deserves it.

Kelly deserves it.

I deserve it.

"Just take a deep breath, and relax," I remind myself two days later as I hear the rumble of Beau's bike pull into the drive. "You want this. No, you need this." I place the rope I found in Beau's draw at the end of the bed.

It's not like I'm trying to convince myself to do it, because I know I want this, but more to calm my nerves. I've been planning and probably overthinking it. We both know it's been a long time coming; however, with Mia staying with us on and off and the work with the shelter, we've had no time.

I hear the front door click open and my body locks.

Shit.

"Kenzie?" Beau's voice comes down the hall.

"Down here!" My voice shakes with nerves, not believing this is about to happen. His footsteps grow louder along the wooden floor while I take my position.

"What you doing in here, darlin'?" Beau pushes the door open and stops short when he notices me.

"Hi," I whisper, watching his eyes darken with need, lust and hunger.

"What the fuck you doing, Kenzie?" His Adam's apple bounces up and down three times before he slowly swallows.

"What does it look like?" I arch my back a little, pushing my breasts out a bit more. I'm fucking nervous, but I'm adamant I won't let him see it.

He hasn't moved his body, his eyes traveling from my naked body to the rope at the end of the bed.

"Mackenzie." He groans, and then takes one step toward me.

"I want this," I rush out, not wanting him to reject me or stop this. "I need this." He slowly takes another step toward me, licking his lips in a slow, sensual way. The last couple of days I've been going over everything in our relationship, and I didn't know what was holding me back. Until I realized I never gave Beau full control. It kind of became lost in the mess our life has become.

"Haven't had my cock in you since Kelly's accident and you want me to do this?" I can see his apprehension and possible confusion, but I can't have him second-guessing this. I need the controlling man I fell in love with.

"Beau, I need this. I need you to make me feel. Make this doubt go away." He drops his cut to the floor and rips his shirt over his head.

Leaving his jeans in place, he takes four large steps to the end of the bed, places his knee to the comforter and crawls up over me.

"Doubt?"

"That I'm not good enough for you." I hold his stare, willing him to take it away.

"You're more than enough."

"I believe you believe it, but I need you to show me." He closes his eyes and sits back on his heels.

"You sure you want this?" His eyes darken as he looks down at me.

"Never been surer. I'm ready." He doesn't reply. Instead, he leans back and reaches for the rope.

"Are you going to listen to everything I say, Kenzie?" he asks, looping the rope around my left wrist and pulling it up over my head to secure it to the headboard.

"Yes, Beau." I nod as he pulls it harder. The rope rubs against my skin, the friction making this all the more real. This is going to happen.

He reaches for my other hand and secures it next to the one above my head.

"I'm not going to do your feet tonight, darlin'. Want you to wrap these long legs around me later," he tells me. My breath hitches when his mouth moves to my erect nipple, pulling it into his mouth and sucking hard.

"Ahh!" I arch at the sharp pain, before exhaling in pleasure.

"Who's this body belong to Mackenzie?" He pulls back, circling my wet nipple with his finger.

"You, always you," I answer, knowing it's the truth.

"And who controls this body, Kenzie?" He lowers his mouth just above my other nipple, waiting for my answer.

"You, Beau. Always you." His lips wrap around my nipple when I answer correctly, sucking it with the same intensity as the first one. Pain sears through me before he strokes me back to pleasure.

"You have the prettiest nipples I've ever seen." He draws back, and gently blows a breath over it. My hands pull on my restraints, my natural instinct to touch him takes over. I blow a frustrated breath realizing I just gave my control up. No touching.

"Tsk, tsk." He sits up and watches me with a deep hunger before reaching over into his nightstand and pulling out a small package. "I got these for you a couple of weeks back," he murmurs, pulling out a small black box. My eyes grow wide seeing the image on the package.

Nipple clamps.

"Are you going to use them on me?" He reaches in and pulls out what looks like a long metal chain with a clamp on either end.

"Yes," is all he says, before throwing the empty box to the side and coming back to hover over me.

"Been dreaming about using these on you since the first

time I had you." He dips his head low, and pulls my nipple between his teeth for a few seconds before letting it go.

"Holy shit." I breathe through the light sting. "Is it gonna hurt?" I watch him trail the cool metal over my breasts and around my nipple.

"No, darlin'. It's gonna feel good. Everything I do to you is gonna feel good." He clicks his tongue against his teeth as he reaches for my nipple. Squeezing it tightly between his thumb and finger, he uses his free hand to press one of the clamps open then places it over my erect nipple. The smooth metal tingles to begin with as he releases the clamp, letting it squeeze down slowly before slightly tightening it with a small screw on the side.

I draw in a sharp breath through my teeth, the sting unlike anything I've ever felt before pushes me out of my comfort zone.

"How's it feel?" he asks, pulling back to have a better look.

"It stings." I start to pant, not sure if I'm in pain or highly turned on, and have no idea what I'm talking about.

"Good." He moves over to my other nipple. Repeating the same actions, he squeezes my nipple between his thumb and forefinger, before slowly and gently releasing the clasp onto my swollen nipple. He fiddles with the tightening screw before resting back.

"Fucking hell, darlin'." His finger circles my left nipple, trailing it over the clamp, down the metal chain over to my right nipple. "It's even better in real life." He leans down and flicks his tongue over my nipple.

His cock grows harder against my stomach, but I can't give it too much thought. I'm lost in a haze. He repeats the same action back over to my left nipple.

When he's happy with his work, he slides down my body, trailing soft, wet kisses on my skin. His beard scratches along my stomach, as every inch of me comes alive. Every touch and each breath brings me to the crest of something bigger.

"Spread wider for me, darlin'," he orders. When he settles his body between my legs, his warm breath dances over my skin. Doing as I'm told, I part my legs, exposing myself to him.

A hiss passes his lips as his eyes settle on my exposed pussy.

"I want you to come on my face. Been thinking about it every day for the last month," he tells me before running his nose between my legs, breathing me in.

"Oh, God, Beau." My hips leave the bed as I squirm against him, seeking more friction.

"Ass to the bed or I will tie your feet." He looks up, his eyes glass over with a new level of power and I drop my ass fast. "Good girl." He takes his gaze back to my pussy before ever so lightly flicking his tongue over my clit. It's like it almost didn't happen.

"More," I whimper. Forcing my ass to stay on the bed, I pull against my restraints instead.

I'm like a starved woman, just needing to be touched.

"Patience, Mackenzie." He grins back up at me, and I have to curb my desire to kick him.

"Beau." I can barely recognize my own voice. My plea sounds pained.

"Trust me, darlin'. This is going to be worth every agonizing second." He dips his face back between my legs and blows a warm breath over everything except my clit.

Fucker.

I'm so wound up, I don't know if I can keep it up.

"Please, Beau." I'm at his mercy and the longer he keeps playing with me, the more my mind starts to daze.

"What do you need, darlin'?" His fingers wrap around my ankle, before slowly sliding up my leg.

"Yes, more. I need more." His hand rises over my knee, up the inside of my thigh, before slightly grazing my bare lips.

"Ughhh." I release a pissed-off groan when he doesn't apply any pressure. His soft chuckle tells me this isn't going to end any time soon.

"The more you fight this, the more I'm gonna hold this off." I still my body, and try to clear my mind.

Okay, I can do this. Relax.

I let a slow and deliberate breath out, forcing my body to focus on what he's doing and not what I need. Every delicate stroke, every almost brush, it's like every spot he's not touching is more alive than where he is.

"That's it, darlin', let me play you like you were made to be played." He presses his lips on the inside of my thigh, and carefully guides himself up. His beard draws out the anticipation. Where his lips or tongue don't touch, the rough hair scrapes, bringing a whole new level of sensation.

"Mmmm." Pleasure pulls a low moan past my lips as heat blankets me in a heavenly fog. He's barely touching me, yet I'm certain any minute now, I'm about to come.

"You're fucking beautiful, Kenz. Lying there tied to my bed. Nipples pulled tight with these clamps." His fingers slide up over my stomach in a slow leisurely pace and lightly tug on the cord

"Ahhh!" The sharp sting lights a new fire in me, burning a

371

path straight to my clit.

"Relax into it, darlin'." He tugs a second time, igniting the path over again.

"Please. Oh, God, please." I arch as he pulls, relaxing when he releases.

"Again." He pulls one last time just as his finger enters me. I'm sure I come out of my skin as his finger hooks and finds my favorite spot.

"Yes!" My breath catches as his mouth lowers over my needy clit. Stars burst in front of my eyes. Every nerve ending comes to life in a dance of seduction, passion and need before I'm pushed over the edge of reason.

Wave after wave of ecstasy cascades over me.

"Eyes." Beau's demand pulling me out of my trance. Before I can look down my body, the swell hits and my orgasm surges through me.

His tongue laps it up, every drip that spills from me. His eyes find mine as his fingers tug on the chain for a fourth time and before I know what's happening, I'm coming again.

"Oh, my god, Beau." My head falls back, the pleasure too intense to hold my head up and watch. Beau's moans of approval are enough to tell me I gave him what he wanted. What he'd been searching for.

"I don't think I'll ever get sick of seeing it." Beau's voice has me lifting my neck back up to watch him climb up over my body.

I don't have anything left in me to reply so I just watch as he slaps his cock on my clit a couple of times. The cool metal of his cock rings, reminding me just how much I've missed them. How much I've missed him.

"You doing okay, darlin'?" My eyes flick up to his just as he lines himself at my entrance. I'm doing more than okay. I'm floating, dancing on air.

"Yeah." I spread myself wider to let him in.

At my answer, he pushes himself all the way in, burying himself balls deep, before sliding out and repeating his actions.

His piercing, his balls, his body, skin to skin, all connects me to him as he strokes himself into me.

It's too much.

It's perfect.

I'm unraveling.

"Kenz." His breath quickens as he rocks inside of me. My wrists start to burn with the friction of the tight rope rubbing against me. "Tell me you love me." He thrusts deeper.

"I love you," I answer, thrusting my own hips up to meet him.

"Again." He reaches down and pulls at the chain. Fire spreads through me.

"Oh, God, it's too much."

"No it's not," is all he says, before pulling out again. It's all it takes before I'm seized by a rush of sensations so intense, I scream out.

"Beau!" My body tenses for a brief second before I'm coming apart in a convulsive release. Wave after wave of pain mixed with pleasure rips through me.

"Look at me." I hear Beau's voice over the roar of my orgasm and my eyes fly open.

He drives in harder, faster, matching the range of emotions tearing through me.

"Fuck, I missed this." He pumps once, twice, then a third

time before an uninhibited cry of satisfaction rips from his throat and he releases. Our eyes stay locked as we both ride out our pleasure, neither one of us lost to ourselves. Our ragged gasps become out of sync when Beau's strokes slow and come to a stop.

"Jesus Christ." He pants, dropping his body to mine.

"Ahh!" I suck in a startled breath when he lands on the nipple clamps. "Clamps," is all I say before his fingers are pressing down and slowly releasing my nipples from their pleasurable torture.

"How do you feel?" He presses a gentle kiss over the red swollen flesh.

"I don't know." My words become caught in my throat as he moves on to the other nipple, showing it the same attention and ending with a soft kiss.

"*You* are amazing." He pulls back slightly, letting his still hard cock fall from me. I can barely talk. My body is spent, my mind lost to itself.

I force my eyes to stay open as he reaches over me and releases my right hand from its restraints.

"Next time, I might just let you sleep in these." He takes my wrist and soothes the burn with soft kisses.

"Oh, God, no." I shake my head.

"Yes, darlin'." He moves on to my other wrists, releasing it from the rope then bringing it up to his mouth and soothing the burn.

"I wouldn't be able to touch you," I mumble, my eyes becoming too heavy to fight the pull.

"But I'll be able to touch you," he whispers, rolling me to my side and coming in behind me. "Whenever I want." He wraps his arms around me and mumbles more positives of having me tied to his bed, but I stop hearing them. I've given up the fight against sleep. Before I know it, I've succumbed to my first ever peaceful after-sex slumber.

Limbs heavy, mind relaxed, I fall deeper into blissful darkness knowing we will never come back from what just happened.

I don't want to.

It is etched into my mind and will be the moment we draw all comparisons from. We will revisit it, try to replicate it, but nothing will ever compare.

Because it is the first time I gave myself entirely to Beau.

He owns me, and for the first time in my life, I realize I don't want to be owned by anyone other than him ever again.

I WAKE THE FOLLOWING MORNING TO AN EMPTY BED,
the lingering smell of coffee, and visions of having my woman
tied naked to my bed.

"Fuck me." I sigh into my pillow, not ready to let the image
go. I didn't think Mackenzie and I would ever get to that point,
but now I know what she's capable of, I can't wait to play some
more.

"Shit, shit, shit." Mackenzie's cursing floats down the hall,
bringing me out of my daydream and back to the moment.

Giving up the comfort of my bed, I pull on some pants, tie
up my hair, and make my way down the hall and into the
kitchen.

"Morning, beautiful." I step into the kitchen and watch her

head whip around.

"W-what are you doing up? Go back to bed. I was making you breakfast in bed." She starts to panic. Turning back to the stove, she bumps the pan, almost spilling a mess everywhere. Her hair sits up on her head in a messy bun. She's wearing one of my club tees and she's barefoot in my kitchen trying to make me breakfast when we both know the woman is shit at breakfast.

Jesus, I need to marry her as soon as fucking possible.

"You okay, darlin'?" I keep my distance, watching her become flustered.

"NO! You're making me nervous. Go away."

A deep laugh rumbles from my belly and she turns her head back my way and narrows her eyes.

"I told you, breakfast is my gig, darlin'." I shrug, not at all bothered if she's pissed. We've been over this so many times. The woman just can't do eggs. It's that simple.

"Yeah, well, maybe I want it to be my gig." She huffs, trying to fix up something that resembles an omelet. *A bad omelet.*

"Not gonna happen." I step all the way into the room and move to her.

"No, you stay right there, mister. I'm doing this." She points back to me but I don't listen. "Please, Beau," she begs when I step in behind her and press my front to her back.

"You really want the breakfast gig?" I lean and whisper into her ear. I don't know why it's such a big deal for her.

"You know I do. Why else do I set my phone alarm to try to beat you?" She whips her head around and I raise my brow at her confession. "I normally snooze it, but still." I spin her the rest of the way around so she's facing me.

"Fine, you can do breakfast." Her face transforms into something else when her smile of victory takes over. "When you marry me." Her eyes fly up at my stipulation. Shock, and confusion flicking over her face.

"Beau." My name falls from her lips in a mixture of not understanding and frustration. "Quit messing." She tries to pull out of my grasp, but I place my hands on either side of her face and hold her in my space.

"I'm only going to ask you one more time, darlin'. You think I was fucking around last week. I wasn't. No one will work harder to make you happier than me. Let me be your family. Marry me." I don't even have a fucking ring, but I don't care. I need to do this now. I'm not waiting.

Her eyes squeeze shut, forcing the tears down her face.

"This here, right now. This is all you're going to get, because I'm not waiting another second, Kenzie. Let me give you everything you want. Everything you deserve." I hold her gaze and watch a flurry of emotions take over. Hope, love, wanting, even need. Each one flashing so fast I nearly miss it, but they're there.

"Mackenzie, say yes," I whisper her name in a plea.

"Yes, Beau, I will marry you."

"Yes?" I repeat, just to be sure.

"Yes. Yes. Yes." She shakes her head, tears rolling down my hands. Not knowing what else to do, I crash my mouth to hers, needing more than anything a deeper connection to her. She opens instantly. Her tongue finds mine with the same need. Keeping the kiss going, I release her face, bend at the knees and pick her up. She wraps her legs around my waist as I lean forward and turn the stove off, and then stumble my way back to bed.

"Breakfast," Kenzie mumbles against my lips, but I ignore it. Breakfast is the last thing on my mind. I need to be with her. *Inside of her.*

I take us back to bed and gently lower her down.

"Shirt off," I tell her, while dropping my pants then working on her panties. She helps me along, lifting her ass so I can pull them easily down. When we're both naked, I climb over her and maneuver myself on top of her.

"I love you, darlin'."

"I love you, more." She threads her fingers through my hair and yanks out my hair tie.

"Not possible." I shake my head, releasing my hair.

"How about I show you." She manages to roll me to my back then straddles me. Her bare pussy rests against my stomach, and her arousal seeps against my skin.

"You gonna ride me, baby?" I slide my hands up the outside of her thighs and over her waist.

"Yeah," She lifts herself up, grabs my hard cock, then slides herself down my cock, taking me whole.

We hiss in pleasure at the same time as she rolls her hips to adjust to me.

"You have until the first orgasm. Then I'm taking control," I tell her as she builds her movements.

"Second," she argues, pinching her nipples while picking up her pace.

Fucking little tease.

"Fine, but then I'm bringing the rope out." Her walls clench in response to my plan.

"Deal," she agrees in a weak cry as she rides out her first

orgasm over my cock. Willing my balls to hold it together, I fold my arms behind my head and lie back to enjoy the show.

This woman, this incredible, sexy, funny, and strong woman is mine.

Forever.

I don't know what to do with that knowledge.

Forever seems like a long time, but looking up at her now, wild, free, riding my cock, I know forever isn't going to be long enough.

Nothing we have would ever be enough.

But I will take whatever we have, because anything less will hurt more. And we both have too much hurt already in our pasts.

From now on, it will only be goodness. It is a vow I know I will keep, because I won't accept anything else, not when it comes her.

Not ever.

"I don't think we should tell them," Kenzie tells me when we pull up outside the hospital later that afternoon. After I let her ride me to her second orgasm, I took over. Giving her one more before I had her hands tied behind her back and fucked her from behind.

"Not yet anyway," she adds before I can respond.

"Whatever you want, darlin'." I kick the stand down and wait for her to climb off my bike before following her.

"You're not angry, are you? That I want to hide it from everyone?" Her hands bunch up at the bottom of her shirt and

I know she's probably been worrying about this on the whole ride over.

"Do you want to hide it because of Brooks and Kelly, or because you're having second thoughts?"

"Because of Brooks and Kelly. I'm not second-guessing my choices, Beau. I just don't want to upset anyone. Not when everything is still so unknown."

"Then I'm not angry. It's why I love you." I pull her body to mine and kiss her. Maybe it's selfish I asked her to marry me when Brooks is dealing with his shit. When her friend, Heidi, is still missing. When we have so much shit to deal with at the shelter. But I don't care. Because in a normal day, I wouldn't factor how me asking Mackenzie to be my wife would affect anyone else's life but ours. I'm not about to start now. Especially not when I've worked so hard making sure Kenzie doesn't either.

"It will just be until things settle down." She pulls back, still worrying about it.

"Darlin', I'm not angry. But fair warning, when my ring goes on your finger it's not coming off."

"Noted." She reaches up and kisses me again. This time skimming her tongue along my lips.

Yeah, I fucking need a ring today. No fucking way I am keeping this shit locked up.

"Where the fuck you been?" Nix's question interrupts our kiss, bringing us back to the hospital parking lot.

"We had shit to deal with for the opening at Missy's." I look down at Kenzie and give her a wink. He doesn't need to know we were off the grid because I needed to fuck my new fiancée.

"Kelly's awake."

I look up just as Mackenzie's body recoils at the news. "Oh my God."

I reach around Mackenzie, not trusting her to keep standing. "Good news, darlin'," I remind her as she breaks down into sobs.

"Yeah, it's great." We both look up at Nix's tone, and notice he doesn't share the same excitement.

"What's wrong?" Mackenzie beats me to it.

"She doesn't know who she is." He rubs his forehead.

"What? What do you mean?" I hold Kenz tighter, not sure this is the news we were hoping for.

"I don't know. That's all Brooks could tell us before he went back. He hasn't come back out. They're running some tests."

"Oh my God, Beau." Kenzie twists to look up at me.

"Don't think about it like that, darlin'. This is good news. For all we know, it's temporary."

"But what if she doesn't remember? What if she never remembers?" Her mind moves straight to the worst possible outcome.

"What if she didn't wake up, Kenz? You can't keep on this track. She woke up. It's a start and you have to believe it's gonna be okay." I take either side of her face in my hands. "She's gonna remember, darlin'. And if she doesn't, then we'll find a way to remind her." A tear falls down her cheek, but I don't take this one away. She needs to feel this if she is going to believe it.

It might not have been the news we hoped for, but we're closer to having our family back, and we have to hold on to what we are given.

Infatuation

Because what is the alternative?

Epilogue

Mackenzie
four months later

"THIS CAN'T BE HAPPENING NOW." I LOOK UP AT MY reflection and try to talk myself down. "This is what you wanted," I remind myself, watching the damn wrinkle crease between my brows. "If you don't relax, your makeup is going to be messed up." I nod, feeling myself calm a little. I don't want to have to ask Holly to fix up my face or my hair. Not when she just spent two hours making me perfect. "You can totally do this. No, you have to do this." I level my stare at myself just as another wave of nausea has my head in the sink. I pray I don't bring up my lunch.

"Shit, I can't do this."

"Are you okay in there?" A knock at the door pulls me out of my trance and back to the room.

"Err yeah, just give me a second," I call back, before taking some deep breaths then placing the pregnancy test in my bag so no one finds it.

"You still need to put your dress on, Kenz. Hurry up," Kadence shouts through the door, rushing me along. Not wanting to run any later, I shake the nervousness off and force myself out of my panic.

"Sorry. I'm here." I open the bathroom door and step out into the room in front of my friends.

"Come on, everyone's ready." Kadence stands from the bed first and rushes toward me.

"I know. I know, I'm coming." I drop my bag on the bed then let her help me out of my silk dressing gown so I can step into a strapless, fit and flare ivory dress with a sweetheart neckline.

I didn't want anything too fancy, but with friends like Kadence, Holly and Bell, I knew the dress shopping would turn into a huge deal.

"Oh my, Mackenzie, it's so beautiful," Bell whispers from the bed as I hold the front of my dress up, allowing Kadence to carefully zip me.

"Thanks." I smile, watching all the girls come to stand around me. The last four months they have really gone above and beyond. With still no news on where Heidi is, they have shown me all the support I could ever imagine helping to organize my wedding.

"I wish Kelly and Heidi were here." I blink a couple of times, fighting the tears.

"I know with everything in my being both of them would want to be here." Bell reaches for my hand and offers me a light squeeze.

"Now, no more tears today. We have buttons to deal with." Kadence drops to her knees and starts fastening each one of the thirty buttons.

It's the best and the worst part about the dress.

"Thanks." I sigh, my anxiety coming back full force as she fiddles more with it.

"Are you okay? You seem tense." Holly gazes at me through the makeup mirror as she touches up her lipstick.

"Yeah," I lie, trying to keep my breathing under control. I'm not okay, but I can't tell them. Not now.

"How much time do we have?" I ask, starting to second-guess my choice on this dress. The buttons are amazing, but a pain in my ass.

"Okay. Done." Kadence steps back and allows me to take a closer look in the floor-length mirror.

"Wow." I look at myself, my hand instantly touching my stomach.

I'm going to be a mom.

Beau's going to be a dad.

I don't even see myself as a bride on my wedding day, making sure everything is perfect. All my eyes see is my hand on my stomach holding in the biggest secret.

"Beau is going to freak." Bell pulls me out of my head and I turn to look back up at her.

Would he? I know she's not talking about the *news*, rather how I look, but all I can focus on is the life growing inside of me.

"Mackenzie?" I look up at Kadence's voice as the music starts to play, signaling the beginning of the ceremony.

"Oh my, God, girls." I inhale deeply, only to stop when a sharp pain halts me, radiating through my chest.

"What's wrong?" Kadence steps forward, offering me her arm.

"I can't breathe." My heart beats fast and my hands start to sweat.

"You can, just slow your breathing down." She tries to calm me by holding me, but it doesn't help. I'm too worked up. Holly steps forward, followed by Bell, but each one of their panicked faces only pushes me into anxiety.

"No, I can't. It hurts, something's wrong." I inhale again, only to be restricted by the same sharp pain. "I can't do this." I step out of Kadence's embrace and pace. "What am I doing here, guys?" I know I'm overthinking it, but I can't help it. Everything that's happened over the last four months has happened so fast.

Between Kelly coming out of her coma, Missy's place taking off and needing so much of our attention, Beau asking me to marry him and now this— everything feels rushed.

"I can't. Oh, God, I can't." I sit on the floor, my legs becoming too unsteady to stand. "I can't breathe. I literally cannot breathe." The sharp pain in my chest grows as I struggle with short pants. "It hurts."

I briefly hear Kadence talking to someone before tunnel vision kicks in and I'm spiraling out of control.

Is this too soon? What if we aren't ready? Question after question spins me further out of control. I can hear Kadence and Bell's voice try to pull me back, but I can't latch on to them. I'm too focused on what's happening inside of me.

"Mackenzie." The deep timbre of Beau's voice breaks

through my panic and a quick sharp burst of air accompanies it. "Come back to me, darlin'." He enters my headspace and slowly starts to coax me back. "Slow your breathing and come back to me, now." I'm moved from the floor and pulled into the warmth of his lap.

Not understanding what's happening, I focus on his smooth comforting voice and follow his orders.

"That's it, darlin', nice slow breaths." I do as I'm told, drawing strength and comfort from him. After a few more silent minutes, I'm finally able to open my eyes.

"Beau?" I look up, the room coming back to me.

"Welcome back." He pushes some curls from my face and leans forward to gently kiss me.

"I'm so sorry." I close my eyes, realizing I just totally freaked and caused him to come running back here.

"Talk to me. What happened?" I look up briefly, noticing we're alone.

"Where are the girls?"

"I kicked them out." He lifts his shoulder in a shrug, and for the first time since he's come in, I notice his outfit.

"You look handsome." I run my eyes over him. He's wearing his leather Rebels cut over a clean white dress shirt that pulls tight over his arms, and black pants.

When we started planning our wedding, Beau only had two requests. First was he would not wear a tux and second, he wanted to be married at the clubhouse. It didn't bother me either way where we got married, but I was a little disappointed I wasn't going to see him in a suit. Now I've seen his alternative, I'm not so torn up.

"Glad you approve." He grins his sexy grin as I look back

up at him. His hair is pulled back in one of his messy buns, which makes his beard look longer, and my knees weak. "I'm trying not to look at you, darlin', but from what I can see, you're taking my breath away." I smile at his ability to always say the right thing. We both know I'm a hot mess right now. I mean, he just pulled me up from the floor of my old room in the clubhouse.

"Seriously, did I just ruin our wedding?" I dab under my eyes with the pad of my finger.

"I don't know why you would say that? I think it's normal for the groom to come back and talk the bride down from having a panic attack."

"Don't joke right now." I shift a little in his lap, my dress less restricting now I'm not in the middle of a full-blown freak out.

"What happened?" His voice lowers with his question and I know we're being serious now.

"I just panicked. I don't know." He rests his forehead to mine and lets me try to gather my thoughts.

"You wanna get out of here?"

"What? No!" I pull back, almost shocked he even suggested leaving. Not only do we have forty people waiting outside for us to be married, I want this.

"Then talk to me. What's happening?"

"I'm pregnant." I blurt the news out without even thinking about the consequences. His body tenses underneath mine while he processes my words.

"Darlin'." His hands come up and cup my face. "Are you fucking with me?" I shake my head. "You have my baby inside of you?"

I nod.

"I just found out. Like ten minutes ago. I took a test."

"This why you panicked?"

I nod again.

"This is what you want, right? Why you stopped taking the pill?"

"It is, but I wasn't expecting it so soon." I only stopped taking the pill last month, thinking we would have some time to enjoy married life before I would be peeing on sticks.

"You having second thoughts?" His brows dip low as he tries to figure me out. It's not like we haven't discussed it. As soon as he put his ring on my finger, he's talked about starting a family. I just wasn't expecting to find out right here, on my wedding day.

"No. Never. I want this so much. I just think with everything happening I'm a little overwhelmed. You know?"

"I know, darlin'. Things have been hectic, but that's all gonna change. Life is settling down now. Missy's place has found its pace, and you have my baby inside of you." He pulls me tighter against his chest, and wraps his arms around me in a tight embrace. "I've got ya, darlin', whenever you need me. Even minutes before you're meant to be marrying me." He chuckles when I groan. I'm never going to live this down. I just know it.

"I love you, Beau."

"And I love you, darlin'." He holds me for a little while before pulling back, "So, you still wanna marry me?" The corner of his mouth rises, waiting for my reply, and I smile back at his playfulness.

"Yeah." I nod, letting him kiss me briefly.

"Come on. I'll walk you down the aisle." He stands, taking me with him.

"You can't do that." I wasn't planning on having anyone walk me down, but now he's offered, the thought actually sounds appealing.

"I can do what I want. My wedding." He moves to the door, opens it, and almost has to catch Holly and Kadence as they fall forward.

"Sorry." They fight to hold their laughter in as they look from me to Beau. Bell hangs back, holding her own laugher.

"We're ready. We're walking down together, so go take a seat," Beau tells them, unimpressed they were eavesdropping, but he doesn't call them out.

"Does she need to be fixed up?" Holly peaks past Beau for a better look. "Yeah, she needs me." She pushes past him and comes to me.

"Rule one, no crying before the ceremony." She shakes her head and sets about making me pretty again. It only takes a few minutes, before I'm back to being presentable. Holly and Kadence leave, but not before Beau warns them to keep their mouths shut about anything they heard. They both act like they have no clue what he's talking about. That is until they both give up their act and embrace us with congratulations and hugs.

Something tells me our news will be public before the night ends.

"You ready?" Beau asks when we're left alone.

"Never been more ready." I take his hand, letting him guide me out of the room, down the hall, and through the empty clubhouse. The soft hum of Hunter's guitar grows louder as we exit the clubhouse and walk toward one of the large marquees

Beau rented. It's just gone dusk, and the fairy lights hanging from the marquee glow against the warm sky, setting the mood,

Everyone comes to a stand as we walk hand in hand down a small aisle covered in white rose petals.

I know it's not traditional with Beau walking me down the aisle and with no bridesmaids, but it couldn't be more perfect. Just the two of us, doing this together.

We come to a stop and face each other in front of Brie, our social worker and friend who works with us at Missy's, who also happens to be qualified to officiate weddings. *Our* wedding.

Over the last four months, Brie and I have grown close. When she found out I was looking for someone to marry us, she offered herself.

I couldn't think of anyone or anything more perfect.

"Welcome to all who have gathered here this evening to share in this marriage ceremony of Beau McIntyre and Mackenzie Morre," she begins as everyone takes a seat around us. Most of our guests are from the club, with a few new faces from Missy's Place.

"These words, spoken today between Beau and Mackenzie are indeed important and sacred, but they are not what joins these two together, nor is this marriage ceremony. We are not here to witness the beginning of their relationship, but to acknowledge and celebrate a lasting bond that already exists between them. Beau and Mackenzie have already joined their hearts and chosen to walk together on life's journey, and we have come to bear witness to a symbolic union and a public affirmation of the love they share."

She pauses, letting it all sink in, but I'm too lost in Beau and his eyes on me. I'm barely keeping up.

"Mackenzie and Beau, the pledge you make today expresses your devotion to one another and to the love you share, and the words spoken here will support your marriage if you are able to sustain your commitment through the inevitable hardships you'll face together. Today, in the presence of your families and friends, you pronounce your love for each other and make a commitment that will define the next phase of your journey. The vows Mackenzie and Beau recite today have been written by them. Written from the heart and spoken to the soul. Beau, would you like to go first?" She looks to Beau first. Beau nods, then clears his throat before beginning.

"Mackenzie, you know me better than anyone else in this world and somehow you still manage to love me. There's still a part of me today that can't believe I'm the one who gets to marry you." He reaches forward and wipes away a lone tear as it falls down my cheek. "When I held you in my arms that night in the back of the van, something in me clicked. It's as if my body knew you were mine before my heart did, but then I let you go. I drove away when every part of me told me to stay. I'm never letting you go again, darlin'. Today, I choose you as my family. I promise to love you without reservation, and communicate fully and fearlessly. To never hurt you in anger and to always hold you with care. I have no greater gift to give but my word. As your trust is my strength, accept my heart as your shelter and my arms as your home. I give you all I am, and all I shall become."

"Oh God, that's so beautiful." I lean forward and whisper so only he can hear.

"No, you're beautiful." He smiles down at me before I'm told it's my turn.

"Mackenzie, please recite your vows," Brie interrupts our chat, causing a soft chuckle from our guests.

"Beau,"—I steady my voice and hold his hand tighter—"because of you my feet dance, my heart beats, and my eyes see. I laugh, I smile, and I dare to dream again. You've saved me in more ways than one." My voice wobbles and I take a second to gather myself.

"You're doing good, darlin'," Beau encourages, bringing me back.

"You showed me what love feels like and because of that, I choose you to be none other than yourself. Loving what I know of you and trusting who you will become, I promise you my deepest love, my fullest devotion, and my tender care. Through the pressures of the present to the uncertainty of the future, I promise to always be faithful, to love you with actions, not just words. From this day forward, you won't ever walk alone. As you have given me your heart to hold, I give you my life to keep."

"I love you," he whispers leaning down and kissing me before he's meant to.

"The rings?" Brie shakes her head at our inability to stick to the rules. Nix steps forward and hands Beau the rings.

"Beau, please take Mackenzie's hand and repeat these words after me. I give you this ring as a symbol of our love."

Beau takes my hands and looks down at me. "Mackenzie, I give you this ring as a symbol of our love." His rough voice washes over me as he slides the gold band down my finger.

"For today and tomorrow, and for all the days to come. Wear it as a sign of what we have promised on this day."

"For today and tomorrow, and for all the days to come.

Wear it as a sign of what we have promised on this day." He brings my hand up to his mouth and presses his lips to my ring.

"And know my love is present, even when I am not."

"And know my love is present, even when I am not, darlin'." I smile at his slip in of darlin'.

"Mackenzie, please take Beau's hand and repeat these words. I give you this ring as a symbol of our love, for today and tomorrow, and for all the days to come." I follow her instruction word for word, while keeping my eyes firmly on Beau, only taking my eyes off him to slide his ring on his finger.

"Wear it as a sign of what we have promised on this day. And know my love is present, even when I am not."

"Wear it as a sign of what we have promised on this day. And know my love is present, even when I am not." He winks down at me when I look back up.

"Mackenzie and Beau, you have professed your love by exchanging your vows and you have symbolized your commitment by exchanging rings. With those two important things out of the way, there are a couple of questions I need each of you to answer." Brie smiles at both of us before turning to Beau.

"Beau, do you take Mackenzie to be your wife, to live together in the covenant of marriage? Do you promise to love her, comfort her, honor and keep her, in sickness and in health; and, forsaking all others, be faithful to her as long as you both shall live?"

"I do." He gives his answer, no reservations, just pure total honesty.

"Mackenzie, do you take Beau to be your husband, to live together in the covenant of marriage? Do you promise to love him, comfort him, honor and keep him, in sickness and in health; and, forsaking all others, be faithful to him as long as you both shall live?"

"I do." His hands squeeze mine briefly before a smile breaks out over his face.

"By the power vested in me, I now pronounce you husband and wife. Beau, you may kiss your bride. Again." Not needing to be told twice, Beau pulls me into his embrace, dips me back and takes my lips against his for the first time as my husband officially.

Once and for all, finally claiming me as his.

"JUST GIVE ME FIVE MINUTES," I WHISPER INTO HER EAR as I push her up against the brick wall of the clubhouse. It's late and we should be cutting cake, but I dragged Mackenzie out of the marquee and around the far side of the clubhouse for some privacy.

"You, last five minutes?" she sasses as she shimmies her panties down her legs like I asked.

"Not gonna fuck you, darlin', just warming you up for when I get you home." I move my mouth over her jaw and slowly make my way down her neck. Nipping along her smooth skin.

"I'm going to need these back." She hands me her panties then tilts her neck back, giving me better access.

"You're not having them back tonight," I tell her, and pocket the flimsy lace.

"You're going to make me cut our wedding cake panty-less?" I reach down and hike her wedding gown up, sliding my hand along the inside of her thigh.

"You'll be lucky if we make it to the cake." My fingers find their prize. Pushing past her bare lips, I'm met with her arousal.

A soft whisper of pleasure flies out of her mouth and I push her further by sliding my finger into her tight heat.

"Beau." Her hands move to my shoulders, her fingers pressing in as I push into her faster.

"Shh, darlin', or we're gonna have an audience." I remove my finger and replace it with two. It's not like we're completely exposed, but if anyone looks, they'll find us.

Her hips come forward at my intrusion, and I pick up my pace, wanting to pull just one orgasm out of her before we eat cake.

"Ahh, we so shouldn't do this." Her hips roll in time with my fingers, while her head rests back on the brick wall.

Her mouth says we shouldn't, but her slick, wet cunt is telling me otherwise.

"Come on, darlin', fuck my fingers." I ignore her reservations and continue my pace.

"Beau, yes, there." My fingers zone in on her favorite spot as my thumb finds her clit. Her breathing labors just as her walls tighten. Dropping my mouth to her neck, I run my tongue in a line of swirls, before biting down.

"Beau!" she shouts out, and I have to cover her mouth with mine to stifle her screams as she explodes over my fingers. Her pussy convulsing over and over again.

"Shh!" I pull back and chuckle at her inability to be quiet. Not even a little.

Her soft moans fade away as she eventually comes back to herself.

"Seeing you like this never gets old." I slow my fingers, sliding them in and out of her at a lazy pace.

"You're telling me." She brings her arms up around my neck and pulls me down to meet her mouth in a deep hungry kiss. My cock is hard against my slacks, pre-cum wetting the inside of my boxers.

"What do you want from me, Brooks?"

I pull my lips back from Mackenzie and still my fingers as Kelly's voice interrupts our impromptu make-out session. Mackenzie freezes, her thighs squeezing my hand to hold me in place.

"I don't know, Kelly? How about you show me you're trying." Brooks follows her around, both of them walking past us and continuing around the front of the clubhouse. We weren't expecting Kelly at the wedding today, but we were pleasantly surprised to see her hanging at the back of the marquee when the ceremony was over.

"I'm here, aren't I? Came when I told you I didn't want to." A small gasp whispers over Mackenzie's lips and I move my free hand over her mouth to stop her from revealing our presence.

They clearly don't know we're here, and it's not like I want to listen in on them, but I also don't want to interrupt them.

"I know this is hard for you, Kell. I'm trying to understand it all, but how do you expect me to act when you're not open to wanting to remember." Kelly doesn't answer right away and I wonder if they've walked further around, until she responds.

"Maybe I don't want to remember, Brooks." Tears on my hand bring me back and I look back down at Mackenzie and realize she's crying.

"The woman I married wouldn't say that. She wouldn't give up on her daughter." His voice cracks in desperation, and I find myself holding my breath waiting for her to react.

"That's not fair."

"No, what's not fair is that my wife is standing right in front of me, close enough for me to touch, but she won't let me. You think you're the only one who's hurting through this, Kell? I'm fucking here. I'm doing everything I can to save us, and you don't give a fuck."

"We shouldn't be listening to this," Mackenzie whispers against my hand, bringing my attention back to her. She's right. We shouldn't. The last four months have been rough for Brooks and Kelly. The last thing they need is more people knowing how much they're struggling. I nod once and slide my fingers from her, then quietly step back. She straightens her dress, takes my hand and we silently retreat back around the clubhouse without being noticed.

"Beau," Mackenzie starts when we've made a clean break.

"Not our business, darlin'." I already know what she's going to say, how she's going to react. It's just not what we need right now. Not tonight. Not on this day.

"I just wish there was something we could do."

"We're doing everything we can." I bring my finger up to my nose and breathe her scent in.

"Beau, be serious!" She slaps my hand away while I grin down at her.

"What?"

"Don't do that, Beau." She looks around like someone might be watching us.

"Why the hell not?" I breathe her in again, watching her blush a new shade of pink.

"'Cause it's gross." I pull her into my chest and wrap my arms around her.

"Nothing gross about the smell of my wife's pussy." She tilts her head back and looks up at me.

"Say it again."

"Nothing gross about the smell of my wife's pussy."

"Not that part." I grin down at her when I realize what she means.

"Wife, your pussy is fucking delicious." She shakes her head, but I see the flash of excitement come to life in her eyes.

"You're terrible." She drops her head to my chest and I silently high five myself for getting her mind off Brooks and Kelly.

"You ready for cake, wife?" I press my lips to the top of her head.

"Yeah, I'm ready." She steps back, takes my hand, and locks her fingers through mine.

"Do you think Brooks and Kelly—"

"I think Brooks and Kelly are capable of sorting their own shit, darlin'. Now let it go, wife. We have a cake to cut so we can fuck off out of here." I give her a wink before guiding us back over to the marquee. She doesn't reply, 'cause she knows it won't get her anywhere. Instead, she keeps in step with me, and lets me take control.

Today is our day, and yeah, Kelly and Brooks are in a bad

place, but I don't want them on her mind. I'll do anything to make sure this doesn't touch her.

She's my wife.

The mother of my unborn child.

The woman who controls every part of me and in return, handed over every part of herself.

Though we lost our families we were born to, we found an even greater one in each other. In our club.

Through the pain and suffering of our pasts, we've become what was stolen away from us.

She is my family, and I, hers.

Nothing and no one will ever change it.

The Facts

Domestic Violence, Family Violence and Intimate Partner Violence all fall under the same umbrella. It is violence and abuse that occurs within the family unit and intimate partner relationships.

It occurs when a family member or partner exerts power and control over their family member(s) or partner. The relationship can include spouses, partners, siblings, parents and children. It can take many forms and includes physical, verbal, emotional, psychological, financial and sexual abuse. It does not have to occur within the home or between people who are living together.

It affects people of all ages, races, religions, socioeconomic backgrounds, gender, sexual orientation, cultural and ethnic backgrounds.

On average, 24 people per minute are victims of rape, physical violence or stalking by an intimate partner in the United States — more than 12 million women and men over the course of a year. 1 in 4 women (24.3%) and 1 in 7 men (13.8%) aged 18 and older in the United States have been the victim of severe physical violence by an intimate partner in their lifetime.

(*The national Domestic Violence Hotline.)

If you are experiencing domestic violence, or know someone who is, there are many organizations that can help.

Over the page are some useful links and helplines:

Safe Horizon – USA

www.safehorizon.org/page/call-our-hotlines-9.html

White Ribbon –AU

www.whiteribbon.org.au/finding-help

National Domestic Violence Hotline – UK

www.nationaldomesticviolencehelpline.org.uk

Acknowledgments

Alissa Evanson-Smith: Sorry, Lissy, you didn't get Beau, but I have someone even more special for you because you deserve it. I love you, lady.

Brie Burgess: Brie, Brie, Brie. Lady, you are amazing. Don't ever leave me. Ever. 'Cause I will find you and lock you up so you can only beta for me! Hahaha! I love you, lady. You rock my world. Thank you for all your help, your encouragement, for being my voice of reason, for pushing me. I honestly wouldn't have finished this book had it not been for you.

Cassia Brightmore: Girl, you know I love you. I'm sorry I haven't been around so much for you. One word. December. You and I. I love you. YOLO.

Gillian Grybas: Gikky, oh, Gikky. I think writing Beau turned me into Ed, eh? Holla. You really are such a beautiful person. Thank you for being amazing and helping me. I love you.

JJ: Sister, wife, JJ. You've been there from the start. You are such a truly beautiful lady. I better see your ass in New York.

Tania: Thank you for your sound advice, for talking me down from my freak outs. I wouldn't be able to function without your touch on my boys.

Marci: I love you, crazy lady. Thank you for being part of my team. New York, baby!

Abbey: Thank you for pushing me harder. For showing me where I need to fix and make better. I hope you achieve what we talked about. Hahahhha.

Priya: Thank you, thank you, thank you, thank you. You are amazing and I appreciate everything you have done with Beau and Kenzie's story. Love ya lady.

Fiona: Thank you for all your work on Beau and Kenzie, I appreciate all your time.

Louisa from LM Creations: Thank you for working on this beautiful cover. It's by far my favorite.

Becky Johnson: ANOTHER ONE! Wow, what a year! Thank you for all your support on this amazing journey. No way would I be able to do any of this on my own. You really are amazing. Thank you.

To my Rebels: I know heaps of authors say this, but all the others are lying. I truly have the best readers. You all rock!

To ALL the Bloggers: Thank you for your support. I wouldn't have been able to get my name out without you guys pimping my work, reviewing, and loving the Knights Rebels boys just as much as I do.

My Mr. Savage: To my husband. Dude, sixth book. I know you weren't impressed with the last books acknowledgments. You don't love me like a love song? Okay, so short and sweet isn't your taste. Thank you for really stepping up with this book. I honestly couldn't have finished it without you. It was tense there for a bit. Thank for being the best daddy to our girls. Thank you for being the best husband. But most of all, thank you for being the best person I know.

I love you with everything I am. I hope I make you proud.

About the Author

An avid reader of romance and erotic novels, River's love for books and reading fueled her passion for writing. Reading no longer sated her addiction, so she started writing in secret. She never imagined her dream of publishing a novel would ever be achievable. With a soft spot for an alpha male and a snarky, sassy woman, Kadence and Nix were born.

RIVER WOULD LOVE TO HEAR FROM YOU
You can contact and/or follow her via...

Email: riversavageauthor@gmail.com

Facebook: www.facebook.com/riversavageauthor

Follow River on **Twitter:** @RiverS_Author

WANT TO KEEP UP TO DATE
WITH ALL THE NEWEST NEWS?

Come hang out with River's Rebels
www.facebook.com/groups/1513339432229460/

Sign up to River's newsletter
http://goo.gl/ECbNq5